DISENCHANTED

DISENCHANTED

(DÉSENCHANTÉES)

BY

PIERRE LOTI

TRANSLATED BY

CLARA BELL

New York

THE MACMILLAN COMPANY

LONDON: MACMILLAN & CO., Ltd.

1906

C, 17

Norwood Press
J. S. Cushing & Co. — Berwick & Smith Co.
Norwood, Mass., U.S.A.

HR

This is a purely imaginary tale. Any endeavour to find real names for Djenan, Zeyneb, Melek, or André would be waste of time, for they never existed.

The only real thing in it is the high level of culture now prevailing in the harems of Turkey, and the suffering which comes of it.

This suffering, more striking perhaps to my eyes as a foreigner, is already an anxiety to my dear friends the Turks, and they would fain diminish it.

I, of course, do not pretend to have discovered the remedy which profound thinkers, there on the spot, are still seeking. But I, like them, feel sure that there is one, and that it will be found; for the wonderful Prophet of Islam, who was above all else compact of light and charity, cannot have desired that the rules he dictated of old should become in the lapse of time a cause of suffering.

PIERRE LOTI.

I

ANDRÉ LHÉRY, a well-known romance writer, was
wearily opening his letters one cheerless spring
morning in a little house on the shore of the Bay
of Biscay, in which his latest whim had held him,
more or less settled, since the previous winter.

'So many letters this morning,' he sighed. 'Too
many letters!'

To be sure, on the days when the postman
brought him fewer he was no better pleased,
suddenly fancying himself isolated in the world.
Letters from women for the most part, some signed,
others not, breathing the incense of delicate intellectual adoration of the author. Almost all began
in the same strain: 'You will be much surprised,
Monsieur, to see the writing of a woman who is
unknown to you ——' André always smiled at
this opening phrase; surprised! oh no; he had
long ceased to be surprised. And then each new
correspondent, generally believing herself to be
the only woman in the world bold enough to
take such a step, never failed to add: 'My soul is
the younger sister of yours; no one, I can con-
fidently assure you, has ever so fully understood
you as I.' And at this André did not smile, in

spite of the stale repetition of the assurance; on the contrary, he was touched. And besides, the consciousness of his power over so many beings, widely scattered and for ever remote from him, the consciousness of a certain responsibility for their mental evolution, often gave him pause.

Among these letters, too, there were some so spontaneous, so trusting, such earnest cries for help, sent out, as it were, to an elder brother who could not fail to hear and pity! And those André Lhéry would put away — after tossing the pretentious and commonplace effusions into the paper-basket — would keep, in the firm intention of replying to them. But generally, alas! time was lacking, and the poor letters grew into a pile, drowned ere long under the tide of their successors, and finally quite forgotten.

Among the letters this morning was one with a Turkish stamp, and a post-mark showing in clear definition the word which always brought a thrill to André: 'Stamboul.'

Stamboul! what powers of evocation lay in the mere name! Before tearing open this letter, which might in itself be utterly indifferent, André paused, suddenly thrilled by the emotion — the same, and of a kind essentially impossible to put into words, as he had always experienced whenever Stamboul was unexpectedly brought before him from the depths of his memory after many days of oblivion. And again, as often already in dreams, a phantom city rose before his eyes which had seen all the world and gazed at its infinite variety — the city of minarets and domes, majestic and unique, unrivalled still even in its irredeemable decay, standing out high against the sky, with the blue waters of the sea of Marmora circling the horizon.

About fifteen years since there had been among his correspondents a few of the idle fair in Turkish harems; some had been vexed with him, while others had remorsefully delighted in him, for having told, in one of the books of his earliest youth, the story of his adventures with one of their humbler sisters. They clandestinely sent him confidential pages in French, incorrect but often quite adorable; and then, after the exchange of a few letters, they lapsed into silence and inscrutable mystery, dismayed at the thought of what they had dared, as though it were a deadly sin.

At last he tore the envelope stamped in that dear *beyond* — and the contents made him at first shrug his shoulders: No, really, this lady was certainly playing with him. Her language was too modern, her French too perfect and easy. It was all very well to quote the Koran, to sign herself Zaideh Hanum, to beg for an answer by return of post, *Poste-restante*, with as many precautions as a Red Indian on the warpath; she could only be a traveller visiting Constantinople, or the wife of some attaché — who could tell? or, perhaps, some Levantine educated in Paris.

And yet the letter had a charm which was irresistible, for André, almost in spite of himself, answered it at once. Indeed, he could not but show his thorough knowledge of the modern world and say, with all due courtesy of course: 'You, a Turkish lady! Nay, you cannot take me in!'

The charm of the letter was in fact indisputable, in spite of its improbability. Until the morrow, when he naturally ceased to think about it, André had a vague feeling that this was the beginning of something in his life, of something which would lead him on — on to sweetness, danger, and sorrow.

And it was, besides, like a call from Turkey to the man who of yore had loved it so well, but who had never gone back. The Biscay sea, on that doubtful April day, under the still wintry light, suddenly revealed itself to his sight as intolerably melancholy; a dim green sea, with the long rollers of almost unceasing surge, a vast, gaping void open to an infinite distance, at once alluring and appalling. How tenderer far was the sea of Marmora as he saw it in remembrance, how much more soothing and lulling, with the mystery of Islam on its embracing shores. The Basque country, which had so often captivated him, no longer seemed worth lingering in. The spirit of the past, which he had formerly imagined was surviving yet in the Pyrenean highlands and the rugged hamlets near at hand, nay, even below his window here in the ancient city of Fuentarabia, notwithstanding the invasion of impertinent villas — the old Basque spirit — no, to-day he could no longer discern it. But there — far away — in Stamboul — how much more of the past still lived, of the primal human dream, lingering in the shade of the great mosques, in the oppressive silence of the streets, and in the widely pervading region of graveyards, where tiny lamps with a thin yellow gleam are lighted up at night by thousands for the souls of the dead. Ah! those two opposite shores! Europe and Asia, displaying to each other's eyes minarets and palaces along the banks of the Bosphorus, under constantly changing aspects in the play of Eastern light and shade! After the magic of the Levant what could be more dismal, more repellent, than this Atlantic gulf? Why did he stay here instead of going there? How preposterous to waste the numbered days of life, when over there lay a land of airy enchantment, and the sad delicious intoxication which takes no note of the flight of time.

Still, it was here, on the shore of this colourless bay thrashed by the gales and by the tides of ocean, that his eyes had opened to the spectacle of the world, that consciousness had been given to him for a few fugitive years; hence, in spite of all, he passionately loved the things he belonged to, and he knew that he would miss them when he was away from them.

And so, on this April morning André Lhéry was once more alive to the incurable anguish of having scattered himself over many lands, of having been a wanderer over the whole earth, attaching himself to more than one place by his heart strings. Dear Heaven! why must he now be so bound to two native lands: this, of his birth, and that other, his oriental home..

II

THE April sun, in that same April but a week later, fell, subdued by blinds and muslin curtains, into the room of a sleeping girl. The morning sun, bringing with it, even through curtains, shutters, and latticed screens, the ephemeral gladness, the perennial delusion of earthly renewal which, ever since the world began, has always ensnared the soul, complicated or simple, of every living creature — the soul of man, the soul of beasts, the tiny soul of piping birds.

Outside, the flutter and twitter of newly arrived swallows could be heard, and the hollow thud of a tambourine beaten to an Eastern rhythm. Now and again a sound as of some monstrous, bellowing beast rent the air: the voice of the hurrying liners, the hoot of the steam-sirens, revealing the existence of a harbour somewhere near, a great harbour in frenzied stir; but these cries of the ships sounded very remote and came up from below, and this gave a sense of loftiness and peace, as of a hill-top far above the sea.

The room into which the sun shone on the sleeping girl was elegant and white; very modern, furnished with pretentious simplicity and the

6

affectation of archaic taste, which at that date (1901) represented one of the latest refinements of French decadence, and was styled *l'art nouveau*. In a bed enamelled white — on which flowers were vaguely sketched with a mixture of primitive artlessness and Japanese freedom, by the hand of some fashionable London or Paris decorator — the girl was sleeping quietly; a very small face in the midst of a dishevelled tumble of fair hair, an exquisitely oval face, so perfect that it might have been modelled in wax, really too perfect to seem quite real; a small nose with nostrils almost too delicate and the faintest aquiline curve; large Madonna-like eyes, and very long eyebrows, curved down towards the temples like those of our Lady of Sorrows. Rather too much lace, perhaps, frilled the sheets and pillow-cases; too many sparkling rings were on the slender hands that lay lightly on the satin coverlet; too much magnificence, as we should think, for a child so young; but for that, everything about her was quite in harmony with the latest ideas of Western luxury. But there were iron bars to the windows, and besides these the chequered wooden screens — closely fastened, never to be opened — which gave a sense of restraint to all this elegance, the oppression almost of a prison.

In spite of the brilliant sunshine and the glad excitement of the swallows outside, the girl slept on late, with the heavy torpor that suddenly falls after a sleepless night, and there were dark lines under her eyes, as though she had yesterday shed many tears.

On a small, white-enamelled writing-table a forgotten taper was still burning, amid a litter of written papers and finished letters in envelopes with a gilt monogram. There was music-paper too, on which notes were dotted down as in the fever of composition. Some books lay about, with fragile Dresden china ornaments; the last poems of the Comtesse de Noailles, side by side with those of Baudelaire and Verlaine, Kant's *Philosophy* with Nietzsche's. Evidently there was no mother here to weed the reading, and moderate the over-heating of this maiden brain.

And strange indeed in this room, where any spoilt and petted Parisienne would have found herself at home, a text in Arabic characters hung in the very place where, with us, the Crucifix might still be suspended; words embroidered in gold thread on bright green velvet, a passage from the book of Mahomet, the letters flourished and interlaced with antique and elaborate elegance.

The more excited chirping of two swallows, both at once, as they boldly clung to the very sill of the window, suddenly made the large eyes half-open in the small face — so small and infantine in its lines; eyes with a large greenish brown iris, at first seeming to crave mercy from life, to implore reality to come and quickly drive out some intolerable dream.

But reality and the hideous dream were apparently too intimately one, for the eyes grew darker and sadder as thought and memory came back; and they settled altogether into gloom, as if hopelessly resigned to the inevitable, when they fell on certain objects which brought irresistible evidence to her mind—a diadem sparkling in an open jewel-case, and spread out on chairs a white silk dress, a wedding dress, with orange flowers down the hem of the long train.

Like a gale of wind, and without knocking, a woman rushed into the room, thin, with eager, disappointed eyes, in a black dress and a shady black hat, elegantly simple, severe, yet with just a hint of extravagance. She was almost an old maid, but not quite — a governess as might be guessed, very highly educated and of a good but impoverished family.

'I have it! We have it, dear child!' she said in French, showing with childish triumph an unopened letter which she had just brought from the *poste-restante*.

And the little princess in bed replied in the same language without the slightest foreign accent:

'Not really!'

'Yes, yes, really. Who should it be from, child, but from him? Is this envelope addressed to *Zaideh Hanum*, or is it not? Well, then. Oh, if you have given the same password to others — then indeed!'

'You know I have not ——'

'Well, then, you see ——'

The girl was sitting up in bed, her eyes now very wide open and a faint flush in her cheeks — like a child who has been very unhappy and to whom such a wonderful toy has been given that for the moment all else is forgotten. The toy was the letter; she turned it about in her hands, fingering it hungrily, and yet afraid, as if it were a crime only to touch it. And then, just as she was about to tear the envelope, she paused to say in a coaxing tone:

'Dear Mademoiselle, sweet Mademoiselle, do not be vexed by my whim, but I want to be quite alone when I read it.'

'Certainly, of all odd little creatures there is none more odd than you, my darling. But you will let me see it afterwards, all the same? That is the least I deserve, it seems to me. Well, well! I will go to take off my hat and veil, and will come back.'

An odd little being no doubt, and, moreover, curiously coy, for she now felt that the proprieties necessitated her rising and putting on some clothes and covering her hair, before she could open a man's letter, for the first time in her life. So hastily slipping on a light blue morning wrapper, made in the Rue de la Paix by the right maker, and covering her fair head in a gauze veil of old Circassian embroidery, with trembling hands she broke the seal.

A very short letter; ten very simple lines, with a touch of the unexpected that made her smile in spite of her disappointment at finding nothing more confidential, more fraught with meaning — a polite and friendly response, and thanks which betrayed some weariness; that was all.

But at any rate there was his signature, very legible, very real — André Lhéry. This name, in his own hand, went to her brain like a fit of giddiness. And just as he, in the far West, on receiving the letter with the Stamboul post-mark, had felt as if something were beginning, so she here had a presentiment of some indefinable delight and disaster as the outcome of his answer, arriving on such a day — the eve of the great event of her whole life. This man, who had for so long reigned supreme in her dreams, this man, as far sundered from her, as inaccessible as if they were the inhabitants of different planets, had this morning really come into her life, by the mere fact of these few lines written and signed by him for her.

Never had she so keenly felt herself imprisoned, and rebellious, and longing for freedom, and space, and flight into the unknown world. It was but a step to the window where she was wont to rest on her elbows and gaze out; but no, there were the carved lattices, the iron bars, which exasperated her. She turned away towards a door that stood ajar — kicking the train of the wedding-gown out of her way, where it lay on the handsome carpet — the door of her dressing-room, all lined with white marble, a larger room than the bedroom, and with windows unscreened and very wide, opening on the garden with its patriarchal plane-trees. The letter still in her hand, she rested her arms on the sill of one of these windows to see the open sky, the trees, the splendour of the first roses, to feel on her cheeks the soft touch of the air and sun. But ah! what high walls enclosed the garden! Why such high walls, like those built round the yard of prisons

for solitary confinement ? With buttresses at
intervals to prop them up, they were so enor-
mously high! their height contrived expressly to
hinder any one in the tallest house in the neighbourhood from ever seeing who might be walking
in that secret enclosure.

In spite of its dismal seclusion the garden was
very lovable, because it was very old, with moss
and lichen growing on its stones, and because its
walks were invaded by grass between the box-
edges; a jet of water danced in a marble basin of
antique fashion, and it had a little kiosque, much
the worse for time, to dream in under the shade
of the gnarled and knotted planes crowded with
birds' nests. All these had this garden of old;
and above all it held a soul, a sweet, homesick
spirit, a soul breathed into it little by little in the
course of years, the sadly exhaled repining of
cloistered women, of youth and beauty here kept
captive.

This morning four or five men, beardless
negroes, were there in their shirt-sleeves, working
at the preparations for the great event of to-
morrow, one stretching an awning between the
trees, another spreading splendid Asiatic rugs on
the ground. Catching sight of the girl at the
window, they greeted her with a twinkle of the
eye full of covert meaning, and a 'Good day' at
once familiar and respectful, which by an effort
she returned with a frank smile, not at all scared
by their gaze; till suddenly she started back in
dismay at the aspect of a young peasant with a
fair moustache, who came in loaded with baskets

of flowers, and who must almost have seen her face.

But the letter! She had in her hands a letter from André Lhéry — a real letter. For the moment this alone mattered. Last week she had committed the audacious freak of writing to him, so completely had the dread of this marriage, fixed for to-morrow, thrown her off her balance. Four pages of innocent self-betrayal, things which to her had seemed quite terrible; and to conclude, a request, an entreaty, that he would reply at once, *poste-restante*, to an assumed name. She had sent this off forthwith, for fear lest reflection should bring hesitancy, sent it off more or less at the mercy of good luck, having no exact address, with the complicity and assistance of her former governess, Mademoiselle Esther Bonneau — Bonneau de Saint-Miron, if you please, holding the diploma of the University and a qualification of Public Instruction — the lady who had taught her French, and added, for the fun of it, as a crowning accomplishment, a little slang studied in the works of 'Gyp.'

It had reached its destination, that child's cry of distress, and the poet had replied, with a little undercurrent of suspicion and irony, but on the whole quite nicely, in a letter which could be shown to the most sarcastic of her friends, and would be enough to make them jealous. And then, all of a sudden, she was fired with impatience to make her cousins read it — cousins who were like sisters, — for they had declared that he would not answer. Their home was quite close, in the same high, lonely quarter of the city, so she could go in her wrapper without wasting time in dressing; and at once, in the languid imperious tone of a child addressing some over-indulgent old nurse, she called to some unseen attendant, 'Cadine!' And again, more sharply, 'Cadine!' evidently being accustomed to know that some one was always waiting to serve her caprices; then, as Cadine did not appear, she pressed the knob of an electric bell.

Finally Cadine came, a figure even more incongruous in such a room than the text from the Koran in gold embroidery above the bed: a perfectly black face, a head wrapped in a veil spangled with silver — an Ethiopian slave, whose name was Kondjé-Gul (Rosebud). Her young mistress addressed her in some far-away tongue, an Asiatic language, amazing surely to the hangings, the furniture, and the books.

'Kondjé-Gul, you are never on the spot!' but the reproof was spoken in a tone of affectionate melancholy which greatly mitigated it. And it was indeed a base reproach, for Kondjé-Gul was, on the contrary, always a great deal too much on the spot, like a tiresomely faithful dog, and her mistress was, in fact, rather the victim of the custom of the country which allows no bolts to the doors; permitting the women of the household to walk in at any hour, as if all the rooms were theirs, so that no one is ever sure of an instant of solitude. Kondjé-Gul, entering on tip-toe, had come certainly twenty times that morning to be at hand when her young mistress should

wake. And how strongly she had been tempted
to blow out the burning taper. But then! It
was on the writing-table, and she was forbidden
ever to touch anything there; it was to her a
shrine of dangerous mysteries, and she feared
lest by extinguishing that little flame she might
break who knows what spell.

'Kondjé-Gul, my *tcharchaf*,[1] quick. I want to
go to see my cousins.'

And Kondjé-Gul proceeded to wrap the girl
in black. Black was the skirt she put on over
the wrapper made by the right maker, black the
long cape she threw over her shoulders, and black
the thick veil fastened by pins to the hood she
pulled down over her face to hide it as under
a cowl. As she trotted to and fro to shroud her
young mistress, she murmured sentences in her
Asiatic tongue, talking to herself, as it seemed,
or chanting a song — childish, lulling things, as
not taking a serious view of the little bride's
melancholy.

'He is fair, he is handsome, is the young Bey
who will come to-morrow to carry away my sweet
mistress. And how happy we shall be in the fine
palace to which he will take us both!'

'Be silent, Cadine; ten times have I told you
I will not hear him mentioned!'

And the next moment: 'Cadine, you were
there, you must have heard his voice the day
when he came to talk to my father. Tell me,
what is the Bey's voice like? At all soft?'

'As soft as the music of your piano, the music

---

[1] Enveloping veils worn on the street.

you make with your left hand, you know, at the
end where the notes cease. As sweet as that —
oh, and he is so fair and handsome, that young
Bey ——'

'Well, well; so much the better,' interrupted
the girl in French, with a mocking accent that
was almost Parisian.

And she added in the Asiatic tongue:

'Is my grandmother up, do you know?'

'No, the Lady said she would stay in bed late
to look the fresher to-morrow.'

'Well, when she wakes, let her be told I have
gone to my cousins. Go and tell old Ismaïl to
escort me — you and he — I will take you both.'

Meanwhile Mademoiselle Esther Bonneau (de
Saint-Miron), upstairs in her own room — the
room she had had in former days when she lived
in the house, and that she had come back to now
to be present at to-morrow's high function —
Mademoiselle Esther Bonneau had some prickings
of conscience. It was not she, of course, who
had brought Kant's works to find a place on the
white writing-table, nor Nietzsche's, nor Baudelaire's even. For eighteen months past, since her
pupil's education was regarded as finished, she
had been settled under the roof of another Pasha
to teach his little girls, and not till then had her
first charge emancipated herself in the matter of
reading, since there was nobody to check her
vagaries. Still, all the same, the governess felt
herself to a certain extent responsible for the
erratic flight taken by that youthful mind. And
this correspondence with André Lhéry to which

she had lent herself — to what might it not lead ?
Two persons, to be sure, who would never meet;
that, at least, was quite certain; custom and
barred windows would hinder that. And yet ——

When she presently went downstairs again, she
found herself face to face with a little figure
bundled up like a black bogey to go out in the
street, very excited and in a great hurry.

'And where are you off to, my dear?'

'To see my cousins and show them this.'
This was the letter. 'You must come too, of
course. We will all read it together there.
Come, let us be trotting.'

'To your cousins ? By all means — I will get
my hat and veil again.'

'Your hat! That means an hour — Drat it!'

'Come, my child, come!'

'Come? Where, what? Even if you don't
say it you "drat it" too, when you are in
a temper. Drat the hat! and drat the veil,
and drat the young Bey — drat the future, drat
life — death — drat everything!'

Mademoiselle Bonneau had a suspicion that
a flood of tears was threatening, and to effect a
diversion she clasped her hands, bowed her head
in the attitude sacred on the stage to tragic
remorse, and said:

'And to think that your unhappy grandmother
paid and kept me for seven years for such a
result!'

The black bogey, in fits of laughter under her
veil, in the twinkling of an eye had thrown a lace
kerchief over Mademoiselle Bonneau's head, and

c

now dragged her off with her arm round her waist.

'That I should be bundled up is one thing; I must, it is the law. But you, who are not compelled — and to go two yards — and in this part of the city, where you never see even a cat.'

They ran downstairs two steps at a time. Kondjé-Gul and old Ismaïl, an Ethiopian eunuch, waited for them at the bottom to attend them; Kondjé-Gul muffled from head to foot in a green shroud spangled with silver, and the man buttoned and belted into a black European frock coat, in which, but for his fez, he might have been a country attorney.

The heavy door was thrown open; they were outside on the hill, in the bright sunshine of eleven o'clock, looking down on a wooded cemetery, thick-set with cypresses and tombs with tarnished gilding, which sloped gently down to the deep bay crowded with shipping.

And beyond the inlet of the sea at their feet, on the other side, half-hidden by the cypress trees in the sad, peaceful wood, high up against the sky in the clear, limpid air, the mass stood outlined of the city which for twenty years had haunted André Lhéry with longing. Stamboul sat enthroned, not dim in twilight, as in the poet's dreams, but sharp, luminous, and real.

Real — though veiled in a diaphanous blue mist, in remote silence and splendour, Stamboul was there, Stamboul the immemorial, still the same as when the old Khalifs had looked out on it; as when Suleyman the Great had imagined

and created its noble outline by adding the finest
of the cupolas.   Of all this vast number of
minarets and domes standing up in the morning
air none seemed to be in ruins, and yet over all
there was an indescribable impression of Time.
In spite of distance and the rather dazzling light,
it could be seen that it was very, very old.   The
eye was not deceived; a ghost, a magnificent
ghost of the past, is this city, still standing, with
its endless spindles of stone, so slender, so light,
that how they have lasted is a marvel.   Minarets
and mosques have faded in the course of years to
various tints of whiteness streaked with neutral
greys; and as to the myriad wooden houses
crouching in their shadows, they are yellow ochre,
russet brown, subdued by the almost unceasing
haze exhaled from the all-surrounding sea.   And
the vast prospect was mirrored in the glassy waters
of the gulf.

The two women, the one veiled and the other
with the lace kerchief tied anyhow on her head,
walked quickly, followed by their negro attend-
ants, and scarcely glancing at the wonderful view
which was the background to all their days.
They took a path with paving stones in wild
disorder along the hill, between old and aristo-
cratic mansions mummified behind their gates on
one hand, and on the other the hillside cemetery
of Kassim Pacha, the fairy magnificence of the
view gleaming between its gloomy trees.   The
swallows, which had built their nests everywhere
under the barred and shuttered balconies, were
chirping deliciously, the cypresses exhaled a good

smell of resin, the ancient earth, full of the bones of the dead, exhaled a fresh smell of spring.

They did not, in fact, meet a creature in their short walk, no one but a water-carrier in his oriental dress, who had come to fill his water-skin at a very old cistern by the roadside, of ancient marble sculptured with exquisite arabesques.

On arriving at a house with closely barred windows, a pasha's house, a tall, moustachioed porter, dressed in red and gold with pistols in his sash, opened the door without uttering a word; and they, as intimates and privileged, without a word on their part, went upstairs to the harem.

A vast white room on the first floor, whence, through the open door, came the voices and laughter of young women. They were amusing themselves by talking French, no doubt because they were discussing dress. The point in question was whether a certain bunch of roses on a bodice would look best placed on this side or on that. 'Six of one and half-a-dozen of the other,' said one.

'Much of a muchness, only more so,' asserted another, a little red-haired damsel with a skin like milk, and saucy eyes, whose governess had been past mistress of slang.

This was the bedroom of the cousins, two sisters of eighteen and twenty-one, for whom the bride of the morrow had reserved the privilege of first reading the great man's letter. There were two white enamel bedsteads for the two girls, each with its Arabic text, embroidered in gold on a

velvet panel, hanging above it against the wall.
On the floor, other beds had been improvised,
mattresses with coverlets of blue or pink satin, for
four girls invited to the wedding festivities. On
the chairs — white enamelled chairs with Pompa-
dour flowered silk — their dresses for the great event
but just arrived from Paris, lay in light masses of
gay colour, all the usual disorder of a day before
a function; an encampment it might have been —
an encampment of little gipsy maidens, but very
fashionable and very rich. As the Moslem rule
prohibits women from going out of doors after
dark, the pleasant custom has grown up of their
remaining in each other's houses for days or even
weeks together, with or without any reason, sometimes merely to pay a visit; and dormitories are
arranged, with much chat and laughter. Oriental
veils were lying about, wreaths of flowers, and
jewels by Lalique. The window bars and carved
wood lattices gave a sort of clandestine note to all
this strewn luxury, all intended to charm or dazzle
other women, but which no eye of moustachioed
man might ever be allowed to gaze on. And in
one corner two negress slaves, seated at their ease,
were singing their native songs, beating out the
time on a little muffled drum. Our vehement
democrats of the West might learn lessons of
fraternity in this easygoing land, where, in practice,
caste and social differences are not recognised, and
the humblest servants of either sex are always
treated as members of the family.

The arrival of the bride-elect startled and
amazed them all. She was certainly not expected

that morning. What could have brought her?
Black, entirely in her street wrappings, how
mysterious and ominous she appeared in the
midst of all this white and pink and pale blue,
all these silks and muslins. Why had she come
in this unexpected way, to see her bridesmaids at
home?

She threw back her mournful veil, showing her
dainty features, and in an airy, uninterested way
she explained in French — a language evidently
familiar in the harems of Constantinople:

'A letter I want to show you.'

'A letter — from whom?'

'Ah! guess now.'

'From the aunt at Adrianople, I wager,
promising you a set of brilliants.'

'No.'

'Then from the aunt at Erivan, who is sending
you a pair of Angora cats as a wedding present.'

'No, again. It is from a stranger. It is — from
a gentleman ——'

'A gentleman! How dreadful! A gentleman, you little wretch!'

And she held out the letter, satisfied with the
effect she had produced; two or three pretty
golden heads — real gold and artificial gold — came
together at once to see the signature.

'André Lhéry! — No! Has he answered you?
— Is it from him? Impossible!'

All the little circle had been taken into confidence as to the letter to the author. There is
such a consentaneous spirit of revolt among the
Turkish women of to-day against the severe rule

of the harem, that they never betray each other; if the delinquency were ever so serious, instead of quite innocent as in this case, there would be the same secrecy, the same silence.

They crowded up to read it together, head against head, including Mademoiselle Bonneau de Saint-Miron, all holding on to the paper. At the third sentence they shouted with laughter.

'Oh, do you see? He will not believe you are Turkish. That is too good! He knows all about us so well, it would seem, that he is quite sure you are not.'

'But that really is a triumph, my dear,' said Zeyneb, the elder of the cousins. 'That shows how keen your wit is and the elegance of your style.'

'A triumph!' retorted the red-haired girl, with a pert nose and an expression of comic mockery. 'A triumph! If he takes you to be a Perote, thank you for nothing, I say.'

The tone in which the word *Perote* was said (an inhabitant of Pera) was a thing to hear. In the mere pronunciation of it she had infused all her scorn as a pure-bred daughter of the Osmanli for the Levantines — Armenians, Greeks, and Jews — of which the Perote is the prototype.[1]

'Poor Lhéry,' added Kerimeh, one of the young visitors; 'he is behind the times. He must be still in the Turkey of the novels of 1830 — narghilehs, sweetmeats, and the divan all day.'

[1] While heartily agreeing with the Osmanlis as to the Perotes in general, I must admit that I have known many amiable exceptions to the rule; men of perfect respectability and breeding, women who would be exquisite in any country and any society. — P. L.

'Or even,' added Melek, the saucy, red-haired maiden, 'merely in the Turkey of his own youth. He must be getting a little wrinkled, you know, must your poet.'

It was certainly true, indisputably true, that André Lhéry could no longer be young. And this fact intruded itself for the first time on the fancy of his little unknown adorer, who had never thought about it; a rather disappointing fact, disturbing her dream, and casting pale melancholy on her worship of him.

But in spite of their pretence at laughter and irony they were all in love with the man, so remote and almost disembodied — all who were there; they loved him for having loved their Turkey and spoken with respect of their Islam. A letter written by him to one of them was an event in their cloistered lives, in which nothing ever happens till the great annihilating catastrophe of marriage. It was read aloud. Each one was eager to hold the sheet of paper on which his hand had rested. And then, all being students of character from writing, they tried to unveil the mystery of his handwriting.

But a mamma appeared, the mamma of the two sisters, and at once the subject was changed and the letter was conjured away. Not that this was a very strict mamma with her placid face, but she would have scolded all the same, and, above all, she would not have understood, she was of another generation, spoke but little French, and had read nothing since Alexandre Dumas *père*. A wide gulf lay between her and her daughters, an abyss of at least two centuries, so fast does the world progress in Turkey nowadays. Even physically she was a different being; her fine eyes were soft, with a rather vacant calm which was far from the admirers of André Lhéry; she had, in fact, restricted her part on earth to being a tender mother and a blameless wife, and had asked no more. Besides this she wore her European clothes badly, and was awkward in over-trimmed dresses; while her daughters, on the contrary, already understood how to be elegant and refined in very simple materials.

Next the French governess in the house made her appearance — on the same pattern as Esther Bonneau, but younger and even more romantic. And now, as the room was really too crowded with so many persons, and gowns lying on the chairs, and mattresses on the floor, they went into the larger adjoining room, in 'modern style,' the drawing-room of the harem.

Here entered presently, without knocking, for the door always stood open, a fat German lady, wearing spectacles and a hat loaded with feathers, leading by the hand Fahr-el-Nissa, the youngest of the guests. And at once the whole bevy of girls began talking in German, with as much ease as before they had spoken in French. This portly lady was the music mistress, and a woman of indisputable talent; she and Fahr-el-Nissa, who already played like an artist, had just been practising a new arrangement of Bach's fugues, for two pianos, and each player had thrown her whole soul into it.

They talked German with no more difficulty than Italian or English, for these young Turkish damsels read Dante, Byron, and Shakespeare in the original. Better cultivated than most girls of the same class in the West, as a consequence, no doubt, of their strict seclusion and long quiet evenings, they had devoured alike ancient classics and modern degenerates, and in music were equally enthusiastic for Gluck, and for César Franck, or Wagner, or for reading the scores of Vincent d'Indy. Perhaps, too, they profited by the long repose and mental slothfulness of their mothers and grandmothers; in their brain matter, newly tilled, or at least long fallow, every seed sprouted and grew, as rank weeds and beautiful poisonous flowers run wild in virgin soil.

The drawing-room of the haremlik that morning, grew fuller and fuller. The two negresses, with their little drum, had followed their mistresses. After them came an old lady, whom all rose to greet with respect — the grandmother. Then they all spoke in Turkish, for she knew nothing of Western languages, and what did she care for André Lhéry, this ancient dame? Her dress, embroidered in silver, was of the old Turkish make, and a Circassian veil covered her white hair. The gulf of non-comprehension between her and her grand-daughters was for ever unfathomable, and at meals she had more than once horrified them by the habit she had not quite lost of eating rice with her fingers, after the manner of her forebears, though even as she did it she was all the while a great lady to

those finger-tips, and always an imposing personage.

So, out of deference to the old lady, they all
spoke Turkish, and at once the hum of voices
sounded more harmonious — as soft as music.

Presently a lady came in, slender and un-
dulating in her gait; she came from outside, and,
of course, looked like a black spectre. This was
Alimeh Hanum, a diplomaed professor of philosophy in the college for girls founded by His
Imperial Majesty the Sultan. She came regularly
three times a week to give lessons to Melek in
Arabic and Persian literature. There was no
lesson to-day, of course, on the eve of the
wedding, when everybody's head was turned;
but when she had removed her cowl-like veil,
showing her pleasant, serious face, the conversation turned on the old poets of Iran, and Melek,
now quite grave, recited a passage from the 'Land
of Roses,' by Saadi.

No signs here of odalisques nor of narghilehs,
no sweetmeats in this Pasha's harem, consisting of
a grandmother, a mother, the daughters, and two
nieces with their governesses.

And, in fact, with two or three exceptions
perhaps, every harem in Constantinople is of the
same type; the harem in these days is neither
more nor less than the female part of a family
constituted as our own families are, and educated
in the same way, with the exception of their seclusion, of the thick veils worn out of doors, and of
the improbability of ever exchanging ideas with a
man, unless it be the father, or the husband, or

a brother, or, in some cases, by special grace, a very intimate cousin who was a playfellow in childhood.

They were now speaking French again, and discussing dress, when a voice, so clear and pure that it might have been from Heaven, was heard outside as if dropping from on high; the Imam of a neighbouring mosque was calling from the top of a minaret, bidding the faithful to midday prayer.

On this the little bride, remembering that her grandmother breakfasted at noon, fled like Cinderella, followed by Mademoiselle Bonneau, who was the more alarmed of the two at the idea that the old lady might be waiting.

III

It was a silent meal, this last breakfast in her old home, as she sat between two women so obscurely hostile as the governess and her stern grandmother.

When it was over, she went to her room, and only wished she could lock and double-lock herself in, but Turkish women's bedrooms have no locks; she could only give orders through Kondjé-Gul to all the servants and slaves, who were for ever on guard, day and night, as is the custom, in the halls and the long passages of her suite of rooms, like so many tame and intrusive watch-dogs.

During this last supreme day, still her own, she wanted to prepare herself as if for death, sort her papers, and a thousand little treasures, and, above all, burn things, burn them for fear of the eye of the unknown man who in a few hours would be her master. There was no haven of refuge for her distressful soul, and her terror and revolt increased as the day went on.

She seated herself in front of her writing-table and relighted the taper which was to communicate its flame to a host of mysterious little letters that lay sleeping in the white enamelled drawers;

letters from friends just married, or quaking in anticipation of marriage; letters in Turkish, in French, in German, in English, all proclaiming rebellion, all poisoned by the deep pessimism which, in our day, is ravaging the harems of the Turks. Now and again she re-read a sentence, hesitated regretfully, and then, after all, put the little sheet into the colourless flame — a hardly visible glimmer in the sunshine. And all these treasures, all the little secrets of beautiful young women, their suppressed indignation, their vain laments — all turned to ashes, piled up and mingled in a copper brazier, the only oriental object in the room.

The drawers emptied, the letters destroyed, there still lay before her a large blotting-case with a gold snap, crammed full of note-books written in French. Should she burn these too? No, she really had not the courage. They were the whole history of her girlhood, her private diary, begun on her thirteenth birthday, the fatal day when she had *donned the tcharchaf*, to use the phrase of the country; that is to say, the day when she was condemned for ever to hide her face from the world, to take the veil and become one of the innumerable black spectres of Constantinople.

Nothing earlier than this veiling was recorded in her journal. Nothing of her infancy as a little barbaric princess, far away in the remotest plains of Circassia, the obscure realm over which her family had ruled for two centuries. Nothing, either, of her life as a little girl in the fashionable world, when, she being about eleven years old, her father had come to settle in Constantinople, where the title of Marshal of the Court had been conferred on him by the Sultan; that had been a time of wonders, of elegant tutelage, with lessons, too, to be learnt and exercises to be written. For two years she had been seen at fêtes, at tennis parties, at the Embassy dances; she had waltzed like a grown-up girl with the most fastidious partners of the European colony; her card was always full, for she charmed them all by her sweet little face, her grace, her luxurious elegance, and also by an inimitable expression—a look at once very gentle and very capable of revenge, very diffident and very haughty. And then one fine day, at a ball given for children at the English Embassy, some one asked: 'Where is the little Circassian?' and the men of the country had replied quite simply: 'Ah, of course, you did not know. She has taken the Tcharchaf.'

'Taken the Tcharchaf!' as much as to say buried, smuggled away by the stroke of a wand, never to be seen again. If by chance you should meet her going past in a shuttered carriage, she will be a mere black shape, impossible to recognise. She might as well be dead.

So, her thirteen years complete, she had passed, in obedience to an immutable law, into the veiled world which lives in Constantinople on the confines of the other, which you rub up against in the streets but may never look at, and which at sunset is shut up within prison bars; the world

of which you are aware all about you, a disturbing
and attracting influence, but impenetrable, while
it watches, conjectures, criticises, and sees many
things through its immovable shroud of black
silk, and guesses all it does not see.

Thus, suddenly imprisoned at the age of
thirteen, with a father who was always on duty at
the Palace, and a stern grandmother devoid of all
show of tenderness, alone in a vast house at
Kassim Pacha, a quarter of old mansions and
cemeteries, where at nightfall silence and terror
were all pervading, she had devoted herself
passionately to study. And this had lasted till she
was now within a few days of two-and-twenty —
this ardent desire to know everything: literature,
history, transcendental philosophy. Among the
young women her friends, themselves very highly
educated in this propitious seclusion, she was
regarded as a sort of star, whose erudition and
opinions and innocent audacity were quoted, while
her expensive elegance was copied; especially
was she the standard-bearer of female insurrection
against the discipline of the harem.

No, after all, she would not burn this diary,
begun on the first day of the tcharchaf. She
would rather confide it, carefully sealed up,
to some trustworthy and rather independent
friend, whose drawers were not liable to be over-
hauled by a husband. And, who could tell? In
the future, perhaps, she might ask for it back
again, and carry it on further. She clung to it,
because she had almost fixed in its pages the details
of the life which must end to-morrow, the happy

moments of the past, certain spring days more strangely bright than others, evenings of more delicious languor in the old garden of roses, and excursions on the enchanted waters of the Bosphorus with the cousins she so fondly loved. All this would seem more irrevocably sunk in the abyss of time if that poor diary were destroyed. Writing it had been her chief resource against the melancholy moods of an immured maiden, and suddenly she was moved to write in it again at this very moment, and divert the distress of this last day. So, still sitting at her writing-table, she took up her pen, a little rod of gold with a ring of rubies. When, in the first pages of this record, now nine years old, she had adopted the French language, it was to make sure that neither her grandmother nor any one else in the house should find amusement in reading it. But for the last two years, the French, written with the utmost care and elegance, had been intended for the eye of an imaginary reader. A young woman's diary always is intended for a reader, fictitious or real, but necessarily fictitious when the writer is a Turkish woman. That reader was a remote, very far-away person—for her, indeed, he hardly existed — the author, André Lhéry. It was all written now for him, to him, even in quite involuntary imitation of something of his manner. It assumed the form of a letter addressed to him in which, for more complete illusion, she called him by his name, André, as if he were a real friend, a big brother.

So, that evening, this was what the little hand,

D

loaded with too splendid rings, traced upon the paper:

April 18, 1901.

'I have never told you anything about my childhood, have I, André? And you must know this: I, whom you have thought so civilised, am by nature a little barbarian. Something will always survive in me of the child of open spaces, who once used to gallop on horseback to the clatter of arms, or dance in the lamplight to the tinkle of her silver girdle.

'And in spite of a veneer of European culture, when my newly found soul of which I was so proud, my soul as a thinking being, my self-conscious soul, when this soul of mine suffers too acutely, these memories of my childhood come back to haunt me. They rise up dominant, vivid and brilliant; they show me a land of light, a lost paradise, to which I cannot — nay, and *would not*— return; a Circassian village far from hence, far, far beyond the Konieh, known as Karadjemir. There my family has reigned ever since it came from the Caucasus. My ancestors in their own land were the Khans of Kiziltopeh, the Sultan of that time gave them as a fief the territory of Karadjemir. There I dwelt till I was eleven years old. I was free and happy. Girls in Circassia are not veiled; they dance and talk with young men, and choose their husbands by the guidance of their heart.

'Our house was the finest in the village, and on all sides long avenues of acacias led up to it.

Acacias stood round it, too, in a wide circle, and
the least breath of wind bowed their branches as if
in homage; then the scented petals fell like snow.
In my dreams I see a rapid river, from the living-
room I could hear the song of its hurrying
ripples. Oh! how fast they rushed on in their
flow to the unknown bourne! When I was little,
I laughed to see them foam in a rage against the
rocks.

'By the side of the hamlet, in front of the
house, stretched a wide, open space. There we
were wont to dance in the Circassian mode to the
sound of our old-world instruments. Two and
two we formed in chains, all draped in white silk,
with garlands of flowers in our hair. I can see
them now—my companions of those days. Where
are they? They were all lovely and gentle, with
long eyes and bright smiles.

'As day fell in summer my father's Circassians,
the youths of the village, left their labor and rode
on horseback across the plain. My father, an old
soldier, placed himself at their head, and led them
as to a charge. When I was little, one of them
would perch me on his saddle; I was intoxicated
with speed, with the passion that had been silently
rising all day from the burning soil to break out
in the evening in the clatter of arms and wild
songs. The sky would presently change colour;
first came the purple hour of an evening battle,
and the riders shouted battle songs to the winds.
Then came the rosy, opal-tinted hour ——'

She had got so far as this opal-tinted hour,

wondering if the epithet might not be too pretentious to satisfy André, when Kondjé-Gul, in spite
of prohibition, burst into the room.

'He is there, mistress, he is there!'

'He is there? — Who?'

'He, the young Bey. He has been to call on
the Pasha, your father, and he is just going away.
Quick, run to your window and you will see him.'
To which the little princess replied, without
moving, and with an icy indifference which quite
stupefied good old Kondjé-Gul:—

'And you disturb me for that? I shall see
him too soon! To say nothing of seeing him as
often as I want till I am an old woman!'

This she said to emphasise, in the presence of
the servants, her disdain of the young lord. But as
soon as Kondjé-Gul had disappeared in deep confusion, she tremulously went up to the window;
he had just mounted, in his handsome uniform as
a staff-officer. She had time to see that his
moustache was in fact fair, rather too fair for her
taste, but that he was a handsome youth with a
fine stalwart figure. He was none the less the
enemy, the master forced upon her, who should
never be admitted to her secret soul. Then,
determined to think no more about him, she went
back to her table — her cheeks flushed and tingling,
nevertheless — to go on with her journal, her letter
to the unreal confidant.

'The rosy hour (merely rosy, that was certain;
opal-tinted was erased) when memory awakes and
the Circassians would recall the country of their

ancestors; one would chant a song of exile and the others would draw rein to listen to the single mournful voice. Then the hour was violet, tender and sweet; the whole plain would ring with a hymn of love. And then the horsemen hastily turned their steeds and spurred them to a gallop to ride home. The flowers drooped in the road, exhaling their last fragrance. The riders glittered, seeming to bear with them on their weapons all the liquid silver that floated in the summer twilight.

'In the distance a glare of fire marked the little spot where the acacias of Karadjemir were grouped in the midst of the level, silent steppe. The flame grew and soon became a flare of tall flames licking the first stars; for those who had remained at home lighted bonfires, and round about these were girls dancing and singing, accentuated by waving white robes and floating scarves. The young people amused themselves, while men of riper age sat out of doors smoking, and mothers, looking through the window screens, watched the coming of love to their children.

'In those days I was a queen. My father, Tewfik Pasha, and Seniha, my mother, loved me above all else, for their other children were dead. I was the Sultana of the hamlet; no one else had such rich dresses or such finely chased belts of gold and silver, and when by any chance a merchant from the Caucasus passed that way, with his sacks full of gems and bales of silk spangled with gold, every one in the neighbourhood knew that he must call first at our house; no one would have dared to buy so much as a scarf till the Pasha's daughter had taken her choice of the treasures.

'My mother was wise and gentle; my father was kind, and was known to be just. Every passing stranger might knock at our door; the house was his. Though poor he was as welcome as the Sultan himself. An exile, a fugitive — and I have seen such — the shelter of the house would have protected him till his hosts were killed. But woe to the man who should have tried to make use of Tewfik Pasha to help him in any base or even doubtful action; my father, though so kind, could be a ruthless judge. I have seen him ——!

'Such, André, was my childhood. Then we lost my mother, and my father would not stay at Karadjemir without her, so he brought me with him to Constantinople to my grandmother's house, near my cousins.

'Now, my uncle, Arif Bey, governs there in his stead. But hardly any change has taken place in that obscure corner of the world, where the days pass on, silently linking into years. I believe a mill has been erected on the river; the little waves which used only to play at being furious, are now trained to be of use, and I fancy I can hear them bewailing their lost liberty. But the fine old house still stands among the trees, and this spring, once again, the acacias will have shed their snows on the roads where I sported as a child. And some other little girl, no doubt, goes riding in my place with the horsemen.

'Nearly eleven years have passed since then.

'The gay and thoughtless child is now a grown-up girl, who has shed many tears. Would she have been happier if her old life had still gone on? But it was written that she must leave it because she had to be transformed into a thinking being, and her orbit was destined one day to cross yours. Oh, who will tell us the wherefore, the supreme reason for such meetings, when souls scarcely touch and yet never again forget each other? For you, André, you too will never forget me.'

She was tired of writing. And, in fact, the brief vision of the Bey had disturbed the flow of her memory.

What could she do to finish this last day? Ah! the garden; the dear garden, haunted by her youthful dreams; she would linger there till nightfall. Quite at the end there was a certain bench under the venerable plane-trees against the old moss-grown wall; there she would sit alone till the close of the April day, which seemed to her to promise no to-morrow. She rang at once for Kondjé-Gul to give the necessary warning of her coming; orders to all the gardeners, coachmen, male domestics of every kind, that they must leave the paths clear, so as not to profane by a glance the little goddess who meant to walk there unveiled.

Nay, on second thoughts she would not go out; it was always possible that she might meet some eunuch or women servants with their meaning smiles at the bride-elect, and in their presence she would have to assume the rapturous expression required by etiquette in such circum-

stances. And then, how exasperating to see all
the preparations for the fête, tables laid under the
trees and fine rugs spread on the ground.

So instead she took refuge in a little room next
her bedroom, where there was an Erard piano.
She must bid farewell to music too, since there
would be no piano in her new home. The young
Bey's mother — a 1320,[1] as these old-fashioned
ladies are called by the young flowers of hothouse
culture brought up in modern Turkish homes —
an unmitigated 1320, had, not without mistrust,
allowed the library of new books in Western
tongues and the illustrated magazines, but the
piano had evidently shocked her; they had not
dared to mention it again. The old lady had
come several times to see her son's betrothed,
overwhelming her with coaxing ways and little
old-world compliments which fretted the girl,
staring her out of countenance with persevering
attention, so as to be the better able to describe
her to her son. So, no more piano in her home
after to-morrow, her home over there, across the
bay, in the very heart of old Stamboul. Seated at
the instrument, her strong, swift little hands,
wonderfully accomplished and supple, ran over the
keys, at first improvising vague and extravagant
impromptus with neither head nor tail, to an
accompaniment of sharp rattling taps, each time
her heavy loose rings knocked against the flats and
sharps. Then she took off her rings, and after
a moment's thought she began a very difficult

[1] The nickname given to any one who recognises no dates but from the
Hegira, instead of using the European calendar.

arrangement by Liszt of an air by Wagner; and by degrees she ceased to be the girl who was, on the morrow, to be married to Captain Hamdi Bey, aide-de-camp to His Imperial Majesty; she was the betrothed of a young warrior with long hair, who dwelt in a castle on the heights, in the darkness of the clouds, overhanging a broad tragical river; she heard the symphony of old legendary ages in the deep forests of the north. But when she ceased playing, when the glamour had died away with the last vibration of the strings, she noticed the sunbeams already reddening and coming in almost level through the eternal chequers of the windows. Yes, the day was ending, and she was suddenly seized with a terror of being alone on this last evening, though just now she had wished it. She flew to her grand-mother to ask permission, which was granted, and wrote in haste to her cousins, begging them dis-tressfully, come what might, to visit her and keep her company — but only the two sisters, not the other little damsels encamped in their room; only Zeyneb and Melek, her bosom friends, her con-fidants, the sisters of her soul. She feared their mother might not allow it on account of their many visitors; she feared lest the hour were too late, the sun too low, for Turkish women do not go out after it has set. And from the barred window she looked after old Ismaïl, who hurried off with the message.

For some days past, even with her cousins, who had been hurt by it, she had been silent on all serious matters, reserved, and almost haughty;

even with those two she had cherished the decency of her misery; but she could no more: she wanted them, to weep on their shoulder.

How fast it sank — the sun of her last evening! Would they have time to come? To know as soon as possible, she leaned over the street as far as the bars and wooden lattice would permit. It was now the 'purple hour of evening battle,' as she had written in her childhood's diary, and thoughts of flight and open revolt raged in her indomitable and dainty little head. And yet what serene peace, what a fatalistic, resigned calm reigned around. An aromatic fragrance came up from the great funereal wood lying so quiet under the windows — the odour of the old, unchangeful soil of Turkey, of short grass and tiny plants that had basked all day in the April sun. The black-green of the trees standing out against the fiery west was here and there pierced, as it were riddled, by shafts of light. Here and there touches of ancient gilding flashed on the tops of those monumental milestones, stuck in haphazard in the ample space, scattered among the cypresses. The Turks have no terror of the dead; they do not exile them; they lay them to rest in the very heart of the cities. Beyond the melancholy objects in the foreground, and the spires of dark foliage standing up as straight as towers, in the intervals between them the distance could be seen — the matchless view: all Stamboul and the gulf, in the broad blaze of a fine sunset. Below, far below, the waters of the Golden Horn, down to which the graveyards sloped, were red and fiery as the sky itself;

hundreds of caïques furrowed their surface — the perennial to and fro following the closing of the bazaars; but from so high up no sound could be heard of their rippling wake or the splash of the oars; they looked like long insects creeping across a mirror. And the opposite shore, the shore of Stamboul, changed while she gazed. All the houses down by the sea, all the lower strata of the enormous pile, were blurred and blotted out, as it were, by the eternal violet haze of the evening, a mist of vapour and smoke. Stamboul changed like a mirage; no details were now visible, neither the decay nor the misery, nor the hideousness of some of the modern structures; it was a mere mass in outline, dark purple with edges of gold, a colossal city in cut jasper, bristling with spires and domes, set up as a screen to shut out a conflagration in heaven.

And the same voices as had sounded at noon in clear celestial tones sang out again in the air, calling the faithful Moslems to the fourth prayer of the day — the sunset hour.

The little prisoner, soothed in spite of herself by the glory and the peace, was growing uneasy about Zeyneb and Melek. Would they be able to come in spite of the late hour? She looked more eagerly towards the end of the road, shut in on one side by the old barred houses, and on the other by the beautiful home of the dead.

Yes, they were coming. There they were, two slender black spectres with no face, just emerging from a great dusty gateway, and hurrying on, attended by two negroes with long sabres. They had settled it quickly, and were very soon ready, poor little things! And as she identified them hastening to respond to her cry of despair, she felt her eyes fill; tears, but comforting tears this time, rolled down her cheeks.

As they came in, raising their veils, the bride threw herself weeping into their arms.

They clasped her to their young hearts with tender pity.

'We fancied somehow that you were not happy. But you would not say a word. We did not dare to speak of it. For many days past we felt you were so secret with us, so cold!'

'Well, you know my way. It is silly, but I am ashamed that any one should see me in distress.'

She was fairly sobbing now.

'But why, my dearest, did you not say "No"?'

'Oh, I have said "No" so often. The list of men I have refused is really too long, it would seem. And consider, I am two-and-twenty, almost an old maid. After all, what does it matter, this one or another, since I must end by marrying somebody?'

Before now she had heard others talk in this way on the eve of marriage, and their submission had disgusted her; now she had come to the same end. 'Since I have not chosen and loved the man,' one had said, 'what does it matter whether he is called Mehmed or Achmed? Shall I not have my children to console me for his presence?' Another, a quite young girl who accepted the first

comer that offered, had excused herself by saying,
'Why not the first as much as the second, of whom
I shall know no more than of this one? What
can I say in refusing? And then all the to-do;
think of it, my dear!' The apathy of all these
girls had seemed to her incomprehensible, allowing
themselves to be married off like slaves! And
here was she consenting to just such a bargain,
and to-morrow—to-morrow—was the dreadful day
of reckoning. Weary of constantly refusing, constantly contending, she, like all the rest, had at
last spoken the 'Yes' which had been her ruin,
instead of the 'No' which would have saved her
at least for a little while longer. And now, too
late to retreat, she stood on the very edge of the
abyss; it was to-morrow!

They wept together, all the three, shedding the
tears which had been repressed for many a day by
the pride of the betrothed, weeping the tears of
bitter separation, as if one of them were condemned
to death.

Melek and Zeyneb, of course, were not to go
home this evening, but to sleep here in their cousin's
room, as is customary when women go out at
nightfall, and as they had constantly done during
the last ten years. The three girls, always together,
like inseparable sisters, were in the habit of sleeping together in one house or the other, but generally
here with the young Circassian.

This evening, when the slaves, without even
asking for orders, had spread on the carpet the
silken mattresses for the visitors, and the three
girls were left to themselves, they felt as if they

were keeping funereal watch by the dead. They had asked and obtained permission not to go downstairs to dinner, and a beardless negro with a grotesque over-fat face had brought them on a silver-gilt tray some food, which they had forgotten to eat.

Downstairs, their grandmother, the Pasha, father of the bride, and Mademoiselle Bonneau de Saint-Miron ate without talking in the silence of catastrophe. The old lady, more offended than ever at the conduct of her daughter's daughter, knew well whom to blame, and abused modern education and the governess. She loved the child, a daughter of her impeccable Moslem race, but who had proved to be a sort of prodigal whose return to hereditary tradition was never to be hoped for; loved her in spite of all, though she had always felt that severity was a duty; and now, face to face with this wordless and incomprehensible rebelliousness, she meant to be harder and sterner than ever. As to the Pasha, he, who had always petted and spoiled his only child like a Sultana of the *Arabian Nights*, and who had been so sweetly loved by her in return, could understand her no better than his old '1320' mother-in-law; indeed, he too was angry; this last caprice was really too much! To set up for a little martyr because, now that it was high time she should have a master, a handsome young fellow had been chosen for her, rich, of good family, and in favour with His Imperial Majesty. And the hapless governess, guiltless at any rate of this betrothal, who had always been the confidential friend of her beloved pupil, sat in silent consternation. Since she had been invited to the house for the wedding, why would the girl have none of her company up in her own rooms this last evening?

No, the three fantastic little damsels — not dreaming, indeed, of the pain they gave her — had wished to be alone on the eve of such a separation.

The very last, this, of their evenings together in the room which to-morrow would be deserted, and to which they must bid farewell! To make it a little more cheerful they had lighted all the wax candles in the candelabra, and the tall pillar lamp, with its shade in the newest fashion that year, as large as a parasol, and made of flower petals. And they went on turning over, sorting, and sometimes destroying a thousand trifles which they had long treasured as precious souvenirs. Here were the tufts of gold or silver thread with which it is the custom to deck the hair of a bride, and which the attendant maidens preserve till their turn comes; there were several of these, glittering where they were hung by knots of ribbon to the mirror-frames and the white walls, and they raised visions of the pale, pretty faces of friends now in durance, or perhaps dead. In a closet were the dolls they had once loved so dearly; broken toys, withered flowers, the sad little relics of their childhood and early youth spent together within the walls of this old house. There were, too, in frames painted or embroidered by their own hands, photographs of the ladies of the Embassies or of young Moslem ladies in evening dress; they would have passed for Frenchwomen of fashion but for the little scrawl below in Turkish characters, a sentiment or a name. Finally, there were the dainty trifles won in past winters in the lotteries got up by Turkish ladies in the cause of charity during the long evenings of Ramazan; they were not of the very least value, still they recalled some past moments of the life which was ending to their acute sorrow. As to the wedding presents, some of which were splendid, arranged by Mademoiselle Bonneau, and displayed in an adjoining drawing-room, they did not care a fig about them.

They had hardly ended their task when once more above the roofs came the sweet, clear voices calling the faithful to the fifth prayer of this last day.

The three girls, to hear the better, seated themselves by the open window, and there inhaled the soft coolness of the night, smelling of cypress and aromatic herbs and the salt sea. The window though open was of course barred, and besides the iron bars were screened by the all-pervading chequered lattice, through which alone a Turkish woman may look on the outer world. The voices in the air still chanted their call near at hand, and others seemed to answer from afar, a host of others, ringing down from the tall minarets of Stamboul, and across the sleeping waters, borne on the hollow bass of the waves. It seemed indeed as if the sound came from the sky itself, a sudden outburst of clear voices calling, calling, in a very airy chant intoned on all sides at once.

But it was soon over, and when all the

Muezzins had sung out, each to the four points of the compass, the religious bidding of immemorial tradition, utter silence suddenly fell. Stamboul now stood out between the thickly set black cypresses as a blue mass against a dimly moonlit sky, a filmy shape, larger than ever, a city of giant cupolas; and its ancient, unalterable silhouette sparkled with endless lights reflected in the waters of the gulf. The girls admired it, gazing through the tiny squares in the imprisoning screen; they wondered whether the famous cities of the West, which they knew only from prints and would never see, since no Moslem woman is allowed to go out of Turkey, whether Vienna, Paris, or London could give such an impression of beauty and vastness. They even put their fingers out through the lattice, as prisoners always do to amuse themselves, and a wild longing came over them to travel, to see the world — or merely once to take a walk by night, on such a night as this, through the streets of Constantinople — or even to go only so far as the cemetery, there beneath the window. But at night no Moslem woman may stir out.

Silence, total silence, gradually enwrapt the old suburb of Kassim Pacha and its closely shut houses. Everything around them grew deadly still. The noise of Pera, where there is a life of the night as in European cities, died out before it could reach them. As to the strident howls of the steamships which lie in swarms under Seraglio Point, there is always respite from them even before the hour of the fifth prayer, for all navigation is stopped on the Bosphorus as soon as it is dark. In this oriental hush, unknown to our towns, one sound alone was heard from time to time, a sound essentially characteristic of the night in Constantinople, resembling no other in the world, though for centuries the Turks have known it always the same: tap, tap, tap, tap, on the old pavements; a tap, tap made resonant by the funereal echoes of streets where no one passes along. This was the watchman of the district, who, making his slow rounds in slippers, struck the stones with his heavy iron-shod staff. In the distance other watchmen responded, doing the same; and the sounds rang out at no great distance apart throughout the vast city; from Eyoub to the Seven Towers, and along the shores of the Bosphorus, the sea of Marmora, and the Black Sea, saying to the inhabitants: 'Sleep, sleep on; we are here open-eyed till morning, on the lookout for thieves or fire.'

Now and then the three girls forgot that this was the last evening. As so often happens just before the great crises of life, they allowed themselves to be deluded by the calm of long-familiar things; here, in this room, everything was in its place and looked as it was wont to look. But sudden reminders struck them each time with a death-chill; to-morrow the parting, the end of their sisterly intimacy, the fall and ruin of all the cherished past.

Oh! that morrow! For her, the bride, a whole day when she must act a part, as custom demanded, and act it well, whatever it might cost her. A whole day when she must smile like an idol, smile at friends by the dozen, smile at the endless tribe of inquisitive gossips who, on the occasion of a grand wedding, invade the house. And then she must find pleasant things to say, receive congratulations with a grace, wear happy looks from morning till night, keep them set on her lips, in her eyes, in spite of revolt and terror. Yes, yes, she would smile through it all; her pride indeed required it of her; to be seen as victim would be too humiliating to her, the unsubdued spirit who had boasted that she would never be married against her will, who had preached to others the crusade of womanhood. But the morrow's sun would rise on a day of irony and cruel fate.

'And if only with the end of the day it might all be ended!' said she. 'But no; afterwards there will be months and years, a whole lifetime to be enslaved, spurned, tormented by this unknown owner. To think that not a day, not a night, will ever be my own again, and that simply because this man has had a fancy to marry the daughter of a Marshal of the Court!'

The gentle little cousins, as they saw her stamp with nervous vexation, suggested as a diversion that they should make some music for the last time. They all went together into the room where the piano had remained open. Here there were quantities of objects lying on the tables, the consoles, the rugs, which showed the mind of the modern Moslem woman eager to try everything in her seclusion, to possess and know everything.

There was even a phonograph, with the latest
improvements of that year; they had amused
themselves with it for a few days, being introduced to the noises of a Western theatre, to the
insipid music of an operetta, and the imbecilities
of a café concert. But there were no memories
bound up with these incongruous toys; they
might stay where chance had dropped them,
uncared-for lumber, the delight of the eunuchs
and serving women.

The bride, seated at the piano, hesitated for a
moment; then she began a concerto of her own
composition. Besides having studied harmony
under excellent teachers, she had a vein of spontaneous inspiration, often a little wild, and almost
always delicately charming; now and then, perhaps, a reminiscence of the galloping Circassian
horses on her native steppe, but no others. She
went on to an unfinished nocturne, begun the
previous evening; it opened with a sort of gloomy
whirlwind, but the peace of the neighbouring
cemeteries got the upper hand in the end. And
a sound from outside was heard now and then,
accentuating the music — the sound peculiar to
Constantinople — the taps of the night-watchman's
stick in the reverberating silence, now as deep as
that of the tomb.

Zeyneb then sang to the accompaniment of her
young sister Melek; like all Turkish women, she
had a rich, rather tragical voice, which she infused
with passion, especially in the fine deep notes.
She, after hesitating too in her choice, opened a
score by Gluck, and gave out magnificently the

immortal invocation: *Divinités du Styx, ministres de la Mort!*

The past generation lying in the cemeteries below, the Turks of old, sleeping among the roots of the cypress trees, must have been greatly astonished at this window open so late, and shedding a bright shaft of light on their gloomy domain; a harem window, no doubt, since it was latticed and barred, and from it came such melodies as were very strange to them.

Zeyneb, however, had hardly ended the defiant words: *Je n'invoquerai point votre pitié cruelle,* when the pianist stopped in alarm, striking a wrong chord. A human figure, which she was the first to perceive, stood by the piano; a tall, lean figure in dark draperies, who had appeared noiselessly like a ghost!

It was not a Divinity of the Styx to be sure, but hardly more reassuring. Much of a muchness, to use the expression which had amused little red-haired Melek. It was Madame Husnugul, the terror of the household. 'Your grandmother,' said she, 'orders you to go to bed and put out the lights.' And she went away as she had come without a sound, leaving them all three frozen with alarm. She had a gift of appearing always and everywhere without being heard; this is easier no doubt in a harem than anywhere else, since the doors are never shut.

Madame Husnugul (the Beauty of the Rose) was a Circassian slave who, thirty years ago, had come to be almost one of the family, having borne a son to the Pasha's brother-in-law. The child died, and she was given in marriage to an intendant in the country. Her husband presently died, and one fine day she made her appearance here again, on a visit, bringing quantities of clothes in blanket bags, in the old Turkish way. And this 'visit' had now lasted for nearly five-and-twenty years. Madame Husnugul, half lady-companion, half superintendent and spy over the young people, had become the right-hand of her former mistress; she was a well-educated woman, and now, on her own account, visited all the ladies of the neighbour-hood; so complete is the feeling of indulgent equality in Turkey that she was received even in the best circles. Many a family in Constantinople has under its roof a Madame Husnugul — or Gulchinassa (Handmaid of the Rose), or Chemsigul (Rose of the Sun), or Purkiémal (the Perfect), or something of that kind — who is always a scourge. But the old '1320' ladies appreciate the services of these duennas, who accompany the young people when they go out and report on them when they come home.

The orders transmitted by Madame Husnugul left no opening for discussion; the three unhappy girls silently closed the piano and blew out the candles.

But before going to bed they threw themselves into each other's arms for a final farewell; they wept for each other as if the events of the morrow meant eternal parting. For fear of bringing back Madame Husnugul, who was no doubt listening outside the door that stood ajar, they dared not speak; but as to sleeping, that was impossible,

and from time to time a sigh or a sob was heard
from one of the little bursting hearts.

The bride herself, in the deep stillness of the
night, which favoured the prescience of despair,
grew more and more distraught at the thought
that every hour, every minute, brought her nearer
to the culminating humiliation and disaster.
With barbaric vehemence she now abhorred the
stranger, whose face she had scarcely seen, but
who would so soon and for ever be the irresponsible owner and master of her person. Since
nothing was done yet, an overwhelming temptation came over her to make some supreme
attempt, no matter what, to escape him at all risks.
But what, how? What human succour could she
look for, who would have pity on her? It was
too late to throw herself at her father's feet; he
would not yield now.

It was near midnight; the moon shed its pale
light into the room, its beams fell through the
inexorable bars and lattice, outlining them on the
white walls. They fell, too, on the text from the
Koran over the little princess's head, the 'Ayet'
which every Moslem woman must have above her
pillow. Her text was on bright green velvet, an
antique and exquisite piece of embroidery in gold,
designed by a famous writer of a past period, and
the words, as mild as those of the Christian
gospel, were these: 'My sins are as great as the
seas, but thy pardon, O Allah! is greater still.'[1]

Long after the girl had ceased to believe, the
holy words that guarded her slumbers had still

[1] Gârih Bahr-i isyauim, Dâhilek yâ ressoul Allah.

had their influence on her soul, and she had retained a vague trust in supreme goodness, supreme forgiveness. And now — all was over; henceforth she looked for no mercy, however indefinite, either before death or after; no, she must suffer alone, protect herself unaided, and be alone responsible. So at this moment she felt prepared for extreme resolves.

Again, then, what steps could she take? She had no weapon in her room, besides, such a solution of the difficulty would be too vulgar; and, indeed, what she craved for was to live! Then she must fly; but whither — and how? At midnight, at random, rushing through the terrifying streets? And where could she take refuge, not to be caught?

Zeyneb meanwhile, who could not sleep, was saying something in a whisper. She had just remembered that it was the day of the week known to the Turks as Vazar-Ghuri, corresponding to our Sunday, on the eve of which day they pray for the dead as well as on the eve of Tcharchembeh, corresponding to our Thursday. Now they had never omitted this duty; it was indeed one of the very few religious traditions of Islam which they still faithfully observed; for the rest, they were much like the other Moslem women of their generation and social rank, touched and scorched by the influence of Darwin and Schopenhauer and other writers. Their grandmother would often say to them: 'It is a sad thing in my old age to see that you have done worse than if you had been converted to Christianity, for

after all God loves all who profess some religion.
But you are really the infidels whose time, as the
prophet so wisely foretold, was certain to come.'

Infidels they were indeed, more sceptical and
hopeless than the average of girls in Western lands.
But still, praying for the dead remained a duty
they dared not fail in, and it was a soothing duty
too.   Even in the course of their walks in the
summer, in the villages by the Bosphorus that
have delicious graveyards under the shade of
cypress and oak, they had often stopped to pray
over some humble and nameless tomb.

So they noiselessly lighted a very small night-
light; the little bride took up her Koran, which
lay on a console near her new-fangled bedstead —
the Koran, always wrapped in a silk handkerchief
from Mecca scented with sandal-wood, which
every Moslem woman must keep by her pillow on
purpose for these prayers that are said at night;
and they all began to murmur in a low voice,
becoming soothed as they went on, for prayer
refreshed their spirit as cold water cools a fever.

But in a few minutes a tall woman in dark
draperies, as noiselessly as before, came in with no
sound of opening doors, and like a spectre stood
beside them: 'Your grandmother orders you to
put out the night-light.'

'Very well, Madame Husnugul. Have the
kindness to put it out yourself, since we are in
bed, and be good enough to explain to my
grandmother that it was not out of disobedience —
but we were reading the prayers for the dead.'

It was near two o'clock in the morning.

When the night-light was extinguished, the three young creatures, exhausted by their emotions, their regrets, and their rebellious rage, went to sleep at once, sound, peaceful sleep, like the sleep of the condemned the night before the fatal morning.

IV

FOUR days later. The bride is in the heart of the
very old and very lordly dwelling of her young
master; alone in the room of the harem which
has been given to her as her private sitting-room
— a Louis XVI. drawing-room in pale blue and
gold, freshly fitted and furnished for her. Her
pink dress, imported from the Rue de la Paix, is
of an impalpable material, looking like an enveloping cloud, in obedience to the fashion that spring,
and her hair is dressed in the last-invented
fashion. In one corner is a white enamelled
writing-table, very much like that in her room at
Kassim Pacha, and the drawers can be locked,
which was her dream.

It might be a lady's room in Paris, but for the
lattices, of course, and the Moslem inscriptions
embroidered on the loveliest old silks which adorn
the walls here and there: the name of Allah and
texts from the Koran. There is, to be sure, a
throne, which would seem strange in Paris; her
marriage throne, very splendid, and standing on a
platform raised by two or three steps and covered
with a canopy, from which hang curtains of blue
satin richly embroidered with flowers in silver.
And finally, here again is old Kondjé-Gul, any-

thing but Parisian in appearance; she sits by a window crooning in very low hum a song of her own black race.

The Bey's mother, the rather silly lady of '1320' with her old pussy ways, has turned out to be in fact an inoffensive creature, rather kind, and who might be really excellent but for her blind idolatry of her son. She is entirely bewitched by the charms of her daughter-in-law, so much so, that only yesterday she came of her own accord to offer her the longed-for piano; post-haste, in a closed carriage, the bride, escorted by an eunuch on horseback, had crossed the Golden Horn to choose one in the best shop in Pera, and two relays of porters with poles to carry it had just been ordered to fetch it to-morrow morning, bearing it on their shoulders up to this elevated spot of rather difficult access.

As to the young Bey—the enemy—the smartest captain of the Turkish army, where so many officers wear the uniform smartly, he was certainly a very handsome fellow, with a soft voice, as Kondjé-Gul had said, and a somewhat feline smile inherited from his mother — he had hitherto, with the most refined delicacy, half sportively, half respectfully, paid his court most discreetly to his wife, whose superiority he fully appreciated, and, as is the rule in good society in the East, tried to win her affection rather than assert his rights. For, though a Moslem marriage is roughly handled and no consent invited before the ceremony, after it, on the contrary, there is an

amount of consideration and delicacy quite foreign
to our Western manners.

Hamdi Bey, on daily duty at the Yildiz
palace, comes home every evening, is formally
announced to his wife, and at first behaves as a
visitor. After supper he takes a seat more intimately by her side on the sofa, and they smoke
together thin, light-coloured cigarettes, while each
studies and watches the other like fencers on
guard; he tender and insinuating, with pauses
full of suggestive agitation; she witty and brilliant
so long as they merely chat together, but dis-
arming him at once by an assumed slave-like
submission if he attempts to draw her to him or
to kiss her. Finally, when ten o'clock strikes, he
withdraws, kissing her hand. If only she had
chosen him, she would probably have loved him,
but the little unbroken princess of the plain of
Karadjemir will never bend to a master who is
forced upon her. Besides, she knows full well that
the moment is near and inevitable when her lord,
instead of bowing himself out respectfully, will
follow her to her room. She will not resist, far
less entreat him. She has achieved the sort of
duality of identity which is common to many
Turkish women of her age and rank, who say:
'My person is delivered over by contract to an
unknown man, and I devote it to him because I
am an honest woman; but my soul, which was
not consulted, is still my own, and I keep it with
jealous reserve for an ideal lover — whom I may
never meet with, and who in any case will never
know anything about it.'

So she is at home alone all the afternoon, this young bride.

To-day, while awaiting the return of the enemy from Yildiz, the idea occurs to her of continuing for André her interrupted diary, and to take it up at the fateful date of the 28th of Zil-Hidjeh 1318 of the Hegira, the day of her marriage. The earlier sheets are coming back to her to-morrow; she has asked the friend who took charge of them to return them, regarding her new bureau as safe enough to keep them in.

She began to write.

The 28th of Zil-Hidjeh 1318.
April 19, 1901, in the Frankish calendar.

'My grandmother herself came to call me; I had gone to sleep so late that night. "Make haste," said she; "you forget that you are to be ready by nine o'clock. You should not sleep so late on your wedding-day!"

'How stern was her tone! It was the last morning I was to know in her house in my own dear little room. Could she not avoid severity but for one day? On opening my eyes I saw my cousins, who had already risen noiselessly, and were putting on their tcharchaf to go home at once and make their toilet, which would be a long business. Never again should we all wake up together there, and once more we took a long farewell. We could hear the swallows piping in the joy of their hearts; we could feel that spring was radiant out of doors; a bright day of sunshine had risen on my sacrifice; I felt like one drowning whom nobody would rescue.

'Before long the house was full of an infernal turmoil. Doors opening and shutting, bustling footsteps, the rustle of silk trains, women's voices, and then the falsetto tones of the negroes, tears and laughter, sermonising and lamentations. In my room there was a perpetual coming and going; relations, friends, slaves, a whole rout of women offering their advice as to how the bride's hair should be dressed. Every now and then a big negro in attendance called them to order, and besought us to make haste.

'Nine o'clock; the carriages were ready, the procession waiting: my mother-in-law, sisters-in-law, and the young Bey's guests. But the bride was not dressed; the ladies about her pressed their services upon her, but it was, in fact, their presence which complicated matters. At last, quite too nervous, she declined all help, and begged to be left to herself. She dressed her own hair, hastily put on her dress trimmed with orange-blossom and three yards of train, fastened her diamonds, her veil, and the long skeins of gold thread in her hair. Only one ornament she had no right to touch — her diadem.

'The heavy diamond tiara, which with us takes the place of the wreath of flowers worn by Europeans, must, according to custom, be placed on her head by a young wife chosen from among her friends, who has been but once married, has not been divorced, and is notoriously happy in her wedded life. This chosen friend must first recite a short prayer out of the Koran, and then crown the bride, while expressing good wishes for her happiness, and more especially that she may thus be crowned once only in her life. In other words, you, André, will understand, no divorce, no second marriage.

'Among the young women present one seemed so particularly fitted for this office that she was unanimously chosen — Djavideh, my very dear cousin. What had she not, that fortunate woman? Young, lovely, immensely rich, and married eighteen months since to a man who was reputed delightful!

'But when she came up to me *to endow me with her happiness*, I saw two large tears in her eyes. "My poor darling," said she, "why is this my part? I am not indeed superstitious, but I can never cease to regret having endowed you with *my* happiness. If in the future you should be doomed to suffer as I suffer, I shall feel as if it were my doing, my crime." So she, too, apparently the happiest of us all, she too was in distress. Oh woe is me! Would no one hear my cry for mercy before I left that house?

'But the diadem was fixed; I said, "I am ready." A tall negro came forward to carry the train of my dress, and I made my way along the passages to the stairs — those long corridors, watched night and day by women or slaves, and which lead to our rooms, André, so that we live in a mouse-trap.

'I was conducted downstairs to the largest of the reception rooms, where I found the whole family assembled. First there was my father, of whom I was to take leave. I kissed his hands. He made some appropriate speech, which I did

not hear. I had indeed been enjoined to thank
him publicly here for all his kindness in the past,
and above all for that of to-day — the marriage he
had arranged for me. But no, that was beyond
my powers; I could not. I stood before him
speechless, frozen, not looking up, and not a word
could I utter. It was he who had concluded the
bargain, who had surrendered me, ruined me; he
was responsible for everything. How could I
thank him when in the depths of my soul I cursed
him? Was it possible — this fearful fact that I
suddenly felt a mortal grudge against the being I
once most dearly loved? Ah, it is an awful
moment when the tenderest affection turns to the
acutest hatred! And all the time I was smiling,
André, because on one's wedding day one is
expected to smile.

'While some old uncles were giving me their
blessing, the ladies of the party, who had been
having refreshments under the plane-trees in the
garden, began putting on their tcharchaf.

'The bride alone could not put one on, but
negroes held up screens of damask silk to enclose
a sort of passage and hide her from the eyes of
the people in the street, between the door of the
house and that of the closed landau with windows
darkened by wooden shutters pierced with little
holes. It was time to start, and I passed down
between the silken walls. Zeyneb and Melek, my
bridesmaids, both wearing blue dominos over their
elegant dresses, followed me and got in with me,
and there we were in a tightly closed case, impenetrable to every eye.

F

'After thus being put into the carriage, which to me seemed like being put into my hearse, there was a long pause. My mother-in-law and sisters-in-law, who had come to fetch me away, had not finished their glasses of *sirop*, and kept everybody waiting. Well, so much the better! It was so much gained, a quarter of an hour less sacrificed to the *other*.

'However, the long line of carriages started at last, mine leading the way, and we began to jolt over the street pavement. My companions and I did not exchange a word. On we went in our dark cell, in perfect silence, seeing nothing. Oh how I longed to smash everything, to wreck everything, to fling open the doors, and cry to the passers-by, "Save me! I am being robbed of my happiness, my youth, my life!" I clenched my hands, I felt my face redden and the tears start to my eyes, while the two poor little things in front of me were stricken by my too evident misery.

'Then there was a change of noise; the carriage was rumbling on wood, on the endless floating bridge over the Golden Horn. In fact I was going to live on the other shore. And then began the pavement of Stamboul, and I felt myself yet more abjectly a prisoner, for I must be rapidly approaching my new cloister, so abhorred in anticipation. What a long way through the town; by what endless streets we drove, up what impossible steeps! Heaven, how far away I should be, in what sinister exile!

'At last we stopped. The carriage door was opened. In a flash I saw a waiting crowd in front of a gloomy doorway, negroes in uniform, cavasses blazing with gold lace and medals, intendants with the *chalvar*, down to the night-watchman with his long rod. And at once the silken screens stretched by stalwart arms, as at my departure, shut me in; I was again invisible, and again could see nothing. I rushed madly through this corridor of silk, and at the end found myself in a large hall full of flowers, where a fair young man in the full-dress uniform of a cavalry captain came forward to meet me. With smiles on our lips we exchanged an inquiring glance and a flash of intense defiance; it is over; I have seen my master, my master has seen me.

'He bowed, offered me his arm, and conducted me to the first floor, to which I mounted as if dragged there; he led me to the end of a large drawing-room, where a throne stood raised on three steps. On this I seated myself, and he bowed again and went away; his part was over for the rest of the day. I watched him as he went; he met a tide of ladies pervading the stairs and rooms, a surge of light gauze, flowers, jewels, and bare shoulders; not a face was veiled nor the diamond-decked hair; every tcharchaf had been left at the door. It might have been a crowd of Western ladies in evening-dress, and the bride-groom, who had never before seen, and never again will see, such a sight, seemed to me disturbed in spite of his easy manner — the only man, drowned in this flood of women, and the object of interest to all these curious eyes.

'His part was played, but I had to remain, the

rare and curious creature on view all the day, on my seat of dignity. Near me on one side was Mademoiselle Esther, on the other were Zeyneb and Melek, who had also shed the tcharchaf, and were dressed in bodices open at the throat with flowers and diamonds. I implored them not to desert me while all the company passed before my throne, an interminable procession : relations, friends, mere acquaintances, each one asking me the exasperating question, "Well, my dear, what do you think of him?" How was I to know what I thought of him? — a man whose voice I had scarcely heard, whose face I had scarcely glanced at, and whom I should not recognise in the street. Not a word could I find in reply; only a smile, since a smile is indispensable — or rather a grimace resembling a smile. Some of these women as they asked me had an ironical or sneering expression; these were the embittered and rebellious wives; others thought proper to assume an air of encouragement — the docile and resigned. But in the eyes of the rest I read most clearly a look of irremediable sadness, and pity for the sister who had fallen this day into the common pit, and become their comrade in humiliation and woe. And still my lips smiled. Marriage, then, was just what I had thought it. Now I knew. I read the truth in the eyes of each one of them all. And sitting there on my bridal throne I began to reflect that there is a way after all of getting free, a way permitted by Allah and the prophet: yes, I would get a divorce. Why had I not thought of it sooner? Isolated now in the midst of the crowd, and concentrating

my thoughts though still smiling, I eagerly plotted
my new plan of campaign; I already counted on
that blessed divorce; for, after all, a marriage in
our country, if only one is bent upon it, is so easily
undone.

'But after all, that procession was a pretty sight.
I should really have been very much interested if
I myself had not been the melancholy idol which
all these women had come to stare at. Nothing
to be seen but lace, gauze, bright and delicate
colours. Not a black coat, of course, to make an
inky spot, as at your European parties. And
indeed, André, from the little I have seen of them
at the Embassies, I do not think your entertain-
ments can bring together so many charming faces
as are seen at ours. All these Turkish women,
never seen by men, are so slender, elegant, bewitching — as lithe as cats. I mean, of course, the
women of this present generation — the least good-
looking have something to attract; all are pleasing
to behold. And then there are the old "1320"
ladies, mingling with the young whose eyes are
deliciously melancholy or restless, the good old
women, so amazing now with their placid grave
looks, their superb hair in heavy plaits, never
thinned by intellectual toil, their gauze turbans
edged with flowers worked in crochet, and their
rich silks, all purchased in Damascus, so as to put
no profits into the hands of the infidel merchants
of Lyons.

'Now and again, when a guest of distinction
came past me, I had to rise and return her bow
with one just as low as she had chosen to make to

me,[1] and if she were young, to beg her to be seated by me for a few minutes.

'I really believe I was by this time beginning to be thoroughly amused, as though the procession of guests had been in honour of some one else, and I had nothing to do with it. The scene, in fact, had suddenly changed, and from my raised seat I was well placed to lose nothing of it. All the doors on to the street had been thrown wide open; all might enter who would; invited or no, any woman was admitted who wished to see the bride. And such extraordinary figures came in, utter strangers passing by, all in yashmak or tcharchaf, all spectres with their faces hidden in the way peculiar to the province they came from. The old houses in the neighbourhood, latticed and barred, were emptied of their residents or their chance inhabitants, and fine old materials had been brought out of every chest. There were women wrapped from head to foot in Asiatic silks curiously wrought with tinsel of gold or silver; there were gorgeous Syrians, and Persians robed entirely in black; there were even old women of a hundred leaning on their sticks. "A gallery of costume," said Melek in a whisper, very much amused too.

'At four o'clock came the European ladies; this was the most unpleasant episode of the day. They were kept a long time at the refreshment tables, eating little cakes, drinking tea, and even smoking cigarettes, but at last they came on in a crowd towards the throne of the strange creature.

[1] The Temenan.

'I must tell you, André, that they almost always have with them some foreign stranger for whose presence they apologise, some English or American tourist passing through, who is extremely excited by the idea of seeing a Turkish wedding. This person comes in a travelling dress, perhaps even in Alpine climbing boots. With those haggard eyes which have looked down on the world from the summit of the Himalayas, or contemplated the midnight sun from the North Cape, she stares at the bride. As a crowning touch, my traveller, she whom fate had reserved for my wedding day, was a writer, a journalist, who had on her hands the dirty gloves she had worn on the steamship; impertinent and inquisitive, caring only for copy for a newly started paper, she asked me the most astounding questions with absolute want of tact. My humiliation was complete.

'Very disagreeable and odious were the ladies of Pera, who came extravagantly over-dressed. They had been to fifty weddings at least, and knew exactly how everything should be done. This, however, did not hinder them from asking the stupidest, ill-natured questions.

'"Of course you are not yet acquainted with your husband? It really is very funny, you know! What a strange custom! But, my dear child, you ought to have cheated, just cheated! And you did not, really and truly, no? Well, I can only say that in your place I should simply have refused him."

'And as she spoke she exchanged satirical glances with a Greek lady by her side, a Perote too, and giggled compassionately. I smiled to order all the time, but I felt as if these rude minxes were slapping my cheeks till the blood came.

'At last all were gone, all the intruders in tcharchafs or in hats. Only the invited guests remained.

'The candelabra and lamps that were now lighted illuminated none but the most splendid dresses — none black, since there were no men; none dark or sober, a crowd of beautiful and varied colours. I do not believe, André, that you in the West ever see such an effect; at any rate, what I used to see at the Embassies when I was a little girl did not come near this in brilliancy. Mingling with the exquisite Asiatic silks displayed by the grandmothers, there were quantities of Paris dresses that looked even more diaphanous; they might have been made of blue or pink mist. All the latest *creations* of your famous dressmakers (to use their imbecile phraseology), worn to perfection by these little ladies, whose governesses have transformed them into French women, or Swiss, or English, or Germans, but whose names are, nevertheless, Khadija, or Tcheref, or Fatima, or Gulizar, and on whom no man has ever set eyes!

'I was now allowed to come down from my throne, where I had been perched for five or six hours; I might even leave this blue drawing-room, where the old ladies were for the most part assembled, the "1320" fanatics and scorners, severe and rigid of spirit under their flat braids of hair and small turbans. I wanted rather to join the

throng of young women, the "unbalanced" like
myself, who were crowding now into an adjoining
room where a band was playing.

'It was a stringed orchestra accompanying six
singers, who took it in turn to recite passages of
poems by Zia Pasha, Hafiz, or Saädi. You,
André, know how melancholy and impassioned is
our oriental music; indeed you yourself have
tried to express it, though it cannot be put into
words. The musicians — men — were hermetically
screened off by a vast curtain of Damascus silk;
only think of the scandal if one of them should
get a glimpse of us! And my friends, when I
joined them, had just arranged a séance of fortune-
telling by song. This is a sort of game played at
wedding parties where there is a band. One says,
"The first song shall be for me"; another says,
"I will take the second," or the third, and so on.
And each regards the words of her song as pro-
phetic of her fate.

'"The bride will take the fifth," said I as I
went in. And when the fifth was to be sung all
came close, eager not to miss a word, their ear
against the silken screen, leaning on it at the risk
of bringing it down.

'" I who am Love

— the voice of the invisible singer recited —

> burn with too fierce a fire.
> Even if only I pass and touch the soul
> Life is not long enough to close and heal the wound.
> I pass, but my touch for ever leaves its mark.
> I who am Love burn with too fierce a fire."

'How rich and thrilling was the voice of this
man, whom I felt quite near, but who remained
hidden, so that I might attribute to him any
features, form, and eyes that I chose to fancy.
I had come in to amuse myself like the others;
the oracle so often suggests some absurd inter-
pretation that it is hailed with laughter in spite of
the beauty of the words. But this time the performer had sung too well, with too much passion.
The girls did not laugh — no, not one of them, —
but looked at me. For my part, I felt as I had
felt in the morning, that my youth was buried that
day. Yes, in one way or another, I would be
separated from the man to whom I was delivered
over, and I would live my own life elsewhere,
where I knew not, and I would seek and find
"Love burning with too fierce a fire." And
everything was transfigured before me in the room,
where I ceased to be aware of the women who
crowded round me; the mass of flowers in the
large vases seemed suddenly to fill the air with
heavy perfume, and the crystal chandeliers to
beam like stars. Whether from fatigue or ecstacy
I did not know, but my head swam. I saw no
one, nor what was going on around me, and I felt
indifferent to everything, because I now knew
that some day in the course of my life I should
find Love — and if I die of it, so much the worse!
'A minute later — a minute or a long time, I
know not which — my cousin Djavideh, the same
who in the morning had "set her happiness" on
my head, came up to me. "Why, you are all
alone! The others are gone down to supper, and

are waiting for you. What can you have been
doing to absorb you so?"

'It was true; I was alone; the room was
empty. The others had gone. When? I had
not even perceived it.

'Djavideh had with her the negro who was to
bear my train and cry "Destour" as I went, for
every one to make way. She took my arm, and
as we went down the stairs she asked me in a low
voice, "My dear, tell me the truth I entreat you,
of whom were you dreaming when I came up?"

'"Of André Lhéry."

'"Of André Lhéry? No! You are mad or
making game of me. Of André Lhéry! Then
what I was told of your fancy for him was true."
She was laughing now, quite satisfied. "Well, so
far as he is concerned, at any rate, it is certain
there is no fear of your meeting. But in your
place I should indulge in a better dream than
that. Why, I have been told that there are
charming men up in the moon. You might work
out that idea, my dear. A moon-man, it seems to
me, would be the very thing for a little lunatic
like you."

'We had to go down about twenty steps, gazed
at by those who were waiting for us at the bottom
of the stairs; the trains of our gowns, one white
and the other lilac, were held together in the
gloved hands of our ape. Fortunately, my dear
Djavideh's moon-man — such an unexpected sug-
gestion, made me laugh as she did, and our faces
both wore the appropriate expression as we entered
the supper-rooms.

'At my request the younger ladies were seated at tables apart; round the bride there were about fifty guests under five-and-twenty, almost all of them pretty. Also, by my desire, the cloth was decorated with white roses laid closely side by side, without leaves or stems. You know, André, it is no longer the custom here to lay the table in the Turkish manner; here were French silver plate, Sévres porcelain, and Bohemian glass, all bearing my new initials; our old oriental magnificence was not to be seen at this marriage feast, excepting in the array of silver candlesticks, all alike, which were placed all round the table, touching each other, like the roses. I forgot, to be sure, the crowd of slaves who waited on us, fifty of them at least in one room for the young people alone; all Circassian girls of the best type and wonderfully pleasant to look upon: calm, fair beauties, moving with a sort of native majesty, like princesses.

'Among the Turkish ladies seated at my table — most of them of middle height and fragile grace, with brown eyes — some ladies of the Imperial palace who had come, the "Serailis," were distinguished by their goddess-like stature, lovely shoulders, and sea-blue eyes. These also were Circassians, daughters of the mountain or the plain, of labourers or of shepherds, purchased as children for their beauty, and after serving many years as slaves in some seraglio, turned by the touch of a wand into great ladies of amazing elegance by marrying some chamberlain or other magnate. They look down with pity, these splendid women, on the little city-bred ladies with frail forms, dark lines round their eyes, and wax-like skins; they call them degenerate. It is their function — theirs, and that of thousands of their sisters brought here every year to be sold — to bring into the old worn-out city an infusion of their rich, pure blood.

'The company was extremely gay. They talked and laughed at everything. A wedding supper among Turkish women is always an occasion for forgetting trouble, for relaxation and enjoyment. Besides, André, we are gay by nature, I assure you; if the merest trifle leads us to forget our restrictions, our daily humiliations and sorrows, we plunge very readily into childlike, heedless laughter. I have heard that it was so in the convents of the West, the most strictly secluded nuns sometimes playing and amusing themselves with the sports of a little girls' school. And a French woman of the Embassy, on the eve of returning to Paris, said to me one day: "It is all over; never again shall I laugh so heartily, and so innocently too, as in your harems at Constantinople."

'The supper being ended with a toast to the bride's health, the ladies at my table proposed to give the Turkish orchestra a respite and to play some European music. They were most of them good pianists, and some of them quite admirable; their fingers, which have so much time for practising, generally achieve the most faultless execution. Beethoven, Grieg, Liszt, and Chopin are familiar to them, and in singing, Wagner, Saint-Saëns, Holmès, or even Chaminade.

'Alas! I was obliged to confess with a blush there was not a piano in the house. Amazement indeed among my guests, and they looked at me as if they would say: "Poor little thing! They must be '1320' indeed in her husbands' family. Life in this house promises to be very enjoyable!"

'Eleven o'clock. We hear the horses of the fine carriages pawing the horribly dangerous pavements, and the steep old street is full of negroes in livery carrying lanterns. The guests are putting on their veils and preparing to depart. The hour was in fact very late for Moslem women, and but for the exceptional event of a grand wedding they would not be out. They began to take leave, and the bride, still eternally standing, must curtsey and thank each lady for having "condescended to be present at this humble entertainment." When my grandmother in her turn came up to bid me good-bye, her satisfied expression clearly said: "At last we have married off this fantastic girl. What a good thing done!"

'They were all gone, I was left alone in my new prison; there was nothing now to stun my brain. I was left to the reflection that the irremediable deed was done.

'Zeyneb and Melek, my beloved little sisters, had remained till the end, and came now to kiss me last; we dared not look at each other for fear of tears. Then they also were gone, dropping their veils over their faces. It was all over; I was sunk in an abyss of loneliness, of the unknown. Still, I had found the will to escape from it. I was more alive this evening than I had been in the morning, and ready for the struggle, for

I had heard the call of "Love of the too fierce fire."

'At this point I was informed that the Bey, my husband, in the blue drawing-room upstairs had been waiting for some minutes for the pleasure of a few words with me. He had just come in from my father's house at Kassim Pacha, where there had been a dinner given to men. Well and good! I too was eager to see him and to face him. I went up with a smile on my lips, armed with craftiness, and determined to amaze him, to dazzle him at first, but my spirit was seething with hatred and schemes of revenge. . . .'

A rustle of silk behind her and quite close to her made her start; her mother-in-law had come in with the velvet footfall of an old cat. Happily she could not read French, being quite of the old school, and, moreover, she had forgotten her eye-glasses.

'Come, my dear child, you really write too much! You have been sitting at this table for very nearly three hours. I have been in several times already on tiptoe. Our Hamdi will be coming in from Yildiz, and your pretty eyes will be quite heavy to receive him. Come, come, rest a little; put those papers away till to-morrow.'

She needed no asking to put away the papers, to lock them quickly by in a drawer — for another figure had just appeared at the door of the room — one who could read French and had piercing eyes: the fair Durdaneh (the Pearl), a cousin of Hamdi Bey's, who was lately divorced and had been staying in the house for two days. Her eyes were touched with henna, her hair was dyed with henna, her face was too pretty, but her smile malignant. The bride had already felt that she was perfidious. It was quite unnecessary to warn her to look her best when Hamdi should come in, for she was vanity itself, especially in the presence of her handsome cousin.

'Here, my dear child,' the old lady went on, giving her a worn jewel-case; 'I have brought you a necklace of my young days; it is oriental, so you cannot say that it is out of fashion, and it will look well on the dress you are wearing to-day.'

It was a fine old necklace, and she put it round the girl's neck; emeralds, of which the green harmonised delightfully with the pink costume.

'It suits you, my child! It suits you to perfection. Our Hamdi, who has such a taste in colours, will think you irresistible this evening.'

She herself, she must own, was anxious that Hamdi should think her attractive, for she relied on her charms as her chief weapon in rebellion and revenge. But nothing could humiliate her more deeply than the mania they all had for dressing her up from morning till night. 'My dear child, just put that lock of hair a little higher — there — above your ear. Hamdi will think you prettier than ever. My dear child, put this tea-rose in your hair. It is our Hamdi's favourite flower.' Treated all the time as an odalisque, a beautiful doll for her lord's greater enjoyment.

Blushing scarlet, she had scarcely thanked the old lady for the emerald necklace, when a huge

negro in attendance came to announce that the
Bey was in sight; he was coming on horseback
and had turned the corner of the mosque hard by.
His mother rose at once. 'We have only time
to make a retreat, Durdaneh, you and I. We
must not be in the way of the new-married couple,
my dear.' They fled like two Cinderellas, and
Durdaneh, looking back from the door before
she disappeared, bestowed on her a spiteful parting
smile.

The bride went to look in a glass. The other
day she had arrived at her husband's home, as
white as her dress and train, as pure as the water
of her diamonds; throughout her former life,
wholly devoted to study, secluded from contact
with young men, no sensual idea had ever even
crossed her imagination. But Hamdi's increas-
ingly tender courtship, the wholesome savour of
the man, the smoke of his cigarettes were beginning,
in spite of herself, to arouse in her a nervous excitement which she had never dreamed of.

On the stairs the click of a cavalry sword — he
was coming, close at hand; and she felt the hour
was near when their two personalities would be
merged in such intimate communion as she could
not picture to herself. And now, for the first
time, she was aware of an unconfessed wish for
his presence — and the shame of wishing for anything this man could give her aroused in her spirit
a fresh impulse of rebellion and aversion.

G

V

Three years later; 1904.

André Lhéry, who was loosely and inter-
mittently connected with the Embassies, had, after
much hesitation, just asked for and obtained an
appointment for about two years at Constantinople.
He had hesitated, in the first place, because any
official position means a chain, and he clung to his
freedom; also because two years of absence from
his own country seemed to him longer now than it
had been of yore, at a time when almost all his
life lay like a high road before him; and above
all, because he dreaded the disenchantment of
modernised Turkey.

However, he made up his mind to it; and one
March morning, in gloomy wintry weather, a ship
had landed him on the quay of the city he had
loved so well.

At Constantinople the winter lingers long.
The wind, blowing from the Black Sea was wild
and icy that day, driving flakes of snow before it.
In the squalid cosmopolitan district where the
vessels discharge their passengers, in itself a sort
of warning to newcomers to depart quickly, the
streets were gutters of sticky mud, through which
Levantines and mangy dogs splashed their way.

And André Lhéry, sick at heart, his imagination stricken, took his seat like a condemned criminal in the vehicle which conveyed him up streets almost impossibly steep, to the most commonplace of the hotels designated as 'Palaces.'

Pera, where his position compelled him to reside, is a lamentable sham of an European city, separated by an arm of the sea, to say nothing of many centuries, from grand old Stamboul, the city of mosques and of our dreams. There, notwithstanding his impulse to fly, he was fain to find a residence. He perched himself as high as he could go in the least pretentious quarter of the town, not only to remove himself as far as possible from the smart Perote set that lived and moved below, but also to enjoy the vast prospect, to see from every window the Golden Horn with the mass of Stamboul projected against the sky, and, breaking the horizon, the solemn array of cypresses, the great cemeteries, where for twenty years now the unknown Circassian girl who had been the friend of his youth lay sleeping under a fallen stone.

The costume of Turkish women had changed since his first stay here. This was one of the things that first struck him. Instead of the white shroud which showed only the eyes, and which was known as the *yashmak*, and the long straight mantle of some light hue called the *feridjeh*, they now wore the *tcharchaf*, a sort of domino, almost always black, with a short veil, also black, concealing all the features, even the eyes. To be sure, they occasionally raised this veil, showing the whole oval of the face, which to André Lhéry seemed a revolutionary innovation. But for this, they were, as of old, spectres, with whom one rubs elbows, but with whom all communication is prohibited, and at whom one is forbidden to look — recluses of whom one can learn nothing — unknowable, non-existent one might say, the mystery and charm of Turkey.

André Lhéry, long ago, by a series of happy favouring chances impossible to recombine a second time in one man's life, had, with the audacity of a boy who knows nothing of danger, been thrown into contact with one of them — contact so close that he had left a piece of his soul clinging to her for ever. But as for repeating any such adventure, he never even dreamed of it for a thousand reasons; he saw them pass as one sees shadows or the clouds.

The wind off the Black Sea blew incessantly for some weeks, and the cold rain or snow continually fell, and acquaintances invited him to dine and to evenings at the clubs. And he began to feel that this world, this life, was not only making his new visit to the East an empty and disturbing thing, but also threatened to destroy his past impressions, perhaps even to blur the image of his poor little sleeping friend. Since his arrival in Constantinople his remembrance grew less vivid every hour, drowned out by the pervading vulgar modernity; he felt that the people about him profaned it, trampled on it every day. So he decided to go away. The loss of his appointment at the Embassy, it need hardly be said, was a secondary consideration. He would go.

Since his arrival, nearly a fortnight ago, a thousand unimportant matters had so filled up his leisure that he had not even crossed the bridges over the Golden Horn to go into Stamboul. The great city, which he could see from the top of his house, generally wrapped in the persistent winter fog, was still almost as remote and unreal as before his return to Turkey. He would go away — that was finally settled. Just time to make a pilgrimage over there, to Nedjibeh's grave under the cypresses, and then, leaving all else, he would return to France. Out of regard for the beloved past, and pious respect for *her*, he would escape before the disenchantment was complete.

The day, when at last he could set foot in Stamboul, was one of the most dismally cold and dark days of the year, though it was in the month of April.

On the other side of the water, as soon as he had crossed the bridge and stood in the shadow of the great mosque beyond, he felt himself another man, the André Lhéry who had been dead for years, and who had suddenly revived to youth and consciousness. Alone, free, unknown to any one in the crowd, he knew every nook and turning of the city as though he had come back to a former existence. Forgotten Turkish words rose up in his memory, phrases formed in his brain, he once more belonged to the place — really belonged to Stamboul.

At once he was uncomfortable in wearing a hat, almost felt himself ridiculous. Less from a

foolish shyness than from the fear of attracting
the attention of some watchman in the cemetery,
he bought a fez, which, according to custom, was
carefully pressed to the size of his head, in one of
the hundred little street shops. He also bought a
rosary to carry in his hand like a good Moslem.
And now, suddenly in a hurry and excessively
impatient to see the tomb, he jumped into a little
carriage and said to the coachman, 'Edirneh
Kapoussouna ghetir' ('Drive to the Adrianople
gate'). It was a very long way to the Adrianople gate in the great Byzantine wall, beyond
quarters of the city now being abandoned, through
streets dying of inanition and silence. He had to
cross almost the whole of Stamboul, and first to
climb steep lanes where the horses slipped and
slid. At first these were the swarming parts of
the town, full of street cries and things to sell, all
round the bazaar and familiar to tourists. Then
came the sort of steppes, deserted to-day in the
icy wind, which occupy the central plateau, where
the eye sees minarets and cupolas on every side.
And at last the roads bordered with tombs
and funereal kiosks and delicious fountains — the
avenues of old where nothing had changed; the
great mosques one after another with their clustered
cupolas, dimly grey against the still wintry sky;
their vast enclosures full of the dead, and their
squares with the old-world little cafés where the
dreamy worshippers assemble after prayer. It
was the hour when the muezzins call the faithful
to the third service of the day; their voice came
dropping from above, from the light balconies so

high up that they seemed close to the cold, gloomy clouds. Ah, Stamboul still existed! André Lhéry, finding it as he had known it, and shivering with an indescribable and delicious pang, felt himself going back by degrees to his own youth; he was more and more like a being brought to life again after years of oblivion and non-existence. And it was she, the little Circassian, whose body was now destroyed in the earth, who had preserved the power of casting a spell over this land — she who was the cause of all this, and who at this moment reigned triumphant.

As by degrees they drew near to the Adrianople gate, which leads out on the endless stretch of cemeteries, the street became very quiet, running between old barred houses and old crumbling walls. In consequence of the bitter wind no one was sitting in front of the humble cafés, almost in ruins. But the inhabitants of the quarter, the rare passers-by, who looked frozen, still wore the old-fashioned long gown and turban. A dejection as of universal death seemed that day to be exhaled by all earthly things, to be shed from the murky sky, to pervade everything—an intolerable sadness, a melancholy to weep over.

Having arrived under the horseshoe arch of the city gate, André prudently dismissed his vehicle and passed out alone into the country — that is to say, into the wide region of neglected tombs and ancestral cypresses. To right and left along the colossal wall, its half-ruined dungeon towers visible in long perspective, there were only tombs, endless gravestones sunk in solitude, and,

as it were, drunk with silence. Assuring himself
that the driver had gone away, and that no one
would follow and spy upon him, André turned to
the right and went downhill towards Eyoub, walking under the huge cypresses, with their branches
as white as dry bones and almost black foliage.

Tombstones in Turkey are like milestones, with
turbans or flowers carved at the top, at a distance
vaguely like human beings with a head and
shoulders; in the first instance they are planted
upright and quite straight, but in the course of
time earthquakes and heavy rains undermine them;
then they lean in every direction, one against
another, like dying creatures, and at last fall on
the grass, where they lie at rest. And the very
ancient cemeteries where André was now wandering have the melancholy disarray of a battlefield
the morning after a defeat.

There was hardly any one to be seen to-day
along by this wall in the vast realm of the dead.
It was too cold. A goatherd with his flock, a
troop of prowling dogs, two or three old beggar
women awaiting a funeral procession to beg alms
— no other creature, no eye to be feared. But
the tombstones in their thousands were like a
watching crowd, a crowd of stunted grey people
tottering and drooping. And the crows hopping
in the grass began to caw in the wintry wind.

André, guiding himself by landmarks once
familiar, made his way to the resting-place of her
whom he had called 'Medjeh,' among so many
others almost exactly alike which covered this
wilderness from end to end. It was one of the

little group out there; he recognised the growth and shape of the cypress trees. And it was this one, this very one, in spite of its look of being a hundred years old, this one with the uprooted stone lying prone on the earth. How quickly destruction had done its work since he last was here, hardly five years ago. Not even these humble stones would Time leave to the poor little dead thing, so utterly lost in oblivion by this time, that perhaps not a soul in the place re-remembered her at all. In his memory alone and nowhere else did the youthful image survive, and when he should die, not the faintest impression would remain anywhere of what her beauty had been, not a trace in all the world of her anxious artless soul. On the headstone sunk in the grass no one would ever read her name — her real name, which, indeed, would have ceased to mean anything. In former days he had often thought himself profaning her by revealing, though under an invented name, something of her being to a thousand indifferent readers in a too unreserved book which ought never to have seen the light; but to-day, on the contrary, he was glad he had done this, for the sake of the pity it had aroused for her, a pity which it might yet arouse for some few years to come in souls unknown to him; nay, he was sorry that he had not given her real name, for then, he fancied, all that pity would have more immediately touched the beloved little spirit. And, who knows? one or another of her Turkish sisters, passing by the fallen stone, as she read the name might have paused to think of the dead.

The light faded rapidly this evening over the expanse of graves, the sky was so overcast with piled-up clouds without a rift anywhere. Under the wall — the ruins of this endless wall which seemed to be that of a city of the dead — the solitude grew acute, terrifying; a vast expanse of grey monochrome, with scattered cypress trees, and peopled, as it were, with small, decrepit figures, some standing, some leaning over, and some fallen — the memorial stones. And for years she had slept here, that Circassian girl who had once trusted that her friend would return; slept through the winters and summers, and would lie there for ever, alone in the silence, alone during the long December nights under her winding-sheet of snow. Now, indeed, there could be nothing of her there. But he shuddered at the thought of what she still might be, so close to him under the coverlet of earth; no, certainly nothing, a few bones crumbling still amid the deeper roots, and that globular thing, more slow to decay, which represented the head, the spherical cell in which her soul had dwelt, her loving thoughts.

The wreckage of this tombstone really enhanced his heart-broken attachment and remorse; he could not bear it, he could not endure to leave it thus. Being so familiar with the country he knew what difficulties and dangers beset the Christian who should touch the tomb of a Moslem woman in a holy cemetery. He would have to employ all the cunning of a criminal, in spite of his pious purpose. However, he decided that it must be done. He would remain in Turkey for so long as might be needful, for months if necessary, and would not leave till the broken stones were renewed and the tomb restored and consolidated to last.

On his return to Pera in the evening he found Jean Renaud in his rooms, one of his friends at the Embassy, a very young man, who was amazed at all he saw here, and with whom he had become intimate on the ground of their common admiration for everything Eastern.

He also found the French mail lying on his table, and a letter with the Stamboul postmark, which he at once opened.

This was the letter:

'SIR — Do you remember that a Turkish woman once wrote to you to tell you of the emotions stirred in her soul by reading "Medjeh," and to beg for a few words in reply written by your own hand?

'Well, this Turkish woman has grown ambitious, and now wishes for something more. She wants to see you, to know the delightful author of that book which she has re-read a hundred times, and always with increasing emotion. Will you consent to a meeting on Thursday at half-past two by the Bosphorus, on the Asiatic side between Tchiboukli and Pacha Bagtcheh? You could wait for me in the little café near the sea at the head of the bay.

'I shall come in a dark tcharchaf, in a talika.[1] I will get out of the carriage, and you will follow me, but you must wait till I speak first. You know my country, so you know the risks I run.

---

[1] A Turkish hired coach, commonly used in the country; it is also called a mohadjir.

For my part I know I have, in you, to deal with a gentleman. I trust in your discretion. ———

'But perhaps you have forgotten "Medjeh"? Perhaps you are no longer interested in her sisters?

'If, however, you care to read the soul of the "Medjeh" of to-day answer me — and till Thursday.   MME. ZAIDEH.

   ' Poste-restante, *Galata*.'

He laughed as he handed this letter to his friend and took up the others.

'Take me with you on Thursday,' implored Jean Renaud, as soon as he had read the note. 'I will be very good,' he added in a childlike way, 'very discreet. I will not look ——'

'Do you really suppose I am going, my boy?'

'Oh! what, miss such a thing? But you will go, surely?'

'Not if I know it! It is some trick. The lady is no more Turkish than you or I.'

Though he made difficulties, it was chiefly that he might let himself be overruled by his young companion, for in his heart, though he was still opening his letters, he was thinking more of the lady than he chose to show. Preposterous as the assignation might be, he felt the same unreasonable attraction that, three years ago, when he received her first letter, prompted him to reply. Besides, what a strange thing it seemed that the appeal should come to him in the name of 'Medjeh,' on this very evening when he had but just come in from his visit to the cemetery, with his soul so deeply moved by her memory.

VI

On Thursday April 14, rather before the appointed hour, André Lhéry and Jean Renaud had taken their seats in front of the little café, which they easily recognised on the seashore on the Asiatic side, between the two hamlets named by the mysterious Zaideh. It was one of the few solitary and still wild nooks by the Bosphorus, which almost everywhere now is hemmed by houses and palaces; the lady had chosen well. Beyond lay a deserted field with a few plane-trees three or four hundred years old — Turkish plane-trees with prop-roots like the baobab — and close by, sloping down from the heights to the quiet strand, an outlying spur of the forests of Asia Minor, which still harbour brigands and bears.

An ideal spot certainly for a clandestine meeting. The men were alone in front of the ruined and perfectly isolated building in which the café was kept by a humble old fellow with a white beard. The plane-trees had scarcely yet uncurled their leaves, but the meadow was already so bright with flowers, and the sky so beautiful, that it was strange to feel the icy wind blowing without ceasing — the almost perpetual wind from the Black Sea, which spoils the spring in Constantinople.

Here, on the Asiatic shore, there was as usual some shelter from it, but opposite, on the European shore, it was blowing hard, though the thousand houses with their feet in the water were basking in the sunshine.

They awaited the appointed hour in this lonely spot, smoking the humble narghilehs which the old Turk produced for their use, though he was astonished and almost suspicious of two fine gentlemen in hats who had condescended to his shop for boatmen or shepherds, in unsettled weather and such a searching wind.

'It is very nice of you,' said Jean Renaud, 'to put up with my company.'

'Do not burthen yourself with gratitude, my boy. I brought you, please understand, merely to have some one to abuse if she does not come, if things turn out badly, if ——'

'Oh, then I must make it my business to see that they turn out well,' said he, affecting alarm, with the pretty smile which betrayed his childlike soul. 'There, see, just behind you. I wager it is she, bringing herself along.'

André looked behind him. A talika was, in fact, emerging from an avenue of trees, jolting over the villainous road. Between the curtains, blown by the wind, two or three female figures were visible, entirely black, faces and all.

'There are a dozen of them at least packed in there,' André objected. 'Do you suppose, my young friend, that a whole party like that comes to keep an assignation? Callers in a body?'

The talika meanwhile was coming near. When

it was quite close, a little hand in a white glove came from under a black veil and waved a signal. Here she was then! But there were three of them! Three, what an amazing adventure!

'Then I leave you,' said André. 'Be discreet as you promised and do not look. And settle our account with this old fellow; that is your business.'

And he followed the talika at some distance, till presently, in the deserted road, it drew up under the shade of a clump of plane-trees. Three black spectres, black from head to foot, at once sprang out on to the grass. They were nimble spectres, light and slender, with long silk skirts; they walked on against the wind, which blew hard and made them bow their heads; but they went slower and slower, as if to invite their follower to come up with them.

No one who has not lived in the East can conceive of André's agitation and astonishment, or the novelty of the experience of thus walking up to veiled Turkish ladies, when he had always learnt to regard that class of women as absolutely unapproachable. Was it really possible? They had invited him; they were waiting for him; he was about to talk to them.

When they heard him close behind them they turned round.

'Monsieur André Lhéry, are you not?' asked one of them, whose voice was wonderfully sweet, youthful, and shy, and who was certainly trembling.

He merely bowed in reply, and then from under the three black tcharchafs he saw three little hands appear in long buttoned gloves; they were held out to him, and he bowed over each in turn.

Their faces were at least doubly veiled; they were three enigmas in mourning; three inscrutable Parcae.

'You must forgive us,' said she who had already spoken, 'if we say nothing, or mere trivialities — we are dying of fear.' This, in fact, was very evident.

'If you could but know,' said the second, 'all the management needed to get here — the negroes and negresses we have dropped on the way ——'

'And then the coachman,' said the third, 'a man we do not know and who may be our destruction.'

Silence. The icy wind eddied in the black silk, and took away the breath. The waters of the Bosphorus, visible between the trees, was white with foam. The few fresh leaves on the trees, though scarcely open, were snatched off and swept away. But for the flowers in the grass that nodded under the long silk skirts, it might have been midwinter. They mechanically walked back all altogether, like friends taking exercise; but this remote spot, this evil weather — all was dismal and of rather melancholy augury for the meeting.

She who had first spoken, and who seemed to be the leader of the perilous scheme, began to talk, just to say something to break the embarrassing silence.

'As you see, there are three of us ——'

'It is true; I can see that,' said André, who could not help smiling.

'You do not know us, and yet you have been our friend for years.'

'We live with your books,' added the second.

'And you will tell us if the story of Medjeh is true?' asked the third.

And now, after the first silence, they all talked together; three little women eager to ask a number of questions in an interview which could not but be brief. The ease with which they expressed themselves in French surprised André Lhéry, no less than their scared audacity. And the wind having almost raised the veils from one face, he caught sight of the under part of a chin and the top of a throat, details which sooner than any other betray advancing years in a woman, and which were exquisitely youthful with no sign of a wrinkle.

They all talked together, and their voices were like music; the high wind and the thick veils somewhat muffled the sound, to be sure, but the pitch in itself was delightful. André, who at first had wondered whether he were not the object of a practical joke by three Levantines, now no longer doubted that the ladies were assuredly Turkish; the softness of their voices was an almost certain certificate of their nationality, for three Perotes all talking together would have reminded him at once of the cockatoos in the Zoological Gardens.[1]

'Just now,' said she who most interested André, 'I saw you laugh when I told you we were three. But you did not let me finish my sentence. My point was to explain to you that we are three to-day and shall still be three next time, if you

---

[1] There are, I am happy to state, some pleasing exceptions.

again obey our invitation; always three, as inseparable as those parrots, you know — though they
indeed are but two. And you will never see our
faces, never. We are three little black shades and
that is all.'

'Souls,' said another, 'merely *souls*, you understand; to you we shall always be souls and nothing
more; three poor souls in torment who need your
friendship.'

'It is useless to try to know one from another;
still, just to see — who knows whether you can
guess which is she who wrote to you, she who is
called Zaideh, you remember. Come, tell us, it
will amuse us.'

'You yourself, Madame,' replied André, without seeming to hesitate. And he was right, and
from under the veils he heard exclamations of
surprise in Turkish.

'Well, then,' said Zaideh, 'now, since we are
old acquaintances, you and I, it is my part to
introduce you to my sisters. When that is done
we shall have accomplished all the formalities in
the most correct way. So listen. The second
black domino there, the tallest of us, is Nechedil —
and very spiteful. The third, a little way off at
this moment, is Ikbar — very sly. Be on your
guard. And from this moment take care not to
mistake one for another of us three.'

These names, it hardly need be said, were all
assumed, and André suspected it. There was no
Nechedil, or Ikbar, or Zaideh. The second tcharchaf hid the serious regular features and rather
rapt gaze of Zeyneb, the elder of the cousins of

the bride. As to the third, said to be so sly, if
André could have lifted the black veil, he would
have seen the little pert nose and large merry eyes
of Melek, the red-haired damsel, who had declared
long ago that 'the poet must be rather wrinkled.'
Melek, it is true, was altered since those days by
early sorrows and nights spent in tears; still, she
was so fundamentally gay by nature that even her
long griefs had not altogether extinguished the
mirth of her laughter.

'What idea can you have formed of us?' said
Zaideh, after the silence that followed the intro-
ductions. 'What kind of women do you suppose
us to be, of what social rank, of what position?
Come, tell us.'

'Dear me, I can tell you that more precisely
by and by; still I will not conceal from you that
I am beginning to suspect that you are not mere
waiting maids.'

'Ah! And our age? That, to be sure, is of
no importance, since we mean only to be souls.
But at the same time it really is my duty to confess
to you at once, Monsieur Lhéry, that we are old
women, quite old women.'

'That, too, I had detected, if I may say so.'

'Of course, of course,' echoed Ikbar (Melek)
in a tone of deep melancholy with a most successful quaver in her voice. 'Of course! Old age,
alas, is a fact that can always be detected as you
say, in spite of all precautions to conceal it. But
figures, if you please, be exact — let us see if you
are a good physiognomist.'

In regard to their thick veils the word *physiog-nomist* was emphasised as a little funny.

'Figures! But will you be hurt by the figures I may guess?'

'Not in the least. We have so entirely abdi-cated, if only you knew. Go on, Monsieur Lhéry.'

'Well, you at once struck me as being grand-mothers, whose age must range between — at the least, the very least — between eighteen and four-and-twenty.'

They laughed under their shrouds, not very sorry to have missed their mark as old women, but too entirely young to be quite flattered.

In the gale which blew colder and colder under the clean-swept sky, scattering twigs and leaves, they walked to and fro like old friends. In spite of the wind which carried away their words, and the roar of the sea tossing close beside them on the edge of the road, they began to speak their real thoughts, abandoning forthwith the half-mock-ing tone by which they had covered the embarrass-ment of the first moments. They walked slowly, keeping a keen lookout, and obliged to turn round when a blast lashed them too roughly. André was amazed to find how much and how well they understood, and also to feel himself on almost confidential terms with these strangers.

And protected by the bad weather and pro-pitious solitude, they thought themselves fairly safe, when suddenly, just before them, as they turned at the further end, Bogey stood before them in the form of two Turkish soldiers out for an airing, with canes in their hands such as our own soldiers are in the habit of cutting in the copses. This was a most perilous encounter, for these brave fellows, imported for the most part from the wilds of Asia Minor, where there is no compromise with ancient principles, were capable of going to any lengths in view of a proceeding so criminal in their eyes: Moslem women with a man from the West. The soldiers stood still, rigid with amazement, and then, after exchanging a few brief remarks, they took to their heels, obviously to give notice to their comrades or to the police, or perhaps to rouse the inhabitants of the nearest village. The three little black phantoms, thoroughly frightened, jumped into their carriage, which set off at a break-neck gallop, while Jean Renaud, who had watched the incident from a distance, hurried up to offer his assistance; and as soon as the talika, at a tearing pace, was lost to sight among the trees, the two friends turned off into a narrow cross-road which led up to the thick brushwood.

'Well, what are they like?' asked Jean Renaud a minute after, when, the alarm being over, they were walking quietly among the trees.

'Simply astounding,' replied André.

'Astounding! In what way? Attractive?'

'Extremely. And yet no; a more serious word would be more appropriate, for they are *souls* you must understand, nothing but souls. My dear fellow, for the first time in my life I have conversed with souls.'

'With souls? — but, after all, in what form? Are they respectable women?'

'Oh, as for respectable, all that is most correct. If you have been planning in your fancy a love affair for your old friend, you may put that aside, my dear boy, till another time.'

André was in his heart anxious about their return home. What they had ventured to do, poor little Turks, was so extravagantly contrary to all the laws of Islam. Still, was it not in fact of lily-like purity: three together, conversing without the very smallest double meaning about abstract ideas with a man who was not allowed even to suspect what their faces were like? He would have given a great deal to know that they were safe and immured behind the lattices of their harem. But what could he attempt to do for them? Fly, hide, as he had just done — that was all. Any intervention, direct or indirect, could only lead to their ruin.

VII

THIS long letter was mysteriously delivered to André Lhéry on the following evening:

'You told us yesterday that you knew nothing of the Turkish woman of to-day, and we quite believe you, for who can know her when she does not know herself?

'And what foreigner could penetrate the mystery of her soul? She could more easily betray that of her face. As to foreign women, some few, it is true, have seen our homes; but they know only our drawing-rooms, which are now exactly like those of Western Europe; the mere surface of our life.

'Well, shall we help you — you alone — to read our souls, if it is possible to read them? Now that we have put it to the test, we know that you and we can be friends; for it was a test; we wanted to be sure that there was something more than cleverness under your chiselled phrases. Can we have been mistaken in supposing that at the moment when you quitted the black spectres in peril some emotion stirred within you? Curiosity— disappointment — pity, perhaps; but it was not the indifference produced by an ordinary assignation.

'Above all you felt — of that we are quite sure — that those bundles devoid of shape and grace were not women, as we told you, but *souls* — *a soul :* that of the modern Moslem woman, whose intelligence is liberated — and suffers from it, but who rejoices in that emancipating suffering, and who yesterday went forth to meet you, a friend of yesterday.

'And now, to be still the friend of to-morrow, you must learn to see in that soul something more than a pleasing incident in your travels, a pretty image marking a stage in your life as an artist. No more must it be to you the young creature over whom you have yearned, nor the lover so easily made happy by the charity of your affection. If you really care that this soul should love you, you must meet half-way the first quiver of its tardy awakening.

'Your Medjeh is in her grave. We thank you in her name, in the name of us all, for the flowers you have strewn on the tomb of the little slave. In those days, when you were young, you culled happiness without an effort where it lay within reach of your hand. But the young Circassian who rushed and fell into your arms is a thing of the past; the time has come when even to the Moslem women instinctive love and subject love have given place to love by choice.

'And the time has come when you too must discover and describe something more than the picturesque and sensual aspects of love. Try now, to-day, to send out your heart so far as to make it feel the bitterness of the intolerable suffering which is ours, of having nothing to love but a dream.

'For we are condemned to love that and nothing else.

'You know how our marriages are arranged? Still, this mockery of an European home which has become usual since, during the last generation, Western ideas have prevailed in our houses, where formerly odalisques reigned on satin couches, even this represents a change which gratifies us, though such a home is still but a frail joy, liable at any moment to be wrecked by the whim of a capricious husband, or the introduction of a strange woman. In short, we are paired without our consent, like yearling sheep or fillies. Very often, no doubt, the man thus allotted to us by fate is gentle and kind; but we have not chosen him. In time we can become attached to him, but this is not the affection of love; feelings are born in us which presently take wings and sometimes alight far, far away, where, no one ever knows but ourselves. Yes, we can love. But we love with our souls, loving another soul; our mind weds another mind; our heart is enslaved by another heart. Such love as this remains a dream, because we are honest women, and even more because the dream is too dear and precious for us to risk its existence by trying to realise it. And it remains for ever innocent, like our walk yesterday at Pacha Bagtcheh when it blew so hard.

'And this is the secret of the Moslem woman's soul in Turkey in the year 1322 of the Hegira. Our modern education has led to this duality in our lives.

'This declaration will strike you as more extra-

ordinary than our rendezvous. We amused ourselves beforehand by imagining what your surprise
would be. At first you thought it was a practical
joke. Then, still doubting, you were tempted to
fancy it was an adventure — perhaps you hoped it
might be; you vaguely expected to meet Zaideh
attended by subservient slaves, curious to see a
celebrated author, and not too reluctant to lift her
veil.

'And all you met were three souls.

'These souls will be your faithful friends if
you will be theirs.

'ZAIDEH, NECHEDIL, and IKBAR.'

VIII

THE young Bey's love-making, which had become more and more acceptable, had gradually lulled to rest her schemes of rebellion. While keeping her soul to herself, she had surrendered all else very completely to her handsome lord, though he was no more than a great spoilt child, whose selfishness was veiled by much gracious elegance and inviting ways.

Was it for André Lhéry that she still guarded her soul? She herself hardly knew, for, as time went on, she did not fail to discern how childish her dream was. She now seldom thought of him.

She was almost resigned to her new cloister, and life would have been very endurable but that Hamdi, at the end of their second year of married life, took it into his head to marry Durdaneh and have two wives in the old fashion. Then, to avoid an unseemly quarrel, she had simply asked and obtained permission to withdraw for two months to her grandmother's house at Kassim Pacha, to take time for consideration of the new situation, and calmly prepare herself to face it.

So she went quietly away one evening, determined, however, to do anything rather than return
to this house and play the part of an odalisque, to
which she was gradually being subdued.

Zeyneb and Melek had also come home to
Kassim Pacha. Melek, after months of misery
and tears, had at last been divorced from an
impossible husband, and Zeyneb, released from
hers by death, after a year and a half of wretched-
ness spent with an invalid who was repugnant to
every sense; both thus irremediably blighted in
their early youth, weary, widowed, like derelicts
of life, had nevertheless been enabled to resume
their intimacy as sisters, and feel it the closer for
their utter dejection.

The news of André Lhéry's arrival in Constantinople, which they had seen in the Turkish
newspapers, had been utterly astounding; but at
the same time their idol of yore fell from his
pedestal. What, this man was like any other
man; he would have functions, duties as a sub-
ordinate in an Embassy; he had a profession;
above all he had a definite age? And Melek
forthwith amused herself by depicting to her
cousin the hero of her dreams as an old man,
bald, no doubt, and probably obese.

'André Lhéry!' said one of their friends from
the English Embassy, who had happened to see
him, and whom they eagerly questioned a few
days later. 'André Lhéry? Well, as a rule, he
is quite intolerable. Whenever he opens his lips
he seems to think he is doing you a favour. In
society he is ostentatiously bored. As to stout or

bald, no, that he is not.   I must grant that he is not at all ——'

'And his age?'

'His age? he has no age. It ranges over twenty years from one hour to the next. He takes the most extreme care of his person, and still makes you believe he is young, especially when he happens to be amused, for he has a child's laugh and teeth. Indeed a child's eyes too, as I have noticed in such moments. At other times he is arrogant, full of airs, and half in the moon. He has already been most severely criticised.'

In spite of this report, they had finally decided to dare the audacious adventure of going to meet him, to break the dreary monotony of their life. In the bottom of their hearts, some of their former adoration still survived from the days when he had been to them a soaring spirit, a being dwelling in the clouds. And also, to give themselves the semblance of a reason for running into such danger, they said, 'We will ask him to write a book in favour of Turkish women as they now are; in that way we may help hundreds of our sisters who are crushed as we are.'

IX

AFTER the crazy expedition to Tchiboukli spring
rushed on apace, the sudden, exquisite, and transient spring of Constantinople. The unceasing
frozen gale from the Black Sea suddenly granted
truce. And there came the delightful surprise of
discovering that this land, as far south as Central
Italy and Spain, could be at times deliciously luminous and warm. Along the Bosphorus the marble
steps of the palaces and the old wooden houses that
rise out of the water were steeped in hot sunshine.
And Stamboul, in the dry clear atmosphere, wore
its indescribable air of oriental torpor. The Turks,
a dreamy and contemplative people, lived out of
doors once more, seated outside the thousand quiet
little cafés, or round the sacred mosques, near the
fountains, under the young vine leaves and the
wistarias on the trellises, or the shady plane-trees;
myriads of narghilehs exhaled their enticing fragrance at the side of the streets, and swallows piped
in a frenzy of joy round their nests. The ancient
tombs and grey cupolas slept in an unutterable
peace which seemed immutable, sempiternal. And
the remote shores of Asia, and the placid sea of
Marmora, visible between the buildings, blazed
with colour.

André Lhéry drifted back into Turkish orient-
alism with even deeper melancholy perhaps
than in the days of his youth, but with quite as
deep a passion. And one day when he was
sitting in the shade, among hundreds of turbaned
dreamers, far from Pera and its modern turmoil,
in the very heart, the fanatical heart, of old
Stamboul, Jean Renaud, now his usual companion
in these Turkish hours, asked him point-blank:

'Well, what about the three little spectres of
Tchiboukli? No further news?'

They were outside the mosque of Mehmed
Fatih, on an old-world open place where Europeans never come, and at the moment the muezzins
were chanting, as if they had been lifted up to
heaven, at the very top of the gigantic stone
shafts of the minarets; mere voices, quite remote,
coming from so high above all earthly things, and
lost in the limpid blue above.

'Ah! The three little Turkish ladies,' replied
André. 'No, nothing since the letter I showed
you. Oh, I fancy the adventure is at an end, and
they are thinking no more about it.'

As he spoke he affected an air of indifference,
but the matter had troubled his meditative peace;
for each day that passed without any further sign
from his unknown friends made the notion more
painful that he might never — no, never, again hear
Zaideh's voice of singular sweetness beneath her
veil. The time was past when he could feel sure
of the impression he could produce; nothing
tortured him so cruelly as the flight of his youth,
and he sadly told himself, 'They expected to see

me a young man, and they were too greatly disappointed.'

Their last letter had ended with the words, 'We will be your friends if you choose.'

Certainly he asked nothing better; but where was he now to find them? In such a vast and suspicious labyrinth as Constantinople, to seek three Turkish ladies whose names and appearance were unknown to him, was as much as to undertake one of those impossible quests which the malignant spirits of old tales were wont to propose to the hero.

X

BUT on that very day and at that same hour the mysterious little lady who had planned the expedition to Tchiboukli was scheming to cross the redoubtable threshold of Yildiz to cast a supreme throw. On the other side of the Golden Horn, at Kassim Pacha, behind the oppressive lattices, in the room she had occupied as a girl, and to which she had returned, she was very busy in front of a mirror. A dress of grey and silver with a court train, which had arrived the day before from a great house in Paris, made her look more slender even than usual, more fragile and pliant. She meant to be very pretty to-day, and her two cousins, as anxious as she was about the issue, helped her to dress in oppressed silence. Decidedly the dress was becoming, and the rubies were becoming too on the grey cloudiness of the material. At any rate, the time had come. Her train was looped up by a ribbon to her waist, as etiquette requires in Turkey when approaching the Sovereigns; for, though the train is indispensable, no woman who is not a princess of the blood is permitted to let it sweep behind her over the magnificent carpets in the palace. Then her fair head was covered up in a yashmak, the white muslin veil which great ladies still wear in their carriage or their caïque on certain special occasions, and which is compulsory, like the train, for those who enter Yildiz, where no woman would be admitted in the tcharchaf.

The time had come. Zaideh, after kissing her cousins, went downstairs and took her seat in her brougham—all black, with gilt lanterns, and drawn by black horses with gold plate on the harness. So she started, the blinds closed and two eunuchs on horseback behind the carriage.

This was the disaster — easily foreseen, of course — which now threatened her. The two months of seclusion agreed to by her mother-in-law were at an end; Hamdi now insisted on his wife's return to their home. This was a matter of money, perhaps, but it was a matter of love too; for he had not been slow to perceive that she, in fact, was the light of his house, in spite of the empire exerted by the other over his senses. And he wanted to have both.

Now, then, for divorce at any cost. But to whom could she turn to obtain it? Her father, who had gradually regained her fond affection, would no doubt have supported her petition to His Imperial Majesty, but for a year now he had slept in the holy cemetery of Eyoub. There was her grandmother, too old now to take such steps, and far too '1320' to understand; in her time two wives under the same roof or three, or even four — why not? This newfangled notion of being the only one had come from Europe — with governesses and infidelity.

So in her misery it had occurred to her that she might throw herself at the feet of the Princess Sultana-mother, who was known for her kindness, and the audience was at once granted to the daughter of Tewfik Pasha, Marshal of the Court.

Having entered the vast expanse of the park of Yildiz, the black brougham brought her to a closed gate, that of the Sultana's private garden. A negro bearing a large heavy key came to open it, and the carriage, followed now by an escort of the Sultana's eunuchs in livery to help the visitor to alight, made its way through flowery avenues and stopped in front of the great outside staircase.

The fair petitioner knew all the ceremonial of the Court, having been several times to the great receptions held by the kind Princess in Bairam. In the hall she found, as she expected, thirty or more little fairies — very young girl slaves, miracles of beauty and grace, all dressed alike like sisters, and drawn up in two lines to receive her. After a deep curtsey these fairies flew about her like a flight of light billing birds, and bore her off to the room of the yashmaks, where every lady must shed her veils. There, in the winking of an eye, with consummate dexterity, the fairies, without a word, took off the enveloping gauzes which were kept in place by innumerable pins, and she was ready, not a hair out of place, under a very tall, very light gauze turban which rests on the top of the head and is indispensable at Court, princesses of the blood alone having the right to appear there

bareheaded. An aide-de-camp then came in to
welcome her and conduct her to the ante-room —
a woman, of course, since there are no men
about a Sultana — a young Circassian slave,
always chosen for her tall figure and faultless
beauty, who wears a military tunic with gold
aiguillettes, a long train looped up to the waist,
and a little officer's cap with gold braid. In the
ante-room another woman, the Sultana's treasurer,
came in as custom requires to keep her company;
a Circassian it need not be said, since no Turkish
lady is admitted to any function in the palace, but
a woman of high birth as holding so important a
post; and with her, a woman of the world and
indeed a very great lady, conversation was impera-
tive. All these delays were of mortal length, and
her hopes and her confidence dwindled rapidly.

As she entered the sitting-room so difficult of
access, where the mother of the Khalif would
receive her, she was trembling as in a violent
fever fit.

It was a room of purely European luxury, alas!
but for the exquisite carpets and the Moslem
texts; a bright, gay room, high up, and looking
out on the Bosphorus, which could be seen shining
and luminous through the latticed windows. Five
or six ladies in court dress, and the kind Princess
herself seated at the end of the room, rose to
receive the visitor. Three deep curtsies must be
made as for the sovereigns of the West; the third
a prostration, down on both knees, the forehead
bent low as if to kiss the hem of the lady's dress;
but she at once, with a kindly smile, held out her

hands to raise the suppliant. There was a young prince present, one of the Sultan's sons, who all, like the Sultan himself, have the right to see women unveiled. There were two princesses of the blood, fragile, graceful creatures, with their trains displayed and their heads bare. And, finally, three ladies wearing small turbans on their very fair hair, and their trains looped to their waists; three Serailis, formerly slaves in this very palace and become great ladies by marriage. They had been on a few days' visit to their former mistress and benefactress, having acquired the right, as Serailis, of arriving at the house of either of the princesses without an invitation as if they were members of the family. This is an accepted view of slavery in Turkey, and more than one wife of an uncompromising Western socialist might with great advantage come to a harem to learn to treat her maid, or her governess, as the Turkish ladies treat their slaves.

All real princesses, with rare exceptions, have the charm of being simple and gracious, and none certainly excel those of Constantinople in gentle simplicity and modesty.

'My dear child,' said the white-haired Sultana cheerfully, 'I bless the good wind that blows you here. And you know we shall keep you all day; indeed we shall call upon you to give us a little music, you play too delightfully.'

Some more fair girls who had not yet appeared, the young slaves who had charge of the refreshments, now came in carrying, on trays of gold, cups of gold and boxes of gold, containing coffee, sirops, and preserved rose leaves, while the Sultana turned the conversation to one or another of the matters of the day, which never fail to filter into the seraglio, however hermetically it may be closed.

But the visitor could ill conceal her distress; she was longing to speak, to beseech, that was only too evident. The prince, with polite discretion, withdrew; the princesses, and the beautiful Serailis, under the pretence of seeing something in the distance on the Bosphorus, went to gaze out of the windows of an adjoining room.

'What is it, my dear child?' asked the Sultana in a low voice, as she leaned with motherly kindness over Zaideh, who fell at her feet.

The first minutes were full of increasing and agonising anxiety when the little rebel, who was evidently and eagerly studying the effect of her petition, saw in the Sultana's face that the princess did not understand and was a little startled. Still those kind eyes did not speak refusal; they seemed only to say, 'A divorce, and with so little justification! That is a difficult matter indeed! Well, I will try. But in such a case my son will never grant it.'

And Zaideh, reading this refusal though it remained unspoken, felt as though the carpet, the floor, were sinking under her knees, and thought herself lost, when suddenly something like a religious thrill of awe seemed to run through the palace; soft shuffling feet flew along the corridors, every slave fell prostrate with a fuss of rustling

silk, and a eunuch rushed into the room, announcing in a voice sharpened by dread, 'His Imperial
Majesty!'

He had hardly spoken the words at which
every head must bow, when the Sultan appeared
at the door. The suppliant, still on her knees,
met and for a second felt his gaze, which looked
straight into her eyes, and then lost consciousness,
sinking like a dead thing, ghastly pale, into
the silvery cloud of her dress.

The man who had just come into the room
was perhaps in the whole world the most un-
approachably incomprehensible to Western minds
— the Khalif, whose responsibilities are super-
human; the man who holds all Islam in the
hollow of his hand, and is bound to defend it
alike against the undeclared concert of all Christian nations, and against the consuming fire
of time; the man who, to the remotest desert
ends of Asia, is known as the 'Shadow of the
Almighty.'

On the present occasion he had merely come to
visit his venerated mother, when, in the expression
of the kneeling woman, he read such anguish and
ardent entreaty. And that look went to the
mysterious heart which hardens sometimes under
the burden of his solemn pontificate, but on the
other hand is always tender with a secret and
exquisite compassion that none can know. With
a wave of the hand he pointed out the swooning
lady to his daughters, who, bowed to the ground
in deep prostration, had not seen her fall; and the
two princesses in their flowing trains raised in their

arms the lady of the looped-up train as tenderly as if she had been their sister. She, unwittingly, had gained her suit by her eyes.

When Zaideh came to herself some time after, the Sultan had left. Suddenly remembering it all, she looked about her, doubting whether she had really seen, or only dreamed of that awful presence. No, the Khalif was not there. But the Sultana-mother, leaning over her and taking her hands, said affectionately: 'Rouse up, my child, and be happy; my son has promised to sign to-morrow an Iradeh which will set you free.'

And as she went down the marble stair she felt so light, so excited, so tremulous! Like a bird which finds its cage door open. She smiled at the fairy-maids of the yashmak, following her in a sheeny group, hastening to cover her up; and in a hand's turn, with no end of pins, they had rearranged over her hair and her face the time-honoured white gauze shroud.

And yet, as she sat in her black and gold carriage, while the horses proudly trotted back to Kassim Pacha, she felt a cloud rise to dim her joy. She was free, oh yes, and her pride was avenged. But now she was conscious of an obscure longing, binding her still to Hamdi from whom she had believed herself detached for ever. 'This is vile and humiliating!' said she to herself; 'for the man has never been loyal or tender, and I do not love him, no! How utterly he must have profaned my soul, how mercilessly have debased me, that I should still dream of his embraces! Ah, do what I may, I am no longer wholly my own, since this memory can stain me still. And if, by and by, another man should cross my path whom I should really love, nothing worthy to be offered to him is left to me but my soul; and never will I give him anything else, never!'

XI

On the following day she wrote to André:

'If the day is fine on Thursday shall we meet at Eyoub? We shall arrive at about two o'clock in a caïque, at the steps by the water, exactly at the end of the avenue paved with marble, leading to the mosque. You can see us land from the little café there, and you will recognise us I am sure, the three poor little black spectres of the other day! As you like to wear a fez, put one on; it will be a little less risky. We will go straight to the mosque and go in for a moment. You must wait for us in the courtyard. Then walk on, we will follow. You know Eyoub better than we do; find some place, perhaps up the height of the cemetery, where we may talk undisturbed.'

And the weather was beautiful that Thursday, with a far-away sky of melancholy blue. It had turned suddenly hot after the long winter, and the Eastern aroma, which had been dormant in the cold, had everywhere come to life again.

The advice to André to wear a fez when going to Eyoub was quite unnecessary: he would never have been seen in anything else in that part of the

town where he was most at home. This was his
first visit here since his return to Constantinople,
and as he stepped out of his caïque and set foot on
those unchanged marble steps, it was with deep
emotion that he recognised everything in this
favoured nook, as yet ualtered. The little old
café, a hut of worm-eaten wood, standing out over
the water on a foundation of piles, had remained
untouched since the days of his youth. When,
accompanied by Jean Renaud, also wearing a fez,
and strictly charged not to speak at all, he entered
to take a seat in the ancient little room, open on
all sides to the pure air and coolness of the sea,
they found, lying on the divans covered with often
washed calico print, a party of comfortable cats
sleeping in the sun, besides two or three men in
long robes and turbans, contemplating the blue
sky. This motionless calm was all-pervading, this
indifference to the flight of time, this resigned and
very gentle philosophy, which are nowhere to be
found but in the lands of Islam, under the isolating
influence that emanates from sacred mosques and
vast burial grounds.

He and his accomplice in this dangerous adventure seated themselves on the calico-covered
benches, and the smoke of their narghilehs soon
mingled with that of the other dreamers; these
were Imams who had saluted them in the Turkish
fashion, not imagining them to be foreigners, and
André was amused by their mistake, which favoured his purpose.

There, just under their eyes, was the quiet little
landing-place where the ladies would presently

arrive; an old man with a white beard, who was in charge of it, kept ineffectual guard over it, guiding the approach of the rare caïques with his long pole; and the water scarcely rippled in the secluded little inlet where there was no tide, as it lapped against the old marble steps.

This is the end of the world, the last curve of the Golden Horn; no one comes by to go any farther; it leads nowhere. Nor on the shore is there any road beyond, here everything comes to an end; the arm of the sea, and the turmoil of Constantinople. Everything is old and abandoned here at the foot of the barren hills as brown as the desert and full of tombs. Beyond the little café on piles, where they were waiting, there were a few more huts of crumbling wood, an ancient convent of dancing dervishes, and then nothing but tomb-stones in perfect solitude.

They watched the light caïques which came in from time to time from the Stamboul shore, or from Kassim Pacha, bringing the faithful to worship in the mosque or to visit the tombs; or sometimes the inhabitants of the peaceful suburb. They saw two dervishes land and then some spectral women all in black, but bent and slow of pace, and then two pious ancients in green turbans.[1] Above their heads the reflection of the sun from the dancing surface of the water played on the wooden ceiling, like the changeful lights on watered silk, whenever another caïque disturbed the glassy pool.

At last, far away, something came in sight

[1] Worn by the Hadji who have made the pilgrimage to Mecca.

which looked very like the visitors they expected, three slight black figures against the luminous blue of the gulf, elegant and slender even at a distance.

Yes, here they were. They stepped out close to the café, recognised the men no doubt in spite of wearing triple veils, and slowly made their way up the white flagged path towards the mosque. The men, of course, had not stirred, hardly daring to follow them with their eyes up the deserted avenue, so sacred, so surrounded by eternal sleep.

After a long pause, André rose with an air of indifference, and as slowly as they themselves took the beautiful path of the dead which lies between funereal kiosques — circular buildings of white marble, and here and there between arcades like porticoes closed by iron railings. If the passer-by stops to look in through the windows of these kiosques he can see inside, in the dim light, tall bright green catafalques hung with ancient embroidery. And behind the railings of the porticoes there are tombs under the open sky, a crowd in wonderfully close array; tombs that are still magnificent, tall marble slabs, each touching its neighbour, mysteriously beautiful and covered with gilt arabesques and inscriptions; and all about them is a thicket of verdure, of pink roses, wild flowers, and tall grass. And the grass grows, too, between the flagstones of the echoing avenue, and close by the mosque the trees interlace and form a vault of green twilight.

On reaching the sacred court André looked about him, seeking them there. No, nobody yet.

This court lay in deep shade under its cloister and
the ancestral plane-trees; here and there on the
walls gleamed antique porcelain tiles; pigeons and
storks, dwellers in the neighbourhood, picked their
way about the pavement, quite confident in this
peaceful spot where man comes only to pray.
Presently the heavy curtain over the door of the
sanctuary was raised, and the three black spectres
emerged.

'Walk on, we will follow,' Zaideh had written.
So he took the lead, and rather hesitatingly turned
off down silent funereal side paths, still between
railed arches through which the myriad tombstones
could be seen, towards a more humble, much more
ancient and decrepit part of the cemetery, where
the dead lie in what seems a virgin forest. Then,
having reached the foot of the hill, he proceeded
to mount it. About twenty paces behind came
the three ladies, and, further away, Jean Renaud,
who was to keep watch and give the alarm.

They climbed the hill without leaving the
endless graveyards which cover all the heights of
Eyoub. And by degrees there rose around them
a prospect befitting the *Arabian Nights;* they
would presently see the whole of Constantinople
on the horizon, rising up above the tangle of trees
as if it were mounting with them. Up here there
was no longer a grove as in the valley round the
cemetery; on this hill the grass lay smooth,
and there only grew among the endless tombs,
giant cypresses with ample space and air between
them, affording a good view.

They were now quite at the top of this quiet

solitude; André stopped, and the three slender, black figures with no features came round him.

'Did you expect ever to see us again?' they asked almost together in their pretty, cajoling voices, offering him their hands.

To which André replied a little sadly:

'How could I tell whether you would ever come again?'

'Well, here they are once more — the three little souls in torment who are so daring through thick and thin! But where are you leading us?'

'Why, no further than this if it suits you. See, those four tombstones — they seem placed on purpose for us to sit upon. I see no one on either side — besides I am wearing a fez; we will talk Turkish if any one comes by, and you will be supposed to be out with your father——'

'Oh!' cried Zaideh, eagerly, 'our husband, you mean.'

And André thanked her with a little bow.

In Turkey, though the dead are held in so much respect, no one hesitates to sit among them, even on their tombstones; and in many cemeteries there are walks laid out and seats in the shade, as in gardens and squares with us.

'This time,' said Nechedil, seating herself on a fallen stone, 'we would not name a meeting place so far away as on the first day; your kindness would at last have been tried too far.'

'Eyoub is perhaps a somewhat fanatical spot for such an adventure as ours,' remarked Zaideh. 'But you are fond of it, you are at home here. We too love it, and we shall be at home here by and by, for here, when our time comes, is where we hope to rest.'

André looked at them in fresh amazement. Was it possible that these three little persons, whose extremely modern spirit had been brought so near to him, who read Madame de Noailles, and could on occasion talk like young Parisian women too familiar with the writings of Gyp, these little flowers of the twentieth century, should be destined as Moslems, and no doubt of high rank, to sleep some day in this sacred grove, there — down there — among all the turbaned dead of the early ages of the Hegira, in one of those inscrutable marble kiosques ? There each would have her green cloth catafalque hung with a pall from Mecca, on which too soon the dust would gather, and, as for all the others, a little oil lamp would be lighted for her at dusk. Ah! still the perpetual mystery of Islam which enwrapped these women, even in broad day-light when the sky was blue and the spring sun shining brightly.

They sat talking, on these old, old stones, their feet in the fine grass which was gemmed with small, delicate flowers, the friendly growth of a dry, undisturbed soil. They had here a wonderful spot for their conversation, a site unique in the world and consecrated by centuries of the past. Former generations without number, Byzantine emperors and magnificent Khalifs, had laboured for centuries to complete for their sole use and pleasure that fairy-like scene: here lay all Stamboul in almost a bird's-eye view, its crowd of mosques standing out against the distant blue of the sea;

Stamboul seen foreshortened, in close array, domes
and minarets piled one above another in profuse
and magnificent confusion, and behind them the
sea of Marmora, a dizzy circle of lapis-lazuli. In
the foreground, close to them, were thousands of
tombstones, some upright, some already leaning,
but all strange and attractive with their gilt
arabesques, gilt flowers, gilt inscriptions. There
were cypress trees four centuries old with trunks
like church pillars, of stone colour, and black
sheaves of foliage rising up to the brilliant sky like
black steeples.

The three souls without features seemed almost
gay to-day — gay because of their youth, because
they had succeeded in escaping and felt free for an
hour, and because the atmosphere here was mild
and light, with the fragrance of spring.

'Now repeat our names,' ordered Ikbar; 'just
to see that you do not mistake one for the
other.'

And André, pointing to each in turn with his
finger, pronounced their names like a schoolboy
obediently saying his lesson : 'Zaideh, Nechedil,
Ikbar.'

'Good, very good! But these are not our real
names at all, you know.'

'Believe me, I suspected as much, especially as
Nechedil of all names is that of a slave.'

'Nechedil, quite true, yes. Ah, you know so
much as that!'

The high sun fell full on their thick veils, and
André, under this strong light, tried to discover
something of their features. But no — nothing.

K

Three or four thicknesses of gauze made them quite inscrutable.

For a moment he was put off the track by their tcharchafs of poor black silk somewhat frayed, and by the rather shabby gloves they had thought it wise to put on so as not to attract attention.

'After all,' thought he, 'perhaps they are not such great ladies as I fancied, poor little things!' But then his eye fell on their very elegant shoes and their fine silk stockings. And then, their evidently high culture and perfect ease of manner.

'Well, and since that last day,' asked one, 'have you made no inquiries to identify us?'

'An easy task, indeed, to make inquiries; and, besides, I do not care a pin. I have three charming little friends, that much I know, and as to their names I am quite satisfied.'

'But now,' proposed Nechedil, 'we may very well tell him who we are. We have entire confidence in him ——'

'No, I would rather not, indeed,' André put in.

'Do not do anything of the kind,' said Ikbar. 'All our charm in his eyes lies in our little mystery. Confess, Monsieur Lhéry, if we were not veiled Moslem women, if each time we meet you it were not at the risk of our life — nay, of yours too, perhaps — you would say: "What do those three little fools want with me?" and you would not come again.'

'No, no, come ——'

'Yes, yes. The improbability of the adventure and the danger are all that attract you, I know.'

'No, I assure you — no longer.'

'So be it, do not go too far,' said Zaideh decisively, after a moment's silence. 'Do not urge the discussion, I would rather. But without affording you particulars of our birth and parentage, Monsieur Lhéry, allow us to tell you our real names. While preserving our incognito, I feel as if that would make us closer friends.'

'I am very willing,' said he. 'I believe I should even have requested it. Assumed names are a sort of barrier.'

'Well, then: "Nechedil's" real name is Zeyneb; the name of a wise and pious lady who taught theology once upon a time in Bagdad, and it suits her very well. "Ikbar" is Melek,[1] and how dare she have such a name, I wonder, such a little plague as she is. I, "Zaideh," am called Djenan,[2] and if ever you should know my history you will see what a mockery it is. Now repeat them: Zeyneb, Melek, Djenan.'

'Quite unnecessary, I shall not forget. But, since you have gone so far, you must tell one essential thing; in addressing you must I say *Madame*, or else——'

'You must say nothing whatever but just Zeyneb, Melek, Djenan, nothing more.'

'Oh! and yet——'

'That shocks you. But what can we say, we are little barbarians. However, if you insist, it must be *Madame* — Madame, alas! to all three. But our acquaintance is already so antagonistic to all the formalities; what can a little more or less matter now? And you see our friendship may

[1] Meaning an Angel.   [2] Meaning Well-beloved.

know no to-morrow; such terrible dangers hang
over our meetings that when we presently part we
do not know that we shall ever meet again. Why
then, during this short hour which may never be
repeated in all our lives, why not allow us to
believe that we are indeed your intimate friends?'

Strange as it was, the proposal was made in a
perfectly honest, frank, and well-bred manner,
with purity above suspicion, soul speaking to
soul. And André remembered the danger, which
he had in fact forgotten, so completely did this
enchanting spot wear every appearance of peace
and security, and so sweet was the spring day.
He remembered their courage, which had faded
from his mind, their daring to be here, the bold-
ness of desperation; and instead of smiling at this
request he felt how anxious, how pathetic it was.

'I will address you as you wish,' he replied,
'and thank you. But you on your side, you will
drop the *Monsieur?*'

'Ah! But then what can we say?'

'I see no alternative but to call me André.'

On which Melek, the child of them all, remarked:

'So far as Djenan is concerned, it will not be
for the first time, you know.'

'Melek, my dear, for pity's sake!'

'No, no, let me tell him. You cannot imagine
how much we have lived with you in our thoughts,
and she especially. And long ago, in the diary
she kept as a girl, written as if it were a letter
addressed to you, she always wrote to you as
André.'

'She is an *enfant terrible*, Monsieur Lhéry; I
assure you she is exaggerating wildly.'

'Ah, and the photo!' exclaimed Melek, suddenly changing the subject.

'What photo?' he asked.

'Of you with Djenan. It was as a thing
beyond all possibility, you understand, that she
had a fancy to possess it. Be quick, let us do it
at once; such a moment may never recur. Stand
beside him, Djenan.'

Djenan, with her languid grace and supple
rhythm of movement, rose to obey.

'Do you know what you are like?' said André.
'Like an elegy, in all that light trailing black, with
your head bent, as I see you there surrounded by
tombs.'

Her very voice was an elegy when she spoke
a little mournfully; its pitch was musical, extra-
ordinarily sweet, emotional, and yet far away.

But this little embodied elegy could be suddenly
very gay and saucy, and full of the most original
fun; she was evidently capable of childish nonsense
and irrepressible laughter.

Standing by André she arranged herself gravely,
with no sign of raising her veil.

'Why, do you mean to stand so — all black, with
no face?'

'Of course. Just a silhouette. Souls, you
know, need no features.'

Melek, going away a few steps, drew from under
her austere Moslem tcharchaf a little kodak of the
latest pattern and adjusted it. Snap! a first print;
snap! a second.

They never suspected how dear to them, in the unforeseen events of days to come, how dear and sad, these vague little shadows would be, recorded for mere amusement in such a spot at a time when the sunshine and reviving nature made all things gay.

Melek, to make sure, was about to take another snapshot, when they caught sight of a large pair of moustaches under a scarlet fez, which rose up from behind the tombs quite close to them; a passer-by, amazed at hearing an unknown tongue and seeing Turks taking photographs in a cemetery.

He went away, indeed, without making any remark, but with a look as much as to say, 'Only wait a minute. I shall return; we must find out the meaning of this.' And so, as on the first occasion, the meeting ended by the flight of the three gentle spectres — the flight of terror. And it was high time, for down at the foot of the hill the stranger was making a stir.

An hour later, when André and his friend, watching from afar, had assured themselves that the three Turkish ladies, making their way by devious paths, had succeeded in gaining unmolested one of the water-steps on the Golden Horn and securing a caïque, they themselves took a boat at a different landing-place and quitted Eyoub.

All was calm and safe now in the slender caïque, where they sat, almost reclining in the fashion of the place, and they floated down the bay shut in by the immense city, at the hour when the magical evening light was in its glory. Their boatman hugged the shore under Stamboul in the vast shadow cast at sundown, century after century, by the pile of houses and mosques over the imprisoned and placid waters. Stamboul, towering above them, was sinking into solemn monochrome, with the splendour of its cupolas against the blazing west. Stamboul grew imperial again, weighted with memories, an oppressor, as at the great periods of its past history; and under the beautiful, mirror-like sheet which was the surface of the sea, one could picture in its depths corpses piled up, and the refuse of two sumptuous civilisations. While Stamboul sank into gloom, the city that sat in tiers, on the opposite shore — Kassim Pacha, Tershaneh, and Galata — looked as if on fire; even Pera, the commonplace, perched on high and bathed in copper-coloured beams, played its part in this marvel of the closing day. There is hardly another city in the world which has such a power of magnifying itself under the favouring light and distance, so as to produce a sudden splendid spectacle, an apotheosis.

To André Lhéry these excursions in a caïque along the shore, in the shadow of Stamboul, had of old been of almost daily occurrence when he had lived at the top of the Golden Horn. At this moment it seemed to him that that long ago was but yesterday; the interval of twenty-five years was as nothing. He remembered everything, down to the merest trifles and long-forgotten details; he could hardly persuade himself that, if he turned back now, he would not find his secluded house in the old place and the faces he had known. And without quite knowing why, he vaguely associated the humble Circassian girl who slept beneath her tombstone with Djenan, who had so lately dropped into his life; he had a sort of sacrilegious sense of the continuity of one with the other, and in this magic hour, when all was peace and beauty, enchantment and oblivion, he did not feel remorseful over thus confounding the two. What could they want of him, these three little Turkish women? How would this comedy end, so delightful, and so beset with danger? They had said hardly anything beyond playful or indifferent things, and yet they had already attached him, at least by a tendril of affectionate anxiety. Their voices perhaps had bewitched him, especially that of Djenan; a voice which seemed to come from *beyond*, from the past, perhaps, and differed, he knew not how, from the common sounds of earth.

They moved on, floating as if they lay on the water itself, so low down does one lie in these light caïques almost devoid of gunwale. They had left behind them the mosque of Suleyman, which lords it over all the others on the highest point of Stamboul, chief of all the giant cupolas. They had passed that part of the Golden Horn where old-world sailing boats still are moored in a close crowd: tall hulls gaily painted, and an inextricable forest of slender masts all bearing the crescent of Islam on their red flags. The gulf widened before them to the opening into the

Bosphorus and the sea of Marmora, where number-less steamships lay before them, transfigured by embellishing distance. Now it was the Asiatic shore which suddenly came into sight in no less splendour. Scutari, yet another town twinkling with light; its minarets, its cupolas rushed into view, as red as coral. Scutari on most evenings produced the illusion of being on fire in its old Asiatic quarters; the small panes of the Turkish windows, tiny panes in myriads, each repeating the intense refulgence of the half-vanished sun, might make any one who was not prepared for this customary effect believe that all these houses were in flames within.

XII

In the course of the following week André Lhéry received this letter, in three handwritings:

Wednesday, April 27, 1904.

'We are never so silly as when we are with you, and afterwards, when you are gone, we are ready to cry over it. Do not refuse to come once more, for the last time. We have arranged everything for Saturday, and if you knew with what Machiavelian cunning! But it will be a farewell meeting, for we are going away.

'Study carefully what follows, so as not to lose the clue.

'Come to Stamboul, to the front of the mosque of Sultan Selim. Standing facing it, you see on your right a little deserted-looking alley between a convent of dervishes and a small cemetery. Turn up it and it will lead you, at about a hundred paces distant, to the courtyard of the little mosque of Tossoun Agha. Exactly in front of you, in that courtyard, you will see a large house, very old, and formerly painted a reddish brown. Go round to the back of it and you will find a rather dark alley with latticed houses on each side and projecting balconies. On the left-hand side, the third house, the only one with a double door and a copper knocker, is the place where we shall await you. Do not bring your friend; come alone, it is safer.

'DJENAN.'

'At half-past two I shall be on the watch behind the door, which will be ajar. Wear a fez and a coat as nearly as possible of the colour of the wall. The little house where we must say good-bye is of the very humblest. But we will try to leave you with a good impression of the shades that have crossed your path, so swift and so light that perhaps in a few days you will doubt whether they were real.   MELEK.'

'Still, light as they are, they were not mere thistledown wafted to you by a whim. You were the first to feel that the hapless Turkish woman may have a soul, and they wanted to thank you for that.

'And this innocent adventure, brief and almost unreal as it has been, will not have lasted long enough to weary you. It will remain in your life a picture without a wrong side to it.

'On Saturday, before we part for ever, we will tell you many things if the meeting is not broken up, as it was at Eyoub, by an alarm and flight. So, till we meet, our friend.   ZEYNEB.'

'I, who am the great strategist of the party, was desired to draw this fine map which I enclose in the letter to help you to find your way. Though the neighbourhood has a rather cut-throat aspect, your friend may be quite easy; nothing can be quieter or more respectable.   MELEK again.'

And André answered at once to 'Zaideh,' *poste-restante:*

'*April* 29, 1904.

'Saturday, the day after to-morrow, at half-past two, in the required dress — a fez and a dark stone-coloured cloak, I will be at the door with the copper knocker, to place myself at the orders of the three black spectres. — Their friend,

'ANDRÉ LHÉRY.'

XIII

JEAN RENAUD, who augured ill for the expedition, in vain begged permission to follow his friend. André would do no more than concede that they should go together before the appointed hour to smoke a narghileh in a place that had formerly been dear to him, not more than a quarter of an hour's walk from the fateful spot.

It was in Stamboul, of course, in the very heart of the Moslem quarter, in front of the great mosque of Mahomed Fatih,[1] which is one of the holiest. After crossing the bridge it is yet a long walk uphill to this centre of old-world Turkish life. Here are no more Europeans, no hats, no modern buildings; on reaching it through a series of little bazaars like those at Bagdad, and streets bordered with lovely little fountains, funereal kiosques, and railings enclosing tombs, one feels that one has gently gone down the long ladder of time, retrograding to long-past ages.

They had fully an hour to spare when, emerging from the shady alleys, they found themselves in front of the colossal white mosque, whose minarets, crowned with gold crescents, towered up to the infinite blue heavens. Before the tall

---

[1] Mahomed Fatih or Sultan Fith Mahommed II., the Conqueror.

arched porch, the place on which they found
a seat is a sort of external enclosure, chiefly
frequented by pious devotees faithful to the
costume of their ancestors, the robe and turban.
Antiquated little coffee shops stand open all
round, haunted by dreamy figures, scarcely speaking at all. There are trees there too, and under
their shade simple divans are placed for those who
prefer to smoke outside, and in cages hanging
from the trees are finches, blackbirds, and linnets,
specially appointed musicians in this artless, easy-
going spot.

They sat down on a bench where some Imams
courteously made room for them to be seated, and
there came close up to them first the little begging
children, then the sleek cats seeking a friendly
rub, an old man in a green turban hawking coco,
'as cool as ice,' a party of very pretty gipsy girls,
who sold rose-water and danced — all smiling and
discreet, not insistently urgent. And then they
were left to themselves, to smoke in silence, and
listen to the singing birds. Ladies went by all in
black or wrapped in the Damascus veils which are
of red or green silk with large patterns in gold;
the sellers of cats' meat passed that way, and
then some worthy Turk — even those in robes of
silk and magnificently dignified — would gravely
buy a piece for his cat, and carry it off over his
shoulder, stuck on the ferrule of his umbrella.
Again, here were Arabs from the Hedjaz, on
a visit to the city of the Khalif, and mendicant
dervishes with uncut hair, returning from a pilgrimage to Mecca. An old fellow of at least

a hundred was trotting babies twice round the
little square for about a farthing, in a packing-case
on casters which he had made gaudy with paint,
but which jolted a great deal on the old broken
pavement. As a background to these thousand
trivial things revealing the youthful, simple,
kindly side of the people, the mosque rose up,
seeming all the more grand, majestic, and calm,
superb in its lines and its whiteness with its two
pointed shafts against the clear sky of the first
of May.

Ah! what gentle, honest eyes were to be met
under those turbans, what trustful, tranquil faces
framed in black or fair beards! How different
from the Levantines in short coats who, at this
same hour, were bustling along the side-walks of
Pera, and from the crowds in our Western cities,
with greedy or mocking eyes, scorched by alcohol!
How truly here one might feel oneself in the
centre of a happy people, remaining almost such
as they were in the golden age, by dint of always
temperate desires, of fear of change, and fidelity
to the Faith!

Among the men who sat there under the trees,
content with a tiny cup of coffee costing a half-
penny and the soothing narghileh, many were
artisans, working each for himself at his little old-
world trade in his booth or in the open air. How
deeply they would pity the hapless herds of toilers
in our land of 'progress,' who wear themselves
out in some horrible factory to enrich their masters.
How strange, how deeply to be pitied, they would
think the vinous uproar of our labour exchanges, or

the follies of our political stump-oratory, in a public-house between two glasses of absinthe!

The moment was near. André Lhéry left his companion and made his way alone towards the more distant quarter of Sultan Selim, still amid purely Turkish dwellings, but along more deserted streets, where abandonment and decay could be felt. Old garden-walls, old shut-up houses, wooden houses all of them, and originally painted dark ochre or a russet brown, the hues that give Stamboul its low tone of colour and make the whiteness of the minarets seem more dazzling.

Among so many, many mosques, that of Sultan Selim is a very large one; its domes and spires are visible from afar at sea, but it is also one of the most neglected and decayed. There are no little cafés on the square that surrounds it, no smokers; and on this day there was no one within sight; a melancholy desert lay in front of its arched entrance. To the right André saw the alley described by Melek 'between a convent of dervishes and a little cemetery,' a gloomy spot this alley, the pavement green with weeds. When he reached the humble mosque of Tossoun Agha he recognised the large house, the abode certainly of ghosts, which he was to walk round; and here again there was nobody; but the swallows were piping to the happy month of May, a wistaria hung in garlands, such a wistaria as can only be seen in the East, with branches as thick as a ship's cable, and thousands of bunches now showing their tender violet hue. And at last here was the blind alley, most funereal of all, grass-grown, and in a sort of twilight under old balconies masked by impenetrable iron-work. Not a creature, not even swallows, and total silence. 'It is a cut-throat looking spot,' Melek had written in her post-script; and that it certainly was.

When only shamming Turk and on mischief bent, almost a malefactor, it is uncomfortable to walk under such balconies, whence invisible eyes may so easily be on the watch. André went slowly, fingering his beads, on the lookout, without betraying himself, and counting the closed doors. 'The fifth, a double door with a copper knocker.' Ah, this was it! Besides, it was just a little way open, and through the crack a small gloved hand was seen, drumming on the wood, a small hand with many-buttoned gloves, much out of its element, it would seem, in this uncanny quarter. It would not do to hesitate, for fear of possible spies, so André boldly pushed the door and went in.

The black phantom in ambush within, which certainly had the figure of Melek, hastily shut and locked it, bolted to make sure, and said gaily, 'So you have found us! Go up, my sisters are upstairs waiting for you.'

He mounted a flight of carpetless stairs, dark and rickety. At the top, in a small humble harem, very simple, with bare walls, which the iron gratings and wooden lattice over the windows kept in dismal semi-darkness, he found the other two spectres, who gave him their hands. For the first time in his life he was in a harem, a thing which, knowing oriental life as he did, had always seemed

L

to him impossibility itself; he was inside, behind those lattices of the women's windows, those jealous lattices, which no man but the master ever sees excepting from outside. And the door below was barred, and all this was happening in the heart of old Stamboul, and in what a mysterious dwelling! He asked himself with a little alarm that struck him as very amusing: 'What am I doing here?' All the child-like side of his nature, all of him that was still eager to get outside itself, still in love with what was foreign and new, was humoured to the top of its bent.

Meanwhile the three ladies of his harem were like three tragic ghosts, as closely veiled as they had been the other day at Eyoub, and more inscrutable than ever, with no sun to help him. As to the harem itself, far from oriental luxury, it was only decently poor.

They made him sit down on the faded striped divan, and he looked about him. Poor as the women of the house might be they had good taste, for everything, in spite of the humblest simplicity, was harmonious and Eastern; nowhere were there any of the trifles 'made in Germany,' which are now, alas! invading Turkish homes.

'Am I in your house?' asked André.

'Oh, no,' they exclaimed in a tone suggesting a smile under the veils.

'Forgive me, my question was idiotic for a heap of reasons; first of all because, in fact, I do not care. I am with you; nothing else matters.'

He was watching them. They wore the same tcharchafs as at the former meeting — black silk, frayed here and there. And shod like princesses; and besides, when they took off their gloves, fine gems sparkled on their fingers. Who and what were these women, and what was this little house?

Djenan asked him, in her low voice like that of a wounded siren at the point of death:

'How long can you give us?'

'All the time that you are able to give me.'

'We — we have nearly two hours of comparative safety. But that will seem rather long to you, perhaps.'

Melek brought one of the low tables commonly used in Constantinople for the little meals which are always set before visitors — coffee, bonbons, and preserved rose-leaves. The covering was of white satin embroidered in gold and strewn with real Parma violets; the service was of gold filigree, and this was the crowning touch of incongruous disparity.

'Here are the photos done at Eyoub,' said she, as she helped him like a dainty little slave. 'But they are a failure. We will try again to-day, as we shall never meet any more; the light is bad, still, with a longer exposure——' And she produced two little prints, brown and fogged, in which Djenan's figure was hardly discernible; André accepted them carelessly, little thinking how precious they would be to him later.

'Is it true,' he asked, 'that you are going away?'

'Perfectly true.'

'But you will come back; we shall meet again?'

To which Djenan replied in the vague fatalist words which orientals use when the future is in any way in question: 'Inch Allah!' Were they really going away, or was it an excuse for putting an end to this audacious adventure, for fear of tiring of it perhaps, or of the desperate danger? And André, who after all knew nothing about them, felt them as evanescent as a vision, impossible to detain or to call back, as soon as it was their whim not to see him again.

'And you are leaving soon?' he ventured to inquire.

'In about ten days most likely.'

'Then you will have time to send me a sign once more.'

They held council in an undertone, in highly colloquial Turkish intermingled with Arab words, and too difficult for André to follow: 'Yes, next Saturday,' they said, 'we will try once more — and thank you for wishing it. But do you know what cunning we have to exercise, what complicity we must bribe to be able to receive you?'

And now, it would seem, they must make haste to take the photographs, to seize the reflection of a sunbeam from the gloomy house opposite, which fell into the latticed room, but was slowly rising higher and higher and would soon vanish. Two or three exposures were tried of Djenan by the side of André; Djenan always shrouded in her funereal black.

'And do you know,' said he, 'how new and strange it is to me, almost alarming, to talk with invisible beings? Your very voices are masked by those thick veils. Now and then I am vaguely afraid of you.'

'But it was agreed between us that we were merely souls.'

"True, but souls reveal themselves to other souls chiefly by the expression of their eyes. Now I cannot even imagine what your eyes are like. I fully believe that they are bright and honest, but if they were as fearful as those of ghouls I should not know it. I assure you it really discomposes me, frightens me, repels me. At least do one thing, let me have your portraits unveiled. On my honour, I will return them to you at once, or else, if some disaster should part us, I will burn them.'

At first they were speechless. With their hereditary Moslem traditions, to show their faces seemed to them an impropriety which would at once make their acquaintance with André a guilty thing. Finally it was Melek who spoke, pledging her sisters, deliberately, but in a somewhat arch tone which had a suspicious ring in it: 'Our photos without either tcharchaf or yashmak? That is what you want? Well, give us time to take them and you shall have them next week. But now let us all sit down. It is for Djenan to speak; she has a great favour to ask of you. Light a cigarette; you will find the time less long at any rate.'

'My petition is from us all,' said Djenan, 'on behalf of all our Turkish sisters. Monsieur Lhéry, undertake our cause; write a book in defence of the unhappy Moslem women of the twentieth century. Tell all the world, since you know that it is true, that we now have a soul; that it is no longer possible to break us like chattels. If you do this you will be blessed by thousands. Will you?'

André sat silent, as they had done before at his request for the portraits. He did not see the book at all; and, besides, he had promised himself an idle time at Constantinople, to play the oriental, not to write a book.

'What a difficult thing you expect of me! A book to prove a case? You, who seem to have read me with care and know me well — do you think that would be at all like me? Besides, what do I know of the Moslem woman of the twentieth century?'

'We will inform you.'

'But you are going away.'

'We will write to you.'

'Oh! Letters, written things, you know — I can never tell anything I have not seen and lived in.'

'We shall come back.'

'But then you will be compromised. People will inquire whence I derived such information. And they will certainly find out at last.'

'We are ready to sacrifice ourselves for the cause! What better use can we make of our poor little lives — aimless and unprofitable lives? We are all three eager to devote ourselves to alleviating misery, found a good work, like European women. And even that is forbidden us; we must sit idle and hidden behind our lattices. Well, we mean to be the inspiring spirit of that book; it will be our deed of charity, and if we lose our freedom or our life for it, so much the worse!'

André still tried to escape:

'Remember, too, that I am not independent in Constantinople, I have a place in an Embassy. And there is another thing: I meet with such confiding hospitality from the Turks. Among the men whom you regard as your oppressors, I have friends who are very dear to me.'

'Ah, well, you must make your choice: we or they. Take it or leave it. Make up your mind.'

'Is it so urgent as that? Then, naturally and of course, I choose you. And I obey.'

'At last!' and she gave him her little hand, which he dutifully kissed.

They talked on for nearly two hours, in a semblance of security such as they had never before known.

'But are you not quite exceptional?' he asked, astonished to find them wrought up to such a pitch of desperation and rebellion.

'We are the rule, on the contrary. Take twenty Turkish women where you please — women of the upper class of course — and you will not find one who does not talk as we do. They are brought up as prodigies, blue-stockings, musical dolls, objects of luxury for their father and their master, and then treated as odalisques and slaves, like our ancestresses a century ago! No, we can bear it no longer — we can bear it no longer!'

'Take care lest I plead your cause from the

other point of view; I am a man of the past. I should be quite capable of it, believe me. Down with governesses, transcendental professors, and all the books which extend the realm of human misery! Back to the peace of our forefathers!'

'Well, if need should be, we would make the best of such pleading, especially as any retrogression is impossible, no one can turn the stream of time backward. The essential point is to move the world at last to pity, to make it understood that we are martyrs, we, the women of the transition between those of the past and those of the future. That is what we want you to make heard, and after that you will be the friend of us all — all.'

André still hoped for some unforeseen contingency that might save him from writing *their* book. Still, he felt the bewitching influence of their noble indignation, and their sweet voices thrilling with hatred of the tyranny of man.

By degrees, too, he became used to their having no faces. To give him a light for his cigarette, or hand him the microscopic cup out of which Turkish coffee is sipped, they came and went, elegant, fairy-like, and eager, but still black spectres; and when they stooped, the veil over their features hung forward like a Capuchin's long beard added in derision to these youthful forms of grace.

Their safety was, in fact, merely illusory in this house at the end of the blind alley, which in the event of a surprise was a perfect trap. When, now and then, a step was heard outside on the flagstones fringed with starved grass, they looked out anxiously through the protecting bars: some old turbaned Turk going home, or the water-seller of the district with his goat-skin across his back.

Theoretically, they were all to call each other by their real names and nothing more. But neither of them dared be the first, and they used no names at all.

Once they had a shudder of alarm: the copper knocker on the outer door rang out under an impatient hand, rousing a terrible echo in the midst of the silence of these dead houses, and they all rushed to the latticed windows: it was a lady in a black silk tcharchaf, leaning on a stick and apparently bent by great age.

'It is nothing of any consequence,' they said. 'We had foreseen this. Only she will have to come into this room.'

'Then I must hide?'

'That even is unnecessary. Go, Melek, and let her in, and you will say just what we agreed on. She will only pass through, and we shall see her no more. As she passes you, she may perhaps ask you in Turkish, *How is the little invalid?* And you have only to reply — in Turkish, too, of course — that *he is much better since this morning.*'

A minute later the old dame came through, her veil down, feeling the poor carpets with the end of her crutch. And she did not fail to ask André:

'Well, and is the dear boy better?'

'Much better,' said he, 'since this morning particularly.'

'That's well, thank you, thank you,' and she disappeared through a small door at the end of the harem. André asked for no explanation. He was wrapt in the improbabilities of an Eastern tale; if they had said to him: 'The fairy Carabosse will come out from under this divan, will strike the walls with a touch of her wand, and it will become a palace,' he would have accepted the statement without comment.

After the coming of the lady with the stick they had still a few minutes to spare; when the time came they dismissed him with the promise that they would meet once more at whatever risk: 'Go, friend of us all, go to the end of the alley at a leisurely, dreamy pace, telling your rosary, and we all three, through the lattices, will watch your dignified retreat.'

XIV

AN old eunuch, stealthy and speechless, came on Thursday to bring André notice of a meeting on the day but one following, in the same place and at the same hour, and with it some large portfolios carefully wrapped and sealed.

'Ah!' thought he, 'the promised photographs!' And, impatient to look into their eyes at last, he tore open the paper.

They were portraits, no doubt, without tcharchaf or yashmak, and fully signed, if you please, in French and in Turkish: Djenan, Zeyneb, and Melek. His friends had even got into full dress for the occasion — handsome evening dresses, cut low, and quite Parisian. But Zeyneb and Melek presented their backs very squarely, showing only the edge and tip of their little ears; while Djenan, the only one seen in front, held a large feather fan which hid all her face, and even her hair.

On Saturday, in the mysterious house where they met for the second time, nothing tragical occurred, no fairy Carabosse appeared. 'We are here,' Djenan explained, 'in the house of my nurse, who never in her life refused me anything; the sick boy is her son. The old dame is her

mother; Melek had told her that you were a
fresh physician to see him. Now do you understand? Still I feel some remorse at making her
play such a dangerous part. However, as it is
our last day.'

They talked for two hours without mentioning
the book; they no doubt feared to sicken him of
the subject if they talked too much about it.
And he was pledged; that point was gained.

And they had so much else to say, long arrears
of things, it seemed; for it was true that they had
lived for years in his companionship through his
books, and this was one of the rare instances when
he, who usually was so annoyed now at having
bared his heart to thousands of readers, did not
regret one of his most secret revelations. After
all, how contemptible were the shrugs of those
who do not understand, in the balance against the
fervid affection he had won here and there at the
opposite ends of the earth, from the souls of
unknown women — the only thing perhaps for
which one ever cares to write!

This day there was unclouded confidence,
understanding, and friendship between André
Lhéry and the three little spectres of his harem.
They knew a great deal about him by reading;
and as he on his part knew nothing about them, he
listened more than he talked. Zeyneb and Melek
told him of their wretched marriages, and the hopeless imprisonment that awaited them. Djenan, on
the contrary, told him nothing so far about herself.

Besides the intimate sympathy which had so
quickly allied them, there was a surprise for them

all in finding each other so gay. André was fascinated by the high spirits of their nation, and of their youth, which in spite of everything were still theirs, and which they indulged the more readily now that they had ceased to be shy of him. And he, whom they had pictured to themselves as gloomy, who had been described to them as icy and distant, had at once taken off that mask in their presence, and was perfectly simple, ready to laugh at anything, at heart much younger than his years, with a vein even of childish roguishness. This was his first experience of conversation with Turkish women of rank. And they had never in their lives talked to a man of any class. In this humble house, all decrepitude and shadow, buried in the heart of old Stamboul, amid ruins and sepulchres, they had achieved the impossible merely by meeting there to exchange ideas. Being reciprocally such entirely new elements in life, they were surprised, amazed, to find that they were not altogether dissimilar; but no, on the contrary, they were in absolute communion of feeling and impressions, like friends who had always known each other. For their part, all they knew of life in general, of European things, of the evolution of Western minds, they had learnt in solitude through books. And to-day, in this almost miraculous intercourse with a man from the West, and a man whose name was famous, they found themselves on his level; he treated them as his equals, as intellects, as souls, and the effect on them was a sort of mental intoxication such as they had never experienced before.

It was Zeyneb who served their little repast on the low table, covered to-day with green and silver satin, strewn with red roses. As for Djenan, she sat more motionless than ever, a little apart, never stirring a fold of her elegiac veil; she talked more perhaps than the other two, and her questions especially showed greater depth of thought, but she did not move; she was bent, it would seem, on remaining the most inaccessible of the three, physically the least incorporate. Once, however, her arm raised the tcharchaf, giving a glimpse of one of her sleeves — a wide sleeve, very full, as was the fashion that spring, and made of lemon-coloured silk gauze with a pattern in green — two colours which André's eyes were not to forget, as proofs in evidence another day.

The world without was more melancholy than it had been the previous week. The cold had come back in the full flower of May; they could hear the wind from the Black Sea whistle at the doors, as if it were winter; all Stamboul was shivering under a sky shrouded with black clouds, and there was dim twilight in the dingy latticed little harem.

Suddenly the copper knocker on the outer door, always alarming, made them all start.

'It is they,' cried Melek, leaning out at once to look through the window bars. 'Yes; they have managed to get out! How glad I am!'

She flew down to open the door, and soon came up again, following two other black dominoes with impenetrable veils, who seemed also to be young and elegant.

'Monsieur André Lhéry,' said Djenan, intro-
ducing him; 'two friends of mine — their names
do not matter, I suppose?'

'Two spectre-women, and nothing more,' said
the ladies, intentionally emphasising the word
which André had perhaps used too frequently in
one of his later books; and they held out small
white-gloved hands. They spoke French in very
gentle tones, and with perfect ease.

'Our friends here have told us,' said one of
them, 'that you are going to write a book in behalf
of the Moslem woman of the twentieth century,
and we wished so much to thank you.'

'What is the title to be?' asked the other,
seating herself on the shabby divan, with languid
grace.

'Dear me, I have not yet thought of that.
The whole scheme is so new, and I have, I must
confess, been taken a little unawares. We will
take votes as to the title, if you like. Let me
see! I would suggest "Disenchanted."'

'"Disenchanted,"' repeated Djenan thought-
fully. 'One is disenchanted with life when one
has lived. But we, on the contrary, only ask to
live. We are not disenchanted, we are annihilated,
sequestered, stifled ——'

'Yes, there, I have hit on the title,' cried little
Melek, who could not be serious to-day. '"Stifled!"
And it so well describes our state of mind under
the thick veils we wear to meet you in, Monsieur
Lhéry. For you cannot imagine how difficult it
is to breathe under them.'

'I was intending to ask you why you wear

them. Could you not, in the presence of a friend, be satisfied to dress like all the women we meet in Stamboul? Veiled, of course, but with a certain lightness, allowing something to be guessed: the profile, the brow, sometimes even the eyes — while you show less than nothing.'

'And you know,' added Melek, 'it does not look at all the correct thing to be so hidden. As a rule, when you meet a mysterious personage in the street wearing a threefold veil, you may safely say, she is going where she ought not to go. We ourselves, for instance, to be sure. And this is so well known that other women when they meet them, smile and nudge each other.'

'Come, come, Melek,' said Djenan in gentle reproof. 'Do not talk scandal like a little Perote. "Disenchanted," yes, it sounds well, but the meaning is a little beside the mark.'

'This was my notion of it. Do you remember in the fine ancient legends, the Walküre who slept in her subterranean stronghold; the Sleeping Beauty who slept in her castle in the heart of a wood? But alas! the spell was broken, and they woke up. Well, you Moslem ladies have been sleeping for ages in peaceful slumbers, guarded by tradition and dogma. And suddenly the Evil Magician, the wicked West Wind, has passed over you and broken the charm; you are all waking up at once, waking up to the woe of living, to the suffering of knowledge.'

Djenan, however, was only half-persuaded. She evidently had a title of her own choice, but would not yet tell it.

The new-comers were rebels too, and of the deepest dye. There was much talk in Constantinople that spring of a young woman of rank who had fled to Paris; the adventure had turned all heads in the harems, and these two spectre-women dreamed of it dangerously.

'You, perhaps,' said Djenan, 'might find happiness there, because you have some Western blood in your veins. Their grandmother, Monsieur Lhéry, was a Frenchwoman, who came to Constantinople, married a Turk, and embraced Islam. But I, Zeyneb, Melek, leave our Turkish land! No; so far as we three are concerned it is an impossible form of deliverance. Worse humiliations if they must be endured, harder slavery! But here we must die, and sleep at Eyoub.'

'And how right you are!' exclaimed André in conclusion.

They still said that they were going away to be absent for a time. Was it true? At any rate, when parting from them this time he felt sure they should meet again. He was bound to them by the book, and perhaps by something more, by a tie of a kind quite undefinable as yet, but already tenacious and dear to them, which had begun to grow up between Djenan and himself.

Melek, who had assumed the duties of the doorkeeper of this strange house, showed him out, and during their brief *tête-à-tête* in the squalid dark passage he reproached her for her trick in the faceless photographs. She made no reply, followed him half-way down the tumble-down

M

stairs, to be sure that he knew how to unfasten the bolts and lock of the outer door.

Then, when on the threshold he turned back to bid her good-bye, he saw her above him, showing her white teeth in a smile, smiling with her little pert nose, saucy but not ill-natured, and her fine large grey eyes, and all her delightful little face, and her twenty years. She held up her veil with both hands, showing the golden red curls that framed her forehead. And her smile seemed to say: 'Yes, it is I, Melek, your little friend Melek, whom I beg to introduce to you. And you know it is not as if I were one of the others, Djenan, for instance! I really do not count. Good-bye, André Lhéry, good-bye.'

It was only for the space of a lightning flash, and the veil was dropped. André softly spoke his thanks, in Turkish, for he was almost outside in the gloomy blind alley.

Out here it was cold under the black clouds and the Siberian wind. The day fell as dismally as in December. It was in such weather as this that Stamboul most poignantly brought memories of his youth, for the brief frenzy of his residence at Eyoub, so long ago, had had winter for its background. As he crossed the deserted square in front of the great mosque of Sultan Selim, he recalled with cruel precision having once before crossed it in just such an hour, and just such solitude, under a lashing north wind, one dreary evening twenty-five years since. And the image of the dead girl he had loved completely effaced that of Djenan.

XV

On the following day he happened to be walking
up the high street of Pera in the society of some
pleasant friends from the French Embassy who
had also wandered thither — the Saint-Enogats,
of whom he was beginning to see a good deal. A
black coupé came by, in which he vaguely perceived
the form of a lady in a tcharchaf. Madame de
Saint-Enogat bowed very slightly to the veiled
lady, who at once, a little nervously, closed the
blind of the carriage. This abrupt movement
revealed to André, beneath the tcharchaf, a sleeve
of lemon-coloured silk with a pattern in green,
which he was quite sure he had seen the day
before.

'What, do you bow to a Turkish lady in the
street?' he asked.

'It was quite incorrect, no doubt, to do such
a thing, especially as I am with you and my husband.'

'And who was she?'

'Djenan Tewfik Pasha, one of the flowers of
elegance of young Turkey.'

'Aha! And pretty?'

'More than pretty — exquisite.'

'And rich, to judge by her carriage?'

'They say she has the revenues of a province in Asia. By the way, one of your great admirers, dear Master.' She slily emphasised the words 'dear Master,' knowing that they made his skin creep. 'Last week at the X—— Legation all the men-servants were sent out for an afternoon's holiday, you may remember, on purpose to give a tea without any men to which Turkish ladies could come. She came; and a woman there ran you down — oh, but ran you down!'

'You?'

'Oh, dear no. It does not amuse me to abuse you unless you are by. It was the Comtesse d'A——. Well, Madame Tewfik Pasha took your part, and with enthusiasm — and it strikes me now that you seem greatly interested in her.'

'I — why, how can I be? A Turkish woman, as you know, simply does not exist for us men. No; but I noticed the coupé — very well turned out. I often meet it.'

'Often! Then you are in luck, for she never goes out.'

'Indeed she does; and generally I see two other women with her, who both seem young.'

'Perhaps her cousins, the daughters of Mehmed Bey, the former Minister.'

'And what are their names, these Mehmed Beys?'

'The elder is Zeyneb, and the other Melek — I think.'

Madame de Saint-Enogat had, no doubt, scented something, but was far too sweet and too loyal to be dangerous.

XVI

THEY had certainly left Constantinople, for
some days later André Lhéry received the following letter from Djenan with the postmark of
Salonica:

May 18, 1904.

'Our friend, you who love roses, why are you
not here? You who feel and love the East as no
other Western man can, oh, why cannot you find
your way to the old-world palace where we have
settled for a few weeks, behind high gloomy walls
all hung with flowers?

'We are staying with one of my grandparents,
a long way from the town, in the heart of the
country. Everything around is old — old, men
and things alike. Nothing is young here but ourselves and the spring flowers, and our three little
Circassian slaves, who are happy in their lot and
cannot understand our grievances.

'It is five years since we were here last, and we
had forgotten what our life here was like — compared to this our life in Stamboul seems almost
freedom and ease. Flung back into this atmosphere, from which we are divided by a whole
generation, we feel like foreigners here. We are

truly loved, but our modern spirit is at the same
time hated. Out of deference, and for the sake
of peace, we try to submit to external forms, and
mould our appearance on the fashions and manners
of the past. But that is not enough. The newly
born soul is felt beneath it all, bursting through,
palpitating, vibrant, and it cannot be forgiven for
having emancipated itself, not even for existing.

'And yet what infinite efforts, what sacrifices
and pangs, has that emancipation cost us! You,
a Western, can never have known these struggles.
Your soul has no doubt expanded at ease in the
atmosphere congenial to it. You can never understand.

'Oh! our friend, how incongruous we should
seem to you if you could see us here, incongruous but at the same time in harmony. If you
could but see us in the depths of the old garden,
where I am writing to you in this kiosque of carved
woodwork, inlaid with tiles, while a fountain sings
in its marble basin! All round it are divans in
the old fashion, covered with faded pink silk in
which a few threads of silver still shine here and
there. And outside there is a profusion, a mad
prodigality of the pale roses that flower in bunches,
and which in your world are called bridal bouquets.
Your three friends do not wear European dresses
here, nor modern tcharchafs; they have assumed
the garb of their grandmothers. For, André, we
have rummaged in old chests to exhume the garments which were the pride of the imperial harem
in the days of Abdul Medjib; the lady-in-waiting
who wore them was our great-grandmother. You

know those dresses ? They have long trains, and
sashes which would also train on the ground, but
they are picked up and crossed to enable us to
walk. Ours were once pink, green, yellow — hues
as dead now as those of dried flowers kept between
the leaves of a book, and are no more than a
reflection dying away.

'In these dresses, so full of memories, and
under this kiosque by the water, we have read your
last book, *The Land of Kabul* — our own copy
which you yourself gave us. The artist in you
could not have dreamed of a more fitting scene
for such reading. The infinity of roses falling
on every side made heavy curtains to the windows,
and the spring of this southern land is heady with
perfume. So now we have seen Kabul.

'In spite of this, my friend, I like this book
less well than its elder brothers; there is not
enough in it of *you*. I shed no tears, as I have
so often done in reading other things written by
you, which were not all sad, but which touched
me to anguish nevertheless. Oh, do not write any
more only with your brain ! I fancy you do not
wish to put yourself again on the stage. But
what can it matter what people say of it ? Write
again from your heart; is it too weary, too torpid
now, that we no longer feel its throbs in your
books as of old ?

'Evening is falling, and the hour is so beautiful
in these gardens of stricken stillness, where the
very flowers now seem pensive ! I could stay
here for ever, listening to the tinkle of the thread
of water in the marble basin, though its tune never

varies and tells only of the monotony of the days. This spot, alas! might so easily be a paradise; I feel that in my soul, as well as all around me, everything might be so happy; that life and gladness might be one and the same thing — *with liberty!*

'We must go indoors; I must bid you farewell, my friend. Here comes a tall negro to fetch us, for it is growing late, and the slaves have begun to sing and play the lute to amuse the old ladies. We shall presently be made to dance, and forbidden to speak French — which will not prevent us from going to sleep each with a book by you under her pillow.

'Farewell, our friend. Do you sometimes think of the three little featureless shades?

'DJENAN.'

XVII

In the cemetery under the walls of Stamboul, thanks to the intervention of André's Turkish friends, the restoration of the humble tomb was finished. And André Lhéry, who had not dared to show himself in the vicinity so long as the masons were at work, went on the 30th of the sweet month of May to pay his first visit to the dead under her new flag-stones.

On reaching the sacred wood he could see from afar the tomb so clandestinely repaired, which had the brightness of new things in the midst of the grey decay that surrounded it. The two marble slabs — that which is placed at the head of the dead and that which stands at the feet — rose up straight and white among those near covered with mosses, and leaning over or fallen altogether. The blue painted background, too, had been renewed, between the letters of the inscription, which shone in bright new gilding; the inscription which, after a short verse on death, said '*Pray for the soul of Nedjibeh, daughter of Ali Djianghir Effendi, who died on the 18th of Muharrem 1297.*' Already the recent touch of the workman had ceased to be conspicuous, for all round the thicker slab which served as a base, mint and thyme, and all

the fragrant vegetation of stony soils had hurried
into life under the May sunshine. As to the tall
cypress trees, which had seen the passing of Khalifs
and of centuries, they were exactly the same as
André had always known them, and the same no
doubt as they had been a century ago; in the
same attitudes, with the same petrified gestures of
their boughs, in colour just like dry bones, uplifted
to the sky like long dead arms. The ancient
walls of Stamboul showed in long perspective their
line of bastions and broken battlements in the
sempiternal solitude, now more complete perhaps
than ever.

The day was limpid and lovely. The earth and
the cypress trees smelt sweet; the resignation of
these graveyards without end was attractive to-day,
soothing and restful; it was tempting to linger here,
to share, if possible, the peace of all these sleepers,
resting so deeply under the wild thyme and grass.

André came away comforted and almost happy
at having at last been able to fulfil this pious duty,
so difficult to accomplish, which had for a long
time haunted his night thoughts. For years, in
the course of his travels and the vicissitudes of his
wandering life, even at the furthest ends of the
earth, he had often in sleepless nights thought of
this task, which seemed like one of the impossible
feats of a bad dream: the restoration of crumbling
tombstones in a sacred cemetery in Stamboul. And
now it was done. And now the beloved little
tomb seemed to him to be all his own — now that
it was raised again by his act, and it was he who
had made it strong enough to last.

As his spirit felt quite Turkish in this mild and
limpid evening, and the full moon would ere long
shine bluely on the sea of Marmora, he returned
to Stamboul after nightfall, and went up to the
very heart of the Moslem quarter, to sit in the
open air on the square that had now become familiar to him once more, in front of the mosque of
Sultan Fatih. He would sit there and dream, in
the cool purity of the evening air and the delicious
Eastern peace, smoking his narghileh; with all
that dying magnificence about him, and all that
decrepitude and religious silence and prayer.

By the time he arrived there all the little coffee
shops had lighted their twinkling lamps; lanterns
hanging from the trees, old oil lanterns, also gave
a subdued light, and all around on benches or on
wooden stools, turbaned dreamers were smoking
and conversing in few words and low tones. The
little murmur of the hundreds of narghilehs could
be heard, the water bubbling in the glass as the
smoker draws a deep, steady breath. One was
brought to him with scraps of live charcoal on the
bowl of Persian tobacco, and over him presently,
as over all the men about him, there came a very
soothing languor, quite harmless and favourable
to thought. Under those trees, hung with lanterns
that gave scarcely any light, he sat exactly facing
the mosque, divided from it by the width of the
little square. The square was empty and in deep
twilight, the paving-stones all loose and alternating
with earth and holes; the wall of the mosque, tall,
solemn, and imposing, filled up all the opposite
side, as stern as a rampart and with only one

opening: the arched door, at least thirty feet high, which formed the entrance to the sacred precincts. Beyond, to right and left, in the distance was the confusion of darkness, blackness — trees perhaps, cypress trees, vaguely marking a forest of the dead — darkness stranger than elsewhere, the peace and mystery of Islam.   The moon, which had risen an hour or two ago behind the mountains of Asia, now began to show itself above this mass of the Sultan Fatih; slowly it came up, quite round, a disc of bluish silver, and so entire, so aërial above the huge thing of earth, giving so complete an idea of its vast remoteness and its isolation in space!

The azure-tinted light spread gradually over everything.   It fell on the grave, devout smokers, while the square was still overshadowed by the high sacred walls.   At the same time this lunar gleam brought with it a cool evening mist exhaled by the sea, so diaphanous that it had not been perceptible before, but which now became part of the filmy blue, enveloping everything and casting a vaporous veil over the mosque which had looked so ponderous.   The two minarets, soaring to the sky, seemed transparent, soaked in the moonshine, and it made him giddy to gaze up at them in the haze of blue light, they looked so tall, so frail, and immaterial.

At this same hour there was on the other shore of the Golden Horn — not very far off in reality, and yet at a quite immeasurable distance — a city, called European, just beginning its nocturnal life: Pera.   There Levantines of every nationality, and alas some young Turks too, believing that

they had achieved an enviable degree of civilisa-
tion by wearing the dress of Parisians — more or
less — were crowding into the beer-shops, into
idiotic music-halls, or round 'poker' tables in the
clubs of the 'upper ten'of Pera. What poor creatures there are in this world!

Very poor creatures these, excited, unbalanced,
empty-headed, contemptible, bereft of ideal and of
hope. Very poor creatures, as compared with the
simple sages here, waiting only till the Muezzin
should utter his call high in the air to go and
prostrate themselves in full trust and faith before
the incomprehensible Allah, and ready ere long to
die possessing their soul in peace, as men set forth
on a happy journey.

Now they are beginning their chanting call —
those voices for which they wait. Men who dwell
in the tops of those shafts, lost in the high luminous haze, hosts of the air, near neighbours
it might seem of the moon to-night, suddenly
break into song like birds, in a sort of thrilling
rapture that has come over them. These men
have been chosen for their rare gifts of voice, or
they could not be heard from the summit of those
prodigious towers. Not a sound is lost; not a
word of what they chant fails to come down to us,
clear, fluent, and articulate.

One by one the dreamers rise, go into the
broad shadow which still shrouds the square, cross
it and slowly make their way to the sacred door.
In little groups at first of three, four, five, the
white turbans and long robes disappear into the
house of prayer. And more come, from all sides,

out of dark purlieus, the black shade of trees, of
streets, of shut-up houses.   They come in noiseless
slippers, walking in calm and grave meditation.
The vast archway which invites them all, pierced
in the great stern wall, has an ancient lantern
supposed to light it; it hangs from the centre,
and its feeble flame is yellow and dead under the
splendid glory of moonlight that fills the sky.
And while the voices above chant on, a streaming
procession gathers of heads turbaned in white
muslin, and is presently swallowed up under the
great portico.

As soon as the benches on the square were
deserted, André Lhéry also made his way to the
mosque, the last of all, feeling himself the most
wretched of all, for he had no prayer to say.   He
went in and stood near the door.   Two or three
thousand turbans were there, and had instinctively
arranged themselves in long rows one behind
another, facing the Mihrab.   Above the silence a
voice seemed to float, a plaintive voice, so pro-
foundly melancholy, chanting in a very high pitch
like the Muezzins, that it seemed to die away of
exhaustion; then to revive once more and vibrate
tremulously under the high domes, lingering,
protracted as if slowly expiring, dying at last only
to begin afresh.   This voice was leading the two
thousand prayers of this crowd of men; at its
bidding they first fell on their knees, then prostrate
in yet deeper humiliation, and finally, all at once, as
one man, they struck the ground with their foreheads with a regular movement all together, as if
thrown down by that sad, sweet monotone passing

over their heads, dying away at moments to the merest murmur, but nevertheless filling the vast body of the mosque.

The sanctuary was but feebly lighted by little oil lamps at the end of long wires hanging at intervals from the hollow vault; but for the perfect whiteness of the walls it would have been difficult to see anything. Now and again there was a flutter of wings — the tame pigeons which are allowed to build their nests high up in the clerestory, disturbed by the little lights and the soft rustle of so many robes, took to flight and wheeled about fearlessly over the thousand white turbans. And the devotion was so complete, the faith so deep, when every head was bowed to the incantation of that small feeble voice, that one might have fancied they rose up like the vapour from a censer in that silent and multitudinous orison.

Oh! may Allah and the Khalif long protect and isolate this religious, meditative people, kind and loyal, and one of the noblest in the world; capable of terrible energy, of sublime heroism in the battle-field if their native land is threatened, or if the cry is Islam and the Faith!

Prayer ended, André returned with the rest of the faithful to sit outside and smoke under the glorious moon, still rising higher. He thought with very calm satisfaction of the restored tomb, which at this hour must stand out so white, so upright and pretty in the clear beaming night. And this duty accomplished he now might leave the country, since he had already decided that he

need only wait for that. But the oriental charm
had gradually taken entire possession of him
again; and besides, those mysterious three who
would return with the summer, he must hear
their voices once more. At the beginning he had
felt remorseful over the adventure, considering
the trustful hospitality shown him by his friends
the Turks; this evening, on the contrary, he felt
it no more. 'After all,' he reflected, 'I am
offending nobody's honour. Between Djenan,
who is young enough to be my daughter, and me
— who have never even seen her, and probably
never shall see her — how can there be anything
on either side but a pleasant and singular friendship?'

And in fact he had that very day had a letter
from her which seemed to put everything into the
right point of view.

'One day, for a whim' — she wrote from her
palace in the wood of the Sleeping Beauty, which,
however, did not alter the fact that she was very
thoroughly awakened — 'One day, for a whim, in
deadly moral abandonment, irritated by the impas-
sable barrier against which we were always fighting
and which hurt us so, we valiantly set out to discover what sort of a person you could possibly be.
Our first wish for an interview was just defiance
and curiosity.

'We found André Lhéry very unlike what we
had pictured him. And now the *real you*, whom
you have allowed us to know so well, we can
never forget. Still, I must explain these words

which from a woman to a man seem almost like
humiliating advances. We shall never forget you,
because, thanks to you, we have learnt what it is
that must make life a joy to the women of the
West: intellectual intercourse with an artist. We
shall never forget you, because you have given us
a little friendly sympathy without even knowing
whether we are handsome or old harridans; you
have cared for that better part of us, our souls, of
which our masters hitherto have overlooked the
existence; you have enabled us to perceive how
precious the pure friendship of a man may be.'

It had really all been as he had supposed, a
gentle flirtation of souls, and nothing more; a
spiritual flirtation, with danger in it no doubt, but
a material danger, no moral risk. And it would
all continue to be as white as snow, as white as the
domes of the mosque in the moonshine.

He had this letter from Djenan in his pocket;
it had reached him but just now in Pera; and he
took it out to read it again quietly by the light of
a lamp hanging in a tree hard by.

'And now,' she went on, 'when we are away
from you, how sad it is to relapse into torpor.
Your life, so full of colour and movement, cannot
enable you to conceive of ours — so grey, made up
of the slow years which leave no memories. We
always know beforehand what the morrow will
bring — just nothing; and that every to-morrow
till our dying day will glide on with the same
insipid smoothness, in the same neutral hue. We

N

live a life of pearl-grey days, padded with a
perpetual feather bed which makes us long for
flints and thorns.

'In the novels which come to us from Europe
there are always people who in the evening of life
bewail their lost illusions. But at least they had
had some illusions; they had once in their lives
set out in pursuit of a mirage! Whereas we,
André, have never been allowed a chance of
having any, and when our life is drawing to a
close we shall not have even the melancholy
satisfaction of mourning over them. Oh, how
much more keenly do we feel this since you came
into our lives.

'Those hours in your society in the old house
near the mosque of Sultan Selim! We there
realised a dream, such as we formerly would never
have dared to hope for; to have André Lhéry to
ourselves, to be treated by him as thinking beings
and not as playthings, to some extent, indeed, as
friends, so far as that he revealed to us some of the
secret recesses of his soul! Little as we knew of
European life and the manners of your world, we
appreciated at its true value the trustfulness with
which you met our indiscretions. Oh, for we
were very conscious of them, and without our
veils should certainly never have been so bold!

'Now, in perfect simplicity and sincerity of
heart, we have a proposal to make to you. Hearing you speak the other day of a tomb that is
dear to you, we all three had the same idea,
which the same timidity prevented our uttering.
But now, by letter, we venture. If we knew

where to find this tomb of the girl you loved, we might sometimes go there to pray and take care of it when you are gone, and let you hear about it. Perhaps it would be a pleasure to you to know that that spot of earth, where a piece of your heart rests, is not abandoned in utter indifference. And we, on our part, should be so happy to have this tangible tie to you when you are far away; the memory of your lost friend might perhaps preserve your present friends from being forgotten.

'And when we pray for her who taught you to love our country, we will pray for you — for your deep distress is very apparent to us, I assure you. It is strange that I should feel myself alive to new hope since I have known you — I who had none left. But it ill beseems me to remind you that we have no right to limit our anticipations and ideals to this life, when you have written certain passages in your books. DJENAN.'

For a very long time he had been wishing that he could commend Nedjibeh's tomb to some one on the spot who would take care of it; above all he indulged in an apparently impossible dream of entrusting it to Turkish women, the sisters in race and in Islam of the dead girl. Thus Djenan's offer not only attached him the more to her, but fulfilled his desires, and set his conscience finally at rest in regard to the cemetery.

Under the exquisite night he dreamed of the present; as a rule it appeared to him that, between the first rather childish period of his life in Turkey and the present hour, time had opened a wide gulf;

this evening, on the contrary, he saw them brought into connection in uninterrupted unity. Feeling himself still so alive, so youthful, while she had for so long been a mere handful of earth amid other earth in the darkness of the underworld, he experienced now agonising remorse and shame, and now — in his desperate love of life and youth — a sentiment almost of egotistical triumph.

For the second time that evening he associated in his mind Djenan and Nedjibeh; they were of the same race, both Circassians, and the living voice had again and again reminded him of the other; there were certain Turkish words which they pronounced with the same accent.

Suddenly he was aware that it must be growing very late; he could hear, out by the dark thicket of trees, the bells of mules — bells that always sound so silvery clear in the night of Stamboul — announcing the arrival of market men bringing baskets of strawberries, flowers, beans, salads, all the May produce which the women of the people in white veils come to purchase at break of day. He looked about him and saw that he was left, the only smoker on the square. Almost all the lanterns were out in the little coffee-shops. The dew was falling and wetting his shoulders, and a boy, standing behind him leaning against a tree, was patiently waiting till he had done, to take in the narghileh and shut the shop door.

It was near midnight. He rose and went down towards the bridges over the Golden Horn to cross to the other side where he lived. There was, of course, no carriage to be had at such an hour.

Before quitting old Stamboul, asleep in the moonlight, he had a very long walk to take in the
silence, through a city of dreams, between houses
close-shut and still, where everything looked
frosted by the broad beams of spectral, intensely
white light. He had to pass through quarters
where narrow streets went up or down, crossing in
a maze as if to mislead the belated wanderer, who
would have met no one to put him in the right
way; but André knew every turning by heart.
There were places, too, like deserts round the
mosques, with their wilderness of domes wrapped
by the moonshine in white winding-sheets. And
in all directions there were graveyards, closed by
ancient iron gates of Arabic design, and within,
the tiny yellow flame of little oil lamps here and
there on the tombs. Sometimes a dim gleam was
seen through the window of a marble kiosque, and
these, too, were lights for the dead, and it was
better not to look in; there was nothing to be
seen but crowds of tall catafalques devoured by
time and powdered with dust. On the pavement
lay the dogs, all dusky tan, sleeping in families,
curled into large balls — the Turkish dogs, as
easy-going as the Moslems who let them live, and
incapable of being fierce even when you tread on
them, so long as they understand that you did not
do it on purpose. Not a sound, excepting at long
intervals the thud on the ringing pavement of the
watchman's iron-shod staff. Old Stamboul, with
all its sepulchres, was sleeping in religious peace
that night, as it has done every night for three
hundred years.

XVIII

AFTER the changeful skies of the month of May, when the blast from the Black Sea persistently sweeps up clouds charged with cold rain, the month of June had suddenly spread over Turkey the deep blue of the southern Orient. The annual migration of the residents of Constantinople to the Bosphorus was complete. All along the strait, which is stirred almost daily by the breeze, each Embassy had settled into summer quarters on the European shore. André Lhéry had been obliged to follow the exodus, and to find rooms at Therapia, a sort of cosmopolitan suburb, disfigured by monster hotels, where evening is made hideous by the orchestras of the cafés; but he commonly spent his time on the opposite side, the Asiatic shore, still deliciously oriental, shady, and still.

Often, too, he went back to his beloved Stamboul, only an hour away by boat down the Bosphorus, always crowded with ships and barques going to and fro without ceasing.

In the middle of the strait, between the two banks, which are fringed all the way with houses and palaces, plies the endless procession of steamships, enormous modern liners, or of the fine old-fashioned sailing vessels, working their way in

flotillas as soon as a favouring wind blows. Everything exported from the mouth of the Danube,
from southern Russia, even from far-off Persia
and Bokhara, must pass through this green-
set gulf, driven by the current of air which blows
perpetually from the northern steppes to the
Mediterranean. Nearer the shore there is the
unceasing bustle of smaller boats of every kind:
yawls, slender caïques carrying rowers gaudy with
gold embroidery, electric launches, large barges all
painted and gilt, and pulled by crews of fishermen
standing at their oars and spreading long nets
which catch in everything as they pass. And
amid this confusion of moving things noisy paddle-
boats ply from morning till night, carrying red
fezzes and shrouded women between the various
landing-places in Europe and in Asia.

To right and left along the Bosphorus, twelve
miles and more of houses among gardens and trees
look out through thousands of windows at the
turmoil that never ceases on those green or blue
waters. Open windows, some of them, others the
closely latticed windows of impenetrable harems.
Houses of every date and every style. On the
European side, alas! villas built by delirious
Levantines may already be seen, with mongrel
fronts or even *Art nouveau*, horrible by the side of
the simple buildings of old Turkey, but still lost
and inconspicuous in the beauty of the whole scene.
On the Asiatic side, where hardly any but Turks
reside, scornful of new devices and only craving
silence, you may row your boat close to the shore
without vexation, for it is unspoilt; the charm of

the past and of the East broods there still. At every bight in the shore, at each little bay that opens at the foot of the wooded hills, only old-world things are to be seen; tall trees, haunts of oriental mystery. There is no path along the water's edge, each house having its own marble landing-place in the old way, enclosed and apart, where the ladies of the harem are allowed to sit lightly veiled to watch the ever dancing wavelets at their feet, and the narrow caïques that go by, curved up at prow and stern in a crescent shape. Here and there a shady creek, exquisitely calm, is full of fishing barks with long cross-yards. Very holy cemeteries, where the gilt tombstones seem to have come as close as possible to the edge to look out too at all the passing ships, and follow the movements of the rowers. The mosques stand under venerable plane-trees many centuries old, and there are village squares where nets are drying, hung to the overarching branches, and where turbaned dreamers sit round a marble fountain of unchanging whiteness with gilt inscriptions and arabesques.

Going down towards Stamboul from Therapia and the opening into the Black Sea, the legendary and fairy-like scene gradually increases in splendour till we reach the crowning apotheosis at the moment when the sea of Marmora opens out before us : then, on the left, we see Scutari in Asia, and on the right, above the marble quays and the Sultan's palaces, Stamboul towers up with its mass of shafts and cupolas.

This was the scenery of change and transformations in which André Lhéry was to live till the autumn, awaiting his three friends, the little black shades, who had said to him, 'We, too, shall be by the Bosphorus during the summer,' but who now for many days had given no sign of life. And how could he find out now what had become of them, not having any password to admit him to their old palace buried in the forests of Macedonia ?

XIX

DJENAN TO ANDRÉ

Bounar Bashi, near Salonica,
June 20, 1904 (Frankish era).

'Your friend has thought of you, but for weeks she has been too well guarded to write to you.

'To-day she will give you her grey little history — the history of her married life; endure it, you who listened with so much kindness to those of Zeyneb and Melek at Stamboul, you remember, in my good old nurse's house.

'The stranger whom my father gave me for a husband, André, was neither brutal nor unhealthy; on the contrary, a good-looking officer, fair, well-mannered, and gentle, whom I might have loved. Though at first I execrated him as being the master forced upon me, I feel no hatred of him now. But I could not look upon love as he saw it: love that was nothing but desire, and remained indifferent to the possession of my heart.

'Among us Moslems, as you know, the men and women in one house live apart. This, it is true, is less universal than it was, and I know some fortunate wives who really live with their husbands. But this is not the case in the old

families which, like ours, adhere to the old rules;
there, the harem where we must remain and the
selamlik where our lords and masters live are
quite distinct and apart. I, then, lived in our
fine, princely harem with my mother-in-law, two
sisters-in-law, and a young cousin of Hamdi's
named Durdaneh; she is pretty, with a skin as
fair as alabaster, hair dyed brightly with henna,
sea-green eyes, their glance almost phosphorescent,
but you could never meet her gaze.

'Hamdi was an only son, and his wife was much
petted. I had to myself a whole floor of the vast
old mansion; for my own sole use I had four
luxurious rooms in the ancient Turkish style,
where I was bored to death; my bedroom furniture had come from Paris, with that of a certain
Louis XVI. drawing-room and of my boudoir, to
which I had been allowed to bring my books. I
remember that, as I arranged them in the white
enamelled bookcases, I was so miserable to think
that now, when my life as a woman was about to
begin, it must also end; that it had already given
me all I could expect of it. This, then, was
marriage; petting and kissing which never appealed to my soul; long hours of solitude, of imprisonment without interest or object, and then
those other hours when I was to be a mere doll — or
even lower than that.

'I tried to make my boudoir pleasant and
tempt Hamdi to spend his leisure there. I read
the papers, I talked to him of matters concern-
ing the palace and the army; I tried to discover
what interested him, to learn to discuss it. No,

this only upset his inherited ideas, as I could see. "All these things," said he, "are for men to talk about in the selamlik." He only asked me to be pretty and lover-like. He asked this so often that he asked it too often.

'A woman who could no doubt be lover-like was Durdaneh. She was praised in the family for her grace — the grace of a young panther, lithe in all its movements. She would dance of an evening and play the lute; she spoke little but was always smiling, with a smile at once inviting and cruel, showing her small sharp teeth.

'She often came to my room, to keep me company as she said. But the scorn she poured on my books, my piano, my note-books, and my letters! She always dragged me off, away from them all, into one of the Turkish drawing-rooms, where she stretched herself on a divan and smoked cigarettes, playing eternally with a mirror. To her, I thought, who was still young and had been married, I might confide my woes. But she only opened wide eyes and burst out laughing. "What have you to complain of? You are young, pretty, and you have a husband whom you soon will love!"

'"No," said I, "he does not belong to me since I know nothing of his mind." "What matters his mind? You have him, and you have him all to yourself!" She emphasised the last words with an evil look.

'It was a great disappointment to Hamdi's mother that at the end of a year of married life I had no child. Certainly, said she, a spell must have been cast upon me. I refused to be dragged about to waters and to mosques, and to consult dervishes who were famed for averting such maleficent charms. A child! no, I did not wish for one. If a little girl had been born to us, how should I have brought her up? As an Oriental, like Durdaneh, with no object in life but to sing and be made love to? Or as we have been — Zeyneb, Melek, and I, and so condemn her to cruel misery?

'For you see, André, I know that our sufferings are inevitable, that we are the ladder, we and no doubt our immediate successors, by which the Moslem women of Turkey may rise and emancipate themselves. But a little creature of my own blood whom I had nursed in my arms — I should not have the courage to dedicate her to such a sacrifice.

'Hamdi at that time was fully bent on asking for an appointment abroad in some foreign Embassy. "I will take you with me," he promised, "and there you can live the life of Western women, like the wife of our Ambassador at Vienna, or the Princess Emineh in Sweden." And I fancied that there, in a smaller house, our existence would necessarily become more domestic. And I also thought that in a foreign country he would be glad, perhaps proud, of having a wife who was an educated woman and well informed on all subjects.

'How I worked to keep myself up to date in my information. I read all the important French reviews, all the leading newspapers, new novels, and plays. It was at that time, André, that I came to know you so thoroughly. As a girl I had read *Medjeh*, and some of your books on our Eastern

lands.   I read them again at that time, and understood more fully why we, the Moslem women, owe
you such deep gratitude, and why we delight in
you above so many others.   It is because your
comprehension of Islam constitutes a real relation-
ship of your soul with ours.   Islam, our Faith,
maligned, misrepresented, to which we are, nevertheless, so faithfully attached; for our grievances
are no fault of our religion.   It was not our
Prophet who condemned us to the martyrdom we
endure.   The veil which he allowed us was to
protect us, not to be a symbol of slavery.   Never,
never did he intend that we should be mere dolls
for our owners' pleasure.   The pious Imam who
instructed us in our holy book told us so plainly.
Proclaim this yourself, André; say it for the
honour of the Koran, and to avenge those who
are suffering.   Say it, finally, for the sake of the
affection we bear you.

'After your books about the East I wanted all
the others.   On every page I dropped a tear.   Do
very popular authors, I wonder, ever think as they
write of the infinite variety of the minds into which
their ideas will fall with a rush?   On Western
women, who *see* the world and live in it, the impressions made by a writer no doubt sink in less
deeply.   But for us who live cloistered, you hold
the mirror which reflects the world we can never
know; we see it through your eyes.   We feel, we
live, only through you; can you not understand
that an author we love becomes part of ourselves?
I have followed you all over the world.   I have
scrap-books full of cuttings from papers speaking

of you.   I have heard evil spoken of you which I
have not believed.   Long before I met you I had
an exact presentiment of the man you must be.
When at last I saw you I had already long known
you.   When you gave me likenesses of you
— why, André, I had them all reposing in a
secret drawer in a satin pocket!   And after such
an avowal can you ask to see me again?   No,
such things can be said only to a friend whom one
can never see again.

'Dear me, how far I have wandered from the
little history of my married life.   I had got as far,
I think, as the winter after the great festival of my
wedding.   It was a long winter that year, and
Stamboul was for two months under snow.   I had
grown pale, and languished.   Hamdi's mother,
Emireh Hanum, well guessed that I was not
happy.   She was worried, it would seem, by seeing
me so colourless, for one day two doctors were
sent for, and by their advice I was sent off to spend
two months in the Islands,[1] whither Zeyneb and
Melek had gone already.

'Do you know our islands, and how sweet the
spring is there?   You breathe in a love of life, a
love of love.   In that pure air, under the odorous
pines, I recovered my vitality.   Painful memories,
all the false notes of my life as a wife, were merged
in tender homesickness.   I thought it was crazy
to have been so exacting, so complicated, with
regard to my husband.   The climate and the
April sun had altered me.   On moonlight nights,

[1] Îles des Princes in the sea of Marmora, known in Constantinople as 'the
Islands.'

in the lovely garden of our villa, I often walked
alone, without a wish, without a thought but that
of having my Hamdi at my side, and with his arm
round my waist, to be only and wholly loving.
I bitterly regretted the kisses I could not return,
and pined for the fondness which had wearied me.

'Before the date fixed, without announcing my
return, and accompanied only by my slaves, I went
back to Stamboul.

'The boat in which I crossed was detained by
various accidents, and we did not arrive till nightfall.   Moslem women, as you know, are not permitted to be out of doors after sunset.   It must
have been nine o'clock when I noiselessly went
into the house.   At that hour Hamdi, of course,
would be in the selamlik as usual with his father
and their friends; my mother-in-law, no doubt, in
her room, meditating on the Koran; and my cousin
having her horoscope read by some slave practised
in the lore of coffee grounds.

'So I went straight up to my rooms, and on
going in all I saw was Durdaneh in my husband's
arms.

'You, André, will think such an adventure
commonplace enough, an everyday affair in the
West; and in fact I have mentioned it only by
reason of the resulting sequel.

'But I am tired, my friend, whom I may never
see again, and the sequel must follow to-morrow.

'DJENAN.'

XX

However, the whole month of July slipped away and André Lhéry did not receive the promised sequel, nor any other tidings of the three black spectres.

Like all the dwellers on the Bosphorus in the summer, he lived a great deal on the water, to and fro day after day between Europe and Asia. Being at heart as oriental as any Turk, he had his own caïque, and his rowers wore the traditional costume — Broussa gauze shirts with wide sleeves, and sleeveless jackets of velvet embroidered with gold. The caïque was white, long, narrow, as sharp as a dart, and the velvet of his liveries was red.

One morning he was being rowed in this boat under the Asiatic shore, gazing with a vacant eye on the old houses standing on the very brink, the barred windows of the harems, the hanging verdure above the gates of their mysterious gardens, when he saw a light boat coming to meet him, rowed by three women wrapped in white silk; a eunuch, in a severely buttoned frock-coat, sat in the stern, and the three rowers pulled with all their might, as if in a race. They passed very near him, and turned their heads towards him. He observed that they had fine hands, but their muslin veils were down over their faces, and he could see nothing.

Still he had no doubt that he had met his three little black spectres, who, with the coming of summer, had turned white. On the following day they wrote:

August 3, 1904.

'Your friends have been back for two days to settle on the Asiatic shore of the Bosphorus. And yesterday morning they got into their boat, rowing themselves, as is their custom, to go to Pacha Bagtcheh, where the hedges are full of blackberries and the grass full of blue cornflowers.

'We were rowing. Instead of a tcharchaf and a black veil, we each wore a light silk yeldirmeh and a muslin scarf over our heads. We are allowed this on the Bosphorus, in the country. It was fine, it was young; the weather meant love and the springtide of life. The air was cool and light, and the oars seemed but a featherweight in our hands. Instead of quietly enjoying the lovely morning, some folly possessed us to make us row fast, and our boat flew over the water as if we were hurrying to overtake happiness or death.

'But what we caught up in our haste was neither death nor happiness, but just our Friend, lording it like a Pasha, in a fine caïque with red and gold rowers. And I stared straight into your eyes, which looked at mine without seeing them.

'Since our return here we are feeling a little tipsy, like prisoners let out of a dark cell to miti-gated confinement; if you could imagine what it was there — where we have come from — in spite of the splendour of the roses! Can any one who, like you, has lived in the West, feverish, free, conceive of the horror of our dead-alive lot, of our horizon where one thing alone looms clear: to be borne away to sleep under the shade of a cypress in the cemetery of Eyoub after an Imam has said all the necessary prayers. DJENAN.'

'We live like those precious specimens of glass, you know, which are kept packed in cases full of bran. It is supposed that we are thus preserved from every possible jar, but we feel them all the same, and then the vital fracture, with the two edges in perpetual friction, gives us a dull, deep, dreadful pain. ZEYNEB.'

'I am the only person of sense of the three, Friend André, that you must long ago have perceived. The other two — quite between ourselves, you understand — are a little cracked, especially Djenan, who is willing enough to go on writing to you, but never to see you. Happily I am at hand to arrange matters. Reply to the old address: Madame Zaideh, you remember? By the day after to-morrow we shall have a trustworthy friend at hand who is going into town, and will call at the post-office. MELEK.'

XXI

ANDRÉ replied at once. To Djenan he said: 'Never see you again ? — or rather never hear your voice again, for I have never seen you ? — and merely because you have made me a gentle declaration of intellectual regard! It is absurd! I have received many others, believe me, and it does not excite me at all.' He tried to take the whole matter lightly and confine himself to the tone of an old friend, much her senior and rather paternal. In his heart he was uneasy at the vehement resolutions this proud, perverse little spirit was capable of forming; he distrusted her, and he felt too that she was already very dear to him, and that to see her no more would darken his whole summer.

In his answer he asked for the promised remainder of her story, and to conclude, for the relief of his conscience, told them how by chance he had identified the three.

The answer came next day but one.

'That you should have identified us is a misfortune. Do your friends, whose faces you can never know, still interest you now that their little mystery is worn out, riddled with holes ?

'The rest of my story ? that is simple enough; you shall have it.

'As to our meeting again, that, André, is less simple. Let me think it over.   DJENAN.'

'Well, I, for my part, am to be thoroughly identified, for I will tell you where we live. As you go down the Bosphorus on the Asiatic shore, in the second inlet beyond Tchiboukli there is a mosque; next to the mosque there is a large yali in the oldest style, very much latticed, pompous and dismal, with some grim negro in a frock-coat always guarding the harem landing-place: there we are at home. On the first floor, which projects beyond the ground floor over the sea, the six windows to the left, screened by formidable lattices, are those of our rooms. Since you like the Asiatic side, choose it for your excursions, and look up at these windows — but do not look too long. Your friends, who will recognise your boat from afar, will pass the tip of a finger out of a hole as a sign of friendship, or perhaps the corner of a handkerchief.

'I am arranging things with Djenan, and you may count on an interview in Stamboul sometime next week.   MELEK.'

No urging was needed to lead him to pass that way. The following day, as it happened, was a Friday, the day when the Sweet Waters of Asia were always a resort of fashion, and he never failed to join the throng; and Djenan's ancient residence, easy no doubt to recognise, was on the way thither. Stretched in his caïque, he passed as close as prudence would allow. The yali, built entirely of

wood in the old Turkish fashion, a little the worse
for the hand of time, and painted a dark ochre,
had a grand air, but how gloomy and secret! At
the base it was almost washed by the Bosphorus,
and his captive friends' windows overhung the
sea water, rippled by the eternal current. Behind
it were gardens with high walls, sloping up the
hill till they mingled with the adjoining wood.

Under the house was one of the open tunnels
which were in common use in olden days to shelter
the owner's boats, and André, as he went near,
saw a handsome caïque emerge, manned for an
excursion, the rowers in blue velvet jackets embroidered with gold, and a long hanging of the
same velvet, also embroidered, which trailed in
the water. Were his little friends also going to
the Sweet Waters? It looked like it.

As he passed he glanced up at the windows
described to him; slender fingers wearing many
rings peeped through and the corner of a lace
handkerchief. From the mere way in which the
fingers waggled and the handkerchief was flourished, André could recognise them as those of
Melek.

At Constantinople there are the Sweet Waters
of Europe, a little stream among trees and meadows, to which visitors come in crowds on Fridays in
spring. And there are the Sweet Waters of Asia,
an even tinier river, almost a brook, which comes
down from the Asiatic hills to fall into the Bosphorus; and this is the place of meeting on
Fridays in summer.

At the hour when André arrived there that

afternoon numbers of caïques were being rowed
in from both shores, some occupied by veiled ladies,
others by men wearing the red fez.   At the foot
of a fantastic castle of mediæval Saracen work,
bristling with turrets and battlements, and near a
magnificent kiosque with marble landing-steps, be-
longing to His Majesty the Sultan, ends this tiny
stream of water which week after week attracts so
many mysterious fair ones.

Before turning up it, between banks of reeds
and ferns, André looked round to see whether
they were really coming, and he fancied that he
recognised, far behind him, their three forms in
black tcharchafs, and the blue and the gold livery
of their boatmen.

The place was already crowded when he reached
it: a crowd on the water in boats of every form
with liveries of every hue; a crowd on land, on
the lawns, almost too dainty and pretty, arranged
in an amphitheatre, as though on purpose for
groups who wish to sit and watch the boats go
past.   Here and there were large trees beneath
which coffee-stalls were set up, and where indolent
smokers had spread mats on the grass to recline,
with their narghileh, in oriental ease.   And on
both sides rose the wooded hills, unkempt and
rather wild, enclosing it all between their exquisitely green slopes.   They were chiefly women who
sat on the natural steps on each of the pretty river
banks, and nothing is more pleasingly effective
than a crowd of Turkish women in the country,
not wearing dark tcharchafs as in the city, but
dressed in long gowns all of one colour, pink,

blue, brown, red, and each having her head wrapped in a veil of white muslin.

This very crowd is the strange and amusing part of the excursion, on water so calm, so enclosed and shrouded with verdure, with so many pairs of bright eyes watchful on every side through slits in the veils. Often this is the end of the journey; the oars clash and get entangled, the rowers shout, the caïques bump; then they pull up all quite close together, with plenty of time for gazing. Ladies, featureless, will sit for an hour close under the bank, their boat almost buried in the reeds and water plants, with long eye-glasses in their hands inspecting the passers-by. Others are bold enough to plunge into the *mêlée*, still remaining motionless and enigmatical behind their veils, while their boatmen, blazing with gold, rage and rave. And by proceeding no more than a few yards up the pretty little stream, you find yourself in a thick tangle of boughs, between trees that bend over the water; the boat grates on the white stones at the bottom, and back you must go. Then you turn with great difficulty, for a caïque is very long, and go down-stream — but only to come up again and then back once more, as if you were pacing to and fro in an alley.

When his caïque had been turned in the green darkness, where the stream ceases to be navigable, André reflected: 'I shall certainly meet my friends, who must have reached the Sweet Waters a few minutes later than I.' So he looked no more at the women seated in groups on the grass, or the pairs of black, or grey, or blue eyes sparkling from under the white shrouds; he looked out only at what met him coming up the stream. A procession still enchanting in its whole effect, though now no longer such as it was of old, and though one often has to look the other way to avoid seeing the pretentious American yawls of the younger Turks, and the vulgar hired barges in which the Levantine ladies display scarecrow hats. However, caïques are still in the majority, and on this day there were some splendid boats out with handsome oarsmen in jackets loaded with gold; in them, half-reclining, were ladies in more or less transparent tcharchafs, and a few very elegant women wearing the yashmak as if they were going to Court, showing their foreheads and deeply shadowed eyes. How was it indeed that *they* did not wear the yashmak, these little friends, who were, nevertheless, flowers of elegance, instead of appearing here all black, as he had seen them just now? No doubt, in consequence of Djenan's obstinate determination to remain inscrutable to him.

At last they came into view round a bend in the river. These were certainly the three; elegant little spectres, on a blue velvet rug which caught the water weeds in its gold fringes that hung over the stern. Three are rather many in a caïque; two were royally enthroned at the back on the velvet seat of the same colour as the rowers' jackets — the two eldest, no doubt — and the third, the child of the party, sat crouching at their feet. They passed close enough to touch him. He at once recognised at so short a distance Melek's smiling eyes under the black gauze which to-day

was but single — the eyes he had caught sight of
one day on the stairs; and he hastily looked up
at the two seated in the best places. One of these
two had a semi-transparent veil, which enabled him
almost to distinguish the youthful features, exquisitely regular and finely cut, but not allowing
the eyes to be clearly seen. He had no doubt:
this was Zeyneb, consenting at last to be less completely hidden, and the third, as utterly invisible
as ever, was Djenan.

It need not be said that no sign, no greeting,
was given on either side. Melek alone, the least
strictly veiled, smiled, but so faintly that if he
had not been so close to her he would not have
detected it.

They crossed twice more, and then it was time
to go home. The sun soon shone only on the
tops of the hills and the woods, the air was full of
the delicious coolness that rose from the water at
the close of day. By degrees the little river and
its banks were deserted, to remain so till the
following Friday; the caïques were scattered all
over the Bosphorus, bearing home the fair excur-
sionists, who were bound to be at home before sunset and dolefully incarcerated in the harems all
along the shore. André allowed his friends to leave
long before him, for fear of being suspected of
following them; then he returned, keeping under
the Asiatic shore, and very slowly, to let his oarsmen rest, and to see the moon rise.

XXII

DJENAN TO ANDRÉ

August 17, 1904 (Frankish calendar).

'TRULY, André, do you want to have the end of my story? But it was a wretched adventure of which I told you the beginning.

'What torment is dying love! If only it could die suddenly, all at once; but it struggles, it fights for life, and this is the cruel agony.

'My little bag fell out of my hands, and at the sound of a scent-bottle that broke in the fall, Durdaneh turned her head. She was not disturbed; her sea-green eyes opened wide and she greeted me with her pretty panther-like smile. We looked at each other, she and I, without a word. Hamdi so far had seen nothing. She had one arm round his neck, and she gently made him look round: "Djenan," said she in a tone of indifference.

'What he did I do not know, for I fled, to see no more. Instinctively I took refuge in his mother's room. She was reading her Koran, and scolded me at first for breaking in on her meditations; then she started up in horror to go to them, leaving me alone. When she came back, how long after I do not know, "Go back to your rooms," she said with gentle kindness. "Go, my poor child, they are gone."

'Alone in my boudoir with the doors shut, I threw myself on a couch, and cried till I slept from sheer exhaustion. But oh! the awakening at dawn! To find *that* in my mind, to begin to think once more, to see that I must decide on some course of action. I would have hated them if I could, but there was no feeling left in me but anguish — anguish and love.

'It was very early, the first break of day. I heard steps outside my door and my mother-in-law came in; I saw at once that her eyes had been weeping.

'"Durdaneh is gone," she said. "I have sent her far away to a relation of ours." Then sitting down beside me, she went on to say that such things happen every day in life; that a man's whims are as uncertain as those of the wind; that I must go to my room and dress myself to look lovely and smile on Hamdi that evening when he should come home from the Palace; he was very miserable, it would seem, and would not come near me till I was comforted. In the course of the afternoon I received some silk blouses, lace, fans, and jewels.

'Then I begged that I might only be left to myself in my room. I wanted to see clearly to the bottom of my own soul. Remember that I had come home to the harem the day before, in all the thrilling excitement of a new emotion; I had brought with me the springtime of the Islands, its fragrance and its song, kisses I had plucked in that air, all the palpitation of an awakening to love.

'In the evening Hamdi joined me, very quiet and rather pale. I myself was no less calm, and I simply asked him to tell me the truth: Did he still love me, yes or no? I would go home to my grandmother and leave him free. He smiled and took me in his arms. "What a child you are," said he; "why, how could I cease to love you?" And he covered me with kisses, heaping caresses on me.

'I meanwhile tried to ask him how he could love another if he still loved me. Ah, André, then I learnt the measure of man — of our men at any rate. This one had not even the courage of his love. "Durdaneh! That woman!" No, he did not love her. It was a mere fancy; her sea-green eyes, her supple form when she danced in the evening. And she had said that she had arts and spells to bewitch men, so he had wished to put her to the proof. And after all, what could it matter to me? But for my unannounced return I should never have known anything about it.

'Oh the pity and disgust of my soul as I listened! for her, for him, and for myself, who longed to forgive. However, I suffered less violently now that I was resigned. So it was merely her supple form and her sea-green eyes that Hamdi had loved her for. Well, I was prettier than she, I well knew; I, too, had sea-green eyes, darker and less common than hers, and if all he asked was that I should be lovely and loving I was certainly both just now.

'The campaign of reconquest began. It was not a long business; the memory of Durdaneh soon weighed no more on her lover's heart. But never in my life have I known such distressful days. I felt all that was lofty and pure in me disappear, drop like roses fading in front of a fire. I had no thought but one: to please him, to make him forget the love of another in my greater love.

'But soon I perceived with horror that as my contempt for myself grew, so by degrees did my hatred of the man for whom I was degrading myself; for I had become to him neither more nor less than a doll for his pleasure. I thought of nothing but beautifying myself, to be differently charming every day. Cases arrived from Paris full of evening dresses, elegant wrappers, perfumes, cosmetics; all the tricks of Western vanity added to those of our Eastern beauties were my only object in life. I never went into my boudoir, feeling the reproach of my neglected books; the air was full of such different ideas, alas! from those that occupied me now.

'Djenan the lover might do her utmost, she mourned for the Djenan of the past who had striven to possess a soul. And how can I find words for the agony when I felt at last only too clearly that my blandishments were false, my kisses a lie, that love was dead in me.

'But he now loved me with a passion which became a terror to me. What could I do to

escape from him, to put an end to this degradation? I saw no way out of it but death, and I
had it always by me, ready prepared and close at
hand on the dressing-table at which I now so
constantly sat; a swift and gentle death within
reach of my hand, in a silver bottle exactly like
my scent-bottles.

'I had come to this, when one morning, on
going into my mother-in-law's drawing-room, I
found two visitors just putting on their tcharchafs
to leave: Durdaneh and the aunt who had taken
her in charge. She, that Durdaneh, was smiling
as usual, but with a little air of triumph, while the
two old ladies seemed quite upset. I, for my
part, on the contrary, was perfectly calm. I
observed that her dress of fawn-coloured cloth
was loosely made, and that she seemed to have
grown large and heavy; she slowly fixed her
tcharchaf and veil, said good-bye and went.
"What did she come here for?" I asked simply
when we were alone. Emireh Hanum made me sit
down by her, holding my hands and hesitating to
reply; I saw the tears trickle down her wrinkles.
Durdaneh was going to have a child and my husband must marry her. A woman of their family
could not be a mother without being a wife, and
besides, Hamdi's child had a right to a place in
the house.

'She told me all this weeping the while, and
had thrown her arms round me. But how calmly
I heard her! This meant deliverance, brought to
me when I thought myself lost. I at once replied
that I quite understood all this, and Hamdi was

free; that I was ready to be divorced then and there, and owed no one the smallest grudge.

'"Divorced!" cried she, with a burst of tears. "Divorced! You wish to be divorced? But my son adores you. We all of us love you. You are the joy of our eyes!" Poor woman, she was the only person I regretted when I left that house. And then, to persuade me, she began to tell me of the wives of her young days who could make themselves happy in the like case. She herself, had she not shared the Pasha's love with other women? As soon as her beauty had begun to go off, had she not seen two, three younger wives, one after another, in his harem? She called them her sisters; no one of them had ever failed in respect for her, and it was always to her that the Pasha had recourse if he had any private matter to tell or information to ask, or when he felt ill. Had she suffered from all this? Hardly — for she could only remember one sorrow in her life, and that was when little Saida, the youngest of her rivals, died leaving her baby to her. Yes, Hamdi's youngest brother Ferid was not her own son but poor Saida's; and this was the first time I heard of it.

'Durdaneh was to return to the harem on the morrow. What could the woman matter to me at this juncture of affairs; and after all Hamdi no longer cared for her, and loved only me. But still she was a pretext I must seize, this opportunity must not on any account be missed. To cut the matter short, in my horror of scenes, and still more my fear of Hamdi who would be in a frenzy,

I then and there temporised. On my knees before his weeping mother, I only begged and obtained leave to spend two months in seclusion at Kassim Pacha in my girlhood's home; I needed that, I said, to resign myself; then I could come back.

'And I was gone before Hamdi had come in from Yildiz.

'It was just then, André, that you came to Constantinople. At the end of the two months my husband, of course, demanded his wife. I sent word to him that living I would never again be his; the little silver phial I kept always about me, and it was a fearful struggle till the day when His Majesty the Sultan vouchsafed to sign the Iradeh which set me free.

'Dare I confess to you that for the first few weeks I was still very unhappy? Against my expectation the image of that man, and the kisses I had both loved and hated too vehemently, haunted me for a long time.

'Now all is calm within me. I forgive him for having brought me down almost to the level of a courtesan; I no longer long for him nor hate him. It is all over: I still feel some shame at having believed I had known love because a handsome lad held me in his arms. But I have recovered my dignity, I have found my soul again and resumed my soaring flight.

'Now answer this letter, André, that I may know whether you understand me, or whether, like so many others, you regard me as a poor unbalanced mind in quest of the impossible.

'DJENAN.'

P

XXIII

ANDRÉ wrote to Djenan that Hamdi struck him as very like all men, as much of the West as of the East; but that she was the really exceptional being, the choicer soul. And then he pointed out to her — which was certainly not original — that nothing flies so fast as time; the two years of his residence at Constantinople were all slipping past, and would never come again; hence they ought to take every opportunity of exchanging their thoughts, which must so soon perish, like those of every living creature, in the abyss of death.

He received notice of an assignation for the following Thursday at Stamboul, in the old house at the end of the silent alley beyond Sultan Selim.

On that day he went down the Bosphorus in the morning on a steamboat, and found Stamboul basking in summer, almost like Arabia, so hot and still was the air, and so white the mosques in the burning August sunshine. How could any one imagine that a city like this to-day could linger through such long winters, under such a persistent shroud of snow? The streets were more deserted than ever, because so many people had migrated to the Bosphorus, or the islands in the sea of

Marmora, and oriental smells were aggravated in
the over-heated atmosphere.

To while away the time he went to the square
of Sultan Fatih, to sit in the old place under the
shade of the trees, facing the mosque. Some
Imams there, who had not seen him for so many
days, welcomed him warmly, and then sank into
dreaming again. And the caféji, regarding him
as a constant customer, brought with his narghileh the little household cat Tekir, which had
often been his pet in the spring, and which settled
down at once close beside him, her head on his
knee to be rubbed. The walls of the mosque
opposite were blindingly white. Some children
were dipping water out of an old fountain, and
they poured it on the pavement all round the
smokers, but it was so hot in spite of this that the
finches and blackbirds in the cages were mute and
sleepy, and yellow leaves were falling already,
prophesying the early decline of this glorious
summer.

At Sultan Selim, which he reached at the
crushing hour of two o'clock, the alley was so
empty and resonant as to be quite alarming.
Within the outer door he found Melek on guard,
and she smiled at him like a faithful little comrade,
glad to see him again at last. Her veil was thin
and her face was as visible as that of an European
in a mourning veil. He found Zeyneb upstairs
in the same light shroud, and for the first time he
saw the gleam of her brown eyes, and met their
sweet, grave young gaze. But, as he had expected, Djenan persisted in remaining no more

than a slim, black vision, absolutely without features.

The question she asked him in a knowing tone, as soon as they were seated on the shabby, faded divan, was:

'Well, and how is your friend, Jean Renaud?'

'Perfectly well, thank you; but where did you learn his name?'

'Everything is known in the harems. For instance, I can tell you that you dined last night with Madame de Saint-Enogat, and sat next to a lady in a pink gown; that afterwards you and she went out together and sat on a bench in the garden, and that she smoked one of your cigarettes in the moonlight. And so on, and so on. Everything you do, everything that happens to you, comes to our knowledge. Then you can assure me that Monsieur Jean Renaud is perfectly well?'

'Why, yes; when I tell you ——'

'Then, Melek, you have wasted your pains — it will not work.'

He then learnt that Melek had for some days devoted herself to prayer and a magic charm, to obtain Jean Renaud's death, partly in childish fun, and yet more in solemn earnest, having persuaded herself that he embodied an adverse influence and kept André on the defensive with regard to them.

'There, you see,' said Djenan laughing. 'You wanted to know oriental women — that is what we really are. Scratch the veneer and we are little barbarians.'

'You were entirely mistaken about him, at any

rate. On the contrary, he is always dreaming of
you, poor Jean Renaud. Indeed, but for him we
should never have known each other. On the
occasion of our first meeting at Pacha Bagtcheh,
the day of the high wind, he dragged me there; I
had refused to go.'

'Good Jean Renaud,' cried Melek. 'Well,
listen then. Bring him to-morrow, Friday, to the
Sweet Waters in your handsome caïque, and I will
go myself on purpose to smile at him as we pass.'

In the gloomy, melancholy harem, where the
splendour of the day could hardly be guessed
even, Djenan remained sphinx-like and motionless, even more so than last time. It was evident
that she felt some fresh shyness and constraint
from having so fully betrayed herself in her long
letters; and to see her nervous made André
nervous too, almost aggressive.

To-day she tried to make him talk about the
book.

'It will be a novel, of course?'

'How should I be able to write anything else?
But I do not yet see that novel, I must say.'

'Will you allow me to tell you what my idea
is? A novel, certainly, in which you yourself
will figure.'

'Ah, no, never that!'

'Let me explain myself. You will not write
in the first person: that I know you will never
do again. But there might be an European in
the story, staying at Constantinople for a time, a
singer of the East, who would see with your eyes,
and feel with your soul.'

'And no one would recognise me, you may be very sure!'

'What could it matter? Let me go on, will you? In spite of the thousand inevitable risks, he must clandestinely meet one of our Turkish sisters, and they must fall in love ——'

'And then?'

'And then, he must go away, that is inevitable — and that is all.'

'How new and original such an intrigue would be in a book of mine!'

'I beg your pardon, this might be quite new — that their love for each other remained unavowed and perfectly pure.'

'Ah! And after he has gone — she ——'

'She? — why, what would you have her do? She dies.'

She dies. It was said with such a tone of poignant conviction that André felt a shock all through him that kept him silent.

Then Zeyneb began to speak.

'Tell him, Djenan, the title you had thought of. We thought it so pretty: *The Blue Sky that Kills.* — No? You do not seem to like it.'

'It is pretty, certainly,' said André, 'but perhaps a little — dear me, what shall I say? — a little in the sentimental ballad style.'

'Well, well,' said Djenan, 'say at once that you think it 1830. It is rococo — let us drop it.'

'A little in curl-papers,' said Melek.

He now discerned that it had been a pang to her to be contradicted half ironically in the little literary notions which she had formulated unaided,

with so much toil, and often with such unerring
intuition. She suddenly appeared to him as so
artless and so young — she whom he had thought
of at first as too much sunk in books. He was
distressed to think that he might have vexed her
ever so little, and changed his tone at once to one
of gentleness, almost of affection.

'No, no, my dear little invisible friend; your
title is not rococo nor ridiculous, nor could anything be that you might imagine or say. Only,
let us keep death out of it — do not you think so?
In the first place, for the sake of a change; so
many people have died in my books, you know.
Consider, I shall be taken for a perfect Bluebeard.
No, no death in this book; on the contrary, if
possible, sheer youth and life. With this granted,
I will try to write it in any form you like best,
and we will work at it together, like two comrades, will we not?'

And they parted greater friends than they had
been till this day.

XXIV

DJENAN TO ANDRÉ

September 16, 1904.

'I WAS among the flowers in the garden, and I felt so lonely there, and so tired of my loneliness. A storm had swept past in the night and wrecked the roses. The earth was strewn with them. As I walked over these freshly fallen flowers, it was like trampling down dreams.

'It was in that garden that ever since I came from Karadjemir I spent all my summers as a child and a girl, with your friends Zeyneb and Melek. I cannot say that we were unhappy at that period of our lives. Everything smiled on us. Every one about us enjoyed the negative happiness which consists in peace at the passing moment and security for the next. We had never seen hearts bleed. Our days glided by slowly and quietly between our studies and our little pleasures, leaving us half asleep in the torpor which comes with our always hot summers. It had never occurred to us that we were to be pitied. Our foreign governesses had been very unhappy in their own homes. They found relief among us, and such peace as was like a haven after a tempest. And we sometimes spoke to them of our vague dreams and ill-defined longings to live like European women, to travel and see; they replied by praising the quiet and ease in which we lived. The quiet, the peace of a Moslem woman's life; all our childhood through we heard of nothing else. So nothing from outside had taught us to endure. Then suffering came upon us from within; restlessness and insatiable craving were born in us. My drama really began on my wedding day, when the silver threads of my bridal veil still clung to me.

'Do you remember, André, our first meeting in the flagged path and the blustering wind, and could you then have believed that so soon you would be to us so dear a friend? I am sure too that you are beginning to feel attached to these little Turkish women, although they have already lost the fascination of mystery. A delightful tender feeling has stolen over me since our last meeting, since the moment when your eyes and your tone of voice changed because you were afraid you had hurt me. Then I understood how kind you are, and that you would consent to be my confidant as well as my friend. It will do me so much good to tell you, who will be sure to understand, so many weariful things which no one has ever heard; circumstances in my fate which puzzle me. You, who are a man, and who *know*, will perhaps be able to explain them.

'I have a photograph of you close to me on my writing-table, and it looks at me with its clear gaze. You too, I know, are not far away on the other shore; only an arm of the Bosphorus parts us, and yet what a distance for ever lies between us two, what an abyss of difficulties, with the constant uncertainty of ever meeting again. In spite of all, I could wish that when you have left our country I might not be merely a doubtful spectre in your remembrance. I should like to live in it as a reality, a poor, sad little reality.

'Do you know what the roses I just now trod underfoot reminded me of? A similar destruction in this same garden two years ago or rather more. But it was not the work of a summer tempest; it was autumn. October had seared the trees, it was cold, and we were to go back to town the next day, to Kassim Pacha. Everything was packed up and the house dismantled. We went out into the garden to take leave of it and gather the last flowers. A bitter blast sighed in the boughs. Old Irfaneh, one of our slaves, who is addicted to sorcery and to reading fortunes in coffee-grounds, had declared that this was a good day for foretelling our destiny. She brought us out some coffee, and we had to drink it; it was in a nook at the end of the garden, sheltered by the hill, and I can see her now, squatting at our feet among the dead leaves, anxious as to what she might discover. In Zeyneb's cup and in Melek's she saw only pleasure and presents, they were still so young. But she shook her head as she read mine. "Ah! love is on the watch," said she; "but love is treacherous. You will not come back to the Bosphorus for a long time, and when you return the flower of your happiness will have fallen. Poor thing, poor thing! There is nothing in your life but love and death." It was true; I did not come back here till this summer, after my distressful marriage. Still, is it the flower of happiness that is gone, since I never had any happiness? No, I think not. But her last words never struck me as they did to-day: "There is nothing in your life but love and death."

'DJENAN.'

XXV

THEY met frequently during this delightful summer end. At least once a week at the Sweet Waters of Asia their caïques touched, they giving no sign. Zeyneb and Melek, whose features he could somewhat distinguish, hardly dared to smile under the black gauze. They met, too, in the worthy nurse's house in Stamboul; they were more free on the Bosphorus than in their vast winter homes at Kassim Pacha, and found a hundred pretexts for going into the town and dropping their slaves on the way. Each interview, to be sure, necessitated a tissue of machinations and audacity, which always seemed about to break down and turn an innocent adventure into a tragedy, but which always, by some miracle, turned out happily. And success gave them assurance and made them plot more perilous enterprises. 'You might tell the whole story here in Constantinople,' they would amuse themselves by saying; 'no one would believe you.'

When they were all together in the little house chatting like old friends, Zeyneb and Melek would now raise their veils and show the whole of their faces; only their hair remained hidden under the black hood, and in this way they looked like little nuns, young and graceful. Djenan alone admitted no compromise; nothing could be guessed of her features, perpetually shrouded as funereally as on the first day, and he feared to remark on it, foreseeing that some positive answer might rob him of all hope of ever seeing her eyes.

He now and then ventured, by agreement with them, to go to hear them make music in the still, perfidious nights on the Bosphorus, breathless, warm, and enticing, but which drench you at once in penetrating cold dew. Almost every day during the summer the violent draught of air from the Black Sea rushes down the strait and thrashes it into foam, but never fails to die away at sundown, as if the flood-gates of the wind were suddenly shut. As soon as dusk falls the trees on the banks are motionless, everything settles into stillness and dreams; the surface of the sea is an unwrinkled mirror reflecting the stars, the moon, the myriad lights in the houses and palaces; oriental languor comes down with the darkness on these extreme edges of Asia and Europe facing each other, and the constant moisture of the atmosphere wraps all things in softening and magnifying haze, those that are near as well as those that are far off; the hills, the woods, the mosques, the Greek and Turkish villages, the little creeks on the Asiatic side, more silent than those on the European shore, and more sunk every night in their absolute stillness.

From Therapia, where André lived, to his

friends' yali was about half-an-hour's crossing in
a rowing-boat.

The first time he went in his caïque, for it was
always an enchantment to go about at night in this
little bark, so low as to be able to touch the water,
lying at full length on the pale blue and silver
mirror of the still surface. The European shore,
as it receded, also assumed a semblance of
mystery and peace; all the lights threw on the
Bosphorus innumerable little glittering shafts
that seemed to strike down into the depths below.
The Eastern music from the little outside cafés,
the strange flourishes of the singers pursued him,
carried and harmonised by the deeper tones of the
sea; even the hideous orchestras of Therapia were
mellowed by distance and the magic of the night
till they were pleasing to the ear. And there,
facing him, was the shore of Asia, towards which
he was going so luxuriously. Its thickets of dense
verdure, its hills covered with trees, formed black
masses, which looked gigantic, towering above
their reversed reflection; the lights, fewer and less
garish, came from windows screened by lattices,
behind which he could imagine the women that
none might see.

On that occasion, in his own caïque, André did
not dare stop under the lighted windows, and he
passed by. His oarsmen, whose embroidered
jackets shone too brightly in the moonlight, and
might excite the suspicion of some negro sentinel
on the bank, were all Turks, and, in spite of
their personal devotion, quite capable of betraying
him in their indignation if they had scented the

smallest understanding between their European
master and the ladies of that harem.

So on other evenings he came in the humblest
of the fishing-boats which go out on the Bosphorus in thousands every night. Thus, under
the pretence of laying the nets, he could linger for
a long time; he could hear Zeyneb sing, accompanied by Melek or Djenan; he knew her rich
young voice, such a lovely voice, and so naturally
expressive, especially in the lower notes, but in
which there was now and then the very slightest
huskiness, making it perhaps all the more attractive, as marking it for early decay.

About mid-September they did a most daring
thing — they climbed a hill all rosy with heath,
and took a walk in a wood. This they achieved
without let or hindrance, just above Beicos, the
point on the Asiatic shore precisely opposite
Therapia, to which André came every evening
towards sunset. Impossible to describe the charm
of Beicos, which became one of their favourite
meeting-places least disturbed by alarms. Leaving
Therapia, the pretentious centre of fashionable
folly, he would here find in contrast the silent
shade of tall trees, the meditative peace of a past
age. From a little landing-place of white stone
you step at once into a Garden of Eden, under
plane-trees four centuries old, which do not look
as if they were native to our climate, so much have
they assumed of the growth of the baobab or the
Indian banyan.

This is a perfectly flat meadow, carpeted in
autumn with fine velvety turf, smoother than that

of the best-kept garden; a lawn which seems to
have been created expressly for pacing in moods
of meditation and sage melancholy; it is hardly
half a league across, exactly of the right size to
lie secreted without suggesting imprisonment,
enclosed on all sides by lonely hills overgrown
with woods, and the Turks, struck by its peculiar
charm, give it the name of the 'Grand Signior's
Valley.' It is impossible to suspect that the
Bosphorus is so close, with its constant bustle
which would disturb meditation; the hills hide it
completely. The wanderer is isolated from everything; not a sound is to be heard, unless it be,
towards evening, the pipe of the goatherds col-
lecting their flocks on the hills behind. The
majestic plane-trees, whose roots coil over the
earth like huge snakes, form a sort of sacred wood
at the entrance to this park, but they stand further
apart as you go on, and form into avenues, leaving
open expanses of lawn on which the white-veiled
women walk slowly up and down before sunset.
There is a stream, too, through this valley of the
Grand Signior, a cool rivulet, the home of many
tortoises; it is crossed by little plank bridges; on
its banks, under the shade of a few old trees, the
sellers of Turkish coffee set up booths for the
summer months, and there men sit and smoke
their narghilehs, especially on Fridays, and watch
the women who promenade to and fro on this
meadow of long dreams. They walk in groups
of three, four, to ten, somewhat scattered and a
little lost, for these lawns are to them a very
vast spread of carpet. Their dresses are all in

one form and of one colour, often of Damascus silk, pink or blue, and patterned with gold; these fall in antique folds, and every head is wrapped in white muslin; this costume, in this deeply secluded place, and the spellbound gravity of their walk, remind one, as dusk comes on, of the happy shades of pagan creeds walking in the Elysian fields.

André was a constant visitor to the valley of the Grand Signior; he spent almost every day there during his residence in Therapia.

At the appointed hour he landed under the baobab-like plane-trees accompanied by Jean Renaud, who again was to keep watch, and was always amused at playing the part. His Moslem servants, impossible in these circumstances, he had left on the European shore, bringing with him only a faithful Frenchman, who, as usual, had brought his master's fez in a bag. Since his new friendship he was in the habit of changing his headgear, and the fez had hitherto averted danger; he put it on wherever he happened to be — in a hired carriage or in a boat, or in some deserted side-street.

He saw the three arrive in a talika and alight, and, like three little ladies come out for an innocent walk, they crossed the grass, which was rosy already here and there with clumps of the autumn crocus. Zeyneb and Melek wore the thin yeldirmeh, which is admissible in the country, and the white gauze veil which leaves the eyes visible. Only Djenan had put on the black tcharchaf of the town, to remain still austerely invisible.

Q

When they turned into a certain path they had
agreed upon, a path winding uphill, he joined
them and introduced Jean Renaud, whose hand
they had wished to grasp with their finger-tips as
some amends for having plotted his death, and
who was sent forward as scout. In the exquisite
afternoon they lightly climbed the slope amid
chestnut trees and oaks; the grass was gay with
scabious. Presently they reached the heath, and
under the trees all was pink; and then, higher
still, the distance came into view. On this, the
Asiatic side, there were forests without end; as
far as the eye could see, on hills and mountains
lay the grand wild green covert which still shelters
bears and brigands.

The Black Sea, suddenly extended to an infinite distance, lay at their feet, of a greyer and
colder blue than the sea of Marmora, which is so
near it; it was to-day insinuatingly calm and
pensive under the sun of this late summer day, as
though it were already looking forward to its
perpetual rage and wintry uproar when the fearful
Russian wind should blow again.

The goal of their walk was an old mosque
built of wood, a half-forgotten place of pilgrimage
on a plateau overlooking the sea of storms, fully
exposed to the assaults of the north wind. There,
in a tumbledown hovel, was a very humble café
kept by a white-haired old man. They sat down
in front of it to look at the pale immensity
slumbering below. The few trees surviving here
leaned over, all gnarled, and all on the same
side, having yielded at last to the continuous

buffeting of the same blast. The air was bright and sharp.

They did not talk about the book, nor about anything in particular. Only Zeyneb was at all serious to-day; Djenan and Melek were wholly intoxicated by this clandestine folly, wholly lost in contemplation of the wild magnificence of the mountains, and the cliffs which fell sheer at their feet into the sea. To be alone here with André, the little rebels had dropped two negroes and as many negresses in villages on the road, paying them to keep silence; but their daring, hitherto always successful, no longer gave them any alarms. And the white-bearded old man brought them coffee in his old blue cups, outside, in the presence of the gloomy Black Sea, never doubting that his customer was a Turkish Bey on a pilgrimage with the ladies of his harem.

The air, however, was turning cold after the heat of the valley, and Zeyneb was seized by a little cough, which she strove to conceal, but which told the same ominous tale as the slight huskiness of her voice. The two others looked at each other, and André understood that this was no new subject of anxiety; they tried to draw the folds of her dress over her slender bosom, but the invalid, or merely ailing victim, shrugged her shoulders. 'Never mind,' she said, with the calmest indifference. 'Dear me, what does it matter?'

Zeyneb was the only one of the three whom André fancied he to some extent really knew. Disenchanted in both senses of the word: out

of conceit with life, wishing for nothing, looking
forward to nothing, but resigned with unvarying
sweetness; a being all of lassitude and tenderness,
precisely the soul that fitted her charming face
with its regular features, and her eyes which had
the smile of desperation. Melek, on the contrary,
who seemed to have a kind little heart, never
ceased to be fantastical to excess, sometimes violent,
and then a child again, ready to mock and laugh
at everything. As to Djenan, the most exquisite of
the three, how mysterious she still remained under
her eternal black veil — very complicated, influ-
enced by the literature of all ages; at the same time
uncertain, at once submissive and haughty, not
hesitating at times to reveal herself with an almost
disconcerting freedom, and then shrinking back
into her ivory tower, more distant than ever. 'As
for her,' André said to himself, 'I cannot make
out what she wants of me, nor why I am already
so fond of her. One might sometimes fancy that
we had some memory in common of a remote
unknown past. I shall not begin to read her till
the day when she shows me at last what sort of
eyes she has; but I am afraid she never will.'

They had to go down the hill again early, to
the valley of Beicos, to give them time to pick up
their slaves on the way and get home before night.
So they presently were lost again in the woodland
path, and they insisted that André himself should
pluck for each of them a sprig of the heath which
made the whole hillside rosy; it was to wear, out
of childish bravado, that evening at dinner with
their grandparents and strict old uncles.

On reaching the plain he left them, as a matter of prudence, but watched them as they went, walking at some distance behind them. There were few people now in the valley of the Grand Signior, where the sun was already turning to the redder gold of evening. Only a few women wearing white veils were sitting on the grass in groups far apart. The audacious three went on at a slow and graceful pace; Zeyneb and Melek, in silks of the palest hue, almost white, one on each side of Djenan, an elegy in black; their skirts trailed over the exquisite lawn, over the short fine grass, bending the lilac crocus flowers, and sweeping along the yellow leaves already fallen from the plane-trees. They really looked like three Elysian shades crossing the vale of perfect rest; she in the middle, in her mourning, was a shade not as yet consoled, no doubt, for the loss of earthly love.

He lost sight of them when they reached the great trees, the sacred wood at the further end of the secluded plain. The sun was sinking behind the hills, slowly abandoning this Eden; the sky was clear, with the green transparency of a fine summer evening, and tiny clouds crossing it in long mares' tails looked like orange-coloured flames. The other happy shades, who had been long sitting here and there on the crocus-flowered grass, all rose now to leave too, but very gently, as beseems shades. The shepherds' pipes in the distance began their old-world trilling to call the goats together, and the whole place was preparing for a night of infinite solitude at the foot of the forests, under the stars.

André Lhéry regretfully turned his steps towards the Bosphorus, which he soon saw lying like a sheet of rosy silver between the black masses of the giant planes on the shore. He bade his rowers not to hurry, not feeling eager to return to the European shore at Therapia, where the huge hotels were turning on their electric lights, and tuning, more or less, their blatant bands for the evening of supposed fashion.

XXVI

Letters received by André on the following day:

September 18, 1904.

'Our Friend, do you know there is one point you ought to enlarge upon, and which would afford the most essentially "harem" passage in your book. That is the sense of emptiness which is produced in our life by the necessity of never talking to any but women, of having no intimate friends but women, of living always among ourselves, our fellow-women. Our friends? but, mercy, they are as weak and as weary as we are! In our harems weakness — so many weaknesses rather, combined and huddled together, are sick at heart, suffer the more from being what they are, and cry out for strength. O for some one with whom these poor, neglected, humiliated beings might talk and exchange their little ideas, timid and innocent as they generally are. We so sorely need a man friend, a firm masculine hand on which to lean, and strong enough to uphold us when we are ready to fall. Not a father, not a husband, not a brother; no, a friend, I say.

A being of our own choice, very superior to ourselves, who would be at once severe and kind,
tender and serious, and who would feel for us
a purely protecting friendship. Such men are to
be found in your world, are they not?
                                    'ZEYNEB.'

'An existence in which there is nothing! Conceive of its horror. Hapless souls that have now
found their wings, and which are kept captive;
hearts in which the young sap is fermenting, and
which are forbidden to act, which can do nothing,
not even do good, and devour themselves, or are
worn out by unrealisable dreams. Can you imagine
what dreary days your three friends would be living
through if you had not come? Days all exactly
alike under the vigilant care of old uncles and
old women, whose unspoken disapproval constantly
oppresses them.
'Of all the drama of my marriage of which I
have told you, nothing was left at the bottom of
my heart but rancour against love, at any rate as it
is understood among us — a disbelief in its joys,
and an ineffaceable bitter taste on my lips. At the
same time, I knew that there was in the West
another kind of love than that which had so disappointed me, and I set to work to study it with
passion in literature and in history; and, as I had
foreseen, I found it had inspired many follies, but
also the greatest deeds. I found it at the core of
everything evil in the world, but also of everything
good and sublime. And the more I discerned the
brilliant lot of the Latin woman, the more bitter

was my sadness. Oh, how happy in your Western
lands was the being who for centuries had been
cared for, fought for, suffered for; who might
love and choose as she listed, who had a right to
demand that a man should be worthy of her before
giving herself to him! What a place she filled
in your life, how undisputed was her traditional
supremacy!

'Whereas in us Moslem women almost every
element was unawakened. Self-consciousness and
a sense of our value were scarcely alert, and
every one about us was perversely ignorant
and supremely scornful of the evolution that was
beginning.

'Would no voice uplift itself to proclaim the
blindness of men, kind and tender as they often
were; our fathers, our husbands, our brothers?
For ever, and in the eyes of the whole world, would
the Turkish woman remain a slave, purchased for
her beauty alone, or a Hanum, fair and fat, smoking cigarettes and sunk in perpetual *Kief*.

'Then you came, and you know the rest. We
all three are at your command as faithful secretaries
— we three, and many more of our sisters if we
are not enough — we will lend you our eyes to see
with, our heart to understand with, and offer our
whole soul to serve you.

'We may yet again meet you perhaps once or
twice, here or on the Bosphorus, before we must
return to the city. We have so many trustworthy
friends among the ladies who live on this shore
ever ready to help us to prove an *alibi*.

'But oh, I dread — not your regard for us as

you said, it is above suspicion — but I dread the
grief to come, after you are gone.

'Farewell, André, our friend — *my* friend. May
joy go with you!   DJENAN.'

'Djenan, I am sure, has not told you that the
lady in pink who smoked your cigarettes the other
evening at the house of the Saint-Enogats — Madame de Durmont, not to give her her real name —
has just spent this afternoon with us, on the pretext
of singing Grieg's duets with Zeyneb. But she
only talked, and only of you, with such enthusiasm
that a young Russian lady who was present could
not get over her amazement. We were alarmed
lest she suspected something, and was laying a trap
for us, so we abused you finely, biting our lips to
keep ourselves from laughing, and she was quite
taken in, and defended you vehemently. Which is
as much as to say that her whole visit was a cross-
examination as to our several views of you. What
a lucky mortal you are!

'We have just been concocting no end of
delightful plans for seeing you again. Does your
French servant, who is so much to be depended
on, know how to drive? If you make him also
wear a fez, we might take a drive with you in a
closed carriage, he on the box. But all this we
must arrange *viva voce* the next time we meet.

'Your three friends join in pretty and tender
messages.   MELEK.'

'On no account miss going to the Sweet Waters
to-morrow; we will try to go there, too. As

on former occasions, pass in your caïque under the
Asiatic shore, under our windows.   If you see the
corner of a white handkerchief peeping through
the lattice, it will mean that we shall join you.   If
the handkerchief is blue, it means "Disaster": we
are imprisoned.   M.'

Thenceforth till the end of the season they held
their stolen and wordless meetings at the Sweet
Waters of Asia.   Every time the weather was fine
on a Friday, or on a Tuesday, which is also a day
for an outing on the pretty shady river, André's
caïque met and remet that of his friends, but
without the faintest sign which could have betrayed their intimacy to the hundreds of women's
eyes on the alert on the shore, peeping through
the openings in their muslin veils.   If a favourable
instant presented itself, Melek or Zeyneb ventured
to smile under the black gauze.   As to Djenan,
she adhered to her threefold shroud, as complete a
disguise as a mask; the women in other caïques
were a little surprised at it, to be sure, but no one
thought any harm of it, the spot being ill-fitted
for any wrong doing; and those who recognised
her by the boatmen's livery were content to
remark without ill-feeling that 'little Djenan
Tewfik Pasha always had been eccentric.'

XXVII

September 28, 1904.

'WHAT a new experience it is to us to know that among the crowd at the Sweet Waters there is a man who is our friend. Among the strangers who will remain for ever unknown to us, and who regard us as strange, inscrutable little animals, to know that there is one eye that seeks us — us in particular, not the other similarly shrouded women — that one man bestows on us a thought of affectionate pity. When our boats touched you could not see me hidden under my thick veil, but I was there, and happy to be invisible, smiling into your eyes which gazed in the direction of mine.

'Is it because you were so kind and so simple, so precisely the friend I have longed for, the other day on the hill overlooking the Black Sea, during our almost speechless meeting there ? Is it because I have been aware at last, under the brevity of your letters, of a little true and emotional affection ? I do not know; but you no longer seem so remote from me. Oh, André, if you could but know what an ideal sentiment of tender admiration means to souls so long repressed as ours !

'DJENAN.'

They corresponded frequently this closing
summer, to arrange their perilous meetings. They
could still send their letters without much difficulty
by the hand of some faithful negro, who would
cross to Therapia in a boat, or who followed him
in the evening to the lovely valley of the Grand
Signior. And he, who had no means of reply
but through the post-office at Stamboul, generally
answered by some secret signal as he passed in his
caïque under their forbidding windows. They
took every advantage of these last days by the
Bosphorus, before returning to Constantinople,
where a stricter watch would be kept. But autumn
was felt to be coming on with strides, especially
in the gloomy evenings. Heavy black clouds
sailed down from the north on the blast from
Russia, and squalls would burst, bringing to
naught their most elaborately prepared plans.

Not far from the plain of Beicos, in an unknown and deserted hollow, they had found a
little glade of virgin forest round a pool full of
water-lilies. It was a melancholy but safe retreat,
shut in by steep slopes and a tangle of verdure,
with only one way in, where Jean Renaud kept
watch, with a whistle in case of alarm. There
they met twice by the green stagnant water, amid
huge reeds and ferns, in the shade of the almost
leafless trees. The flowers were in no respect
dissimilar to those of France, and the gigantic
ferns were but the tall osmunda of our marsh
lands; all more luxuriant, perhaps, in consequence
of the damper climate and hotter summers. The
three little black spectres moved about this jungle

somewhat embarrassed by their trains and their too
thin shoes; and they would seat themselves in some
chosen spot in a group round André for a few
moments of serious talk, or of perfect silence,
anxiously watching overhead the swirl of October
storm-clouds, which sometimes darkened the day
and threatened a heavy shower. Zeyneb and
Melek now and again would lift their veil, to
smile on their friend, looking straight into his
eyes with frank confidence; but Djenan, never.

André, with all his voyages in the tropics, had
not for many long years lived so much among
the plants of a cooler climate. These reeds and
harts'-tongues, these mosses and noble osmundas,
reminded him exactly of a marsh in his own
country which as a child he had loved to visit in
solitude, while he dreamed of virgin forests he
had never yet seen. And this Asiatic marsh was
so identically the same as his own that he could
fancy himself at home there, carried back to the
first period of his awakening to life. But then
here were the three little Eastern fairies,
whose presence was such a strange and delightful
anachronism.

It was Friday the 7th of October, the last
Friday at the Sweet Waters of Asia, for the
Embassies were to return to Constantinople in the
course of the following week, and the household
of the three Turkish ladies was preparing to do
likewise. All the houses by the Bosphorus would
now be closing their doors and windows for six
months of wind and rain or snow.

André and his friends had promised each other
that they would do everything in their power to
meet that day at the Sweet Waters, since that
would be the end of all things till next summer,
so full of uncertainty.

The weather was threatening, and he, as he set
off in defiance of everything in his caïque, said to
himself: 'They will not let them escape with this
rising wind.' But as he passed under their windows he saw through the lattice the white handkerchief flourished by Melek, and which meant in their
code, 'Go on; we have leave, and shall follow.'

There was no crowd to-day on the little stream,
nor on the grass-plots where the autumn crocus
bloomed among the dead leaves. Few Europeans,
or none; only Turks, and they chiefly women.
And in the beautiful eyes, which were left uncovered
by the white veils worn country-fashion, there were
melancholy looks, no doubt because of the approach
of winter, the season when the austerity of the
harems is the strictest, and imprisonment almost
unbroken.

They met two or three times. Even Melek's
gaze through her veil, her black veil for town
wear, was full of sadness — the sadness always felt
in the waning season, and when things are wearing
to an end.

When it was time to leave, the Bosphorus, at
the mouth of the little river, had effects of tragical
beauty. The Saracen fortress on the Asiatic shore
by which the boat must pass was crimson in the
low sun, and its battlements flame colour. While
the other castle, much more colossal, opposite on

the European shore, looked, on the contrary, over-poweringly gloomy, with its walls and towers piled up one above the other to the top of the hill.   The surface of the sea was white with foam lashed by blasts that were already keen.   And a calamitous sky spread over it all; bronze or copper-coloured clouds, tossed and rent against a lurid background.

The little ladies happily had not far to go close under the Asiatic shore to reach the old marble quay, always so carefully guarded, where their negroes awaited them.   But André, who had to cross the strait, did not arrive till after dark, his oarsmen streaming with perspiration and salt water, their velvet jackets and gold embroidery soaked and pitiable.   Late in the year, the return passage from the Sweet Waters has such surprises in store, the first aggressions of the Russian wind, and they strike to the heart as the shortening days do.

In his own house, where he brought in the frozen rowers to warm them, he heard on his arrival a curious small music which filled the house; such music as the goatherds had made at sunset in the woods and valleys of Beicos in Asia — a monotonous quick air on low-pitched notes, swifter than a tarantella or a fugue, and at the same time so doleful as to bring the tears.   One of his Turkish servants was blowing with all the power of his lungs into a long pipe, suddenly revealing himself as a great performer of wild and plaintive runs.

'Where did you learn that ?' he asked.

'In my country, among the hills near Eski Chehir.   I used to play that in the evening when

I called in my father's goats.' This alone had
been wanting, such a tune as this, to fill full the
causeless, nameless anguish of such an evening.

And for a long time André would have this
air on the flute played to him by twilight to
bring before him the unspeakableness of all these
things — his return from the Sweet Waters for
the last time; the three black spectres on the
tossing waves, going home in the dusk to their
prison in the dismal harem at the foot of the
mountains and the woods; the first gale of
autumn; the grass strewn with lilac colchicum
and yellow leaves; the end of the Bosphorus
season; the death of the summer.

R

XXVIII

ANDRÉ had been settled in Pera for about a fortnight, and had been able to meet his little friends
once in the old house near Sultan Selim. They
had introduced to him an unknown lady, hidden
under such thick veils that her voice was almost
smothered. On the morrow he received the
following letter.

'I am the phantom of yesterday, Monsieur
Lhéry. I did not know how to speak to you, but
for the sake of the book you have promised to
write for us I propose to give you an account of a
Turkish lady's day. It will be quite seasonable
too, for here we are nearly in November; the cold
and gloom, and above all an increase of weariness
and dark days, loom before us. The day of a
Turkish lady in winter. To begin —
'She rises late, very late. Her toilet is slow,
dilatory; she always has very long hair, too thick
and too heavy to be arranged. And she thinks
how pretty she is in the silvered mirror, how
young and charming; and it makes her sad.
'Then there is the silent walk round the rooms
to see if everything is in proper order; lingering
over a few favourite things, souvenirs and portraits

of which the care seems extremely important.
Then comes breakfast, often in solitude, in a large
room, surrounded by negresses or Circassian slaves;
her hands are chilled as she touches the silver plate
on the table, above all her soul is chilled; she can
talk to the slaves, asks them questions without
waiting for the answers.

'And now what can she do till the evening?
The harems of a past time, when there were
several wives, must have been less dull; they
kept each other company. What then can she
do? Paint in water-colour? We can all paint
beautifully in water-colour, Monsieur Lhéry. Ah,
the screens we have painted, the fans, the hand
screens! Or play the piano, or the lute? Read
Pierre Bourget or André Lhéry? Or do some
embroidery, take one of our long golden strips and
be absorbed, all alone, in seeing our white, dainty
little fingers, loaded with rings, fly over the stitches?
What we want is something new, which we dream
of without hope; something unexpected — a flash,
a thrill, an excitement, but which never comes.
We want to get out walking, in spite of the mud,
in spite of the snow, not having stirred for a fortnight; but we are forbidden to go out alone.
There is no conceivable errand as an excuse,
nothing. We pine for space, we crave air. Even
if we have a garden it seems impossible to breathe
there, because the walls are too high.

'A bell rings. If it were but some catastrophe!
What joy! Or even only a visitor.

'A visitor! It is a visitor; the slaves are
hurrying along the passages. We jump up; a

looking-glass, quick, to make up our eyes, in eager haste. Who can it be? Ah, a charming young friend, not long married. She comes in. Mutual delight, eager hands, rosy lips kissing pale cheeks.

'"Have I come in a good hour? What were you doing, dear?"

'"Being bored."

'"Well, I have come to fetch you for a drive together, anywhere you please."

'A minute later and we drive off in a closed carriage. On the box by the coachman sits a negro, Dilaver, the inevitable Dilaver, without whom we may not stir, and who will report on how we have spent the time.

'The two friends chat. "Well — and do you love Ali Bey?"

'"Yes," replies the bride, "but because I must love some one. I am greedy for affection. This does for the present; if later I see my way to something better ——"

'"Well, I do not love my husband — no, not at all; to love on compulsion, no! I am not one of the women that bend."

'The carriage rumbles on at the full speed of two splendid horses. We must not stop and get out; that would be quite incorrect. And we envy the beggar women who are free, and who look at us as they pass.

'Presently, at the entrance to the Bazaar, there is a crowd of common folk buying roast chest-nuts. "I am so hungry!" says one. "Have you brought any money?"

'"No. Dilaver has some. Dilaver, buy us some chestnuts."

'What can they be put into? We hold out our scented lace handkerchiefs; the chestnuts are handed to us in these, and smell of heliotrope. And this is the great event of the day, this luncheon, which it amuses us to eat like the common women, but under our veils in a closed carriage.

'On our return we embrace again at parting, and repeat the eternal formulas which Turkish women preach to each other: "Now, no chimerical dreams, no vain regrets. Be firm, hold your own!" But it makes us smile, even as we speak, the advice is so familiar and so threadbare.

'The visitor leaves. It is evening; lamps are lighted very early, for night soon falls in a harem in consequence of the close lattices to the windows. Your fourth spectre of yesterday, Monsieur Lhéry, is alone again. But here comes the Bey, her master, announced by the clatter of his sword on the stairs. Then the poor little woman's soul is more chilled than ever. As a matter of habit she looks in a glass; the reflected image is really very pretty, and she thinks: "All this beauty for him! What a pity!"

'He, stretching himself insolently on a pile of cushions, begins a history:

'"To-day, you know, my dear, at the palace ——"

'Oh, yes, the palace, his fellow-officers, his guns, new weapons, these are all he cares for; nothing else, ever.

'She does not listen, she is ready to cry. Then she is told she is "out of sorts." She asks leave to withdraw to her own room, and soon she is sobbing bitterly, her head on a pillow of silk brocaded with gold and silver, while the European ladies of Pera are going to a ball or to the theatre, and are gay and admired under a blaze of lights.

'*   *   *'

XXIX

For the second time since their return from the
Bosphorus André and the three were together in
the secret house in the heart of old Stamboul.

'You do not know,' said Melek, 'where we
are to meet next — elsewhere, just for a change.   A
lady we know, who lives near Mehmed Fatih, your
favourite haunt, has offered us the opportunity of
meeting at her house.   It is quite a Turkish house
with no master; it is a real chance, quiet and
safe.   And I am preparing a surprise for you in
a harem more luxurious than this, and at least
equally oriental.   You will see!'

André did not heed her.   He had made up
his mind to burn his ships to-day, but at any cost
to see Djenan's eyes; and he was thinking only of
that, well aware that if he blundered, and if she
persisted in her refusal, with her inflexible temper,
there would be an end of his hopes for ever.   Now
the eternal black veil over her young face had
become to him an annoyance, an obsession, an
ever growing distress, as by degrees he became
more deeply attached to her.   Only to know what
there was beneath it!   Only to see for an instant
the features of this siren of the heavenly voice,
and stamp it for ever on his memory.   Besides,

247

why should she hide herself, and not her sisters?
What difference was there between them?   What
unconfessed impulse ruled the conduct of that pure
and haughty spirit?   Now and again an explanation occurred to him, but he at once drove it from
his mind as absurd and fatuous.   'Nonsense,' he
always told himself, 'she is young enough to be my
daughter.   It is not common sense.'

And there she sat, close to him.   He need only
put out his hand to raise the piece of stuff which
hung hardly lower than the frill of an ordinary
black mask.   Why was it that an act so simple,
so tempting, would be as impossible, as shocking,
as a crime?

Time was slipping by; it would soon be the
hour of parting.   The beams of the November
sun were rising towards the roofs — that same sunbeam on the opposite wall, of which the reflection
cast a little light into this humble room.

'Listen to me, dear little friend,' he suddenly
exclaimed.   'At any cost I must see your eyes.
I cannot, I declare to you I cannot, go on like this.
In the first place, it is not fair play, since you can
see mine all the while through that double gauze —
triple for aught I know — which protects you.
But, if you choose, only your eyes, understand.
Instead of that heart-breaking black tcharchaf
come next time in a yashmak, as austere a yashmak
as you please, only showing your eyes and the eyebrows which contribute to the expression of your
gaze.   The rest of your face conceal from me
for ever — I submit, but not your eyes.   I entreat
you, I implore you.   Why do you do this?

Why? Your sisters do not. It is want of confidence on your part, and that is cruel.'

She sat a moment speechless. André could
hear the blood throbbing in his arteries.

'Well,' she said at last in a tone of grave determination, 'look, André; am I distrustful?'
And raising her veil, which she flung back, she
uncovered the whole of her face, and fixed on her
friend's eyes, with firm straight gaze, her own
lovely young eyes of the colour of the deep sea.

It was the first time she had called him by his
name, excepting in her letters; and her resolve,
her action, had a sort of solemnity in them, so
that the other two little shades sat mute in surprise,
while André imperceptibly shrank back under the
steady regard of this apparition, as if he had been
a little frightened, or his eyes were dazzled and he
would not let it be seen.

XXX

In the heart of Stamboul, under a November sky.
The maze of ancient streets, of course sunk in
silence, their paving-stones set in funereal weeds,
under low black clouds; the tangle of wooden
houses originally painted a dark ochre yellow, all
tumbledown and askew, but still with doubly
screened windows, impenetrable to the eye from
outside. And it was this, all this worm-eaten
decrepitude which, seen from afar, looked as a
whole like some vast fairy city, but which, seen
close, must bitterly disappoint the horde of tourists.
For André still, and for some others of his mind,
these things, even close at hand, preserve their
charm of immutability, of meditation, and of
prayer. And then, every here and there, is some
exquisite detail; a group of ancient tombs delicately chiselled at a street corner, under a plane-
tree three centuries old; or a marble fountain with
almost effaced arabesques in gold.

André, wearing a Turkish fez, was making his
way through these alleys by the help of a map
drawn by Melek, with notes to guide him. He
stopped once to look at a litter of the little vagrant
dogs which swarm in Constantinople, on which
the good souls in the neighbourhood had, as usual,

bestowed an alms in the shape of a bed of rags
and a bit of old carpet for an awning. They lay
there with an air of amiable contentment. He
did not, however, stoop to pat them, for fear of
betraying himself; for Orientals, though com-
passionate to dogs, would scorn to touch one, and
reserve all their petting for cats. But the mother
came to wriggle at his feet in gratitude, to show
how honoured she felt by his notice.

'The fourth house to the left, past a funereal
kiosque and a cypress tree,' was the spot to which
he was bidden to-day by the caprice of his three
friends. A black figure with her veil down, who
did not seem to be Melek, awaited him within the
partly open door, led him upstairs without saying
a word, and left him alone in a very oriental little
room much darkened by harem lattices; there
were divans all round, and texts of Islam hung on
the walls. In an adjoining room he heard low
voices, light steps, and the rustle of silks.

And when the same veiled figure signed to
him to follow her into the other room, André
could have thought himself Aladdin entering his
seraglio. His three austere little black spectres
were there, metamorphosed into three odalisques
sparkling with gold embroidery and spangles, in
delightful old-world magnificence. Very old
Mecca veils, in white gauze thickly spangled,
covered their hair done in long plaits, and fell back
over their shoulders; they stood up, their faces
uncovered, and bowed to him as to their master,
smiling with all their fresh youth and rosy lips.

These were their grandmothers' dresses and

jewels, brought out for him from their cedar chests;
and with the tact of modern elegance they had
selected from among the dim and faded satins and
archaic embroidery in gold, of flowers in high
relief, exactly such as made the most exquisite
combinations. They presented such a spectacle as
no one now ever sees, and which his European
eyes could never have hoped to see. Behind them,
in the deeper shadow, reclining on the divans, were
five or six trustworthy accomplices, perfectly still,
entirely black, in tcharchafs with the veil down;
and their silent presence enhanced the mystery.
All this, which would never have been done for
anybody else, was an act of unheard-of temerity,
an appalling defiance of danger. And outside, and
around this forbidden meeting, they could feel
the listening melancholy of Stamboul wrapped in
winter fog, the wordless disapproval of a quarter
full of mosques and tombs.

They amused themselves by treating him as a
pasha, and danced before him — a dance like that
of their grandmothers in the plains of Karadjemir,
very chaste and slow, with much waving of bare
arms, to an Asiatic pastoral air played upon a lute
by one of the veiled women, in the gloom at the
end of the room. Lithe, gay, and affecting lan-
guishing airs, they were in these costumes purely
oriental — these three over-cultured little persons
with eager, anxious spirits that had pondered over
Kant and Schopenhauer.

'Why are you not gay to-day?' asked Djenan
of André in a low voice. 'Does this bore you —
this that we arranged for you?'

'On the contrary, you enchant me. But I shall never again see anything so rare and exquisite. No — I will tell you what saddens me when these ladies in black are gone. It may perhaps make you a little anxious, but at least I am sure that it will not distress you.'

The black ladies did not stay long. Among those invited — who were all revolutionary it need not be said — André, as soon as they began to talk, recognised the voices of the two girls who had come one day to Sultan Selim, those who had a French grandmother and dreamed of flight and escape. Melek implored them to raise their veils out of bravado, in defiance of tyranny; but they refused, saying with a light laugh: 'But it took six months to persuade you to lift yours!'

There was also a woman, apparently young, who spoke French like a Parisian, and who was enthusiastic about the book promised by André Lhéry. She asked him:

'You intend, I suppose — and that is what we desire — to show the Turkish woman at the point she has now reached in her evolution? Well, then — if you will forgive an ignorant little oriental for offering an opinion to André Lhéry — if you write a quite impersonal romance with a heroine or a group of heroines as the central interest, do you not run the risk of ceasing to be the impulsive writer we all delighted in? Could it not be rather a sort of sequel to *Medjeh* — your return to the East after the lapse of years?'

'I said exactly the same thing,' exclaimed Djenan. 'But it was so badly received that I hardly dare again explain my humble ideas about the book.'

'Badly received, yes,' he replied, laughing. 'But did I not promise, nevertheless, that, short of putting myself on the stage, I would write exactly whatever you wished? On the contrary; explain to me fully what your ideas are, now on the spot, and the spectre ladies who hear us will perhaps consent to contribute theirs.'

'The romance or the idyl of an Eastern woman is always the same,' said the lady who had already spoken. 'There are always numbers of letters and stolen interviews; love, more or less fulfilled, and at the end death; sometimes, but very rarely, an escape. I am speaking, you understand, of a love affair with a foreigner, the only thing of which an educated Eastern woman is capable — a woman of to-day who has learned what lies within her.'

'How unjust to the men of your own race this spirit of revolt has made you!' exclaimed André. 'Only among those known to me I could name some who are more interesting than we are, and more ——'

But Djenan interrupted him: 'Escape, no,' said she; 'only death. And I come back to what I was suggesting the other day to M. Lhéry. Why not choose a form which enables him, without appearing in person, to set forth his own personal impression? For instance, "*a stranger as like him as his brother*,"[1] a man spoilt by life as he has been, a writer much read by women, comes back to Stamboul one day, a place he has loved

---

[1] ' *Un étranger qui me ressemblait comme un frère* ' — (A. de Musset).

in his youth. Does he revive his youth and
enthusiasms? (It is for you to say, M. Lhéry.)
He meets one of us who has once on a time
written to him, like many another poor little thing,
dazzled by his halo. But now, what twenty years
ago would have been love, is no more than artistic
and curious interest. You understand, I should
not make him a "man of destiny" — they have
gone out of fashion since 1830, but merely an
artist who is amused by every new and rare impression. So he accepts several successive assigna-
tions because they are dangerous and unheard of.
Then what can come of them if not love? But
for her, not for him. He is a mere dilettante, and
sees nothing in the whole business but just an
adventure.'

'Nay!' she suddenly exclaimed, rising with
childish irritation. 'You all sit there listening to
me, and making me speechify like a blue-stocking.
I am making myself ridiculous! I will dance
sooner — another of my village dances; I am an
odalisque, and that will beseem me better.
Chahendeh, will you be so kind as to play the
Ronde des Pastoures that we were practising when
M. Lhéry came in, you know?'

And she tried to take her two sisters by the
hand to dance with her. But every one protested,
and demanded the end of the argument. To
make her sit down they all tried to drag her, the
two houris in spangles, as well as the phantoms in
black.

'Now, you frighten me,' she said; 'really, you
tease me! The end of the story? But it was

finished, it seems to me. Did we not agree just now that for a Moslem woman love has no issue but escape or death? Well, then? My heroine, mine, is far too proud to fly with a foreigner. She must then die; not directly of her love for the man, but, if you like, of the inflexible demands of harem life, which give her no chance of finding consolation in action for her love and dream.'

André watched her while she spoke. Her appearance to-day, as an odalisque in this century-old finery, made her language seem yet more incongruous; her dark sea-green eyes were resolutely fixed on the old ceiling with its complicated arabesques, and she poured out the words with the impersonality of a speaker inventing a pleasing tale but who had no interest in the matter. She was unfathomable!

Presently, when the black ladies had left, she came up to him, quite simple and confiding, like a contented little comrade.

'Now, they are gone. What is the matter?'

'The matter — with me? Your cousins may hear, I suppose?'

'Certainly,' said she, half offended; 'what secrets can we have from them — you and I? Have I not told you from the very first that we three must always be for you but one soul?'

'Well, then, the matter is that as I gaze at you I am bewitched and almost terrified by a likeness I see. Even the other day, when you just lifted your veil for the first time, did you not see me start and shrink back? I saw the same oval face, the same look, the same eyebrows, which she,

however, used to join with a touch of henna. But
I did not then see your hair, which you are showing me to-day, just like hers, in plaits as she used
to wear hers.'

She answered very gravely.

'I am like your Nedjibeh. I! — Ah, it startles
me as much as it does you, believe me. When I tell
you, André, that for five or six years that has been
my fondest dream ——'

They gazed at each other, dumb in each other's
presence. Djenan's eyebrows were a little raised,
as if to open her eyes the wider, and he saw the
gleam of her deep-sea eyes; while the two others in
the harem, where early twilight was creeping on,
stood apart, respecting this melancholy contemplation.

'Stay where you are, André, and do not move,'
she suddenly exclaimed. 'And you two, come
and look at him — at our friend. Standing so, in
this light, would you not think he was hardly
thirty?'

To him, who had quite forgotten his age, as
sometimes happened, and who at that moment had
been feeling, fancying, that he was young again,
this was a cruel blow, reminding him that he was
now in the decline of life, and that that is the
irretrievable descent whence no energy can ever
mount again. 'What am I doing,' he asked himself, 'mixing myself up with these strange little
beings who are youth incarnate? Innocent as it
may be, the adventure into which they have
beguiled me is no mere adventure to me.'

He went away, taking leave more coldly than

s

usual, perhaps, to return, so lonely, through the
vast city where the autumn day was dying. He
had to pass through who knows how many different
quarters and different crowds, through streets that
went up and streets that went down, and across an
arm of the sea, before reaching his temporary
home on the highest point of Pera, which seemed
to him more odious and empty than ever in the
late dusk.

And why was there no light in his room, no
fire ? He called for the Turkish servants whose
duty it was to attend to it. His French valet,
hastening to do their work, came in, throwing up
his hands : 'They are all gone to the great festival.
The Turkish carnival begins this evening; impossible to stop them !'

To be sure; he had forgotten. It was the 8th
of November, corresponding that year with the
beginning of the month of Ramazan, during which
Moslems fast rigidly during the day, but fill the
night with barbaric rejoicings and illuminations.
He went to one of his windows overlooking
Stamboul, to see whether the fairy-like scene he
remembered in his young days a quarter of a
century before was repeated in the year 1322 of
the Hegira. Ah, yes, there it was; nothing was
changed — the matchless mass of the city in the
dim obscurity was beginning to sparkle at distant
points, and then was rapidly lighted up everywhere
at once. All the minarets displayed their double
or triple crowns of lamps, and looked like gigantic
shafts of shadow crossed by bars of flame at various
heights. Arabic inscriptions became visible above

the mosques, traced in the air, and held up by invisible wires, so that at this distance, through the haze, they seemed made of stars, like constellations. And he remembered that Stamboul, the city of silence all the rest of the year, was during the nights of Ramazan full of music, singing, and dancing; in all the crowds, to be sure, no women were to be seen — not even under their ordinary disguise as spectres, which still is pleasing — since all must be immured at sunset behind their window-bars; but there would be a thousand costumes from different parts of Asia, and narghilehs, and old theatres, and puppet-shows, and shadow figures. Add to this that the Perote element, partly from fear of blows and partly from stupid misapprehension, would be conspicuously absent. So, forgetting once more the tale of his years, which had saddened him so deeply just before, he put on his fez, and, like his Turkish servants, went off to the city of light on the other side of the water to keep the Eastern feast.

XXXI

THE 12th of November, the 4th of Ramazan, was at last the day of their visit together to Nedjibeh's tomb. It had been planned some months since, but it was certainly one of their most perilous undertakings; in fact, it had been put off by reason of its difficulty, and its requiring so many hours of truancy, the cemetery being a long way off.

The evening before, Djenan, in writing to him, had said: 'It is so fine and blue to-day that I hope to-morrow, too, will smile upon us.' André, indeed, had always thought of this pilgrimage as being accomplished in one of those still and heady days in November when the sun of Stamboul lends as a surprise a hothouse warmth, gives an illusion of summer, and, as it sets, turns the whole city rose colour, then, at the hour of Moghreb, lights up the coast of Asia opposite with a yet ruddier flush, for a moment only before night brings down with it the chill from the north.

But no. When he opened his shutters in the morning he saw a black and cloudy sky; the wind was blowing a gale, with no hope of a lull. And he knew that at the same hour the pretty eyes of his cloistered friends were in the same way questioning the weather, anxiously gazing through their latticed windows.

However, there was no question as to going; the whole thing had cost infinite pains to arrange, with the help of accomplices, paid and unpaid, who might not again be available. At the appointed hour, half-past one, he betook himself to Stamboul, in a fez and his rosary in his hand, to Sultan Fatih, in front of the house where four days before they had figured as odalisques. He found them ready, all in black, impenetrably veiled. Chahendeh Hanum, the unknown mistress of the house, had wished to join them, so here were four rather excited spectres, rather tremulous at the daring of their proceedings. André, who would have to do the talking on the road, either with the drivers, or, in the event of some unexpected meeting, was a little anxious about his Turkish, his possible hesitancy and foreign accent, for the stake was serious.

'You must have a Turkish name,' they said, 'in case we need to address you.'

'Well,' said he, 'call me Arif without further ado. Of old I used to amuse myself by taking the name of Arif Effendi; by this time I may be promoted — I am Arif Bey.'

A minute later they were walking together in the street, an unheard-of thing in Stamboul, the foreigner and the four Moslem ladies, Arif Bey and his harem. The unrelenting wind brought up blacker and blacker clouds, and was chill with freezing mist; they were shivering with cold. Melek alone kept up her spirits and addressed her friend as *Iki gheuzoum Beyim Effendim* (*Monsieur*

the Bey my two eyes, a common form meaning
'As dear to me as my sight.') But André was
disturbed by her gaiety, for the face of the dead
girl haunted him persistently that day, as if it
were held before him.

On reaching the stand of carriages for hire
they took two, one for the Bey and one for his
four ladies, propriety not allowing a man to ride
in the same carriage with the women of his harem.

It was a long drive, one behind the other,
through the old fanatical quarters of the town,
before they at last left the walls behind them and
reached the funereal solitude, the vast graveyards,
full of ravens at this season, under the black
cypress trees.

Between the Adrianople gate and Eyoub, under
the huge Byzantine walls, they had to get out of
the carriages, for the road, once paved, is no
longer possible. On foot they followed the line
of the ruined ramparts for a short way; through
gaps and breeches they could now and then get
glimpses of Stamboul as if to impress more deeply
on the mind a sense of Islam, here exclusively
predominant: at a less or greater distance a
lordly mosque, or many domes piled up into a
pyramid, or minarets rising from the earth like
groups of spindles, all white against the inky sky.

And this scene of impressive desolation through
which André was now making his way with the
four black-veiled women, was the very same as
when he and Nedjibeh, a quarter of a century
since, had taken their only walk by daylight;
here it was that, young and absorbed in each

other, they had dared to come like two children defying danger; here they had once lingered in the pale winter sunshine to listen to a poor little misguided tomtit singing in a cypress, thinking it was spring; here that, under their very eyes, a little Greek girl had been buried — a face of wax. And more than a quarter of a century had passed over these trivial things, so unique, nevertheless, in their two lives, so ineradicable from the memory of the one who was still living.

They presently left the path under these ancient walls, and plunged into the realm of the dead under an unusually gloomy November sky, among the cypresses and the endless company of tombs. The Russian blast did not spare them, lashing their faces and soaking them with icy vapour. The ravens fled before them, hopping leisurely away.

The slabs of stone over Nedjibeh's tomb came in sight, still very white; and André pointed them out to his companions. The inscriptions, regilt in the spring, still shone brightly new.

And at a short distance from these humble headstones the four gentle spectres spontaneously stood still and began to pray — in the consecrated Moslem attitude with both hands held out open, as if asking a gift — to pray fervently for the soul of the dead. To André this act was so unexpected and so touching that he felt his eyes suddenly blinded by tears, and for fear of betraying himself, he, who had no prayer to offer up, stood a little way off.

He had realised what had seemed such an impossible dream; he had restored this tomb

and placed it in the keeping of other Turkish
women, capable of respecting it and caring for
it. The marble slabs were there, upright and
quite firm, with their fresh gilding; the Turkish
women too were there, like fairies of remembrance
brought round this poor, long-neglected, little
grave, and here was he with them in close communion of reverence and pity.

When they had recited the *fathia* they went
forward to read the shining inscription. First
the Arabic verses beginning at the top of the
stone and sloping downwards. And then, quite
at the bottom, the name and date: 'Pray for
the soul of Nedjibeh Hanum, daughter of Ali
Djianghir Effendi, who died the 18th of Muharrem
1297.' The Circassians, unlike the Turks, use a
patronymic or rather a tribal name; and here
Djenan learnt with deep emotion the name
of Nedjibeh's family. 'Why,' said she, 'the
Djianghirs live in my village. They came
originally from the Caucasus with my ancestors;
they have lived close to us for two hundred
years.' This accounted more clearly for their
resemblance, which indeed would have been
surprising merely as a matter of race; there
was no doubt a tie of blood through the caprice
of some prince in past days. What mysterious
ancestor was he who, himself long since dust,
had bequeathed through who knows how many
generations, to two women of such different rank
those rare and lovely eyes?

The cold was deadly there in the cemetery,
where they had been for some few minutes stand-

ing still; and suddenly Zeyneb's chest, under the
black shroud, was shaken by a fearful fit of
coughing. 'Let us go!' said André in dismay.
'For pity's sake let us go, and walk very fast.'
Before leaving, each of them must need pick up
one of the cypress-twigs which were strewn on the
tomb; and when Melek, whose veils were always
the thinnest, stooped to pick one up he could see
that her eyes were full of tears, and he forgave
her wholly for her levity just now in the street.

On reaching the carriages they separated, so
as not needlessly to prolong the peril of being
together. After they had promised to give him
the earliest possible information of their safe
arrival at the harem, for he was a little uneasy
now the day was closing in, he went off towards
Eyoub, while their driver took them to the
Adrianople gate.

It was now six o'clock. André went home
to Pera. Such an ominous evening! Looking
through his window-panes he watched the vast
panorama sink into the night, and it gave him
one of the most painful reminiscences he had
ever experienced of the Constantinople of old,
the Constantinople of his youth. Darkness had
followed the twilight, but it was not yet the
hour when the minarets light up their crowns
of fire for the fairy-like illumination of a night
in Ramazan; as yet they were scarcely visible, a
darker grey against the grey, scarcely paler, of
the sky. Stamboul, as had often happened, was
a mass as misty and blurred as he had seen it in

his dreams in past years on distant voyages. But on the furthest horizon in the west, there was a sort of black fringe rather clearly cut out against a rosy streak that lingered there, the last reflection of the vanished sun. A black fringe: the cypresses of the great cemeteries. And he was thinking as he fixed his eyes on it: 'She is sleeping in the heart of that immeasurable silence and loneliness, under those humble marble slabs which I have had restored and regilt out of tender pity.'

Yes, yes; the tomb was repaired and entrusted to Moslem women whose pious care might extend over some years yet, for they were young. But afterwards? Could this preserve that period of his life, that memory of youth and love, from falling all too soon into the gulf of rolling years and things forgotten of all men? Indeed, the cemeteries themselves, though so old and venerated, what hope of perpetuity had they? When Islam, threatened on all sides, should be driven back on Asia, what would the newcomers do with this overpowering tract of ancient tombs? Then Nedjibeh's headstone would disappear with so many thousand others.

And now it seemed to him that the mere fact of having accomplished this long-deferred duty, of having paid his debt as it were to the dead, had broken the last tie to the beloved past. Everything was more than ever irrevocably ended.

There were a dinner and ball that evening at the English Embassy, at which he was bound to appear. It would soon be time to dress. His

servant was lighting the lamps and laying out
his clothes. This, after his visit to the cypress-
wood with the Turkish ladies in their black
tcharchafs — what a complete antagonism of
period, of atmosphere, of ideas!

As he turned from the window to go to dress
he saw snowflakes beginning to fall. It was snow-
ing out there, on the vast solitude of the graves.

Next morning he received the letter he had
begged for from his friends to give him news of
their safe return.

4th Ramazan, 9 in the evening.

'We reached home safe and sound, friend
André, but not without tribulation. It was very
late, the last limit of the permitted hour, and then
one of my companions carelessly cut herself. This
was explained, but as it is the old ladies of the house
and the old uncles are suspicious.

'Thank you with all our hearts for the trust
you have shown in us. That tomb now in some
degree belongs to us, does it not? And we shall
often go to pray there when you have quitted our
land.

'This evening I feel you so far from me, and
yet you are so near! I can see from my
window, over there on the heights of Pera, the
lights in the rooms of the Embassy where you are,
and I wonder how you can bear to amuse yourself
when we are so sad. You will think me very
exacting — and so indeed I am, but it is not
for myself but for *her*.

'You at this moment are gay, no doubt, surrounded by women and flowers, your mind and
eyes delighted. And we, in a harem, barely
lighted, warm but very gloomy, we are weeping.

'We are weeping for our own life. Ah! how
dreary and empty it is this evening! This evening
more than on other evenings. Is it the feeling
that you are so near and so remote that makes us
more miserable?   DJENAN.'

'And I, Melek, do you know what I have got
to say to you? How can you be enjoying yourself, when we, before these sprays fallen from a
cypress tree, are shedding tears? There they lie,
in a holy box of wood from Mecca; they have a
sharp damp smell — penetrating, depressing. You
know, I am sure, from whence we brought them.

'Oh! how can you bear to be at a ball this
evening and forget the sorrows you have created,
the lives you have marred on your road. I
cannot conceive that you are not thinking of
these things, when we, your foreign and far-off
sisters, are weeping over them.   MELEK.'

XXXII

THEY had warned him that Ramazan would imprison them more closely, by reason of many prayers, sacred studies, and the long daily fast; and especially of the excitement and bustle of the evening, which assumes peculiar importance, during this lenten month; grand dinners are given called *iftars*, to which large parties are invited to make up for the abstinence of the day.

But, on the contrary, Ramazan seemed to favour their wildest scheme of all, a scheme to shudder at: to receive André Lhéry just once at Kassim Pacha, in Djenan's rooms, two yards away from Madame Husnugul!

Stamboul during the Moslem Lent is unrecognisable. At night fêtes and thousands of lights, streets full of people, mosques crowned with lamps — huge, luminous rings high up in the air, upheld by the minarets which themselves are scarcely visible, so nearly do they match the hue of the night-sky. On the other hand, all the day the world is asleep; the stir of Eastern life comes to a standstill, the shops are shut; in the endless little coffee-booths, which, as a rule, are never empty, no narghilehs, no gossip, only a few sleepers stretched on benches, their faces worn by

long nights and fasting by day. And in the
houses, till sundown the same exhaustion as outside. In Djenan's home especially, where the
servants were as old as their masters, all the
world slumbered, the beardless negroes, and
the moustachioed guards with pistols in their
belts.

On the 12th of Ramazan, the day fixed for
this visit, the grandmother and great uncles, con-
veniently indisposed, kept their rooms, and by
unhoped-for good-luck Madame Husnugul had
for two days been confined to bed by indigestion
brought on by an *iftar*.

André was to arrive at two o'clock, to the
minute, to the second; he was to creep close
under the wall so as not to be seen from the
overhanging windows, and not to venture so far
as the great door unless he saw through a lattice
on the first floor the corner of a white handkerchief — the usual token.

This time he really was alarmed; alarmed for
them and alarmed for himself, not of the immediate danger, but of the universal European scandal
which would ensue if he were caught in the fact.
He approached cautiously, keenly on the lookout.
There were favouring circumstances; there was
no house opposite that of Djenan, which, like its
neighbours, looked out over the great cemetery on
that shore; in front of it was nothing but old
cypress trees and tombs; no eye could spy them
from that side, and this wilderness was wrapped
to-day in November fog.

The white signal was displayed; no retreat was

now possible. He went in, like a man flinging
himself head foremost into an abyss — into a
monumental vestibule in the old style, empty
now of its gilt and armed doorkeepers. Only
Melek, in a black tcharchaf, behind the door,
who exclaimed with her saucy laugh, 'Quick!
quick! Run!'

They went upstairs together four steps at a
time, flew like the wind down the long passages,
and rushed into Djenan's room, who awaited them
with a beating heart and double-locked the door
on them all.

Then came a burst of laughter; their schoolboy laughter, which they flung out as a call of
defiance to all and each whenever some new peril
was safely overpast. And Djenan, with a droll
air of triumph, exhibited the key in her hand; a
key, a lock! What a revolutionary innovation
in a harem. She had acquired it yesterday, it
seemed, and could not get over such a success.
She and Zeyneb, and even Melek, who hastily removed her tcharchaf, were paler than usual, a
consequence of their strict fast. And André saw
them under an aspect quite new to him, for he
had never seen them excepting as odalisques, or
as spectres. They were elegantly dressed as
very fashionable European ladies; the only detail
which gave them still an Eastern touch was
that very small Circassian scarves of white and
silver gauze covered their hair and fell to their
shoulders.

'I thought that you wore no veil at all indoors,' said André.

'Yes, yes always.   But only these small scarves.'

They first took him into the music-room, where they found three more ladies invited to this dangerous meeting. Mademoiselle Bonneau de Saint-Miron, Mademoiselle Tardieu, formerly governess to Melek, and a spectre-lady Ubeydeh Hanum, diplomée of the Normal College, Professor of Philosophy at the school for girls in a town of Asia Minor. Not at all easy were the two Frenchwomen, who had for a long time hesitated between the temptation and the terrors of this visit. Mademoiselle de Saint-Miron, indeed, had quite the appearance of a person who is saying to herself: 'I, alas ! was the first cause of this preposterous disaster ! André Lhéry in my pupil's rooms !'

They talked, however, for they were dying to talk, and it struck André that their minds were both lofty and artless — almost old maids as they both were.   Ladies, too, and very highly educated, but excitably romantic, in a way quite out of date in 1904. They thought they might venture to talk to him of his book, of which they had heard the title and which interested them greatly.

'Several pages of *Désenchantées* are already written, I suppose ?'

'Dear me, no !' said he, laughing. 'Not one.'

'And I am glad of it,' said Djenan, whose voice always surprised André like some super-terrestrial music, even after hearing other voices that were sweet and low. 'You will write that book when you are gone away; then it will at least serve as a bond between us for some months.

When you need some information you will remember to write to us.'

André, thinking that he ought out of politeness
to address some remark to the veiled lady, asked
her in the most commonplace fashion if she was
satisfied with the little Asiatic Turks, her girl-
pupils. He expected some schoolmistress's reply
as obvious as his question. But he was little prepared for what the grave, soft voice said from
behind the veil, in excellent French.

'Too well satisfied, alas! They learn only too
quickly, and are too intelligent. I am sorry to be
one of the instruments to inoculate these women
of the future with the microbe of suffering. I
grieve for all these blossoms, which will fade even
quicker than their simple-minded grandmothers
did.'

Then they discussed Ramazan. The whole
day of fasting, spent, of course, in work for the
poor and pious reading; in the course of this
lunar month a Moslem woman must read her
Koran through without missing a line, and they
had no wish to fail in the task, for, in spite of
subversive and infidel notions, they all venerated
and admired the sacred Book of Islam, and their
Korans were there, with green ribbon markers in
the chapter for the day.

Then after sunset comes the *iftar*. That for
the men in the selamlik, followed by prayer, for
which guests, masters, and serving-men meet
together in the large room, each kneeling on his
carpet with the *mirhab*. In this house, it seemed,
the prayer was chanted every evening by one of

T

the gardeners, the only young man of them all, whose sweet, muezzin-like voice filled the house.

In the harem, the women's *iftar*.

'These meetings of young Turkish women,' said Zeyneb, 'rarely become frivolous in Ramazan, when mysticism has its sway in the depths of our soul; the questions we discuss are those of living and dying. We always begin with the same ardour, the same eagerness; and always end with the same dejection, the same despair, which come over us when, after two hours of discussing every dogma and every philosophy, we come back to the same point and the consciousness of being mere feeble, impotent, helpless creatures! Still, hope is so persistent a feeling that, in spite of the failure of every effort, we still have energy enough to start again on the following day on a new road that may lead perhaps to the unapproachable goal.'

'We young Turkish women,' added Melek, 'are a handful of the seed of a very evil plant, which germinates, survives, and propagates in spite of drought and frost, and even of constant cutting back.'

'True,' said Djenan, 'but we may be divided into two species. Those who, to avoid death, seize every opportunity of diverting their thoughts and forgetting. And those, of finer temper, who take refuge in charity, as, for instance, our cousin Djavideh; I doubt whether among you the Little Sisters of the Poor do more good than she does, or with greater self-sacrifice; and there are many in our harems who do the same. They are, it is true, obliged to do good in secret, and as to

forming benevolent associations, that is absolutely
prohibited, for our masters disapprove of any contact with the women of the lower orders, for fear
lest we should inoculate them with our pessimism,
our eccentricities, and our doubts.'

Melek, whose speciality was inconsequent inter-
ruption, proposed to André to try his hiding-place
in case of any great alarm; it was in a corner,
behind an easel draped with brocade and sup-
porting a picture. 'An excess of precaution,' she
added, 'for nothing will happen. The only active
member of the family at this moment is my father,
and he will not leave Yildiz till gun-fire at the
hour of Moghreb.'

'Well, but after all,' objected André, 'if something unforeseen should bring him home earlier?'

'No one enters a harem unannounced. We
should tell him that a Turkish lady was paying us
a visit, Ubeydeh Hanum, and he would not dream
of coming across our threshold. As easy as lying
— if you know how to manage. No, there is
really nothing to be thought of but your departure
by and by; that will be a delicate matter.'

The piano was strewn with the manuscript
music of a nocturne Djenan had been compos-
ing, and André longed to hear her play it, for
he had never heard her but from a distance when
passing under her windows at night on the Bosphorus. But in Ramazan they hardly dared to
have any music, and then, it would be too im-
prudent to rouse the great sleeping household,
when their slumbers at this moment were so
indispensably necessary.

Djenan's great wish was that her friend should
for once sit down to write at her little writing-table
— that of her girlhood, on which long ago, when
he was to her but a figure in a dream, she had
scribbled her diary while thinking of him.   So they
led him into the large white room where everything
was luxuriously modern.   They made him look
with them through the ever closed chequered
lattice of the windows, at the view familiar to
them from their childhood, and in front of which,
no doubt, a slow, grey old age would gradually
extinguish them — cypress-trees and tombstones
— tombstones of every degree of antiquity; below,
as at the bottom of a precipice, the Golden Horn,
dull and grey to-day like a sheet of lead, and
Stamboul on the other side, drowned in wintry
mist.   He was invited to look, too, through the
unshuttered windows on the inner side, at the old
high-walled garden which Djenan had described
in her letters.   'A garden so deserted,' she had
told him, 'that I can wander there unveiled.   And,
besides, whenever we go into it our negroes are
there to warn off the gardeners.'

In fact, in the distance, where the plane-trees
mingled their enormous leafless boughs, now for-
lornly grey, the place looked like an imprisoned
forest; they certainly might walk there unperceived
by any living being.

André blessed the happy audacity which enabled
him to see, to be acquainted with this home, forbidden to his eyes.   Poor little friends of a few
months, met with so late in his wandering life, and
from whom he must inevitably part for ever!   At

any rate, henceforth, whenever he thought of them, the scene and setting of their sequestered lives would be clear in his memory.

It was now time for him to leave, the perilous hour. Among them André had almost forgotten the strangeness of the situation; but now that he had to get out again he realised once more that he had ventured his skin in a rat-trap, of which the passage, when once he was in, had narrowed and was beset with spikes.

They made several rounds of inspection. All was well; the only person in the way was a certain negro named Yussuf, who persisted in guarding the entrance hall. It was necessary to devise for him a long and urgent message.

'I have it!' Melek presently exclaimed. 'Go into your hiding-place, André. We will bring him into the room, that will crown all!'

And when he came in:

'My good Yussuf,' said she, 'I want this message done really in a hurry. Go at once to Pera and get us a new book. I will write the name on a card; if you must, try every book-shop in the high street, but on no account return without it.'

And this was what she wrote: '*Disenchanted*, the latest novel by André Lhéry.'

One more round of inspection in the passages, after sending orders to one and another to employ them elsewhere; then, taking André by the hand, she dragged him off at a wild run, and rather nervously pushed him out.

He went away, creeping closer than ever under

the old walls, and wondering whether the door, perhaps too audibly shut, might not open again to emit a troop of negroes rushing in pursuit with sticks and revolvers.

The next day they confessed their untruth in the matter of the little Circassian veils.   They never wore them in the house.   But to a Moslem woman it is even more unseemly to let a man see all her hair, and especially the nape of her neck, than to show him her face, and they could not make up their mind to it.

XXXIII

DJENAN TO ANDRÉ

14th Ramazan 1322 (*November* 22, 1904).
'OUR Friend, to-morrow, you know, is Mid-
Ramazan, and Turkish ladies take an outing.
Will you come between two and four o'clock to
the promenade on the Stamboul side, from Bayazid
to Chazadeh Bacheh?

'We are very busy just now with our *iftars*, but
we will ere long arrange a fine expedition together
on the Asiatic shore; the scheme is Melek's, and
you will know how well it is planned.   DJENAN.'

On that morrow the wind was from the south,
there was bright autumn sunshine and a heady
sense of warmth and light — perfect weather for
the veiled fair who have only two or three days
of such liberty in the year.   Their 'outing,' of
course, was in a closed carriage, with an eunuch on
the box by the driver; but they were allowed to
draw up the blinds and let down the windows, and
to remain stationary quite a long time to look at
others, which on ordinary days is forbidden.

From Bayazid to Chazadeh Bacheh is a distance

of more than half a mile, in the heart of Stamboul
and the most Turkish quarter, along old-world
streets, by colossal mosques and shady gardens of
the dead, and sacred fountains. In these usually
silent thoroughfares, ill-suited to modern fashion,
what an anachronism are these lines of carriages
meeting there on the day of Mid-Ramazan. In
hundreds! Coupés and landaus, standing still or
creeping slowly along; they had come from every
part of the vast city, even from the palaces built
on the slopes by the Bosphorus. And in them
none but women, very much dressed, in yashmaks
veiling them to the eyes but transparent enough to
reveal the rest of the face, all the beauties of the
harems almost visible to-day as an exception, pink
and white Circassians and pale Turkish brunettes.
Very few men hung round these open carriage
windows, and not one European, for across the
bridges, at Pera, no one ever knows what is going
on at Stamboul.

André looked about for his three friends, who,
it would seem, had dressed themselves very hand-
somely, to please him; he sought them a long
time but failed to find them, there was such a
crowd. At the hour when the ladies all turned
to go back to the jealous harem, he went away,
rather disappointed; but after meeting so many
bright eyes, radiant with the enjoyment of such a
delightful day, and expressing such artless pleasure
in having for once in a way been allowed to look
about them out of doors, he understood better
than ever before the deadly dulness of their
cloistered life.

XXXIV

The three sisters knew of a little lonely strand on the shore of the sea of Marmora, quite sheltered, they said, from the desolating wind of the Bosphorus, and as warm as an orangery. One of their friends dwelt in the neighbourhood, and undertook to provide a probable *alibi* by declaring stoutly that she had detained them with her all day. So they had decided on going there to try for a last walk together before the coming separation, which might be the fatal, final one. André was ere long to take a two months' holiday in France; Djenan was going with her grandmother to spend the cold season on her estate at Bounar Bashi. They could not meet again till the following spring, and between this and then so much might happen!

Sunday, December 12, 1904, the day chosen for this excursion, after endless plotting and planning, happened again to be one of those days of glory which in that uncertain climate come suddenly in mid-winter, bringing back the summer between two snowstorms. They met on the bridge over the Golden Horn, whence the little steamers start for the Asiatic shore, in the blaze of noon, but without a sign — passers-by that knew not each other; and as if by chance they took the same boat, where, after dismissing their negroes and negresses, the three demurely took their seats in the harem-cabin reserved for Moslem women.

The fine sunshine had brought out throngs of passengers, going to air themselves on the opposite shore. There were above fifty spectre ladies who embarked at the same time, and when they reached the landing-place at Scutari, André lost himself among all the black veils which got off there, and, on a false scent, followed three ladies whom he did not know; this might have led to a terrible disaster, but, fortunately, there was something in their figures less elegant than his trio of friends, who had lingered behind, and in great dismay he left them at the first cross-roads and rejoined his three friends — the right ladies, this time.

They hired a carriage for all four, which is permissible in the country. He, as the Bey, took the best seat, quite contrary to our European notions. Djenan was beside him, Zeyneb and Melek opposite. And the horses once off at a round pace, they laughed with glee under their veils at the trick so successfully played, at the freedom they had achieved till the evening, at their own youth, and the fine weather and deep blue sea and sky. They were, in fact, often adorably gay and childlike, between their gloomy fits; even Zeyneb, who would forget her malady and her wish to die. It was with smiling defiance that they risked everything — perpetual confinement, exile, or, perhaps, some even severer penalty.

As they went on by the shore of Marmora, the keen draught down the Bosphorus was less perceptible. Their little inlet was remote, but bathed in tempered air as they had promised, and so peaceful in its solitude, so reassuring, so absolutely forgotten! It opened due south, and a miniature cliff encircled it like a screen made on purpose. On the fine sand they felt themselves at home, sheltered from prying eyes as effectually as in the walled garden of a harem. Nothing could be seen but the sea of Marmora without a wrinkle, not a ship in sight, and beyond, on the further horizon, the outline of the mountains of Asia. Marmora as absolutely still as on the fine calm days of September, but perhaps too pallidly blue, for its sheen, in spite of the sun, had the sadness of winter; it was like a pool of melted silver slowly cooling. And the distant mountains yonder had already caps of dazzling snow.

As they mounted the little cliff they saw no living soul, nor on the bare and desolate plain all round. So all three, raising their veils as high as their hair, drew deep breaths of fresh air; never till now had André seen their young faces, a little colourless, in the sunshine and free air; never before had they felt themselves in such perfect security together — in spite of the mad risk of the expedition, and the dangers of their return in the evening.

First of all they sat down on the ground to eat some bonbons bought of the fashionable confectioner in Stamboul. And then they pried into every nook of the pretty little bay, their

secret shelter for this afternoon. A wonderful
combination of circumstances, determination, and
audacity had met to this end — in this unusually
sunny December day, almost ominous by dint of
being so lovely, and furtively slipped in between
two days of Russian wind — to bring together
visitors from such dissimilar worlds, whose origin
would have seemed to decree that they should
never meet. André, as he looked at the eyes and
mouth of Djenan, who was to start the next day
but one to go to her palace in Macedonia, understood how much this hour held that was rare and
irrecoverable: the impossibilities that had been
overcome before they could meet here by the pale
wintry sea would be the same again to-morrow and
for ever. Who could tell? They might even never
meet again, at any rate in such security and with
such a light heart. It was an hour in a lifetime,
to be remembered, graven, preserved as far as was
possible from being ever forgotten.

They took it in turn to go to the top of the
little cliff and signal any danger from afar. And
once the sentinel, who happened to be Zeyneb,
announced the approach of a Turk along the shore,
also accompanied by three ladies with their veils
up. They thought there was no danger here, and
that they might risk the encounter, only they, too,
dropped the black gauze over their faces. When
the Turk passed, no doubt some genuine Bey with
the ladies of his harem, his ladies also dropped
their veils before André; but the two men looked
carelessly at each other without suspicion on either
part; the new-comer had at once supposed the

party he found in the bay to be all members of
one family.

Some flat pebbles, that might have been
made on purpose, laid by the quiet waters in a
neat line on the sand, suddenly reminded André
of a game of his childhood; he showed his three
friends how to throw them in such a way as to jump
again from the glassy surface of the sea, and they
set to work eagerly at playing 'ducks and drakes,'
but without success. Ah! how childlike and
merry and simple they were that day, these complicated little souls! Especially Djenan, who had
been at such pains to ruin her life.

After this unique hour they went back to the
carriage, which was waiting a long way off, to go
back to Scutari. Then on the boat they were of
course strangers. But during the short passage
they saw once more the wondrous vision of Stamboul in the light of a glowing evening. Stamboul
seen in front of them and in perspective; first the
ferocious battlemented ramparts of the old Seraglio,
its base bathed in the rose-tinted silver of the sea
of Marmora; then, higher up, the maze of cupolas and minarets against a different rose colour.
A wintry rose too, but less silvery, less pallid,
than that of the sea, and golden rather than pink.

XXXV

'Safe! once more safe! We had dreadful difficulties on our return home, but now the household has calmed down. Did you notice how beautiful our Stamboul looked as you arrived?

'To-day rain and melting snow beat on our windows, the icy blast pipes a doleful tune under the doors. How unlucky it would have been if this weather had burst upon us yesterday. Now that our expedition is well over, and we remember it as a beautiful dream, all the tempests of the Black Sea may rave.

'André, we shall not meet again before I leave; circumstances will not allow of our arranging for another meeting in Stamboul. So I am bidding you farewell, probably till the spring. But would you do one thing I ask of you as a favour? A month hence, when you are going to France, since you intend to travel by steamer, take a fez with you, and choose the Salonica route. The vessel stops there for some hours, and I know of a way of meeting you there. One of my negroes will go on board and give you your instructions. Do not refuse me this.

'All happiness go with you, André, to your own
land.   DJENAN.'

After Djenan's departure, André remained five
weeks at Constantinople, where he again saw
Zeyneb and Melek. When the day came for
him to start on his two months' holiday, he went
by the line she had suggested, taking his fez; but
at Salonica no negro made his appearance on board
the vessel. The stay there was to him but a sad
one, being disappointed in this hope — by reason,
too, of the memory of Nedjibeh, which still
haunted this town, and the barren surrounding
mountains. And he had to leave without any
news of his more recent friend.

A few days after arriving in France he received
this letter from Djenan:

> BOUNAR BASHI, near SALONICA,
> *January* 10, 1905.

'When and by whom shall I ever get this
letter posted, watched as I am here?
'You are far away, and who knows when you
will return? My cousins told me of your meeting
and parting, and how sad they have been since you
left. What a strange thing it seems, André,
when you think of it, that there should be beings
whose fate it is to drag sorrow wherever they go;
a sorrow that casts its shadow on all who come
near them. You are one of them, and it is no
fault of yours. You suffer infinitely complicated
griefs — or are they infinitely simple? But you

suffer; the suspension of your soul is always resolved into a chord of pain. Those who come into contact with you hate you or love you. And those who love you suffer with you, through you, for you. You have this year been a sunbeam in the life of your little friends at Constantinople — a transient gleam, but that they knew beforehand. And now they are wretched in the darkness that has again closed round them.

'For my part, perhaps, I may tell you some day what you have been to me. My anguish is not so much because you are gone, as because I ever met you.

'You were annoyed with me, I daresay, for not having arranged a meeting when you stopped at Salonica. The thing would, in fact, have been possible in this country, which is still as deserted as in your Nedjibeh's day. We might have had ten minutes to ourselves, to exchange a few parting words and grasp each other's hand. My grief, indeed, would not have been comforted, on the contrary; for reasons of my own I kept away. But it was no fear of danger that hindered me. No, far from it! If, to go to you, I had known that Death lay in ambush for me on my way back, I should have felt no hesitation or anxiety; I should have gone to you, André, to bid you my heart's farewell as my heart would bid me speak it. We Turkish women of to-day do not fear death. Does not love drive us to death? When has love ever meant life to us?   DJENAN.'

And Melek, to whom this letter was sent to be

forwarded to France, added a few reflections
which had occurred to her.

'By long thinking of you, our friend, I am
sure I have discovered some of the causes of your
sorrows. Oh, I know you by this time, believe
me. In the first place, you want everything to
last for ever, and never wholly enjoy anything
because you are telling yourself "this must end."
Besides, life has given you so much, you have
had so many good things, so many things, one of
which would suffice to make any one else happy,
that you have let them go because you had too
much. Your greatest woe is that too many
women have loved you and have told you so too
often; it has been too much impressed on you
that you were indispensable to the lives in which
you have played a part; you have too constantly
been met on the threshold; you have never had
to make one step in advance on the road of
feeling; you have always sat still and waited!
And now you feel emptiness in and about you,
because you yourself do not love, you only let
yourself be loved. Believe me, love some one in
your turn, never mind whom of your innumerable adorers, and you will see, you will be cured.
                                                        'MELEK.'

Djenan's letter did not satisfy André; he did
not think it spontaneous enough. 'If her affection were so deep,' though he, 'she would have
wished above everything, and in spite of everything, to say good-bye to me, either at Stamboul

U

or at Salonica. This letter is "literature."' He was disappointed in her, his trust in her was shaken, and that tortured him. He forgot that she was an Oriental, more effusive than an European and far more inscrutable.

He was tempted, in replying, to treat her as a child, as he sometimes did: '"A being who drags sorrow after him." I, then, am the very "man of destiny" whom you declared to be out of date since 1830.' But he feared to go too far, and answered quite seriously, telling her that she had wounded him deeply by allowing him to depart thus.

No direct communication was possible with her at Bounar Bashi, in the Palace of the Sleeping Beauty; everything must be sent *via* Stamboul through the hands of Zeyneb or Melek, to say nothing of other accomplices.

At the end of three weeks he received these few lines enclosed by Zeyneb.

'André, how can I wound you by anything I can do or say — I who am nothing as compared with you? Do you not know that all my thoughts, all my affection, are but a humble tribute that you can trample underfoot; a long-worn carpet, still pleasing in design, on which your feet may tread. This is all I am; and can you be angry or offended with me?   DJENAN.'

Here she was purely oriental, and André, charmed and touched, wrote to her at once, and this time in a burst of sweet affection — all the more so because Zeyneb had added: 'Djenan is ill of a nervous fever which makes our grandmother anxious, and the doctor does not know what to think of it.'

Some weeks later Djenan replied in a little note, very short, and as Eastern as the last:

BOUNAR BASHI, *February* 21, 1905.

'I have for many days been asking myself, "Where is the remedy that will cure me?" The remedy has come, and my eyes, which have been growing too large, devoured it. My poor thin fingers now hold it, and I thank you. Thank you for the gift of a little of yourself, for the alms of your thoughts. Bless you for the peace your second letter has brought me.

'I wish you happiness, my friend, in return for the moment of joy you have just bestowed on me. I wish you happiness, sweet and perfect happiness, that may bring joy to your life like a garden of fragrance, like a bright summer morning.

'DJENAN.'

Ill and worn by fever, the poor secluded creature had gone back to her old self on the plain of Karadjemir, had become a child again. And under this aspect, antecedent to the remarkable culture of which she was so proud, André loved her more than ever.

This time again there was a postscript by Melek to Djenan's note. After reproaching him for the rarity of his always too brief letters, she said:

'We admire your busy-ness, and would ask you
how we can set to work to be busy too, absorbed,
overworked, hindered from writing to our friends.
Teach us how, if you please. We, on the contrary, have all the day to write in, for our sins
and your misfortune.   MELEK.'

When, his leave at an end, André returned
to Turkey early in the month of March, 1905,
Stamboul was still wrapped in a mantle of snow,
but the day he arrived was exquisitely blue.
Thousands of gulls and terns whirled round the
vessel he was in. The Bosphorus was covered
with the white birds, like a sort of snow in very
large flakes; crazy, numberless birds, a cloud of
white plumage fluttering in front of a white city, a
marvellous winter scene with the glory of Southern
sunshine.

Zeyneb and Melek, knowing by what boat he
was to arrive, sent him their *Selams* of welcome by
a negro the same evening, and at the same time a
long letter from Djenan, who was well again, they
told him, but would stay for some time yet in her
remote old palace.

Now she had recovered, the little barbarian of
Karadjemir was wilful and complicated once more,
no longer by any means the thing of nought which
her friend might 'trample underfoot.' Oh, no!
She wrote now in a key of rebellion and anger.
In fact, there had already been a good deal of
talk, behind the lattices of many a harem, about the
book André was to write; a young woman, whom
he had scarcely seen, and only under the thickest

of black veils, had boasted, so it was said, of being
a friend of his and the chief inspirer of the intended
work; and Djenan, cloistered so far away, was
raging with rather savage jealousy.

'André, can you understand what a fury of
impotence comes over us when we fancy that any
one can creep in between you and us? And it is
still worse when the rivalry encroaches on what is
our special domain: your memories and impressions of the East. Do you not know, or do you
forget, that we staked our lives, to say nothing of
our peace, solely to give you such impressions of
our country in full completeness; for it was not
even to win your heart; that, we knew, was weary
and closed; no, it was to inspire your sensibility
as an artist, and set before it, if we may so express
it, a sort of half-real dream. To achieve this,
which seemed possible, and to show you what
without us you could only have imagined, we took
the risk, with our eyes open, of planting in our
own souls eternal grief and regret. Do you think
that many Europeans would have done as much?
'There are times when it is torture to think
that other thoughts will come to you that will
drive away your memories of us, that other
impressions will be dearer to you than those of *our*
Turkey, seen with us and through our eyes. And
what I want is that when you have finished this
book you should never write another, that you
should think no more, that your hard, bright eyes
should never soften for any other woman. When
life is too unbearable I tell myself that it will not

last long; and then, if it is possible for souls in freedom to influence the living, my soul will take possession of yours and draw it to itself, so that wherever I may be yours will have to come.

'I would give all of my life that remains to me to read your heart for ten minutes. I long to have the power to make you suffer — *and to know it;* yes, I, who a few months ago would have given that life to make you happy.

'Good God! André, are you so rich in friendship that you waste it so? Is it generous to inflict such misery on one who loves you, and who loves you from so far, with such disinterested devotion? Do not foolishly destroy an affection which, even if it is a little jealous and exacting, is nevertheless the truest perhaps and the deepest you have inspired in all your life.   DJENAN.'

André was greatly disturbed by this letter. The reproaches were childish and inconsistent, since he had no friends among Turkish women but those three. But the whole tone of it jarred. 'There is no mistake this time,' he said to himself. 'This is really a wrong note, a crashing discord in the harmony of sisterly friendships which I so perversely persuaded myself was indestructible. Poor little Djenan! But is it possible?'

He tried to understand the new situation, which seemed to him insolvable. 'It cannot be,' said he to himself; 'it shall never be, because I will not have it. So much for my share in it; so far as I am concerned the matter is settled.' And when a decision is thus formulated it is a great protection

against agitating thoughts and seductive lan-
guishing.

Not that there was any great merit in such a
decision, for he was perfectly convinced that
Djenan, even if she loved him, would always be
inaccessible. He knew the little being who was
at once confiding and reserved, audacious and
immaculate; she was capable of surrendering her
soul from a distance to a friend who, as she
thought, would never deviate from the part of an
elder brother; but she would certainly veil
her face for ever, and remain irrevocably lost, at
the mere hint of a lingering or agitated grasp of
her hand.

The adventure was none the less sinister; and
certain phrases formerly spoken by her, which at
the moment had hardly struck him, recurred to
his mind with ominous resonance: 'The love of a
Moslem woman for a foreigner can have no issue
but in flight or in death.'

Next day, however, in lovely weather, already
almost spring, things looked altogether less serious.
As before, he reflected that this letter was 'literature,' probably to no small extent, and above all
full of oriental exaggeration. But, in fact, for
some years past, a woman, to convince him that
she loved him, had to prove it by substantial
evidence, so perpetually present to him was the
sum of his years — a cruel obsession.

His heart was lighter than it had been yesterday, and he went off in better spirits to Stamboul,
where Zeyneb and Melek, whom he longed to see

again, awaited him at Sultan Selim. Stamboul, always differently magnificent at a distance, was on that day a pitiable spectacle seen close at hand, in the damp and mud of the rapid thaw; and in the blind alley where stood the house of their meetings, there were still patches of snow in the shade under the wall.

They received him with their veils raised in the humble little harem, where it was very cold, and they were eager and affectionate, as to an older brother returned from a foreign journey. But he was at once struck by their altered appearance. Zeyneb's face, still exquisitely refined and chiselled, had a waxen pallor, her eyes were larger, and her lips colourless; the winter, which had been exceptionally severe, had no doubt aggravated the malady she scorned to nurse. As to Melek, pale too, with an anxious furrow on her brow, she was evidently concentrated, almost tragical, suddenly matured and ready for a supreme effort of rebellion. 'They want to make me marry again!' she said bitterly, without another word in reply to the wordless questions she read in André's eyes.

'And you?' he asked Zeyneb.

'I? Oh, I have my deliverance under my hand,' she replied, touching her chest, shaken now and then by an ominous little cough.

Both were much excited about Djenan's letter, which had passed through their hands only the day before, and which had been sealed, an unprecedented thing among them, for they had never had any secrets.

'What can she have had to say to you?'

'Oh, nothing. Childish reproaches. Some absurd harem gossip which had upset her without reason.'

'Ah, this new talk of some one who has inspired your book, who has risen up apart from us?'

'Exactly that. And it is absolutely without foundation, I assure you, for besides you three, and one or two veiled figures to whom you yourselves introduced me ———'

'We never believed it, my sister and I. But so far away from everything, in such seclusion — what can you expect? Your brain works ———'

'And hers has worked so effectually that she is seriously vexed with me.'

'It is not a deadly hatred, at any rate,' Melek put in. 'At least it would not seem so. See here, what she wrote to me this morning.' And she held out part of a letter, after folding back the lower portion, which, no doubt, he was not to read.

'Tell him I constantly think of him, and to remember him is the only joy in my life. I envy you every minute you spend with him and all of his presence he bestows on you; I envy you for being so near him, for seeing his face, for grasping his hand. Do not forget me when you are together; I demand my share of your meetings and your risks.'

'Certainly,' he said, returning the folded letter, 'that does not look like mortal hatred.'

He did his best to speak lightly, but these few phrases shown to him by Melek, left him more sure and more disturbed than the long and vehement letter addressed to himself. There was no 'literature' here — it was perfectly simple and perfectly clear! How innocently she had written these transparent sentences to her cousins, after taking the trouble to seal so carefully her impassioned reproaches to him.

So this was the turn taken quite against his expectations by the curious, calm friendship of last year, with three women who were for ever to be an inseparable trinity, 'one soul' and 'for ever featureless.' The outcome terrified him, but it fascinated him too; at that moment he was quite incapable of deciding whether he was glad or not that it should be so.

'When is she to return ?' he asked.

'At the beginning of May,' said Zeyneb. 'We are going to spend the summer as we did last year in our yali on the Asiatic shore. Our modest scheme is to enjoy a last summer together, if the despotism of our masters does not divide us by a marriage before the autumn. I say last, because, so far as I am concerned, next winter will no doubt carry me off, and in any case the other two will be married again before next summer.'

'As for that, we shall see !' exclaimed Melek, with gloomy defiance.

For André also this would be the last summer on the Bosphorus. His appointment at the Embassy would end in November, and he had made up his mind to follow the leading of destiny, partly out of fatalism, and also because there are things which it is folly to insist on prolonging, particularly when the issue can only be disastrous or criminal. So he looked forward with deep melancholy to the return of the summer, so enchanting on the Bosphorus, where the light caïques carry one over the blue water, along the two shores with their latticed houses, or up to the valley of the Grand Signior and among the hills on the coast of Asia carpeted with pink heath. This was all to return for one supreme season, but only to end without any hope for the future. Over his meetings with his three friends there would hang, as before, the perpetual dread of spies or of treachery, which might in an instant part them for ever; and added to this the certainty that they could not meet in the following year would be ever present to give increased pathos to the flight of the fine days in August and September, the blossoming of the autumn colchicum, the yellow shower of falling leaves, the first October rains. And over all there would hang this new and unforeseen element: Djenan's love for him, which, though only covertly avowed, nay, suppressed as she could suppress it with her small iron hand, could not fail to make the close of this Eastern dream more breathless and more cruel.

XXXVI

ABOUT the 10th of April André's French servant,
when he called him in the morning, announced in
a gleeful voice, as an event sure to please him:

'I have seen two swallows! Oh, and they were
piping — piping!'

The swallows were already in Constantinople!
And what a hot sun was pouring in at the windows
that morning! Why, the days certainly flew
faster even than of old. Spring already here;
already cut into instead of being in reserve for the
future as André had been able to fancy only
yesterday, in gloomy weather before the swallows
had been seen. And the summer, which would
be here to-morrow, immediately, would be the
last, irrevocably the last of his life in the East — the
last, too, no doubt, of his spuriously renewed
youth. Back to Turkey by and by, in the grey
twilight of his declining years, perhaps. But after
all for what? When one comes back, what does
one retrieve of oneself and of what one has loved?
How disappointing a venture is such a return
when all else is changed or dead. 'Besides,'
thought he, 'when I shall have written the book
for which these poor little things have extorted a
promise, shall I not have closed this country

against myself for ever; shall I not have lost the confidence of my friends the Turks and the rights of a citizen in my beloved Stamboul?'

The month of April sped like a single day. André spent it in pilgrimages to Stamboul, in dreams and long visits to Eyoub or to Sultan Selim, in narghilehs smoked out of doors in spite of uncertain weather, with spells of cold and wind off the snows.

The first of May came, and still Djenan said nothing of leaving her inaccessible old castle. She wrote less often than she had done last year, and her letters were shorter. 'Forgive my silence,' she wrote once. 'Try to understand it; it means so much.'

Still Zeyneb and Melek said she would come, and seemed very sure of it. André saw less of this pair than before; one was slowly giving up life; the other was less evenly sweet, under the threat of a second marriage. Again, surveillance was stricter this year, over all women in general — and perhaps more especially over these two, who were suspected, as yet very vaguely, of illicit coming and going. They wrote often to their friend, who, though he was very fond of them, generally contented himself with replying *in the spirit*, with good intentions only. And then they would reproach him — with much diffidence.

KASSIM, PACHA, *May* 8, 1905.

'Dear Friend, what is the matter? We are uneasy — we your poor, humble, distant little friends. When days go by without a letter from you a heavy cloak of sadness crushes our shoulders, and everything is dismal, the sea and the sky and our hearts within us.

'Still, we do not complain, I assure you, and this is only to tell you once more a very old story that you know full well — that you are our great and only friend.

'Are you happy just now? Are your days strewn with flowers?

'Time flies or lingers according to what life brings us. For us it dawdles indeed. Really, I cannot see what we are here in the world for. Perhaps, indeed, for the sole joy of being your very devoted slaves, faithful till death and beyond it.   ZEYNEB AND MELEK.'

Already the 8th of May. He read this letter at his window in the warm twilight, which invited him to linger there in front of the vast expanse of distance and sky. In his rooms Pera could really be ignored; the turbulent high street was far away; he looked down a wood of fragrant cypress trees which is enclosed in the town and known as the Little Field of the Dead; and the domes of Stamboul stood up in front, on the horizon.

Night came down on Turkey, a moonless night but bright with stars. Stamboul in the darkness draped itself in magnificence and came out, as it does every night, in lordly shadowy outline against the sky. The clamour of the dogs, the thud of the watchman's iron-shod staff began to be heard in the silence. And then it was the appointed hour for the muezzins, and from every part of the phantasmal city rose the usual symphony of minor chants, high-pitched, light, and pure, winged like prayer itself.

The first night this of summer, a night of real glow and enchantment. André at his window hailed it with less joy than melancholy; his last summer had begun.

At the Embassy, on the following day, he heard that the move to Therapia was to take place soon. To him this meant the final departure from Constantinople, since he would return for only a few sad days at the end of the season, before finally leaving Turkey.

Turks and Levantines, too, were already busy preparing for the annual migration to the Bosphorus or the Islands. Houses were being opened all along the Strait on both the European and the Asiatic shores. Eunuchs were rushing to and fro on the stone or marble landing-quays, making ready for their mistresses' summer stay, bringing, in gaudy gilded caïques, hangings of silk, mattresses for divans, and embroidered cushions. Yes, it was the summer, come upon André more quickly than of yore, he thought, and fated certainly to end more quickly still, since spans of time seem to diminish more rapidly in length as we advance in years.

XXXVII

THE first of the lovely month of June! May had slipped away in no time; still Djenan had not come back, and her letters, now always short, gave no explanation.

The first of the lovely month of June. André, who had his old rooms in Therapia, on the edge of the water, looking up to the opening into the Black Sea, woke to the splendour of the morning, his heart gripped at the mere idea of its being June. Just the change of date gave him the sense of a long stride forward towards the end. Indeed, his incurable malady, which was his distress at the flight of the days, never failed to be more acute in the extra-lucid moments of awakening. What he now felt slipping away from him was the Eastern spring, which went to his head as it was wont to do when he was young, and which he would never, never see again. And he reflected: 'All this will end to-morrow, this sun will be extinct for me to-morrow; my hours are strictly numbered till old age comes and annihilation.'

But when he was fully awake, as usual his thoughts went back to the thousand pleasing and amusing things that come into daily life, the thousand little delusions that help us to forget the

march of time, and death. In the first place it
was the valley of the Grand Signior which rose
before his mind; it was over there, opposite,
behind the wooded hills of the Asiatic shore which
he saw every morning as soon as he had opened
his eyes. He would go this afternoon and sit
there as he had done last year, in the shade of the
plane-trees to smoke a narghileh, while he watched
from afar the veiled ladies who wandered there
like Elysian shades. Then he gave his attention
to his new caïque; his man told him it had just
been brought up from Stamboul under his windows,
fresh in its new gilding, and that the rowers begged
to try on their new livery. For this last summer
in the East he wished to be seen in a fine equipage
on Fridays at the Sweet Waters, and he had devised
a quite oriental combination of colours; the oarsmen's jackets and the long trailing carpet were to
be in dark orange velvet embroidered with gold,
and on this carpet the servant who squatted quite
at the end of the slender prow was to wear sky-
blue embroidered in silver. When the men were
dressed in their new splendour, he went down to
see the effect on the water. At this moment the
surface was a scarcely heaving mirror — this water
of the Bosphorus generally rather broken. There
was infinite peace in the air, the joy of the morning and of June in the verdure on either shore.
André was satisfied with the trial, his eye was
pleased by the contrast between the blue and silver
figure and the orange velvet on which he squatted
— the design on the carpet formed the words of
an old Arabic poem setting forth the perfidy of

x

love. And then he stretched himself in the caïque to be rowed over to the Asiatic shore before the heat of the midday sun.

That evening he had a note from Zeyneb appointing a meeting for the next day at the Sweet Waters — only to pass each other in their caïques, of course. Dangers were increasing, she said. The watchers were doubled; they had now been forbidden to take exercise along the shore as they had done last year, rowing themselves, in muslin veils. At the same time, there was never a bitter word in Zeyneb's complaints; she was too gentle to be vexed, besides being too weary; and so resigned to everything, in her certainty of the merciful and approaching death she had welcomed to her bosom. In a postscript she added that poor old Mevlut, an Ethiopian eunuch, had just died in his eighty-third year, and that this was a real misfortune, for he loved them, having known them from childhood, and would never have betrayed them for silver nor gold. They, too, loved him truly; he was like one of the family. 'We nursed him,' she wrote; 'nursed him like a grandfather,' but the last word had been erased, and above it in Melek's pert writing was inserted 'grand uncle!'

Friday came, so he went to the Sweet Waters, for the first time that year, in his boat of more conspicuous colours than those of the past season. He passed and repassed his two friends, who had also changed the colour of their livery from blue to green and gold; they both wore the black tcharchaf, and a semi-transparent veil, pulled down

over the face.   Other ladies of fashion, also veiled
with black, turned their heads to look after him,
ladies who went by lying as it seemed almost on
the water, which was crowded with similar enigmatical figures between the shores fringed with
ferns and flowers; almost all these shrouded ladies,
interested in him from having read his books,
knew him by sight, having had him pointed out
to them by others.   With some he had perhaps
spoken during the previous autumn, without seeing their faces, in his adventurous meetings with
his friends.   He caught an attentive glance now
and again, or a faint smile scarcely perceptible
under a black veil.   And they perhaps approved
of the combination of colours he had devised,
which glided over the green stream — a blaze of
orange and hydrangea blue between the emerald
banks and the shady screens of trees, and were
sympathetically surprised at an European who thus
showed himself so purely oriental.

And he, still at times such a child, was
amused by attracting the attention of these unrecognisable fair ones, at having possibly haunted
their thoughts by the influence of his books, which
were now being widely read in the harems.   The
June sky was exquisitely calm and deep.   The
spectators in white veils, who watched as they sat
in groups on the grassy banks, showed large calm
eyes above the folds of muslin.   There was a
sweet smell of hay mingling with that of the
narghilehs that were being smoked in the shade.
And the summer, he knew, would last for three
months yet, and the season of the Sweet Waters

was but just beginning; so there were still many Fridays to come, and everything would really endure for some little time and not all come to an end to-morrow.

When André left his gay boat for a while among the reeds, to smoke a narghileh himself under the trees, and play the part of spectator in his turn, watching the caïques as they glided over the water, he felt once more the illusion of youth, the intoxication of forgetting.

XXXVIII

A LETTER from Djenan to André the following week.

June 22, 1905.

'Here I am once more by the Bosphorus, André, as I promised you, and I am really longing to see you. Will you come to Stamboul on Thursday, and be at Sultan Selim at about two o'clock in my nurse's house? I would rather see you there than at my friend's at Sultan Fatih, because it was the scene of our first meetings.

'Wear your fez, of course, and take the same precautions as before, but do not come in unless our usual signal, the corner of a white handkerchief, appears through one of the lattices on the first floor. Otherwise the chance will be lost, and probably, alas, for a long time; in that case walk on to the end of the alley and turn back as if you had missed your way.

'Everything is much more difficult this year, and we live in constant alarms. — Your friend,

'DJENAN.'

On that Thursday when he awoke he was more than ever disturbed about his appearance.

'I must have grown much older,' said he to himself, 'since last year; there are silver threads in my moustache which were not there when she went away.' He would have given much never to have disturbed his friend's peace of mind, but the thought that he might fall off personally in her eyes was nevertheless intolerable.

Men such as he, who might have been great mystics but that they failed to find anywhere the light they so earnestly sought, fall back with all the disappointed ardour of their souls on love and youthfulness, and cling to them desperately when they feel them slipping from them. And then begins childish and pitiable despair, when they see their hair turn white and their eyes grow dull, and they look forward in heart-broken dread to the moment when women will look away at other men.

That Thursday came, and André made his way through the fascinating desolation of old Stamboul under the sweet June sky to Sultan Selim, dreading to see her and even more to be seen by her.

On reaching the dismal little street and looking up, he at once saw the guiding speck of white against the dark brown and ochre of the houses; and behind the door Melek was on the watch.

'Are they here?' he asked.

'Yes, both of them; they are waiting for you.'

At the door of the harem stood Zeyneb, her face uncovered, more faded and wasted than ever.

At the end, in the shadow, was Djenan, who came to meet him with spontaneous eagerness like

a girl, and gave him her hand.   Yes, it was she;
he heard once more her voice like distant music.
But the deep-sea eyes, where were they?   The
eyebrows with their pathetic slant like those of
Our Lady of Sorrows, the oval face? nothing
could he see.   The veil had fallen over them all
as impenetrable as in the early days.   Seized with
horror at having gone too far the little white
princess had retired into her ivory tower.   And
at once André understood that no entreaty would
avail, that the veil would never again be lifted —
unless perhaps in some tragical and supreme
moment.   He felt that the stage of freedom and
sweetness was past in this doubly forbidden affection.   Thenceforward they would move on to the
inevitable catastrophe.

XXXIX

STILL a few days of apparent calm were to be allotted to them.

July passed, it is true, without their being able to meet again, even at a distance, at the Sweet Waters. July is, at Constantinople, a month of wind and storms, a time when the Bosphorus is lashed from morning till night into white foam. All through that month Djenan could hardly write to him, so closely was she guarded by a cross-grained old aunt, who had come from Erivan to pay her an interminable visit, and who could not bear to go out in a caïque unless the water was as smooth as a mirror.

But this lady, called by André and his three friends 'Plague Hanum,' took herself off early in August, and the end of the summer, their last summer, was no longer spoilt for them. August, September, and October are the delightful season on the Bosphorus, when the sky is as clear as in Eden, and the days, as they shorten, grow calmer and more sober, but lose nothing of their splendour.

Once more they frequented the Sweet Waters of Asia, and plotted meetings at Stamboul in the house near Sultan Selim. Superficially everything was the same again as in the summer of 1904,

even to the black veil perpetually shrouding
Djenan's face; but in their souls there were
different feelings, thoughts as yet unspoken, of
which they were not yet sure, but which, nevertheless, led to moments of oppressive silence in the
midst of their talk.

Besides, the year before they could say: 'We
have another summer to look forward to.' Whereas
now everything was coming to an end, since André
was leaving Turkey in November; and they constantly thought of the approaching separation, which
seemed to them as final as entombment. Being
old friends now, they had reminiscences in common,
they laid plans for doing once more, before the inexorable end, the things they had already done,
excursions or pilgrimages they had made all four
together. 'We must try once more in our lives
to go together to the little wild wood at Beicos;
and once more, for the last time, we must visit
Nedjibeh's grave.'

To André, whose heart turned cold each time
the name of the month changed, the morning of
the 1st of September marked a long stride down-
ward in this descending slide in life, which gathered
pace like a fall. It seemed to him that the air had
suddenly, since yesterday, acquired an autumnal
clearness and crispness, and that it was more
pervious to sound, an effect generally of the later
year; the deep-toned Turkish trumpets rang out
louder when they were sounded on the opposite
shore at Beicos, where the soldiers have barracks
under the shady plane-trees. The summer was
departing, no doubt, and here collected with a

shiver that the lilac crocuses were flowering now among the dead leaves in the valley of the Grand Signior.

And yet how radiant it all was this morning, and what perfect calm lay on the waters! There was not a breath, and as the sun mounted in the heavens it grew deliciously warm. A long caravan of sailing vessels was now passing up the Bosphorus, towed by a steam-tug — old-world Turkish boats with a high-cabined poop covered with gaudy archaic painting, such ships as are seen nowhere else. With all sails reefed they submissively followed each other towards the Black Sea, to which the passage was visible between two steep mountain shores, and it looked like the most calm and inoffensive sea in the world to any one who did not know it better. Just beneath his windows André saw the sun-smitten little quay by which gay caïques lay moored, his among the number, to carry him in the evening to the Sweet Waters.

The Sweet Waters! Four or five times yet he might be seen there, figuring as an Oriental — on the green-set stream where he was 'dressed in a little brief' royalty, and veiled ladies recognised the livery of his rowers from afar. And for some days yet he might sit at sunset under the giant planes of the Grand Signior, smoking narghilehs in the heart of unutterable peace, while watching the slow, wandering women, happy shades in the Elysian meadows beyond. Thirty or thirty-five summer days yet to come, a really precious respite before the end of everything, which was not immediate after all!

The slopes of Asia above Beicos were brightly pink that morning with full-flowering heath — as pink as pink ribbon. The little houses of the Turkish villages standing quite in the water, the huge green plane-trees, on which for three hundred years the fishermen have hung their nets — all these and the blue sky were calmly gazing at their own reflection in the mirror of the Bosphorus, as perfect as if its beauty never changed. All these things together seemed so confident of the permanence of summer, of peace, of life, and of youth, that André once more allowed himself to be beguiled, forgot the time of year, and ceased to feel the threat of coming days.

So, in the afternoon, he went to the Sweet Waters, where everything shone in an ideal light; he passed his three friends, and met the glances of other veiled ladies. He returned in a matchless evening, creeping along under the Asiatic coast: old houses closely dumb, in which tragedies may be acting which none may know; old gardens, secret gardens under dense leafy shade; old marble quays, jealously watched, where invisible fair ones sit on Fridays to see the caïques coming home. Lulled by the quick measure of the oars he was borne through the softly fanning air; merely to breathe it was intoxicating. He felt rested; he knew he looked young again at this moment, and the zest for life was aroused in him as keen as in his first youth, the same thirst to revel utterly in everything that might come. His soul, usually a dark abyss of weariness, could still change under the voluptuous fascination of outer

things, or of some phantasmagoria that appealed
to his artist's sense, — change, be born again, and
feel ready for a whole chapter of adventures and
love affairs.

He brought back with him in his caïque his
friend Jean Renaud, who confided to him in
burning words his woe in being in love with a
lady of an Embassy, very politely indifferent to
his devotion, and at the same time in love with
Djenan, whom he had never seen, but whose form
and voice disturbed his slumbers. André listened
without even shrugging his shoulders, such
avowals were so completely in the right key this
evening; he felt himself at the same pitch as this
boy, and absorbed in precisely the same ideas;
nothing else counted. Love pervaded the air.
Confidence for confidence, he was tempted to cry
out in a tone of triumph: 'Well, and I — I — am
better loved than you!'

They proceeded on their way in silence, each
man for himself egotistically lost in thought,
chiefly of love; the splendour of a summer
evening on the Bosphorus wrapped them in
reverie. Alongside, the prohibited landings of
the old houses glided by; women sitting at the
very edge watched them pass in the now copper-
coloured light, and it amused them to think that
to these veiled spectators their presence, their
caïque with its quaintly strange colouring, must
have a fine effect under the apotheosis of sunset.

XL

SEPTEMBER is ended. The fine rosy hue of the
heath on the hills is fading day by day, turning to
the colour of rust. And in the valley of Beicos
the lilac colchicum is in profuse bloom among the
grass of the lawns; the strewn leaves of the
planes, a bed of gold, lie everywhere. In the
afternoon, to smoke a narghileh outside the booth
of one of the humble cafés which still remain
though they will soon be gone, a place in the
sunshine is desirable, the last warmth of the
shortening summer; presently when the beams
lie level on the ground, and a red glow like the
reflection of a conflagration lights up the great
boughs of the trees, a sudden chill nips and
distresses you; you start up to go, and the dead
leaves in the grass rustle under your feet. The
heavy autumn rains which leave the meadow
soaked, alternate with days still hot and strangely
clear, when bees hum over the last flowers of the
scabious, till at nightfall cold mists rise from the
ground and the woods.

All this strew of yellow leaves André had
already seen in this same valley the previous year;
and one is attached to a place where twice one has
seen the leaves fall. So he knew what the pain

317

would be of leaving for ever this little pastoral
nook of Asia, whither he had come almost every
day during two sunlit summers. He knew, too,
that this pain, like so many others he had already
suffered, would, alas! be soon forgotten, lost in
the ever greyer gloom of the near future.

All this season André and his friends had
found it impossible to arrange any expedition
together. But they had planned two at all risks,
for the 3rd and 5th of October, the last — the last
of everything.

Their destination to-day, the 3rd, was the little
forest wilderness they had discovered in 1904.
And there they met, on the fringe of the marsh
that lay hidden, as if on purpose, in a fold of the
hills. They took their seats as before, on the
same mossy stones, near the stagnant water where
the tall reeds grew, and the great Osmunda ferns,
like a tropical jungle.

André saw at once that they were not quite
themselves, poor little persons, but nervous and
excessive, each in her own way; Djenan with
exaggerated coldness, Melek with vehemence:
'Now we are all to be married again,' they explained, 'to break up the trio of revolutionaries.
And our proceedings are too independent, it
would appear; we must have husbands who will
break us in.'

'So far as I am concerned,' said Melek, 'the
matter was settled in family council on Saturday.
The executioner is chosen, a certain Omar Bey, a
cavalry captain, a handsome man with hard eyes,

whom they condescended to point out to me one day below my window; so there will be no delay.' And she stamped her foot, looking away, and crumpling all the leaves she could reach between her fingers.

He could find nothing to say, but looked at the other two. He was going to say to Zeyneb, who was next to him: 'And you?' but he dreaded the reply; he could guess too well the gentle melancholy gesture with which she would point to her chest. So it was to Djenan, who alone, as usual, kept her veil down, that he addressed his question: 'And you?'

'I — oh, I,' she said with the rather haughty indifference she had assumed of late, 'I am to go back to Hamdi!'

'But what then will you do?'

'Dear heaven! what would you have me do? I shall probably submit. Since I must be handed over to somebody, it may just as well be to the man who was my husband; it would seem less a degradation than with an unknown man.'

André heard with amazement. The thick veil she wore hindered him from reading in her eyes whether she were sincere or not in this sudden resignation. This unexpected consent to return to Hamdi was the best he could hope for as a solution to an inextricable predicament; but he could scarcely believe in it, and he also perceived that it was a solution full of suffering for him.

They spoke no more on these burning questions, and a thoughtful silence ensued. It was Djenan's soft voice that broke it in this still spot, so calm that they could hear each leaf as it fell. Her tone was quite simple, quite cool, as she spoke of the book.

'Ah, yes,' said he, trying to be less serious; 'to be sure, let us discuss the book. We have thought no more about it for a long time. Now, what am I to say in it? That you pine to go to parties in the evening, to wear hats by day — fine hats with heaps of roses and feathers like the ladies of Pera?'

'No, André, do not make fun of it, to-day — so near the last.'

So he listened to them attentively. Without having the smallest illusions as to what he could achieve for them, at least he was anxious not to place them in an imaginary light, or write anything that did not accord with their own ideas. It seemed to him that they clung to most of the traditions of Islam, and really loved the veil as a habit, if only they might sometimes lift it in the presence of chosen and tried friends. The maximum they claimed was that they should be regarded to a greater extent as thinking, free, and responsible beings; that they should be allowed to see certain men in their homes, veiled, if it were insisted on, but to talk to them — especially when there was any question of marriage. 'With no greater concessions than these,' said Djenan emphatically, 'we would rest satisfied, we and the women after us for at least half a century, till a more advanced stage of our evolution. Say plainly, as our friend, that we ask no more, so that we may not be condemned for folly and rebellion. Moreover, I defy any one to find in the Book of the Prophet any plain text which is opposed to what we demand.'

When he took leave of them as evening came on, he felt that the little hand Melek held out to him was burning.

'Oh!' he exclaimed in alarm, 'but you are in a high fever.'

'Since yesterday — a fever which is increasing. So much the worse for Captain Omar Bey — eh? This evening I am really ill; such a weight in my head — a weight! I felt I must see you again; for nothing else should I have got up to-day.'

She leaned on Djenan's arm. When they reached the plain — the meadow carpeted with lilac flowers and strewn with golden leaves — they must seem not to know him, since there were other people there, and groups of women, those graceful, slow-paced groups, who come in the afternoon to walk in the valley of Beicos. André, as usual, watched them depart, but with the conviction this time that never, never again should he see this scene: at the golden hour of autumn sundown, these three slender creatures of transition and anguish, looking like pagan shades and vanishing down this Vale of Rest, over the bright, unreal-looking grass; one in her black shroud, and the other two veiled in white.

When they had disappeared he turned towards the booths of Turkish coffee, still there under the trees, and ordered a narghileh, though the cool dew of an October evening had already begun to be felt. He sat down to meditate, against one of the

Y

great planes in a fast-dying sunbeam. A cata-
clysm had engulfed him. Djenan's resignation
had destroyed his dream, his last dream of the
East. Without being quite aware of it, he had
so entirely trusted to everything lasting after his
departure. Separated from him, and not seeing
him grow older, she would, he had hoped, have
preserved for him a sort of idealised love which
would long have withstood the shocks and dis-
appointments which kill ordinary love. But no,
taken back by Hamdi, who was young, and who
doubtless still had a hold over her senses, she
would be utterly lost to him, André: 'She did
not love me so much as all that,' thought he. 'I
am very simple and presumptuous still! It was
all very pretty, but it was "literature"; and it is
all over, or to be accurate, it never existed. I am
as old as my years, and this at any rate proves it.
To-morrow I shall be naught at all, either for her
or for any other woman.'

He remained the last smoker left under the plane-
trees. Quite past now was the time of fine warm
evenings which brought so many dreamers from
the neighbourhood to loiter in this valley; the
low red sun had no power; it was cold.

'I still persist in trying to spin out my last
summer,' said he to himself, 'but it is as vain and
absurd as trying to prolong my youth. The time
for such things is past and gone.'

The sun had now set behind the European
shore, and in the distance the goatherds were
piping to collect their flocks. The meadow about
him, deserted now under the scattered yellow

trees, had the look of wild melancholy which he remembered so well from the late autumn last year. The melancholy of twilight and of fallen leaves, the melancholy of parting, the melancholy of having lost Djenan, and going back to daily life,—it was all unendurable, and spoke too plainly of universal death.

XLI

For some few days past they had contrived a very ingenious means of corresponding in case of urgency. One of their friends named Kiamouran had authorised André to imitate her handwriting, which was well known to the suspicious household, and to sign her name; she had also supplied him with several envelopes with her monogram addressed to Djenan by her own hand. Thus he could write to them, in carefully chosen words, however, for fear of letters being opened, and his man-servant, accustomed to wearing a fez and carrying a rosary, conveyed these notes direct to the yali of the three little sinners. Sometimes André sent him at a fixed hour, agreed upon beforehand; then one of the three would happen to be in the vestibule and to have sent away the negroes, so that a verbal message might be given to such a trustworthy messenger.

So on the following day he ventured to send one of these notes, signed 'Kiamouran,' to ask after Melek's fever, and inquire whether they would still make the excursion to the mosque on the hill. In the afternoon he had an answer from Djenan, saying that Melek was in bed with increased fever, and that the two others could not leave her.

Well, even alone, he was bent on the walk on the 5th of October, the day they had named for going there all together for the last time.

The weather was exquisite, that of the Southern autumn; the bees were humming. He believed himself to be less attached to-day to his little Turkish friends, even to Djenan, and he felt that he could take up life once more, elsewhere, where they would not be. He thought, too, that his regrets on leaving would be less for them than for the East itself, the unchanging East which he had so passionately loved from his earliest youth, and for the lovely summer here, now ending; for this pastoral nook of Asia, where he had spent two seasons in the old-world calm, under the shade of the trees, with the fragrance of the leaves and mosses. And what lovely sunshine, again to-day! The oaks, the scabious, the bracken all russet and gold, reminded him of the woods of his French home, to such a pitch that he suddenly was thrown back to the impressions of a long-past time when, at the end of his holidays as a boy, he was obliged at this time of year to leave the country where he had played games for many happy hours under September skies.

As he mounted the hill by the narrow mossy paths through the heath, and the horizon rose before him, his vision of France faded away. This was no longer the thing; the sense of being in Turkey took its place. The reaches of the Bosphorus lay at his feet, the villages and palaces on its shores, and the long lines of slowly moving boats. Inland, too, the aspect was foreign, an

endless chain of hills covered with a dense monotonous cloak of verdure, forests too vast and
silent, such as France has no more.

When he finally reached the plateau, beaten by
all the winds of heaven, which formed the front
court of the old lonely mosque, a number of
Turkish women were there, seated on the grass,
having come on a pilgrimage in very primitive
ox-carts. Quick — as soon as they saw him —
quick with the muslin veils to wrap and hide their
faces. And they were at once a silent company of
shrouded spectres, projected with archaic charm
against the immense expanse of the Black Sea,
which had suddenly come into view, filling the
distance.

And André said to himself that the enchantment of this land and its mystery would survive
everything, even his disillusionment in Djenan,
and the disenchantment of the decline of years.

XLII

On the next day, a Friday, he would not miss going to the Sweet Waters of Asia, for this was indeed the very last time. His agreement for the season, for the hire of the caïque and oarsmen, expired that evening, and the Embassies were to move back to Constantinople in the following week. The season on the Bosphorus was ending.

No day of midsummer was ever so brilliant and so still; but that there were fewer pleasure-boats, perhaps, by the already somewhat deserted shore, it might have been a Friday in a fine August. Out of habit, and attachment too, he would once more, come what might, steer his caïque past the closed windows of his friends' yali. The little white signal was in its place. What an inexplicable surprise! Were they coming out?

At the Sweet Waters the meadows were golden by the side of the pretty stream, so covered were they with fallen leaves, and the trees told plainly of autumn. Nevertheless, most of the handsome caïques that frequented the place came in one after another, full of beauties from the harems, and André, as he passed, met once more, in final fare-well, many a covert smile from beneath a veil.

He waited a long time, looking out on all

sides; but his friends did not come, and the day was waning, and the ladies began to go home.

So he, too, was going away when, just as he got out of the river, he saw coming, in a handsome caïque, with a blue and gold livery, a woman alone, wearing a white yashmak, letting her eyes be seen. She was perched, no doubt, on cushions, for she looked tall, and sat high above the water, as if on purpose to be better seen.

The boats crossed, and she looked at him steadily. Djenan! Those bronze-green eyes and the long tawny eyebrows, which she had hidden from him for a year past, were like no others, and could not ever be mistaken. He shuddered at this apparition an arm's length from him; but he must keep his countenance before the boatmen, and they passed each other motionless, without a sign on either side.

However, he turned his caïque a minute later, to meet her again as she came down the stream. There was hardly any one left when they again crossed each other in a flash; and on this second meeting the form enveloped in the white muslin yashmak stood out against the dark cypresses and the headstones of the old graveyard on the very edge of the water there — for in that land there are cemeteries everywhere, no doubt to keep the thought of death ever in mind.

The sun was low, and its beams already red; they must go. Their two caïques left the little river almost at the same time, and turned up the Bosphorus in the glorious evening, André's boat about a hundred yards behind Djenan's. He saw her, from afar, set foot on her marble steps and go back into her gloomy dwelling.

What she had done told him a tale: to have gone alone to the Sweet Waters, and yet more in a yashmak, to show him her eyes and stamp their expression on her friend's memory. But André, who had at once felt how special and how pathetic this was, remembered presently a passage in *Medjeh*, in which he had related something analogous in speaking of looks solemnly exchanged in a vessel at the moment of parting. 'It was very pretty of her,' he sadly reflected, 'but, again, rather "literary"; she was imitating Nedjibeh. It will not hinder her a few days hence from opening her arms again to her Hamdi.'

He went on his way up the Bosphorus close under the Asiatic shore. Many houses were already empty, hermetically closed; many gardens had their gates barred under a tangle of crimson Virginia creeper; everywhere autumn had laid its hand — departure — the end. Here and there on the little, prohibited landing-places some women who had lingered in the country were sitting by the water on this last Friday of the season; but their eyes — all that could be seen of their features — were sad at the thought of returning, now so soon, to the town harems, and at the apprehension of winter. And the setting sun lighted up all this melancholy like red Bengal fire.

When André was at home again in his rooms at Therapia, his rowers came to make their farewell selam; they had put on their own common clothes, and each man brought back, carefully folded, his fine Broussa gauze shirt and smart orange-velvet jacket. They brought also the long carpet of the same stuff, artlessly advising him to have it well dried, as it was soaked with damp and salt. André looked at the tawdry relics; the gold embroidery had already begun to assume, in the wind and sun, the rich tawny tones of things old and precious. What could he do with them? Would it not be less sad to destroy them than to take them home with him and say to himself in the dreary future, one day when he found the things, 'That was the livery of my boatmen, long ago, in the good time when I lived on the Bosphorus'?

It was growing dark. He desired his Turkish servant, the man who had once been a shepherd at Eski Chehir, to bring his pipe and play the same air again as he had played last year, the sort of wild fugue, which now held to him the unutterable expression of the dying summer in this place and under these particular circumstances. Then, with his elbows on the window-sill, he watched his caïque disappear, the rowers mere poor boatmen, who would pull it down to Constantinople to hire themselves to some new master. For a long time he watched the slender white thing on the ever darkening water, for its disappearance in twilight greyness represented to him the similar vanishing of two oriental summers.

XLIII

On Saturday the 7th of October, his last day by the sea, he received a few lines from Djenan, telling him that Melek's fever was worse, that the old people were uneasy, and that they were returning to the city that very day for a consultation of physicians.

All the Embassies were packing to go. André hurried through his preparations in order to have time to go over once more to the Asiatic shore before nightfall, and bid farewell to the valley of the Grand Signior. It was late when he arrived there, under a sky across which heavy clouds were racing and shedding some drops of rain as they swept by. The valley was deserted, and the little coffee-stalls under the trees had been removed since yesterday. He took leave of two or three humble souls who dwelt there in huts; and of a good yellow dog and a good grey cat, little souls also of this valley; he had known them for two summers, and they seemed to understand that he was going for ever. And then, at a funereal pace, he walked round these quiet, sheltered meadows, now abandoned, where the veils of his friends had so often brushed the grass and the lilac flowers of the colchicum. This walk kept him there till the hour of dusk, when the stars come out and the barking of the wandering dogs begins to be heard. His pilgrimage ended, by the time he found himself under the huge trees, a sort of sacred grove, at the entrance to the valley, it was quite dark, and his feet caught in the roots that lay like snakes under the thick mass of dead leaves. In the gloom he went down to the little landing-place, of which each granite block was familiar to him, and took a caïque to return to the European shore.

XLIV

THE wind has raged all night on the Bosphorus,
the wind from the Black Sea whose lugubrious tones
will ere long be heard almost incessantly during
four or five winter months; and this morning the
blast has gained in violence and shakes André's
dwelling, to add to the sadness of his last waking
at Therapia.

'My word, but this is weather!' exclaims his
man as he opens the shutters. Opposite, on the
hills of Asia, low heavy clouds are being dragged
along, almost touching the storm-tossed trees.

And it was in this threatening gale and the
lashing squalls of rain that he went to-day down
the Bosphorus for the last time, passing his friends'
yali, where everything was closed and shuttered,
while flights of dead leaves danced in a whirl on
the marble steps.

This evening he would be again in Constantinople, but for such a little while before his final
departure! Just fifty days, for he had decided to
take the steamship sailing on the 30th of November
and return to France by sea, just to have a fixed
date before him, unalterable, and to which he must
adhere.

A letter from Djenan at nightfall brought him

the report of the physicians. Brain fever, of a serious type from the first. So poor little Melek, no doubt, was to die, worn out by so much nervous excitement, and the rebellion and horror she felt at this second marriage.

XLV

THE two weeks at the end of October, while Melek lay dying, were almost invariably fine, with a melancholy sun; André, every evening, like a schoolboy, scratched through the day that was gone on a calendar, where the 30th of November was marked with a cross. He spent as much time as possible in Stamboul, in the Turkish life that was so soon to end for him. But here, as on the Bosphorus, the sadness of autumn added to that of his approaching departure; already it was growing cold, almost too cold for narghilehs and dreams in the open air, in front of the sacred mosques under the trees shedding their leaves.

He, of course, saw no more of his friends, for Zeyneb and Djenan never left her who was dying. Towards the end they placed in the lattice of a window an imperceptible scrap of white which meant: She is still alive; and he felt sure that a scrap of blue would tell him: All is over. So, early every morning, and again once or twice in the day, he, or his friend Jean Renaud, or his French servant, went to the cemetery at Kassim Pacha, to look up anxiously at the window.

All that time, in the house where she was

dying, and where perfect silence reigned, Imams, at the request of the old people, were perpetually praying. Islam, old Islam, with its divine care for the dying, was closing in on its recalcitrant child, who yielded gradually to its influence and was falling asleep without terror. In her, indeed, doubt was still a curable evil, a very recent graft on a long-inherited stock of faith and quietism. And so by degrees the crude observances which are to the Koran what, with us, the practices at Lourdes are to the Gospel, nay, even the superstitions of her venerable grandmothers, no longer shocked this little infidel of yesterday, who allowed them to provide her with amulets and submitted to have her clothes exorcised by dervishes; her dainty shifts were blessed in the mosque at Eyoub, elegant garments from the 'right shop' in Paris, or they were sent further still, to Scutari, to the Howling Saints whose breath has the gift of healing, so long as they remain in their ecstasy after long appeals to Allah.

As October ended, she had already been speechless for two days and probably unconscious, sunk in a hot and heavy sleep which the doctors said must end in death.

XLVI

On the 2nd of November Zeyneb, who was watching by her pillow, suddenly turned round with a shudder, for, at the end of the half-darkened room, a voice was heard breaking the persistent silence, a very sweet, young voice saying prayers. She had not heard the girl come in — a girl with a veiled face. Why was she there, Koran in hand? Ah, yes; she understood at once! The prayer for the dead. It is the custom in Turkey when some one is dying in a house, for the girls or women of the neighbourhood to come in turns to read prayers; they enter as a right, without giving a name or raising their veils, nameless and fateful; and their presence is a sign of death, as that of the priest who brings extreme unction, is to Catholics.

Melek, too, understood, and her eyes, for some time shut, opened again. She had reached that mysterious *better* which almost always supervenes in dying persons. She recovered her voice too, which they had thought extinct for ever. 'Come nearer,' she said to the unknown reader; 'I do not hear distinctly. Do not think that I am afraid, come close. Read louder — that I may not lose ——'

Then she desired herself to confess the Moslem faith, and spreading her little waxen white hands in the attitude of prayer, she repeated the sacramental words: 'There is no God but one God, and Mahomet is his Prophet.'[1]

But before she reached the end of the confession, as inaudible as a breath, the poor outstretched hands fell. Then the nameless one reopened her Koran and began to read once more. How sweet is the rhythm, the lulling music of those Moslem prayers, especially when they are chanted by a girl's voice under a thick veil! Till a very late hour the unknown readers carried on their pious task, one after another coming in as silently as shades; but there was no pause in the melodious drone that soothes and helps the departing spirit.

Others, too, would come in on tiptoe, and without speaking would bend over the bed of mortal sleep: the mother, a kind and passive creature, always so much ignored that she hardly counted; the two grandmothers, not resigned, but dumb and almost fierce in their concentrated despair; or the father, Mehmed Bey, his face disfigured by grief and perhaps by remorse, for in his heart he adored his little Melek, and it was his inexorable observance of old customs that had led to her death. Or else, trembling all over, Madame Tardieu, the former governess, sent for a few days since because Melek had wished it, but only tolerated with some hostile

---

[1] La illahé illallah Mohammed Ressoul allah. Ech hedu enné la illahé illallah vé ech hedu enné Mohammedul alihé hou ve ressoulouhou.

feeling, and regarded as a responsible and evil influence. The dying girl's eyes had closed again; but for a slight clenching of her hands now and then, or a twitching of her lips, she gave no more sign of life.

XLVII

It was about four in the morning. Djenan was now keeping watch. A minute since the veiled reader, whose prayers filled the room, had raised her voice a little in the more solemn silence, praying with excited fervour, as if conscious that *something* had happened — something final. And Djenan, who was still holding one of the little transparent hands without noticing that it was growing cold, started with terror when a hand was laid on her shoulder — two little warning pats, ominously gentle. But oh! the fearful face of an old woman she had never seen before, who suddenly stood behind her, having entered without a sound by the always open door; a tall, old woman, broad, but lean and haggard, who without a word signed to her: 'Go.' She had, no doubt, long been waiting in the passage, and then, feeling with professional certainty that her moment had come, she approached to perform her part.

'No! no!' cried Djenan, throwing herself on the dead. 'Not yet! I will not let you take her away. No! no!'

'There, there, gently,' said the old woman, raising her authoritatively. 'I will not hurt her.'

And in fact there was nothing malignant in

340

her ugliness; rather a sullen compassion, and above all utter weariness. So many, so many sweet flowers mown down in the harems! so many she had carried out, this strong-armed woman, this 'Washer of the dead,' as they are called.

She took her in her arms like a sick child, and the fine red hair, all tumbled, fell over her hideous shoulder. Two of her assistants, old hands too, and more terrifying still, were waiting in the ante-room with lights. Djenan and the praying woman followed them along corridors and halls wrapped in the cold silence of dawn — the weirdly woeful group which went on and on towards the stairs to go down.

Thus little Melek Sadia Saadet, at the age of twenty years and six months, died of dread at the idea of being a second time thrown into the arms of a strange master.

Having descended to the lower floor, the old women carried their burden to the door of a large room in the servants' quarters of this ancient dwelling; a sort of serving-room paved with marble, with a deal table in the middle, a large pan of steaming hot water, and a sheet lying unfolded on a tripod. In the corner was a coffin — a light coffin of thin boards, as they are made in Turkey — and finally, on the floor an antique shawl rolled round a pole, one of the 'Valideh' shawls which are used as winding-sheets for the wealthy; and all had been prepared beforehand, for in Turkey no time is lost in burying the dead.

When the old women had laid the girl on the table, which was rather short, the beautiful red hair, not yet fastened up, fell to the ground. Before beginning their task they dismissed Djenan and her veiled companion by a sign. But in fact they withdrew of their own accord to wait outside. And Zeyneb, aroused by some intuition of what was happening, came to join them — Zeyneb, not weeping, but as pale as the dead, her eyes set in purple rings. All three stood there motionless, frozen, following in fancy the processes of this toilet of the dead, listening to the splashing of water and moving of various objects in the echoing room; and when it was all over the tall old woman called them in: 'Come and look at her now.'

She lay sunk in the narrow coffin, wrapped in white all but her face, left uncovered for farewell kisses; they could not quite shut her eyelids nor her mouth; but she was so young, her teeth were so white, that she was still exquisitely pretty, with the expression of a child, and a sort of sorrowful half-smile on her lips.

Then every one was roused to come and kiss her: her father, her mother, her grandparents, her stern old uncles, who for some days now had ceased to be stern, the servants, and the slaves. The great mansion was full of sudden lights, of alarms, hurrying feet, sighs and sobs.

When one of the grandmothers came in, the most violent of the two — she who was also Djenan's grandmother and had for some time taken up her abode in this house — a thorough-going '1320,' an uncompromising Moslem if ever

there was one, only this morning exasperated by
the new evolution which had carried away her
granddaughters — when this old lady came into
the room the shivering governess, Mademoiselle
Tardieu, was on her knees by the coffin. The
two women looked at each other for a moment
in silence, one terrible, the other terrified and
humble.

'Go!' said the old woman in Turkish, quivering with hatred. 'What have you to do here —
you? Your work is done. Do you hear me?
Go!'

But the poor soul, shrinking away from her,
looked up with such honesty and woe in her tear-
filled eyes, that the old woman was suddenly
moved to pity; she understood, no doubt, in a
lightning-flash, what for years she had refused to
recognise: that the governess, all through, was
but the irresponsible tool of Time. Then, holding
out her hands, she cried, 'Forgive!' and the two
women, hitherto enemies, wept and sobbed in each
other's arms. Incompatibility of ideas, of race,
and of period had long kept them apart; but they
were both kind and motherly, capable of tenderness
and of spontaneous reaction.

Meanwhile a pale gleam of light through the
windows announced the end of the November
night. Djenan, remembering André, went upstairs to find a scrap of blue ribbon, as they had
agreed, and tied it to the lattice of the well-known
window.

XLVIII

The man-servant who went to see at break of day came back to Pera quite scared.

'Mademoiselle Melek must be dead,' he said to his master when he called him. 'They have put up a blue signal; I have just seen it.'

The man had more than once had occasion to speak with Melek through a partly open door when he was sent on André's dangerous messages; she had even let him see her face when thanking him. And to him she was Mademoiselle Melek, she looked so very young.

André, hearing from Djenan an hour later that the body would be taken to the mosque at noon, went to Kassim Pacha at eleven o'clock. He put on a fez and the dress of a man of the people, to make more sure of not being recognised, for he was anxious to be able at a given moment to go close up to his little friend and fulfil a pious rite of Islam.

He stood apart at first, in the cemetery near the house; and he soon saw the light coffin borne out, carried on the shoulders of unknown men, as the custom is in Turkey; a valuable old shalw was wrapped closely round it, a 'Valideh' shawl, striped green and red, with a minute Cashmere pattern all over. At the end where the head lay, a little white veil was put to show that the dead was a woman, and by way of a wonderful innovation, a small bunch of roses was pinned to the shawl.

Among the Turks the dead are buried with more haste than among us, and no communications are sent out. Those who please may attend the funeral — relations, friends, all whom the news has reached, servants and neighbours. There are never any women in these chance gatherings, and above all never any bearers; the men in the street give their services.

It was a fine, bright, still day, with a clear November sun. Stamboul was splendid across the Golden Horn in its lofty immutable grandeur, above a thin haze which hung over the sea at its foot.

The coffin was often lifted from one man's shoulder to another's, as various persons met on the way volunteered for the pious task of bearing for a few minutes the unknown dead. Foremost of all walked two priests in green turbans; a hundred or more men followed; men of every degree, and some old dervishes had come, too, with their tall hats, chanting as they went in loud lugubrious voices, like the howling of wolves in the woods on a winter night.

They made their way to an ancient mosque beyond the houses, almost in the country, in a valley that verged on the wilderness. Little Melek was deposited on the flags of the court, and the Imams chanted the prayers for the dead in a very sweet falsetto.

In about ten minutes at most they resumed their march, going down to the sea to embark in boats and gain the opposite shore and the great cemetery at Eyoub, which was to be her last resting-place.

As they got nearer to the Golden Horn their progress was slower, by reason of the crowd which joined the procession; and there little Melek was carried by a number of boatmen and sailors who relieved each other. André, who had hitherto hung back, now at last came near, feeling safe among the crowd in which he was lost; he laid his hand on the antique shawl, put out his shoulder, and felt the weight of his little friend resting on it for about twenty paces as they approached the shore.

After that he stole away, fearing lest his persistent following should be noticed.

XLIX

A week later the two that were left bid him come
to Sultan Selim. They found themselves together
once more in the humble little dwelling, gloomy,
hidden, and unchanging; the last meeting but one
in all their lives, and they were both black and
invisible under equally thick veils which they did
not once raise.

They talked of nothing but of her who was
gone, who was 'free' as they expressed it; and from
them André learned all the details of her death.
It seemed to him that they were tearless under
their black gauze masks; their voices were steady;
they were grave and calm. So far as Zeyneb was
concerned there was nothing strange in this detachment, for she herself was now hardly of this
world. But he was surprised to find Djenan so
composed. At one moment, thinking to please
her, he said with deep, gentle affection: 'I was
introduced to Hamdi Bey last Friday at Yildiz;
he is very gentlemanly, elegant, and good-
looking ——'

But she cut him short with her first show of
excitement. 'If you please, André, we will not
speak of that man.' He then heard from Zeyneb
that the family, quite overwhelmed by Melek's

death, had ceased for the moment to entertain the idea of this marriage.

He had indeed met Hamdi Bey, and had thought well of him. Since then he had tried to say to himself: 'I am very happy to think the husband of my little friend so satisfactory!' But it did not ring true; on the contrary, he suffered all the more acutely from having seen him and recognised his charm, and yet more his youth.

After leaving them for the long walk he had so often taken before, from this house to his own, Stamboul impressed him more than ever as a city of decay, sadly becoming Western, and sinking into the commonplace of hurry and ugliness. Beyond the still undisturbed streets round Sultan Selim, and as soon as he reached the lower region near the bridge, his gorge rose at the swarming turmoil of the crowd, which, down there, never ceases; in the mud, in the darkness of the narrow alleys, in the cold evening fog, these hustling folks, selling and buying a myriad squalid things and horrible food, were no longer Turks, but a medley of all the races of the Levant. Excepting the red fez which they still cling to, half of them no longer wore the dignified national costume; they were tricked out in European second-hand garments, outcast from our great cities, which the trading ships bring out in quantities. Never had he been so keenly aware of the factories sending up their smoke in various spots, nor of the tall stupid houses, plaster imitations of our suburban villas. 'I am absurd in persisting to see Stamboul as it is no more,' said he to himself. 'It is crumbling away, dying out. Now one must constantly and carefully select the things to look at, the nooks to be frequented; up on the heights the mosques survive, but all the lower town is undermined by "progress," which is advancing by long strides with all its squalor, its alcohol, its hopelessness, and its bombs. The evil breath of the West has passed over the city of the Khalifs; it is "disenchanted" now, just in the same way as ere long all the women of its harems will be.'

And then even more sadly he went on to reflect: 'After all, what can it matter to me? I no longer belong to the place; at a fixed date, which will soon be here, the 30th of November, I shall be gone — no doubt for ever. But for the humble gravestones over Nedjibeh out there, about which I shall still be uneasy, what is there here that concerns me? I myself, indeed, in five years, or say in ten — what shall I be but a wreck? Life has no duration, mine is already behind me on the road; the things of this world will soon matter to me no more. Time may still run at its dizzy pace and sweep away the old East that I loved, all the Circassian beauties, with their large eyes of deep-sea green, and may demolish every human race and the world itself, the vast Cosmos — what will it matter to me, since I shall not see it? I, who am almost at an end myself, and to-morrow may have lost all consciousness of being.'

And then, at certain moments, it seemed to him that the 30th of November never could come, so completely was he at home in Constantinople, nay, anchored in his rooms where nothing had as yet been disturbed for his departure. And as he walked on amid the throng, while lanterns innumerable were lighted up, through all the cries from the stalls, the bargaining in every language of the Levant, he felt himself floating rudderless, driven by conflicting impressions.

L

November was drawing to a close; they had met for the last supreme interview. The same sunbeam on the opposite wall again threw its reflected and artificial gleam on them for a few minutes before twilight in this modest little harem in the heart of Stamboul. Pale Zeyneb, unveiled, and Djenan, buried in her black shroud, were conversing with their friend André as calmly as in their former meetings; it might have been supposed that this day would have its morrow, that the last of November, the date that must end everything, was still far off, or would not come at all. Really there was nothing to suggest that never, never again after this once would they hear each other's voices in this world.

Zeyneb, without any visible emotion, was arranging plans for correspondence when he should be in France. '*Poste-restante* is now too closely watched; in these times of terror no one may enter the post-office without giving his name. But our letters will be quite safe by the way I have planned, only it will be a little long; do not be surprised if we do not answer you within a fortnight sometimes.'

Djenan, with much composure, was plotting at

least to see her friend once more on the afternoon of that last November day. 'At four o'clock by the clock at Tophaneh, which is the hour when the steamships weigh anchor, we will both of us drive along the quay, in the commonest hired vehicle, you understand. We will pass as near the edge of the quay as possible, and you, from the poop, watch all the hired carriages closely, so as not to miss us. There is always a crowd there, you know, and as Turkish women are never allowed to stop, our greeting will last but an instant.'

The reflected sunbeam was to mark the hour of their parting. When it vanished above the roof, André was to rise and leave; this had been agreed on from the first; this was to be the utmost limit; after that, all was over.

André, who had been prepared to find them painfully agitated at this supreme interview, was astounded by their composure. Also, he had counted on looking once more into Djenan's eyes this last time; but no; the minutes went on, and nothing changed in the arrangement of the severe tcharchaf or the folds of the veil, as immovable, no doubt, as though it were of bronze over the face of a statue.

At about half-past three, while, for the sake of talking, they were discussing the Book, an almost sudden gloom invaded the little room, and all three were abruptly silent. 'We must go,' said Zeyneb, simply, in her sweet husky voice, and she pointed to the latticed windows no longer illuminated by the reflection from the house opposite —

the sunbeam had disappeared above the old roofs. The hour was come; André rose. During the very last minute, as they were standing in front of each other, he had time to reflect. 'This was the only time, absolutely the only time, when I might have seen her once more before her eyes and mine return to dust.'

To be so sure of never again meeting her, and to leave her thus without seeing her again — no, this he had not expected; but he endured the anguish of his disappointment and grief without a word. He bowed ceremoniously over the little hand she gave him, and kissed it lightly, and that was all.

And now, back through the deserted old streets, the dead streets — alone.

'It is well ended,' said he to himself. 'Poor little captive, it could have no better end! And I had fatuously imagined it would be dramatic.'

It had, indeed, ended too well; for he went away with a deep sense of emptiness and loneliness. He was even tempted to retrace his steps to the door with the old brass knocker, while they might still be there. And he would have said to Djenan: 'We cannot part like this, dear little friend; you, who are so sweet and kind, do not make me so unhappy. Let me look once more into your eyes, and clasp my hand more closely; I should go away less miserable.'

Of course, he did nothing of the kind, but went on his way. But at that moment he loved Stamboul distressfully; its myriad lights of evening were reflected in the waters; something made him cling to it desperately, what, he could not precisely define — something in the air which hung over the immense and various city, an emanation from the souls of its women, no doubt — for that is really almost always what attaches us to places and objects — the souls of the women he had loved, and which mingled in his memory. Was it Nedjibeh's or Djenan's, or both together? — he could not tell.

LI

NEXT day two letters came:

ZEYNEB TO ANDRÉ

'Truly, I did not understand that we met yesterday for the last time, or I should have fallen, a hapless wretch, at your feet, and implored you not to leave us thus. Oh! you are abandoning us sunk in darkness of heart and mind. You — you are going into light and life, and we must vegetate through the lamentable days, all alike, in the torpor of the harem.

'When you had gone we sobbed bitterly. Zerichteh, Djenan's kind nurse, came down; she scolded us, and took us in her arms; but she too, poor soul, wept at seeing us weep.

'ZEYNEB.'

'I have sent you this morning some trifling Turkish souvenirs. The embroidery is sent by Djenan; it is the "Ayet," the text from the Koran which has watched over her bed ever since she was a child. Accept the scarves from me. That worked with roses is a Circassian veil given to me by my grandmother; that embroidered in silver I found in an old chest in our yali. You can throw them over a sofa in your home in France.   Z.'

DJENAN TO ANDRÈ

'I wish I could read your thoughts when the ship goes out round Seraglio point, when at every turn of the screw, the cypresses in the cemeteries, the minarets, the cupolas, will be a little further away. You will watch them till they vanish, I know. And then, far off in the sea of Marmora, your eyes will seek, under the Byzantine walls, the graveyard where we prayed one day. And at last all will be lost in mist before your eyes, the cypresses of Stamboul, all the minarets and the domes, and before long, in your heart, every memory of them too.

'Well, be it so; let mist and confusion envelop them all; the little house at Eyoub, where you lived and loved, and the other humble house in the heart of Stamboul, near a mosque, and the vast melancholy mansion where once you got in by stealth. And all the persons of the past, let confusion blur them too — her whom you loved long ago, who crept by your side in her grey feridjeh, under the wall among the January daisies — I have trodden the path and called up her shade — and the other three later, who yearned to be your friends. Let them mingle all together, but keep them all in your heart — your remembrance is not enough. These, too, these later friends, have loved you, more perhaps than you supposed. I know that there will be tears in your eyes when the last cypress is lost to view — and I also ask for a tear.

'And over there, when you are at home, how will you remember your friends? The spell once broken, what aspect will they assume in your mind? It is horrible to think that, perhaps, they will have ceased to exist for you, that you may shrug your shoulders and smile as you think of them.

'I am in such a hurry, and yet afraid, to read the book in which you will write about Turkish women — about us! Shall I find in it that which I have vainly tried to discuss, ever since we have known each other, the depths of your soul, the inmost truth of your feelings; all that your short letters never reveal, nor your few words. I have felt emotion in you now and again, yes; but so quickly suppressed, so transient. There have been moments when I longed to tear open your heart and head to find out at last what lay behind your cold, keen eyes.

'Oh! André, do not say that I am crazy. I am miserable and alone — unhappy and struggling in darkness. Farewell. Pity me. Love me a little if you can.   DJENAN.'

André replied:

'There is not much left to be discovered, I assure you, behind my "cold, keen eyes"; much less do I know what there is behind yours, dear little enigma. You are always complaining of my silence and reserve. You see I have seen too much of life; when you have lived as long you will understand better.

'And if you fancy that you yourself were not icy — you too, yesterday, at the moment of parting!

'Then to-morrow, at four o'clock, on the dismal quay of Galata. In the wild medley of departure I will keep a sharp lookout; I shall have nothing else to care for, I assure you, but just not to miss the passing of your beloved black form, since that is all you allow me ever to see again.   ANDRÉ.'

LII

THURSDAY, the 30th of November, dawned with ruthless punctuality, as every decisive and fateful day arrives in needless haste. Not only, to each of us, the day of death, but, after us, the days which will see the last of our generation, the end of Islam, the disappearance of our declining races, and then those which will mark the end of all time, the annihilation and wreck of the revolving suns, swallowed up in engulfing darkness.

Fast, fast, came the 30th of November, such a day as any other to the majority of very various beings which Constantinople sees mingling in the crowd; but to Djenan and to André a date marking one of the fateful turnings in life.

The cold, grey dawn woke them both at about the same time; both under the same sky, and in the same town for a few hours yet, parted only by a ravine full of human dwellings, and a cypress-wood full of dead — but, in fact, so very far apart, divided by invisible barriers. He, as soon as he opened his eyes, was gripped by the sense of impending departure, for he had left his house and was camping in the hotel; he had taken a room as high up as possible to avoid the chaotic noise downstairs, the cloth caps of the globe-trotters from America, and the fantastic elegance of Syrian sharpers; but especially to command a view of Stamboul, with Eyoub in the distance.

And both Djenan and André looked first at the horizon, the heavy rack of clouds, the direction of the autumn wind; he from his wide-open window, and she through the penitential, inevitable wooden lattice that imprisons a harem.

They had hoped for a day of bright sunshine, and the haunting glory of the belated sun which sometimes sheds the warmth of a hothouse over Stamboul. He, that he might carry away with him, in his eyes greedy and crazy for colour, a last splendid vision of the city of minarets and cupolas. She, that she might be sure of succeeding in seeing him once more from the quay of Galata, as she drove past the departing ship; for otherwise nothing filled her with deeper melancholy than the pale rose-tinted lights of a fine November afternoon, and she had long since told herself that if, after he was gone for ever, she had to come back and bury herself at home under one of those languid gold-coloured sunsets, it would be more unendurable than in the gloomy fall of a rainy evening. But then in wet weather everything would be doubtful and complicated; what pretext could she invent for going out, and how escape from the increased watchfulness of all the eunuchs and slaves?

And it was going to rain, very evidently all day. A black sky, with clouds whirling and breaking under the Siberian wind; heavy masses sweeping low, almost touching the earth, darkening the distance and drowning everything. Cold and wet.

Zeyneb also, at the open window, was looking
at the sky, careless of her own health, and breathing
in the icy damp air of the Constantinople winter,
which last year had developed in her lungs the seeds
of death.   Then it suddenly struck her that she
was wasting precious minutes.   André was not to
leave till four o'clock in the afternoon; but she
went, nevertheless, to see Djenan as she had promised her yesterday; they wanted to reconsider
their plans, and contrive more infallible arrange-
ments, so as to drive, exactly at the right moment,
past the place of embarkation.   He would be here
for nearly the whole day; the excitement of his
presence, of danger and emotion, still kept them
up; but afterwards — oh! afterwards would come
the sudden plunge back into stagnant calm, with
nothing more in life.

To André, on the contrary, the day began in
rather placid melancholy.   The supreme fatigue of
having lived and loved so much, of having said
farewell so many times, undoubtedly lulled his soul
at the hour of this parting, which he had imagined
beforehand as more cruelly painful.   It was with
surprise, almost with remorse, that he detected in
himself a sort of detachment, even before he had
started.   'It had to be cut short,' said he to himself.   'When I am gone, everything will be better
for her; everything will be forgotten, alas! in
Hamdi's caresses.'

But what a disastrous sky for his last day!
He had intended to go across to Stamboul, to
wander sadly round in the mild November sunshine.   But it was impossible in this wintry

weather, it would leave a too painful last impression. He would not cross the bridge — never again — but stay in uninteresting, muddy Pera, frittering away the day till the hour of departure.

Two o'clock, time to leave the hotel and go down towards the sea. Before starting, however, he had the crowning distress of looking once more out of window towards Eyoub and the great fields of the dead, which he could not possibly see from below, neither from Galata, nor from any other spot; far, far away in the haze, beyond Stamboul, something like a stiff black crest showed against the horizon, a crest of hundreds of cypresses which, in spite of the distance, could be seen to stir, so wrung were they by the wind.

When he had looked out, he went away down to the low quarter of Galata, always crowded by a horrible Levantine mob, the part of Constantinople which is most infected by the perpetual arrival of steamships, and the travellers they bring, and the modern pedlars' rubbish that they unceasingly pour out on the ancient city of the Khalifs. A black sky, alleys padded with sticky mire, filthy wine-shops reeking of tobacco smoke and the anise-flavoured alcohol of the Greeks, a jostling mass of porters in rags, and hordes of mangy dogs. Of all this the magician Sun sometimes makes a thing of beauty; but to-day, what a mockery under the winter rain!

Four o'clock now; the November day is closing in, darkening behind the heavy rack of clouds.

It is the hour fixed for departure — the hour, too, when Djenan is to drive slowly past for the last farewell. André, having chosen his cabin, and seen his luggage on board, took a place on the upper deck at the stern, surrounded by friendly members of the various Embassies who had come to see the last of him, sometimes absorbed and inattentive in his watch for the carriage, and sometimes forgetting those who were to be in it, while he laughingly chatted with the friends about him.

The quay was as usual packed with people. It no longer rained. The air was full of the noise of engines, of steam-cranes, of cries and calls from the porters and the sailors, in every language of the Levant. This wet crowd, hustling and shouting, was a motley of Turkish costumes and European rags, but the fez, worn by almost every one, gave an oriental aspect to the whole scene. The cafés all along the street, behind this crowd, were full of Levantines; faces crowned with red caps were to be seen at every window of the wooden houses, which are perpetually full of oriental strumming and the smoke of narghilehs. And all of them were watching — as they always watch — the departing steamships. But beyond this intrusive quarter, this confusion of costumes and this noise — beyond, and divided from it by the waters of the gulf bearing a forest of ships, Stamboul the great lifted its mosques above the fog; its sovereign mass crushing all nearer ugliness, its silence reigning above the squalid turmoil.

Will they come? Poor little things! For a moment André almost forgets them in the inevitable excitement of leave-taking, bewildered as he is by shaking hands, by answering remarks of careless fun. And, in fact, he is no longer quite sure that it is he who is leaving; he has so often found himself on board one of these vessels, in front of these quays and this same crowd, to welcome or to speed a friend, as is customary in Constantinople. And besides, the city of Stamboul up against the sky has been much his own, almost his home more than a quarter of a century since; is it possible that he is really going away? No; it seems to him now that he will go back there to-morrow as usual, back to the old familiar spots and the well-known faces.

But the second warning bell has rung, the friends who came to see him off go on shore; the stern deck is deserted, only those who are really leaving stand there, looking at each other. There is no disputing it; that second bell, the last, had a funereal tone — and then André pulls himself together.

Ah! that carriage over there must be the very one. A hired coupé — shabby enough, but then she had told him so — moving forward even more slowly than the crowd necessitates. It is coming quite close, the window is down, and there are certainly two women in it veiled in black. And one of them suddenly raises her veil: Djenan! Djenan, who would be seen! Djenan, who for a second looks straight at him, with such a face of anguish as he never can forget.

Her eyes flash through her tears; but they are gone! The veil has fallen; and this time André understands the finality of this veiling, an end for all eternity, as when we hide a beloved face under the lid of the coffin. She did not lean out of the window, she did not wave her hand, she gave no sign; nothing but just that look, which indeed was enough to involve a Turkish woman in serious danger. And the hired coupé went slowly on its way, vanishing through the crowd.

That look had struck André to the heart more than any words or all her letters. The groups on the quay, who were waving adieux with hands and hats, had ceased to exist for him. There was nothing in the world but that carriage in the distance, slowly returning to a harem. His eyes, though he would fain have watched it, were suddenly dim; he saw everything in a quivering mist.

What now? Can he be dreaming? The carriage, still going quite slowly, is fast disappearing, and not in the direction in which the horses are moving. It is going off sideways like a dissolving view, and with it the people, the swarms of figures, the houses, the city! The ship is off: without a sound or a jerk or a throb of the screw. Absorbed in thought, he had not observed. The huge steamship, towed by tugs, was stealing away from land without any sensible motion; it was as if the quay were moving, slipping very quickly away with all its ugliness and its crowds, while high Stamboul, further away, had not yet stirred. The uproar of voices died away, the waving hands were no longer in sight — nor the black shape of that carriage among the myriad red specks that were Turkish fezzes.

Still without any sense of motion on board, in sudden and unexpected silence, Stamboul now began to be lost to sight in the fog and dusk. All Turkey was disappearing, with a sort of funereal dignity, fading into the distance — and into the past.

André did not cease from looking as long as a dim vision of Stamboul could be discerned, a darker grey in the grey of evening. To him on that side of the horizon a charm still dwelt of women's souls and figures — those who but now went away in that carriage, and those others already sleeping in death.

Nightfall on the sea of Marmora. André was thinking: 'By this time they are at home again.' And he pictured to himself their drive back, their arrival at the house under inquisitive eyes, and then their imprisonment, their loneliness this evening.

The ship was not yet far away; that lighthouse just blazing out at a short distance was on Seraglio point. But André had already a sense of infinite remoteness; his departure had cut, as with the stroke of an axe, the threads which had bound the life of Turkey with the living hour; and then that time, really so recent, but now held by no tie, dropped away, falling, falling rapidly into the void where things absolutely past sink into nothingness.

LIII

On reaching France he received this note from Djenan:

'When you were in our country, André, when we breathed the same air, it still seemed as though you belonged to us a little. But now you are lost to us; what concerns you, what surrounds you, is all unknown to us — and your heart, your diverted thoughts escape us more and more. You evade us — nay, rather it is we who are fading, soon to vanish completely. It is so frightfully sad!

'For a little while yet your book will keep us in your mind. But after that? I have a favour to ask you. You will send me as soon as possible the first pages in manuscript, will you not? I shall never part from them; wherever I go, even underground, they will be with me. How sad a thing is the real romance of that romance! It is now the only ground on which I feel sure of meeting you; to-morrow it will be all that is left of a time now past for ever.   DJENAN.'

André immediately sent her the sheets she had asked for. But he had no answer, not a line for five weeks, when he received this letter from Zeyneb:

KASSIM PACHA, 13th of Zilkada 1323.

'André, to-morrow morning our dear Djenan is to be taken to Stamboul to the house of Hamdi Bey for the second time, with all the ceremonial of a wedding. All has been settled strangely, quickly, every difficulty smoothed away. Both families combined to take steps for petitioning His Imperial Majesty to annul the iradeh of separation; no one defended her.

'Hamdi Bey has sent her to-day the most magnificent sheaves of roses from Nice; but they have not yet met, for she requested Emireh Hanum to beg him, as the only favour, to wait till after to-morrow's ceremony. She has been loaded with flowers; if you could see her room — which you did see once — where she has had them all arranged, you would think it an enchanted garden.

'I found her this evening quite amazingly calm, but it is, I feel, only weariness and resignation. This morning, when it was wonderfully fine, she went out, I know, accompanied only by Kondjé Gul, to visit the graves of Melek and of your Nedjibeh, and went up the hill at Eyoub to that spot in the cemetery where my poor little sister photographed you side by side, do you remember? I wished to spend this last evening with her, as we did — Melek and I — on the eve of her former marriage; but I understood that she would rather be alone, so I left before nightfall, my heart aching with distress.

'So here I am at home, indescribably forlorn; I feel she is more utterly lost than she was the first time, because Hamdi mistrusts my influence. I shall be kept away, I shall see her no more. I never believed, André, that such suffering was possible; if you could ever pray, I should say pray for me. But I will implore your pity, your great pity, for your poor friends, the two who remain.

'ZEYNEB.'

'Do not be afraid that she forgets you. On the 27th of Ramazan, the day of the dead, she settled that we should go together to the tomb of Nedjibeh to take her some flowers — and our prayers, all that is left to us of our lost faith. Though you have not had a letter from her for many days it is that she has been ill and wretched; but I know she intends to write you a long letter this evening before going to sleep. She told me so when I left her.   Z.'

LIV

BUT the next day but one André received this written communication,[1] in which, as he tore open the envelope, he fancied he recognised the hand of Djavideh Hanum:

'Allah!

'Ferideh Azadeh Djenan,

'Daughter of Tewfik Pasha Darihan Zadeh, and of Ismet Hanum Kerissen, died to-day, the 14th of Zilkada 1323.

'She was born on the 22nd of Redjeb 1297, at Karadjemir.

'By her desire she is buried in the turbeh of the venerable Sivassi of Eyoub, there to sleep her last.

'But her eyes, which were pure and beautiful, have already been opened, and God, who loved her, has directed their gaze towards the gardens of Paradise, where Mahomet, our Prophet, awaits the faithful.

[1] No printed announcement of death is sent out in Turkey. It is made known to friends at a distance by a notice in a newspaper or a written letter, always worded approximately as above.

'All we who must die send up our prayers to you, O Djenan Ferideh Azadeh, and beseech you not to forget us in your appeal. And we, your humble friends, will follow in the path of light you have shown us.

'O Djenan Ferideh Azadeh,
'May the *rahmet* of Allah descend on you.

'KASSIM PACHA, 15*th Zilkada* 1323.'

He read it in haste and bewilderment; the oriental form of the communication was unfamiliar, and then all Djenan's various names, which he did not know, at first misled him. Some few minutes passed before he finally and completely understood that it was she who was dead.

LV

A LONG letter from Zeyneb arrived three days later, enclosing a sealed envelope on which his name 'André' was in Djenan's writing still.

ZEYNEB'S LETTER

'André, all my sufferings, all my misery, were mere gladness so long as her smile shed its light on them; my blackest days were made bright by her: now I know it, now that she is no more.

'It is almost a week now since she was laid in the earth. Nevermore shall I see those deep grave eyes which her soul shone through, never again hear her voice, nor her child-like laugh; all will be dreary for me till the end. Djenan lies in the grave. I do not believe it yet, André, and yet I touched her little cold hands, I saw her rigid smile, her teeth of pearl between the marble lips. I was the first to go to her, and took the last letter she wrote, her letter to you, all twisted and crumpled in her fingers. I do not yet believe it, and yet I saw her pale and stiff, I held her dead hands in mine. I do not believe it! But it is true. I saw her, and I saw her coffin wrapped in a Valideh shawl with a green Mecca

veil, and I heard the Imam say the prayer for
the dead — for her.

'On Thursday, the very day when we were to
escort her back to Hamdi Bey, I received a note
at daybreak with the key of her room — the key
she was so delighted to have obtained, do you
remember?   It was Kondjé Gul who brought it,
and why so early?   I was terrified even as I
opened the envelope.   And I read: "Come; you
will find me dead.   Come into my room first, and
alone.   Close to me look for a letter; hide it in
your dress, and then send it to my friend."

'I flew there, I went alone into her room.
Oh! André, the horror of it; the horror of the
first glance.   Where would she be?   In what
shape?   Fallen on the floor?   In bed?   There, in
her armchair, in front of her writing-table, her
head fallen back, perfectly white, looking as if she
saw the rising sun.   And I was not to call, to cry
out.   No; the letter — I must find the letter.   I
saw five or six letters lying sealed on the table in
front of her — letters of farewell, no doubt.   But
there were also some scattered sheets, and this
envelope addressed to you.   And the last sheet,
which you will find all crumpled, I took out of her
left hand, which clasped it tightly.   I hid them all,
and when I had done her bidding, I screamed as
loud as I could, and they came in.

'Djenan, my only friend, my sister!   There is
nothing in the world now without her, after her;
neither joy, nor affection, nor light of day!   It is
all gone with her into her grave, where before long
a green slab will mark the place — over there —

you know — at Eyoub which you both loved so well.

'And she would be alive now if only she had still been the little barbarian, the little princess of the Asiatic plains. She would have known nothing of the emptiness of things. It was thinking too much, knowing too much, which poisoned her drop by drop, day by day. It is the West that has killed her, André. If she had been left ignorant, primitive, only lovely, I should see her by me now, and hear her voice. And my eyes would not have wept as they will still weep for her for many days and nights yet. I should not now be in despair, André, if she had remained the little princess of the Asiatic plains! ZEYNEB.'

André had a pious awe of opening Djenan's letter.

This was not like the formal announcement which he had opened unsuspectingly. He knew now; he had worn mourning for her for some days; the grief of having lost her had taken possession of him, slowly and deeply sinking into his soul; and he had had time, too, to reflect on his share of responsibility for this desperate blow.

Before opening her letter he shut himself into a room alone, not to be disturbed by anything in this last *tête-à-tête* with her.

There were several sheets; and the last, the bottom one, was, as his fingers felt it, crumpled and crushed.

He saw at once that the writing was the same

as in all her letters, the same neat, clear hand. She was mistress of herself in the face of death. And she began with the balanced sentences which it was her manner to compose; phrases so calm that André could almost have doubted their finality, since he had not seen her stiff and white, had not held her dead hand.

THE LETTER

'My friend, the hour of our parting has struck. The iradeh by which I believed myself protected has been annulled, as Zeyneb no doubt has told you. My grandmother and my uncles have made every arrangement for my marriage, and to-morrow I am to be handed over once more to the man — you know.

'It is midnight, and in the silence of the sleeping house there is not a sound but that of my pen; nothing is awake except my misery. To me the world is blotted out; I have already taken leave of all I ever loved; I have written my last instructions and my farewell letters. I have divested my soul of all that is not of its very essence, I have driven away every image — so that nothing may come between you and me, so that I may give to you alone the last hours of my life, and that you alone may feel the last dying throb of my heart.

'Because, my friend, I mean to die. A quite peaceful death, like a deeper sleep, that will not disfigure my prettiness. Peace and forgetting are here, in a phial under my hand. It is an Arabian poison, very gentle and sure, which gives to death, they say, the semblance of love.

'André, before departing from life, I have made a pilgrimage to the little tomb that is so dear to you. I went to pray there, and beseech her whom you loved to support me in the hour of death — and also to allow some memory of me to mingle with hers in your heart. And I have been to Eyoub too, alone with my old Kondjé Gul, to entreat my dead to welcome me. I wandered among the tombs, choosing where I would lie; then I rested, all alone, on the spot where we have sat together. The winter's day was as mild as that April when in that same place I surrendered my soul. Over the Golden Horn, as I came home the sky was shedding roses. Ah! my beloved city, so lovely in the evening glow — I shut my eyes to carry the vision with me into the next world.

'Zeyneb advised me to escape when the news came that the iradeh was annulled. But I could not make up my mind to it. Perhaps if I had been sure of finding under another sky some love to shelter me. But I had no right to hope for anything but tender pity. I prefer death. I am very tired.

'A strange calm possesses me. I have had all the flowers sent to me for to-morrow's *fête* brought into my room — my room as a girl which you once were in. I have arranged them round my bed, and on the table at which I am writing, and, my friend, I think of you. I can see you before me. You are my companion to-night. I shut my eyes and I see you, cold, motionless; but those eyes of yours — the eyes of which I shall never sound the mysteries — pierce my closed eyelids and scorch my heart. And when I open mine you are still there, your portrait looks at me from among the flowers.

'But your book — our book — excepting the pages you have given me, and which will go with me to-morrow — I am going away without having read it! I shall never have known exactly what you think even. Have you really understood the sadness of life to us? Have you felt what a crime it is to rouse sleeping souls, and then crush them if they try to soar; what a shame it is to reduce women to the passiveness of mere chattels? Tell them, André, that our lives are smothered in sand, are one long death. Oh, tell them this! Let my death at any rate be of use to my Moslem sisters. I would so gladly have been of use to them living. Once upon a time I cherished a dream of trying to arouse them all — but no! Sleep, sleep on, poor souls. Never discover that you have wings. But the others who have already taken flight, who have had a glimpse of a wider sphere than the harem, these, André, I confide to you; speak of them, and speak for them. Be their advocate in the world where men and women think; and may their tears, may my anguish at this hour, touch the blinded tyrants who love us though they crush us.'

Here suddenly the writing changed, grew feebler, almost tremulous.

'It is now three in the morning, and I must finish my letter. I have wept so much that I can hardly see. Oh! André, André, is it possible to be young and loving and yet be driven to die? Something clutches my throat, is strangling me. I had every right to live and be happy. A dream of life and light still hovers before me. But to-morrow, to-day's sun even, is to fling me into the embracing arms of the master who is forced upon me, and where — where are the arms I could have loved?'

Here there was a break indicating an interval of time. The last hesitation, no doubt, and then the doing of the irrevocable. For a few more lines the letter was in the old tranquil strain; but it was a tranquillity that made him shudder.

'It is done; it only needed a little courage; the phial of forgetting is empty. I am already a thing of the past. In an instant I had stepped out of life; I have only a bitter taste of flowers left on my lips. The world seems far away; everything is confused and vanishing — everything except the friend whom I loved, whom I am calling, who must stay with me till the end.'

And now the writing sloped across like that of a child; then, at the bottom of the next page, the lines crossed in every direction. The poor little hand was no longer firm and steady; the letters were too tiny or suddenly much too large, frightfully large. This was the last sheet, which had been crushed and twisted in the last throes of death, and the crumpling of the paper made it more terrible to read.

'The friend I am calling, who must stay with me till the end. My beloved, come quickly. I want to tell you — Did you not know that I loved you with every fibre of my being? When one is dead one can confess all. The rules of the world are then no more. Why, now I am going, shall I not tell you that I have loved you?

'André, that day when you sat here, in front of the table where I am writing to you in farewell, by chance, as I leaned forward, I touched you; I shut my eyes, and behind the closed lids what lovely visions flashed across. Your arms held me to your heart, and my hands, filled with love, gently touched your eyes and drove out all sadness. Ah! Death might have come then; and it would have come at the first moment when weariness came to you, but how sweet it would have seemed, what a joyful and grateful soul it would have carried away! Now, all is swimming; all is growing dim. . . . I was told I should sleep, but I am not yet sleepy, but everything is shifting; I see everything double; it is all in a whirl; my candles look like suns — the flowers are grown larger — larger; I am in a forest of gigantic flowers.

'Come, André, come near me. What are you doing among the roses? Come close to me while I write. I want your arms round me, and your dear eyes near my lips. So, my love, that is how I want to sleep, close to you, telling you that I love you. Let me see your eyes close to me, for in this other life, where I am, souls can be read through the eyes. I am dead, André —— Is that a tear for me in your deep eyes that I could not understand? I do not hear your answer because I am dead —— That is why I am writing; you could not hear my voice; it is too far away.

'I love you — do you at least hear that? I love you ——'

Oh, to feel this dying anguish in his very hand! To be the one to whom she persisted in speaking even at the last, at the moment of crowning mystery when the soul is released! To possess the last trace of her tender thought, coming already from the realm of death!

'I am going, floating away, André; hold me! —— Will any one ever love you with such devoted love? —— This is sleep — the pen is so heavy —— In your arms —— dear love, dear love ——'

The last words were hardly visible. But, indeed, the reader could see no more, neither that nor anything else. On the page, all crumpled by the poor little hand which could no more, he piously and passionately pressed his lips — and this was their first and only kiss.

LVI

O DJENAN FERIDEH AZADEH, may the *rahmet* [1] of Allah rest upon thee! Peace to thy lofty white soul! And may thy sisters in Turkey at my call for some years yet, before all is forgotten, repeat thy dear name in their evening prayers.

[1] Rahmet: the crowning mercy of Allah, the forgiveness which wipes out all sin. In speaking of the dead the Turks say : 'Allah grant him rahmet,' as we were wont to say: 'God rest his soul.'